SWORD OF THE BUTTERFLY
©2017 Scott Carruba
First Edition
All rights reserved
Edited by Christina Hargis Smith
Cover art by Jeffrey Kosh Graphics
Published by Optimus Maximus Publishing, LLC

This book is a work of fiction. Names, characters, businesses, organizations, places, events, and incidents either are the product of the author's imagination or are used fictitiously. Any resemblance to actual persons living, dead, or otherwise, events, or locales is entirely coincidental.

This book is protected under the copyright laws of the United States of America. Any reproduction or unauthorized use of the material or artwork contained herein is prohibited without the express written permission of the author.

ISBN-10: 1-944732-23-3
ISBN-13: 978-1-944732-23-3

Acknowledgment and Dedication

Ideas often come to me in dreams, but those alone are not enough. Were it not for the support of my family and friends, none of this would be possible. Thank you for helping me realize my dreams. Thank you, Jane, for being there during the entire process. Without your help, this tale would not be.

Many thanks to my publisher, beta readers, and all the readers out there who give me a chance. I hope you enjoy the story.

Thus by blood, were they tempted, lusting in mind and form

SWORD OF THE BUTTERFLY

A Novel by
Scott Carruba

PROLOGUE

The passing of monumental times may be marked with celebrations, an effort to etch them more thoroughly in memory. The wedding party has come early to the Bermuda destination to spend some time in exactly that sort of festivity prior to the "big day". There are ten in all, and they have acquired two large, connecting bungalows on the beach, allowing for gender-exclusive activities as well as an ease of mingling as they may like.

The resort is a very nice one, though not quite as well-known as some more popular destinations. It had not been a question of money or exclusivity so much as just wanting these sorts of accommodations. They are young, vibrant, excited, and they barely give enough time to settling in before bottles are opened, music turned on, and the party begins.

The bride and groom have known each other for some years, having met early in college and started dating, quickly becoming more serious, and with graduation recently behind them, the time has come for another important gateway of their lives. Most of the others are also friends from college, though a sparse few are relatives, the bride's younger sister amongst them. They engage in their interplay and boisterousness, their comradery evident.

One of the bridesmaids has brought along something she thinks will be a fun addition to the celebration, and on the second night of their stay, she waltzes into the large sitting room of the guys' side, wearing her great-great-grandmother's wedding gown. It is a somewhat discolored garment, though still largely intact, having mellowed to a heady ivory as opposed to the white it once showed. Lace and eyelets give the dress a formal, even somewhat overdone, Victorian look. The attempt to hearken to such times is obvious, even if it had been new and worn a few decades past that era.

Everyone stops, looking over, and the moment of silence is broken by whoops and hollers and even gasps and exclamations of wonder. She gives a pirouette, then a little curtsey, showing off the dress.

"Oh, Iris, that is *beautiful*," Kaitlyn comes over, gently taking the girl's hands to open her arms and give the gown a better view.

"Uh oh, careful, or Kat's going to steal it for her wedding," calls out another of the young ladies, and the bride-to-be throws out a smirk.

"She'd better not," Ryan, Kaitlyn's betrothed, remarks.

"Too old-fashioned for you, Ryan? You want to see more cleavage," flings another of the girls, and laughter erupts.

"I was thinking of how much her dress *cost*!" he protests, more laughter bubbling throughout the vibrant group.

Kaitlyn saunters over, sitting in Ryan's lap, arms wrapping about him as she gives him a quick kiss. "Dad's paying for that, not you."

"I know that, but-," and his continued protestations are stifled as Kaitlyn shoves her bosom into his face. The shouts and laughter burst out again, having had little time to breathe.

Their energy is positive, vigorous, and it fills the rooms easily. Still, the dark presence here has resided for some time, and though such a joyful resonance might generally prohibit this sort of occupation, it acts more as a lure now, bait, something to be consumed and converted as though an obscenity to those opposed to such. Those very entities wait now, observing, having held themselves in that readiness like a very patient fisherman. They do not even jerk the hook, even as the school of promising fish dance around it, their lust stoking that of the lurking beasts. This rare moment will not be ruined, no. The flesh and hopefully even the spirits of these here will be spoiled, but the moment shall be milked, fat drops coaxed forth gently until comes the explosive spray.

They hold awareness of these human rituals, especially those of a religious ancestry, and they know what transpires here. This hope and eagerness of young love increases their arousal. They look upon it with envy, jealousy, lust. The bride, the bride will be the one to suffer the most.

The Maiden of Honor, Jordan, heads into the bathroom on the girls' side, her bladder filled with wine and liquor, a casual grin on her lips as she revels in the fun and thinks on what shall transpire in a few days. She

SWORD OF THE BUTTERFLY

sits on the clean toilet seat, the stream of urine flowing out in abundance. Her sense of relief is suddenly interrupted when the scent enters her nose. She blinks rapidly, curling her upper lip. This is not the odor of her expulsion, and it takes her a moment to realize it smells as rot emanating from a sewer. She quickly finishes, flushing, then looks down, observing carefully as the water whirls about and drains. As the bowl refills it shows a darker coloring, a slowly seeping cloud of dense, black ink comes up, its tendrils spreading about as though once empty veins filling.

Jordan's eyes widen, her upper body moving back as though instinctively increasing distance from that odd happening and the growing stink. She blinks again, her disgust becoming more evident, and she waves a hand through the air near her nose, hoping to dispel the odor. Something is clearly wrong with the sewage here. She turns, ready to head back into the fray of the party and call the resort's front desk to alert them. She does not make it.

A sudden rise from a shadow in the corner coalesces, giving birth to a firmer shape, one that looks as though it might be human but something is off, indistinct even, and a sharp length of black snicks out, stabbing through her neck with a quick and quiet ease. She blinks again, stumbling, then looks in the mirror, seeing ... something, but the light of life in her eyes fades quickly. She is not the bride, so she shall not suffer as much.

Whispers, sibilant chattering, even sounds that suggest a different sort of celebration than those coming from the other parts of the cabanas, rise forth. These prove an initial surge of their own to announce the beginning of the meal, the slaughter, and they are ready to rapaciously feed. Though it may prove subtle or even unnoticed by the mundane eye, the shadows begin to grow, spreading out as though a harbinger, giving a hinting mist and darkness to the otherwise bright colors and energies this evening.

The attack continues with a similar subtlety as the best man, Greg, stands near a round table set upon by a myriad of different finger foods. His height and size indicate he is often in need of such fueling, and his athleticism held further evidence by his sports accomplishments in college. He had not proved good enough to be drafted into any elite professional ranks, but his future looks bright.

That light is extinguished as he plops several pieces of cold, spiced chicken into his mouth, chewing quickly before swallowing. The tension rises slowly, another effort at swallowing made, unsuccessful, then his hands come up sharply, the bottle in one dropped, colliding with the tabletop then clattering to the ground, beer gurgling out onto the tiling. His hands are now like claws wrapped about his throat, trying to free the impediment to his breathing. A few of those nearby look over, confusion initially dispersing the festive expressions before urgency takes hold, voices raised, one running over to help.

Another of the groomsmen, Aaron, tries to administer the Heimlich maneuver, and though he executes it with textbook ability, the obstructing food does not come forth. If the recipient, Greg, could speak, he'd say that it feels as though other hands are beneath his, choking him relentlessly. His lack of breathing is not from food in his windpipe.

More voices are raised, shouts and cries, but Greg slumps into unconsciousness soon enough. Aaron continues pushing up on his abdomen, hoping to save his friend's life, but such proves futile.

"Oh my God. Oh my God!" Kaitlyn's sister, Kathryn calls out.

"Someone call for help!" Ryan bellows from where he is trying to help hold Greg as life-saving efforts are continued on the warm corpse.

Colby turns from staring at the scene with an expression of frozen shock and practically sprints for the phone, everyone suddenly oblivious of their mobiles. He bumps into an end table, a glass structure atop it falling, fracturing against the floor but not shattering. Some clipped, startled cries follow this as he picks up the phone, going to press the buttons, but then his brow furrows, and he lowers the receiver.

"The line's dead."

"What?" Kaitlyn asks, defiance in her tone, and she rushes over.

She suddenly stumbles, falling to the side, hard, crying out in pain. Her right foot hangs useless, her bones broken just above the ankle, one spiked horribly through her flesh. She has tripped over the fallen piece of artwork, though it would seem that it has moved from where it fell.

"Kat!"

SWORD OF THE BUTTERFLY

And this is Ryan, relinquishing his place at his best man to run over to his intended. Aaron's hold on the now dead weight of Greg falters, and his hands come apart, a look of abject sorrow on his features.

"Shit, shit, shit," Ryan assesses, trying to hold his girlfriend as she screams out in pain, then he looks over to Colby. "Call someone, dammit!"

Colby looks lost, eyes wide, a miasma of confusion clouding his mind, as though without the functioning telephone, he has no idea what to do. A glance to Kathryn shows she is in worse shape, standing in place, eyes unfocused, frozen in silent panic. Her lips are slightly agape, and a collection of saliva froths slowly at the right side of her mouth.

"Use a cell phone!" Iris grabs up a nearby mobile, and the forces that haunt this place gurgle with excitement, waiting to unleash this opportunity on the one they assume is the bride-to-be. She quickly stabs out 9-1-1, then waits very impatiently for the operator to pick up. Her small motions of unease stop suddenly, her eyes widening as she registers the sound rising up from the device, as though the hearing of it also gives sight, a growing buzz uncurling from a great distance, becoming a cacophony, a swarm of locusts bleeding through an oily fog. She hurls the phone aside after becoming lost and latched to the rising noise.

"What the hell!" Ryan demands, "We need help. Someone get help!"

The remaining groomsman, Joel, nods once, then turns and runs, hoping to hurriedly get to the front desk and have them provide some assistance. He practically rips the front door open, such is the force of his coming to it, but he only gets out a few steps before he stops, halting in a series of stupefied, stuttering footsteps. He looks around at the fog, the thick, low-hanging cloud such an obscurity as to make his immediate locale seem an isolation. He knows there are more buildings out here, he's recently seen them, yet the fog is so thick. He gives little thought to what must be a very strange change in weather, and he picks a direction in which he thinks the main part of the resort lies.

After a time of getting nowhere but deeper into the thick mist, he stops as he glimpses a moving shape in his peripheral vision. He blinks, looking over, but then he sees nothing.

"Is someone there?" he tries, but he gets nothing but the eerie silence in return, "I need help! Is someone there?"

And then a similar glimpse to his left, and he jerks himself that way only to see nothing. He does feel a deep compulsion, though, in that general direction, and he runs. He shortly hears and feels the sloppiness of the ground beneath him, and he wonders that he has reached the beach. He stops, trying to change direction, but his feet feel trapped, heavy. Extreme lethargy moves up him, gripping his thighs, and he drops to his knees, feeling the soggy ground beneath him yield like mud. He doubles over, his hands going to that ground, also sinking.

What's happening, he wonders, *where am I?*

"What's happening to him?" Lindsey cries out, watching as Aaron has tried to administer help to the supine form of Joel, for he collided harshly with the wall beside the front door, physically having never left the room, and he has now gone from quietly leaking blood from his nose and ears to erupting in a series of horrible spasms. The run through the fog to the beach had been in his head, all more tricks from those malignant entities preying on them.

"He's having a seizure," Aaron concludes, but his time in college was not as a doctor-in-training, and his attempts here end as uselessly as those tried on Greg.

Joel's head arches back, hair spread and tousled on the entryway's floor, teeth bared from the tension along with tendons rising in his neck, and an eruption of blood shoots out of his nostrils, a thick, torrential flood resulting.

"Holy shit!" Aaron recoils just as screams peel out from others.

This acts as an alarm, and Colby's eyes blink from their frozen stare, the once white sclera now clouded from a growing red, leaking out from a more vibrant crimson shade at the center. His spine stiffens, mouth opening wide, and he sucks in a loud breath. Everyone who is of sufficient mental focus snaps their attention to him, some looks of confusion but others coated in horror, and as the deep, lengthy intake ends, he unleashes an unbridled yell of rage.

He surges forth with a sudden, almost preternatural speed, rushing over toward the girls. He ignores the panicked and immobile form of Kathryn, and Iris screams, dodging away and running toward the passageway to the adjoining cabana just as the suddenly animate form of Colby reaches Lindsey. He collides with her, taking her to the ground, snarling like a beast as the two are immersed in a tangle of limbs. Aaron springs up, going for the young man, grabbing him by the shoulders. Colby turns at the waist, not giving up his position atop the screaming woman, flinging out with both arms and knocking away the would-be rescuer.

Lindsey claws at him, leaving some furrows and gashes on his face and arms, but these only further anger him, and he looks down, bellowing another loud call of fury. He reaches within the chaotic, defensive flailing of her arms and grips the sides of her head, leaning down with a sudden speed to head-butt her face. A sickening thud rises from this, and he does it again, the next sound even more disturbing as it is enveloped in wetness from her now freely flowing blood. Her arms lull, her consciousness not far behind, and he bares his teeth, leaning down to savagely tear at her throat.

Ryan leaps over, taking up the broken, heavy glass statuette, and he fiercely swings, hitting his cousin on the side of the head. The other man crumbles away from the blow, and Ryan finishes pushing him off Lindsey. The girl is nearly unconscious and nearly dead, her eyes mere slits, mostly whites, her face a red mask, her right orbital socket smashed, rich blood not only coating her face but also leaking profusely from a terrible wound in her throat, her flesh torn and opened like ripped meat.

"Oh, God," he mutters, slamming his hands over the wound, hoping to staunch the flow, giving a quick glance to his fiancé. She has thankfully lapsed into unconsciousness from the stress and pain.

He then looks down at his cousin, noting the rather mean looking wound at his temple, and the copious blood flowing from this. What is happening? What caused Colby to attack Lindsey like that? He keeps the pressure on the wound, even as he looks at Aaron, the two sharing a look of horror at what is happening. His eyes then travel to Kathryn, the slightly younger lady still just standing there, mute, eyes held open, unseeing. He then looks back.

"Aaron?" he says, his voice much calmer than he feels, and the other moves his eyes back, imploring, frightened, "We *have* to get help. Try another phone."

Aaron gives a shaky nod then moves unsteadily, trying to find a mobile. Ryan gives further observation to the area.

"Where's Iris?"

Iris has fled to the ladies' cabana, running with an inexplicable need for safety and protection to the bathroom. She flicks the light on, and a scene of horror awaits.

Jordan lies dead on the ground, blood about the bathroom indicating the loss of such from her. She has been removed of most of her clothing, the fabrics torn through and ripped away, and her nearly nude form displays multiple wounds, her stomach ripped open, guts hanging out, one of her thighs flayed to the bone. There are creatures standing about, the cause of the carnage. The once elegantly appointed and quite generously large bathroom is enshrouded in darkness and a near overpowering stench. The misty shadows that coat the chamber do give up the slavering, hissing forms of these monsters, their general shape similar to human, though resemblance ends there. Their skin is ashen, their bodies more possessed of a scaly hardness or tight rugosity than any hair or semblance of 'normal' covering. Their mouths show deadly crowds of fangs, the digits of their hands and feet adorned in lethal claws. The noisome stench now originates not from the latrine but the large tub, within which stands a thick ooze that lists grotesquely, the gel-like liquid showing blotches of black, floating like tar balls within an otherwise sickening gray.

This mere moment of stunned silence passes, and then Iris unleashes a horripilating scream.

It does not last long, for though the malignant creatures had wanted to draw out the bride's torture, she is here, now, and with a quick attack from one, she is knocked into the ichor. It is corrosive, poisonous, and a hissing of gas rises up as her body is engulfed. There is some attempt at flailing, but the concoction is heavy, thick, and very potent, and those meager struggles soon cease.

The need for subtlety now quite gone, the dark forces lurking in this place increase the intensity of their attack.

SWORD OF THE BUTTERFLY

Drowning, drowning in sludge ... pieces of skin and other material flaking off, floating in the thick soup ... the warmth almost inviting, save for this corrosion ... physical pain like jerks and shocks over the network of nerves, a spasmolytic doll on terrible strings ... this feeling numbs, for the mental torment must rise, much more horrifying than the mundane. Still, time for that later. One thing courses through her mind – survival.

She rises up from the morass, not springing up as though some forced expulsion, but grasping wetly at the sides, hands slipping, then taking hold, carefully, and she pushes, her backside having been upwards, and she raises her head above the sludge, taking in a breath, still careful. She inhales some of the liquid, coughing, sputtering, thick tendrils of it trailing down over her face and hair, seeming like a coat to her, her dark, wet locks looking to have become part of the ooze. This is no mere water, but more like a demented amniotic fluid. Has she been reborn?

She forcefully exhales, spitting a spray of the stuff from about her mouth, then reaching over with her right hand to try to wipe away the more pronounced, stubborn leavings. Her hand is, of course, covered in the slime, and this does not much help. She clambers up onto her knees, the dense liquid rocking with her movement but somehow the more stable of it and her. She looks about, again, carefully, but those ... *things* she thinks she saw are nowhere to be found. If it were not for her own condition and the body of Jordan, she might even wonder if it had not all been some vivid nightmare.

She looks down at the gunk in which she kneels, and it hits her, what she has somehow managed to get out of her mind, and she tenses, jaw clenching. She surges forward on clutching abdominal muscles, retching into the muck. She expels the contents of her stomach, adding it to the disgusting soup, and this motivates her. She again grips the slick sides of the vast tub, finally managing to get to her feet.

She then stands before the mirror, the once polished, pristine surface of it now marred by blood and other, less identifiable stains, abstract swathes of dark liquid, drying, other areas more a peppering of strange dust, as if ash. She looks at herself, a slight trembling to her body, having left the torturous embrace of the acidic soup. Shock has assuredly set in, but she does not completely crumble beneath it. The tattered remnants of her ancestor's bridal gown hang on her now like the saturated leavings of a thick web, clinging wetly to her form.

She reaches forward for the faucet, hands slipping a bit to get hold, and she slowly, methodically, goes through the motions of washing her hands and face, pushing her hair back, feeling more of that slime, and she washes her hands again. She looks pale, as though her flesh has somehow uniformly been bleached from her time in the bath. Her eyes, once a rich dark brown, even look more hazel now. She leans in closer to her image, peering, and she sees some variegations of red throughout, radiating from the center. She might think her eyes bloodshot from her ordeal, vessels burst, but it appears as though the pigmentation itself has been changed.

A terrible scream comes from the other cabana, obviously a man, and she starts, tensing, her trembling now of fright rather than the damp. Her teeth clench, even as her paled lips quiver. She stands there a moment, not wanting to leave, not wanting to stay, wanting to be anywhere but here, yet here she is.

She leaves the bathroom, moving on shambling feet toward the continued sounds – tittering, hissing breaths, some seeming to come from pain, others emerging as though from inhuman throats and mouths. She hears noises like that from the mobile phone earlier, a buzzing that toys at some underlying, animal part of her brain, something she feels could be a language, yet how can she possibly know that?

When her feet finally get her back into the other room, she sees things her brain does not want to accept. She sees those creatures and more. Some of the ones that at least hold a quasi-human shape, though there is no doubt they are the stuff of nightmares, others looking less anthropomorphic, some hovering in the air on leatherine wings, a lack of any noticeable sensory organs, but they all eventually turn their notice to her.

She sees Ryan, held in bondage. He is restrained by something that looks organic, as though one of the very beasts has wrapped itself about him, lengths of its form attached by toothed suckers, the tendrils flexing obscenely, one of them partially covers his face, going over his left eye, fluid leaks, staining him, a dark red, some even black. He is obviously in anguish.

SWORD OF THE BUTTERFLY

The Bride, the Bride ...

She turns about, looking, wondering how she hears this rustling of odd speech, this sense of confusion and excitement coming from the denizens.

"... Iris ...?"

And this is Ryan, and her eyes find him, noting his struggles, his tension and pain, the seething burn and fear so obvious upon his restrained form. She merely stands there, saying nothing, as several of the monsters move to her, getting in close, more observant than ready to touch her.

"How are you ... *alive?*" one hisses out at her in a more solid form of communication than the buzzing whispering she thought she registered before.

She does not answer, and she feels a somewhat chitinous hand grip her right bicep. She tenses, a short breath passing roughly through her nostrils, eyes looking at the culprit. Many eyes look back at hers, and that insanity-inducing horror threatens at her again, and just as before, she somehow manages to quell it. The sharply tapered digits of that hand squeeze at her arm as though testing the ripeness of fruit.

"She *lives* ...," says another voice, then the pitch rising, "The Bride lives." More hands grip her, moving her toward Ryan.

"Look ... look and see. See what we do to your groom, your *love*."

Iris stares, blankly, her body moved like a rag doll to get closer, held by firm, terrible hands and other appendages, made to stand there and observe. Ryan returns that gaze, his single, exposed eye filled with panic, pain, as he drills the remnants of his sight into her, almost as though they may save each other through sheer will. What he does not know is that her mind is not directed the same as his.

The tentacles over him flex again, going thicker as though filling with air or coursing with a rush of blood, and then they constrict. He tenses, teeth bared, then cries out in pain. The tittering and buzzing increases, accompanied by more obvious gurgling laughter from those creatures that possess some capability of a semblance of human speech.

Let him make noise, let him speak ...

"You see? You see?" One of them comes in close, hissing in her ear, its fingers caressing her face and neck. "We will let him keep the use of his mouth until the end. We want him to scream and plead and beg. We want him to *talk* to you."

All she can think is to let it be anyone else but her. Let it be him, if it must, but just *not her*. She even emits a weak, shaky nod.

The torture resumes, more pain applied, more grunts and twitches and tensing and screams. She casts her eyes about, and she sees the crumbled and broken forms of Kaitlyn and Aaron. She figures they have left Ryan alive for this torture, and then she sees Kathryn, still just standing there, looking untouched, still a petrified husk, lost in her mind. The girl's mouth now fully gapes, slack, stains of drool on her chin as fresher expulsions collect and drip into lengthy trails.

She doesn't care, she doesn't feel …

"Look at him!" one of them commands, its voice wet, a spray of whatever fluid resides in its mouth spattering her face as she is roughly made to gaze upon Ryan as the torture continues.

"His skin, his skin," another says, moving in to pet a portion of exposed flesh that has not yet been covered or ruined by the treatment, "His *precious* skin. You *love* that flesh. We will flay him."

A number of the talons displayed on many of the monsters would seem to suffice, and one is brought nearer, its edge promising just the sort of razor sharpness needed. Ryan's eye bugs, craning to look at the direction of the coming operation. It is amazing he retains consciousness.

"He is not my love."

What? …

"What!" cry out many, some more substantial, like a choir with manifest voices over sickly whispers and hums.

"I-I'm not the bride," she says, then she slowly raises her right arm, the slender length of it wracked by trembling, tatters of the torn, lacey garment wriggling from the motion as she points, "Kat … *Kaitlyn*. There. She's the bride. Not me."

Dead, dead … we did kill the Bride …

And she hears cries of anguish from this. She feels she has done herself a disservice by revealing it; her efforts to spare Ryan may only bring her death.

"You *lie* to us," accuses a voice, and then digits that may pass as fingers prick and pull at her, "*You* wear the bridal dress. *You are the offering.*"

"No," she shakes her head, trying to make it more forceful and deliberate than a spasming jerk, "This ... this is m-my g-g-great-great grandmother's dress."

And more of those insubstantial cries erupt into that subconscious part of her hearing, more hisses and yowls and scatterings.

"Then you serve no purpose to us," comes a deeper, much clearer voice, and the others scuttle away.

She turns to see one there who looks more human, definitely masculine, tall, well-muscled, even a length of dark hair emerging in some healthy abundance from his pate. His red eyes stare fixedly on her.

"For your deception, you will be last. You will watch as we kill the others, then you will die."

She drops to her knees, taking the thing's left hand in her own, noting that though it is large, the fingers thicker than one might expect, the nails dense and curved to points like those of a bird of prey, it still looks more human than the others, giving her a strange sense of comfort. She averts her eyes, looking at the floor, much of which is stained with blood and other broken bits of things and people, her friends.

"Please don't kill me," she begs, her voice weak, though she fights the inclination to stammer, trying to give more strength to her fearful words, "I'll do whatever you want, just please don't kill me."

"You are a pathetic thing," the seeming leader declares, pulling his hand away, and she drops her arms in surrender. "Kill them."

A more rejoiceful chattering arises even as the suitable voices emit similar cries on more mundane wavelengths. Many rush over, grabbing her, roughly returning her to her feet, turning her. She watches, stoic, stunned, as time is taken to tease and torment Ryan, eventually ending him. Her efforts to protect him from being flayed prove wasted, even as he eventually expires.

Sweet, sweet suffering ...

They then move to Kaitlyn's younger sister, collecting Kathryn's body, ripping off her clothes, and the lithe, youthful girl is finally brought back to wakefulness with nigh inhuman-sounding screams as they decide to do to her what they intended to the groom, peeling away her virile skin. Iris remains mute throughout, no tears even falling from her vacant, spoiled eyes.

Ambrosial pain, yes, yes ...

She can hear the orgiastic cries that do not so clearly resonate on this plane even as others make obvious sounds of barbaric enjoyment, some huffing in sharp bellows, others yipping like barking animals. The crowd of them seems too numerous for this room, their forms varied beyond nature, beyond sanity. Why has no one else heard this? Why is no help coming? Is she broken?

She wonders this of herself.

She finds her gaze again on the masculine one, its form rippling with dark muscles, veins in unhealthy, inhuman prominence. Her arms and legs are held in steel-like grips of others, and she feels the sickening length of tentacles threading about her, holding her further.

"And now *you*," he says with a steaming coat of eroticism.

Stop ...

He does so, instantly, and she sees something there that strikes her as alien, even more so than the appearance of these beasts, in as much as she has grown to know them. She sees fear.

You are more pathetic than the creature you threaten.

She does not know how she hears this, how she comprehends the unearthly-sounding words. She holds still, listening, watching.

You will not kill her ...

"But she is not the Bride."

You think that because you command this rabble that you are worthy? I could send you to tortures that make what these humans have endured feel like a meaningless pastime ...

The beast stiffens further.

"I merely-."

You are where you are by design! You have been given what meager power you have by design! The girl, she is the Bride ...

Silence ensues, all of them cowed, even Iris. The voice that speaks sounds as though it comes from even further away, yet its malignance and power is undeniable.

She was put in the bath, yes? ...

SWORD OF THE BUTTERFLY

"Yes."
And she did not die ...
No answer comes to this statement, for such is obvious.
What fortitude must a mere human possess to survive thus? ...
Another weighty moment of silence stretches, and this time, it seems the speaker is desirous of an answer.
"I ... don't know."
Fool! She is no mere human. Fool! You will be demoted, marked. You are not worthy of the paltry position you have been given ...
She sees a blink of disappointment on the alien features.
Ask her what she will do to continue to keep her life ...
This infuses the beast, eyes narrowing as it grates out, "What is your life worth to you?"
She again drops to her knees, realizing the hold which once bound her has slackened enough that she is able to lean forward, burying her obsequious face against the tall being's left thigh, her head very near his prominent genitals, something about which she seems to care little, if at all.
"I will serve. I will do whatever I am commanded," she spurts, instinctively, "Please, *please*, don't kill me."
Her instinct to live feels as though a flaring, a pulsing inflammation. Nothing else matters to her, not her friends who now lie dead, not her family, not even what in hell is even going on. She just wants to live.
You see? She endures ...
He nods, slowly, looking down at her, "I s-."
You see nothing*! Were I not bothered by having to keep such a watchful eye on you, you would have killed her, thus denying us her obvious power. Do you see? Do ... you ... see! ...*
And he openly trembles now, and with such a display of fright and such a showing of anger on the part of the speaker, all the others begin to also convey trepidation. She remains on her knees, but she registers this, noting that even with their alien-nature, their obvious power, they may also feel fear.
"I ...," he begins, stumbling on his words, appearing to ponder them, a slow nod coming to his head, "I see."

Good. Now, look closely, for you will never see this again. She shall never again kneel to the likes of you …

And he does indeed stare, taking in the sight.

Others are coming. You will protect her. Nothing will take her away or take her life. Others are coming who are more capable than you, and they shall collect her for us and bring her somewhere safe where she may be used as is her due …

"Yes, Master. Thy Will be done."

Naught but silence now results, and he finally looks back down.

"Get her to her feet," he growls, and hands and tendrils again take her, "But do not harm her. You heard the Master."

And so did she, and she wonders if the Master knows she heard, and she wonders what it all means. What is her *due*?

CHAPTER ONE

He stands alone atop the building, the night a plague to vision, but something in his eyes belies a preternatural focus. A light wind tries to have its way with his trench coat, producing little movement in the well-worn fabric. The color is dark, variance of hues speaking out amongst his other clothing, though all look desaturated, as though old and brethren to the night. A utilitarian aspect hints in his dress, but the main focus is his eyes, peering out beneath the scraggy array of his short hair. His jaw is square, though not overly large, a shadowy forest of whiskers grown up from neglect.

He pauses in his scanning, for there is only so much he may see from atop this broad three-story building. He raises his chin, inhaling deeply. Something catches his notice, and with a brief flex of his legs, he springs away, launching himself into the air in a way that seems humanly impossible.

He is not unused to this, for he has been a tracker and a hunter nearly his whole life. He plies the family trade, and though he is not the best, he is far from the worst. Experience has given him some useful edge, and he hopes to prove successful here. He moves across the top of another night-quiet building in this town, the boots on his feet reporting his progress. The evening takes the sound, eating it, as though the stillness were a sensory famine. The staccato finds interruption as he again leaps through the air.

He's been on this one's trail for a while, hoping to catch glimpses like shadows from fire. Things had proved slow, methodical, taunting, as they are wont to be at times, until this most recent upheaval. They know he tails a powerful one, which is why this is his quarry. It would not do to send the untried to meaningless death.

He stops atop another building, not far now from where he senses the latest disturbance. He slows, walking at a determined pace but mitigating his noise. He doesn't think anyone will look up here, and even if they do, the shadows may well hide him, but he sees no reason to wantonly invite scrutiny. He pauses near the metal structure of an air vent, staying close to it as he peers across the four lanes of the street. He sees the yellow police tape, the real scene inside that other building. He'll not get any closer, though, as the many lights crowning the vehicles announce the continued show. The police are not done with their investigation. It doesn't matter to him. With the trail so fresh, he doesn't need to get any closer. He stares, losing himself in his focus, and then he deeply draws in breath as though suddenly gifted with the ability. He blinks once, then moves his head in the direction he knows he must follow.

A trail which leads to a room, this one constituting a small space. Three of those inside move about freely, but one, the fourth, sits in a chair, his thick, muscled arms pulled back and held by handcuffs. He seems not at all perturbed by this confinement as he looks at the others, his eyes piercing, challenging beneath the tangled, chaotic mess of his short, black hair. His sideburns stretch down to beside his ear lobes, also overgrown and unkempt, and his blunt chin looks as though it might be its own weapon. His overall appearance is one of generous, good health, swarthy in tone, and amused by his situation.

"We got you at the scene, blood on you, so just admit what you did and tell us why."

The suspect's eyes gaze intently into those of the detective, the man's blazer on a hook outside the interrogation room, his shirtsleeves unrolled, one unbuttoned. His tie is loose, the collar of his white shirt undone. He does not look to be entirely past his prime, but he is on the downward slope.

"Do you think having me handcuffed keeps you safe?" the man challenges, the edges of his lips curling into a grin.

The two uniformed officers look from the man to the detective, a shimmer of unease coats them both like translucent oil.

SWORD OF THE BUTTERFLY

The detective walks closer, looking down at the prisoner. "I think you being handcuffed and unarmed while we're armed and trained means we're pretty safe, yes. Now ... the *question*."

The man presses closer, the wood of the chair straining, as he closes the distances between himself and the detective, his prominent chin leading the way. The two officers move in, one on either side of the man, but then he sits back, looking at the pair, grinning more openly.

He then lapses into a soliloquy, and the detective has heard it before. He moves away, wandering about as the man speaks, pausing, looking up at the ceiling in the tiring room.

"... because I can, because I enjoy it, because you are all so *pathetic*," the prisoner says, "and that is why you are not safe around me ... *ever*."

The detective walks back over, his seething contained but not enough to completely conceal. He shares a lingering stare with the man before turning to one of the uniformed officers. "Kovar, go get the shackles for our *guest* here."

The amused twist to the man's lips never leaves, his eyes going from one person to the other, as though hungry, until presently his ankles are held together by much thicker chains and metal than what makes up the handcuffs still about his wrists.

"There," the detective says, arms crossed as he regards his prisoner, "Satisfied?"

The only answer he gets simmers through the ubiquitous grin on the man's face.

"Well?" he continues, "Answer the question."

The man peers up at the detective, eyes moving beneath his suborbital ridge, his mouth opening a bit further, showing more of his yellowed teeth, and then there is a flash of something in those eyes. Something that jars the detective, something he obviously does not want to see.

The moment passes quickly, for it is then that the prisoner flexes his considerable muscles and breaks free from his bonds, lunging from the seat and lashing out with hideous speed, his left hand open, fingers slightly bent, tensed, the nails of those fingers tear through the flesh of the detective's throat, blood erupting from the deep gash. The wounded man stumbles back and falls, his own hands coming up to clutch at his ruined neck as his life pumps out with the spreading spray of his blood.

The two uniformed officers are momentarily stunned, eyes gone wide with shock. One reaches for his revolver, but the man is exceedingly quick, moving over to this nearer cop and again striking out with terrible speed and strength, using the thick nails of his fingers as deadly weapons, slashing at tender flesh. The third manages to pull his weapon, aiming and firing, and the sounds ring out loudly in the confined room. The man has turned, intent on dispatching the last of his interrogators, and he dodges with a deftness perhaps unexpected in one his size.

He closes the distance even as the officer methodically retreats, still firing, but there is nowhere to go in the locked room. A third casualty arises in the chamber, more blood marking the walls and floor, some even splashed up onto the ceiling, such is the ferocity of the killing.

The station is on alert, alarms ringing out to those here at this hour, and they are converging on the room just as the secured, metal door bows and bursts out from within, the reinforced hinges unsuitable to the task of the force applied. The bent piece of metal collides with the wall, and clanks to the ground. The man comes barreling out and into a barrage of bullets.

His speed proves an amazement as he moves toward the firing line, dodging and weaving, though some of the shots find their mark, bloody wounds opening on the man's shoulder, arm, and thigh, but such does not slow him in the least. His face is still that set mask of homicidal enjoyment, teeth clenched and bared, lips curled into some deformity of a smile, and all about lies, darkness, and blood.

It takes a moment to reach the adrenalin-heightened brains of the police, but there is something not "right" about the man. Something in the way he moves and endures the ballistic wounding in his thick muscles, even something now in the way he looks, as though the growing shadow of the beast within has come more unto appearance. Still, these moments are like the flashes of lightning bugs, and out just as quickly, as the man moves systematically from one to another, executing them all, increasing the volume of the blood bath.

SWORD OF THE BUTTERFLY

He finally stops, as though the eye of the storm settling over a broken home. In his hand he holds the limp body of his latest kill, his impressive fist about the torn collar of the uniform. He looks toward the door, his eyes narrowing subtly.

"You," he utters in his basso voice, that determined grin increasing a few scant degrees.

In the doorway stands the man who had been lately leaping across the rooftops, stalking, tracking, and now he has found his quarry. He steps in, holding position, looking with obvious distaste upon the other and the gruesome display he has wrought. He stands ready, his posture relaxed as one familiar with deadly fighting.

The suspect drops the dead cop, turning to fully face the intruder, his lips curing into a smirk. "Dessert," he says, lunging with a shocking suddenness, clawed hands leading the way.

The other, the Hunter, pulls forth twin daggers, the blades nine inches in length, a darkly drawn runic pattern lining the sharp edges of the rich, deep gray metal. He holds his weapons with a practiced ease, moving forward to meet the attack, then aside, not wanting to let those powerful hands find purchase, and he counters with quick swipes, one dagger used more defensively than the other. The two part from their initial test, eyeing one another, neither having found their mark.

Unwilling to offer too much of a respite, the man again attacks, bringing forth a flurry of blows, pressing, trying to use his advantage of size and strength to finish his opponent. The Hunter, though, proves more capable than those who so recently fell victim, dodging, returning the attacks, even suffering glancing blows without faltering. The man replies with his own ability, not allowing the ornately-tooled daggers to find a place in his flesh, and it may be seen how the weapons sometimes glow with luminescent edges in the scant moments before a potential strike.

Despite the evident ferocity and speed, the fight is methodical, calculated, neither willing to make a mistake. The carnage left in the wake of the man's activities this evening incenses the Hunter to no end, but he cannot afford to dim his wits with anger or passion. His face is almost a calm mask, his movement fluid, experienced, as the dance continues. His eyes do not always look directly at his prey as he moves with instinct, the motions almost a thing unto themselves. His opponent keeps his eyes locked on the other, as though they might consume in their eagerness. It seems the very vessels within rise up in great definition, threatening to tear free and lunge out to aid in the fight.

And then, like the sudden snapping of bone, it is over.

The two stop, the man still grinning, and an exhale emerges noisily from his gaping nostrils. The Hunter slumps, his outré weapons clanging to the ground as his fingers lose their tension. With his left hand, the man pushes on his opponent, angling his right downward, and the corpse slides away slowly, revealing the glistening, blood-soaked fist and forearm. The gaping, dark wound in the torso shows where the man has finally hit his mark, punching through his prey.

"I can see your heart beating," the man says, standing over the other as blood pools thickly.

The Hunter says nothing in return.

*****

They move steadily, quietly, through the underground passageways, both wearing dark colors, both suits utilitarian. They had gotten to the entryway wearing reasonable civilian attire, carrying their packs, then geared up once in a more secluded place. Lilja strapped her leg holster over the cargo pants, then the combat harness atop the long-sleeved shirt, slipping on the tactical gloves before arming herself with the pistol and submachine gun. Her vibrant red hair is tied up in a high ponytail, a shemagh-scarf about her neck, the folds showing a dark pattern of black and shades of gray.

Both of them wear combat boots as they trudge as silently as possible along the stone and concrete grounds, sometimes avoiding puddles of fluid, other times forced to move carefully through such when no other options afford themselves. They had come via abandoned metro tunnels to get here, moving along inexorably in a slow, creeping descent, further and deeper. Those footsteps, no matter how much they try, are not always sufficiently low of volume, and they even sometimes create echoes. Doubts may fill minds as to whether all such heard are indeed a reflection of sound waves or perhaps noises made by something else.

SWORD OF THE BUTTERFLY

This far down, they know they are not alone, so they try to make it as difficult as possible to draw the attention of any others.

Skothiam leads the trek, one hand pointing a sleek flashlight, illuminating the way, the other holding his cane, the highly-polished and reinforced ebony promising more of a lethal than balancing function. He carries a custom-modified Walther P99 on the left of a shoulder holster, the other side sporting a pair of extra magazines. She carries her FN P90, leading hand about the fore grip, suppressor and subsonic bullets not part of this mission, such stealth unneeded. She keeps the tactical light on, sometimes adding to Skot's beam, other times moving about and rear as she regularly checks that no one is watching or following. Whenever her angle passes him, Lilja lowers the barrel, her extended right index finger near, but not on, the trigger. She cannot shake the feeling they are being watched and followed.

He knows the way, having been told it by his sister before they set out on this mission. *They have taken him to this plac*e, Nicole revealed, gleaning the information through one of her many inexplicable abilities, the ones that make her seem less of this corporeal world. Charles Felcraft, second cousin, thirty-eight years old, killed in battle, and his body had not been left where they might retrieve it and show it the proper honor. She had even discerned something of the nature of the demon that had slain him, a very powerful one, more powerful than they have encountered on earth in some time.

How did it get here? What does its coming mean?

These questions may be pondered afterwards, but for now, they need to deal with the body of their fallen.

Deeper in the tunnels, and Skot moves his beam aside, peering. Lilja creeps up beside him, angling her barrel away. Her depthful blue eyes look up at him, curiosity on her features, then she stares further, trying to see what he sees.

"What is it?" she whispers.

"There." He points with the hand holding the cane , "A light."

He flicks off his torch, and now she can indeed better see – a faint gleam ahead of them.

They move within a careful pace, though both feel an eagerness to reach the source of the illumination. Once there, it shows that they have found a small underground church or shrine, rock carved into depressed shelves on the curving walls, a table rising up from the center as though grown from stone, its top spreading out, narrowly, the structure in the shape of a 'T'. There are also sigils hewn into the walls. He knows many of them. She feels certain she recognizes some, having come across similar shapes in her capacity as librarian, researcher, and curator of a rare books collection at a prestigious private university.

An ornate, metal brazier stands atop the table, casting an ominous red-orange hue throughout the chamber, smoke wafting up from it, the dark metal appearing to have given way to a good deal of rust. Lilja curls her top lip a bit, blinking, eyes glancing to Skot then back to the outré-seeming blaze. It smells weird to her, making the air blurry, and she pulls her scarf up to cover her mouth and nose. She gives another concerned glance to him, but though he has a history of respiratory illness and sensitivity, he acts unaffected by the smoke.

He is intent on investigating the room, and he moves further in, examining the stone shelves, even the table and the brazier, the flames giving an eerie cast to his features. She knows he is more attuned to the "Shadow World" than is she, and she wonders what he sees. Still, she remains at the door, keeping close eye on the tunnels to her right and left.

She strains to see and hear, knowing full well that an invisible attack is possible. Still, from what she has learned during her own time in training as a Hunter, the more invisible they are, the more difficulty they have in directly affecting the corporeal plane. Their lack of tangibility may be useful for many things but not generally in a straight offensive.

And just as she thinks of this, she remembers their affinity with the shadow and darkness, both of which are in abundance here. She remains calm, alert, swooping her attention about these ways of ingress as well as keeping note of Skot inside the room. She then hears it, jerking her barrel in that direction.

"We have to move," she says, coming up to him.

He retrieves a shiny object from a recessed portion cut within the far wall, a decently-sized amulet on a thin, metal chain that had been draped about a small sculpture, the indistinct object rising from the stone like an unnatural stalagmite. He carefully wraps it in a cloth napkin then nods to her, and they continue moving.

SWORD OF THE BUTTERFLY

They make their way through another passageway, this one angling about in a lazy, rightwards curve. They move with more haste, seeming now to have instinctively decided for increased speed over stealth. Their presence here is known. They both halt when they reach the next room, this one also lit up by a similar brazier as the other, but where the prior had been a shrine, this one is a torture chamber.

There are devices and tools throughout, but what draws their attention, what causes terrifying feelings of shock, is the man hanging lifelessly on the cross, his body nailed in a form of crucifixion. He is naked, covered in blood, and a dark, horrible wound, a gaping hole, shows in his torso at the region of his heart. Small markings can also be spied over most of his flesh, as though he has been branded. The blood gleams with a freshness, and Skot steps closer, eyes narrowing as he focuses, and then the man on the cross suddenly gasps, unleashing a long, horrible moan.

Both of them physically start, then rush over, ostensibly to get him down from where he hangs. She had said Charles was dead. Even within her aethereal investigations, Nicole had seen him dead. *How can he be alive? What has he endured?*

All of these thoughts crash through Skot's mind, but before anything else may be done, things quickly happen. His cousin's head slumps, whatever life may have been sustained within him gone, and Lilja turns back toward the dark, gaping entryway, pointing her gun.

"Something is coming," she hisses out in a whisper, bending her knees to lower her center of gravity, holding her steady aim with clear signs of experience.

Despite that history, despite all she has done and seen, she feels a shroud of dread overtaking her even as she senses *something* rushing towards them within the darkness. A rapid clatter, as though of bone on rock, rises, the wide beam of her tactical light showing as much as it may before the tunnel curves out of sight. She barely has time to register that Skot has not drawn his weapon before a rush of horrible, multi-legged beasts comes into view. She pulls the trigger, bullets expelling rapidly, these now treated in the special way by the Felcraft's Weapons Master, Jericho, giving them more lethality to just such unearthly creatures as now sets upon them.

Black ichor spews up from well-aimed bullets, wounds opening in chests and heads. The things move on many limbs, some even capable of use as arms, making them unusual targets in more ways than one, but she manages to drop several as they near. More shots are fired, her barrel moving minutely to adjust the aim, and then this initial attack is repelled. She has brought along the P90 for not only its ease of use in such tight quarters but also its capacity, and the gun now has about half the 50 round magazine remaining. She squeezes the trigger as others arrive, unleashing more bullets at a renewed approach on the part of the demons.

These are the grayish ones, of ashen pallor, such is their flesh somewhat mottled. Their narrow, elongated heads are hairless, slightly ridged, their pupil-less eyes like shiny red pools inviting insanity into their depths. They wield deadly talons on their hands and feet, their overly-wide maws crowded with pointed teeth, and from what she has been told, these are more of the 'lesser' kind. She saw something similar in the warehouse back in the City when she first learned of the existence of such things, and she is told these are more easily killed.

She does not necessarily find it so, but there is a lull as she empties the magazine, having jerked her Glock free, firing off a few rounds from her sidearm, moving the pistol about, looking for more targets. She re-holsters, then reloads the submachine gun, glancing at Skot, her breath heavier than she had realized, and she sees him pouring a thick substance over his cousin, as though anointing him with the contents of the glass phial.

"What are you-?" she tries, but he speaks.

"Step back," he says, firmly, holding out his left hand, and she does, keeping an eye and ear on the avenue of approach, knowing another attack is imminent.

He murmurs something, something in that language she has heard before, the one that seems as though it may be similar to Latin, but it is not that same tongue. She realizes it must be a prayer of some kind, a benediction, and just then the body lights up, an eldritch blue to the dancing flames, lending more obvious sign to the supernatural origins of the fire.

"What are you doing? He's alive."

SWORD OF THE BUTTERFLY

"Not anymore," Skot says, then he glances at her, noting the bewilderment, "He has been dead for a while. He was artificially, *magickally*, infused with a bit of life. He's bait."

She wants to ask more, but she sees him pull out his pistol, aiming into the hallway. She turns in that instant, seeing as more of the demons round the corner, and they both unload their charged bullets, occasional glimpses of amber flaring forth as though of tracer rounds, though the actual cause is more akin to that which gives life to the blue fire that thoroughly consumes his cousin's corpse.

"We need to get out of here," Lilja says when this attack is repelled, "Are we done down here?"

"Yes," Skot utters, and she sees a shadow pass over his features.

Though she again wishes to know more, such can wait, so she nods once in response to him, both of them reloading, both low on ammunition, and she leads the way out.

*****

"It was a trap, you know?"

They both look at Nicole, both having been given time to clean up, change, and now they sit in this expansive room in the manor, sipping of calming tea. Lilja recalls meeting Skot's sister, Nicole-Angeline Felcraft, and being taken not only by her beauty but also her aspect. The woman, slender of form, tall, seems as though she almost floats and speaks through wind rather than being a normal part of this physical world. Even when she does show expression, a smile or a movement of brow, it proves subtle, as if a continued attempt to speak in a foreign language merely for the benefit of the natives.

She is married, happily so now for a little over fifteen years, mother of three children of her own, but she does not even have a hyphenated surname. Regardless of marriage or gender, the family name always remains.

"And yet we still went," Skot replies, coloring his words with enough sarcasm that they all pick up on it.

Jericho stands to the side of the main area, thick, tattooed arms crossed. He furrows his brow at these words but remains silent. The

Matriarch, Joanne Felcraft, looks about to speak, but her daughter intercedes.

"It was an acceptable risk, and you know that. Otherwise, why did you go? There are any number of resources from which to choose."

Her hair is a rich brown, not quite as dark as her mother's had once been, and it falls down in thick, straight locks to nearly the middle of her back. She wears a dress, also her usual attire, the coloring and accenting pattern elegant, adding to her almost sublime appearance. Her tone, even now when under some stress, always calm. Skot cannot shake the feeling that the more she delves into her power, the less she is of this world.

"Nicole!" and all eyes turn to the mother, "You risked your brother's and Lilja's lives?"

"Mom," Skot begins, but he is spoken over.

"My brother is the Head of the Family, and he is well aware of the risks."

"She's right," he continues, "No one *made* me go."

"Then what about Lilja?" Joanne persists, gesturing with one hand to the woman, seeming quite protective of her, "She's had very little training. Why take her?"

"She *protected* me, Mom," Skot says, "and she had many more kills than I did. She may be new to … *this*, but she is not new to this sort of danger in general."

Joanne smiles warmly, then rises, walking over, giving Lilja a hug, one which is accepted somewhat awkwardly, judging from the young lady's reaction.

"Thank you, dear, thank you for saving my son's life."

"I … uhm." Lilja licks her lips, her pale flesh flushing.

The elder woman rises up from the embrace, giving a pointed glance to her children before moving back to the soft cushion of her chair, taking the nearby crystal glass in hand and having a sip of the Montresor Recioto della Valpolicella wine. Skot glances at Lilja, and when her eyes meet his, he gives her a very sincere smile. She returns it, her bashfulness still evident. He leans forward the short distance to the coffee table, setting his saucer and cup atop it, then slips his right arm about Lilja's shoulders, pulling gently. She leans into him.

SWORD OF THE BUTTERFLY

"They wanted us to find the body," Nicole intones, her slender, tapering fingers held entwined before her, very loose, almost as if not quite touching, the interlacing pattern more an affectation, "The skin wearer was not there."

"Skin wearer?" Lilja asks, confusion taking her face as she looks up at Skot, whispering the question.

He nods, eyes back to her. "Some of the more powerful demons are able to ... shapeshift, for lack of a better term, taking on the guise of a human. It is not possession of a human host. They change their appearance."

"We rarely see it," Nicole adds, "As Skothiam says, only the most powerful are able to do it."

Lilja looks about, noting the heavy expressions writ on everyone present, though they all show it in their own ways.

"Uhm, so something allowed this powerful ... demon," she says, obviously still not comfortable with the terminology, "to get through to our world?"

Skot nods. "Yes, and though we are concerned with that-"

"We need to know where he now is. We have to find him," Nicole finishes.

"So, your cousin," Lilja continues, speaking slowly, carefully, "was ... bait? Why bring us down there? Was that to throw us off the other's trail?"

It takes her a moment to realize that all eyes are now on Skot. She blinks, looking about and back, and he sighs, heavily, an act which does nothing to answer her query or allay concerns.

"Those are very good questions, Lily," he finally speaks, and she wonders if that is all he wanted to say, "We're still looking into that, but it would not be the first time they have laid traps or such plans."

"They're a manipulative lot, the Infernal," his mother comments.

"We should inform the Malkuths."

Joanne's top lip sneers just the barest bit at her son's words, then she covers it with a healthy sip of her dessert wine.

"Prudence seems to dictate that we give them some information regarding the skin wearer," Nicole begins, "It would be helpful to have them also hunting such a demon, and it would serve as a gesture that we'd expect the same from them if they were to learn of such a creature here on earth."

"Hmph."

All eyes turn momentarily to the matriarch, but she merely goes about to sipping more of her wine, choosing to not notice the attention. Once a brief moment has passed, Nicole looks expectantly at her older brother.

"We'll do that. Let them know of the Demon and what it has done. They may even be told it took one of ours, but no more detail than that."

A heavy sigh draws them back to Joanne.

"I'll call Marcella tomorrow, maybe tonight," she says, mentioning Charles' mother, then she sets her eyes back on Skot, "Arrangements will need to be made for the memorial service."

He nods.

"I wish we had the body and could have handled it differently," she continues, looking away, forlorn, which she punctuates with another sip of the wine.

Lilja looks at the woman, suddenly taken with thoughts of all she must have seen in her seven decades. What was it like for her to come into a family like this? Skot has told Lilja more of his brethren in the ensuing months, and she knows that his mother was no Hunter. She married into it, embracing fully the revelations made to her as well as the responsibility and stress, yes, the very deep, real stress. Joanne had lost her firstborn before losing her husband, one to battle, the other to a lingering, debilitating illness that continued to baffle and stymie the doctors throughout.

Skot had explained something of how they forge unions in this family, how there is that rarity in the genes that not only grants some of them the potential of their supernatural abilities but also works on a deeper, more underlying level to bring them together. There are few of them, so very few, and if they remain apart, they might well lose this war, but when they create bonds, love, progeny, they stand a better chance. It is not lost on her what this may mean of the deep attraction the two of them share for one another.

Lilja further studies the elder woman, watching her, knowing that such arrangements as are about to be made are more commonplace in

SWORD OF THE BUTTERFLY

this family than they would like. Do the feelings mingle with the sense of responsibility, or do they become eclipsed by it, she wonders. She understands this, what it may mean, and she experiences a type of fear deep within herself as her musings run their course.

"We would have brought the body back if we could," Skot says, breaking Lilja's train of thought, and she turns her eyes up to him. "If the situation had been less hostile, we would have stayed until a larger team could come for retrieval."

His mother nods, slowly, the tone of his statement not one of defense or explanation but merely conveying an unfortunate circumstance.

"The condition of Charles's corpse," Nicole says, her tone slow, soothing, and all attention is turned to her, "He was not just bait. He was a message."

*****

The two of them sit in the sumptuous chamber, the lighting an elegant accentuation, adding much without drawing undue attention to itself. Artwork is glimpsed in these writhing shadows, bold, some quite evidently erotic. One of the tall walls bears floor-to-ceiling shelves, the topmost holding three statuettes. The rest are crowded with books, and if one were adept at the evaluation of such things, a fortune would be known to reside there.

Three books in particular, though, are missing from that private collection.

He sits, a glass of very fine red wine before him. He sips from it on occasion, keeping his fingertips on the stem. He wears what he considers casual clothes, though most might find them to be rather elegant, perhaps even uncomfortable for more intimate, unguarded moments. But then, rarely is any moment in his life unguarded, and assuredly this one is not.

The other person sitting here, a woman, also mingles some sense of refinement along with relaxation. Her dark hair is long, straight, fine. She wears it parted in the middle, the style almost archaic in its manipulation of simplicity. Her face is well-fleshed, rounded, the body beneath her dressing also alluring of curve. Her genes favor her, and along with many other benefits, she exhibits little effort to maintain her attractive figure.

A similar glass of wine sits on an elegant end table near the equally exquisite chair. As with the overall décor in this room, none of it is ornate, ostentatious, but all of it shows a deep quality for those of a mind to know of these things. She quietly scans over a digital notepad, reading some information, occasionally reaching toward the crystal glass, having a gentle sip, eyes rarely straying from the device. He waits, patiently, having been summoned here. She gave him the barest of acknowledgements when he arrived, merely looking at him with those dark, intoxicating eyes of hers, then silently inviting him to sit. No one had asked if he wanted to join her with a serving of wine, no, it had just been brought.

"It seems a very powerful demon has entered our world," she finally speaks, reaching again for the drink, her eyes finally moving to him as the glass comes to her lips.

He blinks, letting the barest hint of perplexity take his features.

"How powerful?" he finally speaks into the drilling silence of her gaze.

"It wears the guise of a human."

A split second passes, and she senses a touch of fear there, like a gossamer whisper from shadow.

"Where is it?"

"That is not precisely known," she answers, her voice smooth.

"How did we come by this information?"

A curl touches her lips, and in that moment, he knows he will not like the answer, and she gains some sadistic satisfaction from this.

"We received a very thoughtful and astutely political missive from the Felcrafts."

And just as a curl had briefly danced over her lips, giving them a short up-curve, something similarly fleeting also takes his, though in the opposite direction.

"I suppose they want us to also hunt it."

"Come now, Denman, don't sound petulant. It doesn't benefit you."

He stiffens for a moment, one shorter than the fear, the frown, but she still catches it. She is keen to such things, almost as though a hunter

SWORD OF THE BUTTERFLY

of negative emotions, especially ones she may cause, directly or indirectly, and she senses them, as though somehow snatching them up for a dark consumption.

"Of course, they want us to also hunt it," she resumes when he has calmed, "Why would they not? We would do the same if one as rare and powerful as this had been discovered by us. It must be found and exorcised."

He nods once after she spends a time just staring sat him. She continues staring.

"Do you wish me to hunt it?"

She expends some more small instances watching, and she is pleased that she senses no more of the fear, no incredulity.

"I am not yet sure of the course of action. I have just recently received the message."

He doubts that, believing she has invited him here to make this informing to him. He watches his cousin as she goes back to looking over the datapad. She is a few years his junior, but her abilities far outstrip his own, thus is she the Head of the Family Malkuth.

"Mayhap this could be a way for you to make up for your failure regarding the book."

He controls himself, not reacting to this barb. She loves to fling out these stingers, though sometimes, within them, is a sincere way to do some good work. One excels in this family by developing a resistance to the venom, not succumbing to it.

"I would gladly undertake this hunt, if that is your wish." He dips his head once at the end of this declaration.

"We require more information. I'll not send you blindly and alone to take on such a creature."

He moves his head again, another single nod.

"Of course, you were not exactly alone when you went to acquire the book, were you?"

He feels another stab.

"I was not," he admits what is already known to them both.

"We knew the Infernal were active there. We even let you use one of our most powerful dowsers, which you also lost, but in the end, you did not realize how much you were not alone."

He knows she is referring to the Head of the Felcrafts, Skothiam, being there. He also knows she is well aware of his inability to detect such a man, should he so choose to remain hidden. If anything, it shows the lengths to which their rivals were willing to go to acquire the book, efforts not matched by the Malkuths. The book still resides in the university's rare book collection, but it is decidedly under the custodianship of their rivals. A move against it now would be too much an open declaration of war, and they cannot afford to so fight one another, not when a greater threat looms.

"Is it not acceptable that the book remains out of *their* hands?"

She lets a moment linger betwixt them.

"It is," she begrudgingly gives him, "and this way, we may even keep surreptitious watch over it. It is quite an eloquent solution."

He lets a smirk barely touch his lips.

"Did you resign your position there?" she asks, angling more at him, her language evident to one such as him, "or will you be returning this session to … *teach*?"

And her smirk is more open, ending only when the glass again reaches her lips, and another sip of the fine wine is taken.

"I took a leave of absence," he finally says, trying not to give in to her efforts, adjusting himself as though becoming more comfortable.

"What a pity. I am sure many young minds will suffer without your guidance."

"Yes … a pity."

He merely looks at her. She and the family engage in many forms of philanthropy, and all of it is part of their continued effort to help humanity from its lost ways. She sometimes even seems to show sincere sympathy, which confuses him. He supposes it is part of her emotional perversion.

"There are still the other books," she leads, and he wonders why she states the obvious, and just as he is about to speak into another lengthening silence, she resumes, "We have people working on that, but I am curious about this new demon. How, why, where, and *who*. I'd like to know the true extent of its power."

He again gives a single nod, feeling as though he is more concerned with its purpose.

SWORD OF THE BUTTERFLY

"I'll send a reply, letting them know we shall also work to locate it," she concludes, then she fixes him with another look, and he almost squirms under it, "You and Skot worked *so well* together last year, maybe I ought to just lend you out to him to find this one, hmmm?"

He narrows his eyes at her, seething.

"Calm down, Denman," she says, finishing her wine and taking to her feet, which he also does out of courtesy and some defensiveness, "You know how much we feed on the mistakes of our own. For me to tease you is a concession. Had you truly failed, you'd be feeling *much* worse."

Before he may say anything else, she saunters over, placing a hand on his chest, then leaning in the short distance to give a brief kiss to his mouth. She then heads to leave the chamber.

"Asenath?" he halts her, and she turns.

"Hmmm?" she perks her sculpted eyebrows.

"Did you have any specific orders for me?"

She grins, lightly, "I'll let you know."

*****

He is young for what he does, though not so much so that it brings to mind questions of such things as nepotism or even more fantastical fancies like deals with the devil. He has earned his place. The tattoos on his sleekly muscled body tell that tale, dotted throughout his torso, down his arms, even over the top of the segments of his fingers. The stars at his shoulders, the epaulets, just below the collar bones, those tell of his high station within the organization. Some call them the Marks of Cain.

The sleeves of his dark colored shirt are rolled up to near his elbows, and he wears latex gloves. He takes up the hand of the man lying on the table, moving a bit, somewhat indelicately, to get a better hold. He brings the small, sharp clippers to the index finger, worming them into a good position, and he snips, easily cutting through flesh and bone. The first of ten digits falls free of its former connection, resistance evident from the chilled condition of the body. A lack of reaction and blood shows the man is dead.

He is nearly done when the others enter the room.

"I used to do this when I first started," he speaks, his back still to the entryway, "It was more difficult then. I was young, frightened ... determined." His voice carries an obvious accent, his words slow, though not from lack of familiarity with the language but from a lack of need to feel or act rushed. "I am only still one of those now," he continues, almost as an aside, and his head moves with what may pass as a short, introspective chuckle.

He then turns, picking up the smoldering, thin cigar from the nearby ashtray, holding it with the pair of tongs already secured about its body. He takes a lengthy taste as he eyes the men. His brown hair is slicked back high on his head, the styling of it making it appear darker. His pale brown eyes are sloped slightly downward, and as he raises his dimpled chin to better study the arrivals, it almost gives him a gentle cast. Those who know him know there is little to nothing gentle about him. He exhales a thick, piquant plume, still looking at the one man with whom he holds much less familiarity than the others.

"You come alone."

The man to whom he speaks is large, overweight, perhaps even oafish. He nods, the expression somewhat jerky. The other man raises his eyebrows in bid for more.

"My," he begins, then clears his throat, "My partner didn't come. I talked to him about it, but ... I don't think he wants in ... anymore." A flash of eyes is given, as though a plea.

The other nods slowly, thoughtfully, then drags on the cigarillo before setting it back. He returns to his work.

"This man was one of us," he says, gesturing with the clippers toward the pallid face before getting back to the last of the digits.

The "guest" glances inquisitively at the others to his sides, and one gives a somewhat snarling up-nod, indicating to step closer. He listens, but he also peers at the corpse, belying some of his own nature.

"He betrayed us, but we still show him respect. It does not keep him intact, as you can see," the man says, and though it sounds like it might could be a joke, it is uttered with such dryness as to bring that to question.

No one laughs.

SWORD OF THE BUTTERFLY

He then takes up a different tool, this one with longer, slimmer pincers, fine grooves on the inner tips. He opens the body's mouth, getting a good grasp with the instrument, then takes a firm hold across the forehead with his left hand, strong fingers clamping against the temples. Thus stabilized, he begins wrestling with the teeth. It is clear he has done this before, and the guest somewhat cringes as he watches.

"We can't have jackals like you easily identifying him when he is found," the man says, keeping at the chore, depositing the teeth in a small container as they are extracted, "If you stayed out of our business, such dishonor would not be necessary."

The guest looks up from watching, staring at the speaker, but the man seems intent on the corpse. Tense time passes, further dull sounds of ripping and tearing and the clicks of the teeth collecting together in the cup. Then the man turns, removing and discarding the latex gloves.

"What are we to do with you, *Detective* Sladky?" the man asks, then he narrows his eyes, musing, "Sladky? What is this name? Are you Polish? Jewish?"

Alec Sladky shakes his head. "Czech."

The other continues to observe, his steely eyes unfaltering.

"A pity you are not Russian, *Detective*."

"I can still be of service," Alec tries.

"Yes, I am sure," the man says, stepping nearer, raising the already heightened level of tension, "Like you helped my predecessor, Gnegon, hmm?"

Alec nods eagerly.

"The one who is now dead," he adds, perking his eyebrows higher.

"I – I didn't have anything to do with that."

"I know you didn't," the man all but scoffs, moving away, then he turns, leaning back against the table, uncaring of the corpse, "Na vore shapka gorit."

Alec blinks, squinting his eyes, then shakes his head.

"Ah, yes, you are Czech," the other says, waving a hand dismissively, his silver watch gleaming in the dim lighting, "I forget. That is too bad." He lets a moment pass before he speaks again, "It means 'A thief's hat is burning'. It is proverb. It says that a guilty mind betrays itself. *You* betray yourself."

39

Alec raises his hands, palms somewhat outward. His opens his mouth, but before he may speak, the other continues.

"There is another – Bog pluta metit. God marks the crook. Some say these mean same thing. I do not agree." And he holds up his own hands, but his are not to ingratiate.

He angles them outward, displaying the tattoos on his fingers, hands, and forearms.

"Do you see, *Detective* Sladky?" he asks, always giving the title that subtle hint of malice, as though the word is distasteful to him, "I am marked, and I wear it proudly. I have chosen my side. You, though, you wear a burning hat, and you do not see it. That flame will eat you. You are ashamed of your own choices."

"No, I'm-," comes the refutation, but it is clipped as assuredly as the fingers that were once on the nearby corpse.

"*You* ... are ashamed," the voice resumes its usual controlled pace, "You are in turmoil ... Limbo. It is *here*. You have become *slime* in this city. This place is mud pit, pot of boiling sludge. It wants to be progressive, to give everyone equal footing. That makes everyone into *dirt,* unh?" He perks his eyebrows. "We will stand on dirt. No more getting soiled with cooperation; no more *dirty* cops. We do not need police. We will *not* bow. We will not even want your loyalty. If you are loyal to us, then you will *be* one of us ... not police officer."

Alec stammers, stumbling without making a sound or movement, such is his unease obvious.

"You corrupt cops and other *officials* of government, you will never be loyal to us. You will take and take. You are parasite, leech. You think you help us. No. You wish us to pay dues, like some tax, and you will continue to squeeze, draining our blood, and when there is not enough, you will throw us to our doom. Like *him*," he adds, an afterthought, as he turns, gesturing to the dead man, and a very subtle, self-satisfied smirk briefly takes his lips.

"Now that *I* am here," and he raises his left hand, holding up his first two fingers in an indication to himself, "Kazimir Volkov, things will be different."

SWORD OF THE BUTTERFLY

Another moment passes, Volkov staring intently at Alec. The detective has learned to hold his tongue, for once, and he merely waits. The other man, the City's new Russian crime boss, nods a single time.

"Your partner has chosen his side. Good for him. Now, Detective Sladky, you must choose."

Alec does not note the slight change in tone from the man, the sudden loss of venom from the appellation. He sees the obvious indication of dismissal, and he is escorted out, relieved enough that he still breathes, torn over what he shall do. His next stop will be a bar. One in which he feels comfortable, will be treated with respect because of who he is. One where he can drink and drink and drink some more, and try to decide what to do.

CHAPTER TWO

Skot sits in the small bathroom chair, wearing only a towel about his waist, having come from a recent shower. He looks up into the gleaming eyes of the woman sitting in his lap. She wears a thin, white cotton bath robe, the length of it generally not making it very far over her lithe thighs, bunched up now as she straddles him. It also hangs open, her having not even bothered to tie the sash when she finished drying from the shower they had shared. He sneaks his hands in slowly, placing them about her waist, the right holding her somewhat firmly, the left curling the fingers and brushing her supple skin.

"Don't make me lose focus." Lilja smirks, then carefully draws the edge of the straight razor along his throat.

He tilts his head up, offering her better access as she continues to shave him. He breathes in slowly, taking in the intoxicating nearness of her, emitting a very low, light moan as she presses down, leaning in. She has done so to better support and balance herself as she proceeds to finishing up along his sensitive neck, but he feels the movement and presence like an arousing lure. It surges through him despite the recentness of their lovemaking in the shower.

He blinks when he realizes she has stopped, sitting back, and he peers at her.

"What is it?"

"Are you going to let me finish?" she continues, holding out the fine shaving tool in her right hand, wrist bent away, her eyebrows perked.

"Of course."

"I don't want to cut you."

The sound of the metal moving along his short whiskers seems quite loud, and she carries it through with a deft smoothness. The master

SWORD OF THE BUTTERFLY

bathroom in this townhouse is large, but they spent enough time in the shower to have made it feel somewhat humid in here. She had also lit candles, though not for illumination, as their cleaning tryst has occurred in the late morning, but for the scent. This adds to the odors of the soaps and shampoos they used on one another, mingling also with the erotic smells produced by their healthy bodies, creating quite the heady bouquet.

Her long, red hair has been combed into a wet, shiny curtain along her upper back, kept also out of her way in this manner as she uses her left hand to hold his face, having come in very close, touching up her work. She sneaks the edges in the subtle crooks of his throat, up in the more rear, recessed areas of his jawline, being very thorough.

The townhome is one that has seen many years, much upkeep, and relatively recent renovation. It still holds its old world charm even as modern amenities dot throughout its area. When Skot recently acquired it, he'd had further modifications made to suit his needs. The property is ostensibly an investment, as he does not figure to live here indefinitely, but they all know why this has happened - she is here.

Lilja had proven hesitant to accept his invitation of last year to move in with him to the manor in the United States. She explained to him that it was something she felt she wanted to do, but the idea of such a move so soon proved too scary to her. She had also been eager to be sure he knew it was not due to any lacking of emotion toward him or their relationship. She had left her home those years ago for personal reasons, reasons that were not entirely positive, but she does not like to move. She prefers to grow roots, likes to make a place a home and then remain. He understand this, and so he tries to be patient, catering to her concern.

Their relationship continues to blossom, and though she yet maintains her small apartment, she spends nearly all of her time here at the townhouse, even bringing Dali over from time to time, letting him get acquainted with the spacious, fine new digs. She's even made a few decorative touches throughout the place.

He told his family he was taking up a temporary residence here to be nearer to the book and to her. Everyone but his mother proved supportive. She had given him some none-too-subtle hints that she worried he might move there permanently, exchanging the family manor for the city in which his girlfriend lives. He had addressed some of this, though not entirely rising to her bait. Still, he knows the main reason he yet lingers in the City, and she sits on his lap, smiling beautifully at him as she towels his face.

She continues to wear that curve to her lips as she applies the after shave cleanser to a cotton pad then wipes it gently over his freshly shaved skin. There is no alcohol in it, so he feels no sting, just the cooling soothe of it as she carefully applies. Once done, she tosses the pad into the nearby trash bucket, then looks back at him. He moves his hands again, now that she is done, leaning in, reaching down to grip her bottom. She grins, moving nearer, closing the scant distance between them, and they kiss.

It begins as something casual, perhaps a mere punctuation to the shaving ritual, but it quickly grows to much more. Their jaws work as lips move, tasting of one another, flesh against flesh, tongues dancing with a sureness of familiarity, a simmer of need. His fingers clutch more intently, and he presses up with his crotch.

"Are you already ready for more?" she asks, pulling back just a bit, bright eyes on him, a smile on her delicious lips.

The grin is somewhat shy, and he loves that. Even after this time that they have been together, she still conveys that alluring sense of bashfulness from time to time.

"Are you?" he returns, flexing his buttocks as he again pushes up against her more fervently.

She emits a very quiet, short moan, feeling that pressure against her naked pubis as she presses lightly in return.

"If you want," she breathes, the words a whisper, as though carried on a soft breeze of need.

"I do want."

Further kisses are ardently exchanged. He trails his hands around and toward himself, and he parts the robe. She lowers her hands, angling her arms downward, and the soft garment falls to the tiled floor of the bathroom, leaving her naked atop him, her petite, fit body writhing with the motion of her hips as she brings her hands up to gently hold aside his face. He feels a continued stirring at his loins, the towel about his waist now proving a nuisance. He gently coaxes her to stand, and he rises in her wake, the fabric already having become loosened by their movements, and it falls away.

She glances down, briefly, at his turgid member, then her eyes come back up to his, and she bites her lower lip. She then drops gracefully to her knees before him, using her lovely mouth to arouse him to a full readiness. He takes her hand, guiding her back to her feet, leading her to the adjoining master bedroom and the large, sumptuous bed within. Time is taken at making sure both of them are quite ready for more before culminating their union, lingering over one another, expressions of reverence.

Not long later, they lie in each other's arms, aglow in the aftermath of their coupling, quite spent. She places her right hand on the center of his chest, playing absently with the almost gossamer hairs there. After a time, she nuzzles in, feeling a reciprocatory pull from his arm, holding her closer. She just stays there for a moment, feeling the warmth of his chest, listening to his heart beat, but it does not take long for her to sense … something. She looks up at him, noting the distant gaze of his open eyes.

"What is it? What's on your mind?"

"Charles," he finally says.

She rises up onto an elbow, getting closer to his face, and he shifts his eyes down to hers. They look at each for a moment, and he sees a subtle furrowing to her brow, an emanation of sympathy.

"I'm sorry," she then utters, leaning in, and they embrace.

"It is not just the loss of him. Nicole said he was a message, and she was right."

She again rises up, now looking at him with a different sort of focus.

"Okay?"

"That amulet I found. And the marks on his body. Do you remember those?"

She nods again, solemnly.

"Those were not marks of torture. They were made after he died."

"But, he was alive when we got there?" and the touching lilt of her words being a question rises just at the end, as though it has become so in the moment of speaking.

"Not exactly. A force had been applied, a power, an energy ... magick, if that sounds easier," he explains, "to give some animation to his corpse. It was false, a perversion."

Lilja frowns.

"And it was not just done to affect us, though such horrors are certainly well within their normal ... tactics," he pauses very briefly, "They wanted to be sure we'd see the body, *I*'d see it."

"You?" She blinks. "They expected *you* to be there?"

"So it seems. Though it is quite possible this message would have gotten to me if I had sent someone else, but still, it's very personal."

"What message, Skot?" she asks, burning with curiosity, but still speaking softly, having a care for his feelings.

"The markings on the medallion, they look abstract, but when used as a stamp, they may form an ancient script. It's their language, or one aspect of it, at least, and it was used as a brand to make the figures on his body."

She is stunned. She wants to express horror, sympathy, even wonder, and these things war within her so. She merely remains silent, observing.

"I saw enough of it to get the message. So did Nicole. I don't know how she managed that, but she says she saw when I burnt his body. We ... compared notes." He angles his eyes toward her for a moment, as though apologetic of his choice of words. "And there is a very clear message there."

She continues just looking at him, her left hand splayed gently on his chest, her right arm still bent at the elbow, propping herself even as his arm is still somewhat about her. She gazes at him, taking it in, waiting. She nods, again a bid to continue.

He exhales, looking away within a blink, eyes angling downward, then he turns them back to her. "I expected it to be the usual taunts, perhaps about Charles, threats to the family, to the human race. They use those sorts of approaches very often, so much so, really, that it may become white noise, but this was different." He pauses, taking in another breath. "They are claiming to be the cause of my father's death."

She blinks, brow knitting.

SWORD OF THE BUTTERFLY

"I've mentioned he had a rare illness, and the 'official' documentation does specify a known disease, but that was done to keep the paperwork tidy. We were never quite sure exactly what it was or how he got it. It turned out to be non-contagious, and we eventually determined what it was doing to him. No matter what we tried, it could not be cured. We were able to delay it somewhat, but in the end, it was as terminal as we all expected. We had time to come to grips with it. But now, they, the Infernal, are saying they caused it, they gave it to him, through some repeated exposure to them and their influence, like a slow acting poison."

"That's …," she finally speaks, still obviously confused, "Is that possible? Do you believe it?"

"I don't know."

She leans in to him, embracing, and he returns it. They hold each other, feeling one another's presence.

"If it is true, they could, theoretically, do it again."

She nods against him, the motion seeming more conciliatory than real agreement. She then again senses something and pushes herself back up, looking at him.

"And that's exactly what they'd want," she expounds, "Fear from you."

He nods, slowly, contemplatively. "I know. And even if it is true, we won't stop what we're doing. They'd actually be exposing a very real, secret threat to us, which is our first step in thwarting it, so why?"

"To taunt you, just as you said, to give you a reason to fear," then she pauses, looking him over, her eyes gone wider.

"What is it?"

"What if …?" She blinks, her lips straining together, threatening a frown. "What if you've already been exposed?"

He quickly takes her in his arms, holding her close, feeling the near desperate return from her, the tight clutching of her strong limbs. He then realizes their strategy. If they do speak true, then why indeed would they reveal this secret weapon? For this very reason – to cause strain, worry, even hesitancy amongst them. It is far easier to steel one's self in the face of adversity than to realize a loved one may be equally at risk and possibly taken away.

"We have documented symptoms, as best we can, and we do keep an eye out for them. Even though we were not sure what it was, and especially since it did not sufficiently match anything found in popular medical history, we were quite wary. We had not thought to attribute it directly to the active intent of the Infernal, but we are, obviously, exposed to certain … unnatural things, so to speak," he tries to explain and soothe, "We will not stop our work, but will be no more blind than we have to be."

"Lily," he says, and a gravity now weighs in his voice that worries her.

"Yes?" She looks back at him, her courage evident.

He wants to just hold her, not speak of such things, but that sort of naïveté is for adolescent romance.

"My father lived to be almost sixty-five years old," he informs, "For a Hunter, that is long-lived."

She understands what he is saying, and such had been in the deeper, darker places of her mind for a while now, but she is not unfamiliar with risk. Decidedly not so. She gives another nod, and though this one shows slightly weaker, it is still there. She faces her fears.

"Maybe they did poison him," he posits, "Maybe his fortitude and ability proved him to be such a great adversary they had to try something different to defeat him."

And even as he mentions defeat, he recalls the appearance of his father's specter, whether true ghost or some technological apparition, which led him to that rare book more than a year ago. His father was an amazing man, and nothing will change that.

"I'm sorry," she says, and the sincerity of it touches him deeply.

He smiles warmly, if not somewhat wistfully, and he pulls her into another hug.

"Thank you."

When they part, they remain close, and he takes her eyes again in his own.

"I love you," he utters.

"I love you, too."

SWORD OF THE BUTTERFLY

"You help me to feel stronger," he says, and she smiles at this, "But there is still very real danger to my family and how we live our lives. Some much more so than others."

"I know." She nods, the fingers of her left hand again moving as though of their own accord through the light tuft of his chest hair. "This scares me," she admits, "but really not because of that. We all die someday. Life is risk. I'm more afraid of emotional pain than death."

He lets a deep, thoughtful breath pass through him, and she looks up to meet his eyes.

"I promise to do my best to never be the willful cause of such pain to you."

She nods, pondering this, then she again fixes her gaze onto his, her lips curling ever-so-slightly.

"Likewise," she also vows.

*****

The buildings of the campus display a baroque seriousness, not quite the Georgian or Neoclassical styles one might expect of prestigious colleges in other parts of the Western World. This is not the oldest school in the country, nor the most popularly respected, but something of it speaks of mystery. Still, on this reasonably sunny late afternoon, as students clamber over the sidewalks amidst the well-tended greenery, it looks to be just a place of higher learning.

Those funneling into the Morgan building are doing so as part of their freshmen orientation. They find their way into the main room, much more modern than the structure's exterior suggests, built to be something like a small auditorium. It almost appears as though the room descends deceptively into the ground, but it merely takes advantage of the landscape and some creative architecture.

A scant few, small gatherings of the prospective freshmen show that some of those here already know each other, but the majority look lost in the unfamiliar. One in particular, a quite tall young man with stringy black hair hanging down the sides of his face, wanders in, his drab green satchel seeming quite heavy, the color washed out, the thing looking old and well-used. His expression is one of a careful curiosity, nothing though belying a sense of arrogance. He finds a seat in the uppermost rows.

No one here knows him. His intelligence marks him as one easily suited to command admission to the exclusive, expensive university, but his social skills look lacking from the way he carries himself. His dark eyes peer about, not meeting any other gaze for longer than it may take to even realize such a look is joined. They do not dart, though he does feel a weight, but their movement is continuous. He hesitates when a trio sits near him, their conversation marking them as friends of some degree. They prove content to ignore him. His furtive glance at them is not noticed, so he looks longer, taking measure. This suits him, as he goes back to observing over the large chamber and the people gathering within.

The clamor is quieted as three older students walk out onto the obvious area of attention, that portion of the room at the head of the angled seating's intended scrutiny. They prove to be upperclassmen, one a senior working toward a very difficult degree. This gets suitable reactions of awe from most. The curiously tall student continues to watch with a quite aloof air, still appearing as though somewhat guarded and more interested in taking in the crowd than what is being imparted by these "veterans".

His scores on the various entrance examinations had been phenomenal, and though he towers over the average students, his age is actually lower than them, his genetic pedigree obviously giving him accelerated physical growth as well as mental. His age of record is sixteen years old, his height 190 centimeters. He is here on scholarship, his academic abilities garnering him a coveted place in this year's freshman class. His physical size has not lent itself to any athletic accomplishments, and his personal history has not equipped him socially and emotionally to the same degree as other attributes he possesses. He had been home-schooled and quite isolated from those outside his family.

When this session is ended, he lumbers out, moving slowly, eyes cast mostly downward from his impressive height. He does not show any obvious discomfort or imbalance as might be expected from some who experience such radical growth, but he still moves slowly. He receives

SWORD OF THE BUTTERFLY

looks from other students, but if any were inclined to bully or make fun of him directly to his face, his size proves a deterrent. This does not stop the whispers and points on the part of some, but most of these first year college students hardly notice him, more concerned with themselves and their education than the over-dressed student in their midst.

He is not so due to wearing too expensive clothing but because he appears to wear too much, especially for this warm weather. His baggy pants pile atop the heavy, dark boots, the light jacket hanging over his frame, the sleeves so long as to cover more than half of his hands. He looks a bit paunchy in the middle, as though somewhat pear-shaped. He holds onto the strap of his satchel with his left hand, moving steadily to his destination. As he does so, he clambers past the library, hardly sparing it any notice.

Inside that same building, down on the floor that is below ground, Lilja works, tidying up the room that houses the campus' Rare Books Collection over which she holds curatorship. She does not necessarily expect any visitors, but she likes to keep the room clean. She also checks over the security of the more valuable books, paying particular attention to one.

This book's already impressive security measures had been increased when the endowment had come in from the Felcraft group. It does not seem as though the very rare and priceless tome will leave the school's collection for the private one of the distinguished family, but with this donation, they all but possess it. Knowing now what she does, Lilja also acts more overtly as the special book's guardian.

No threats have arisen to it since the initial one last year, but they remain ever-vigilant. Amanda Honeycutt, her assistant, had been moved to another position. It had been a delicate affair. The woman's obvious fraternization with Denman Malkuth, a member of faculty, may not have been enough to get her fired, but the record of her violating protocol and giving him access to the invaluable book had resulted in a serious warning and transfer to a different role at the school.

Marcel had graduated last year, and as if his multiple degrees did not indicate his love for education, his application for the vacant position indicated his desire to stay here. He had not been an automatic approval, but he had stood out above the other few prospects, and Lilja had offered him the job. His training had been rather easy, his taking to the security and other such stringent protocols regarding the collection occurring rapidly. The job really is quite mundane, even considering the value and age of the books here. So long as the demons stay away, and the Felcraft's rivals, the Malkuths, it really is generally common, perhaps even boring.

Even so, she has her precautions – the gun in the new false bottom of her desk drawer, loaded with an eight round magazine of the specially treated bullets. The pistol is an H&K USP45CT, given modifications to better suit Lilja's personal specifications.Skot had even advised her in the use of some sensory systems that might detect the Infernal. It had all seemed like so much magick to her, but he has begun to explain that it all has its own set of rules, those that just prove difficult to understand or not in line with what we know of our accepted, corporeal realm. It is a science *and* an art. They use the term 'magick', just as they do 'demon', 'devil', and 'infernal', but he cautions to not attribute too much of a human-made meaning to such words.

The Book, though, now lies within layers of better protection than it yet ever has, and they hope that the use of these defensive measures shall never see a need.

Ultimately, the goal is to someday, somehow acquire it into the private collection with the first of the trilogy. It also seems that if the school were to ever consider such a thing, the Felcrafts would be the obvious candidates. Still, if it were put to auction, it would not only be subject to that set of rules but also put into a possibly compromising situation. For now, it is watched, closely, and if its utmost safety is accomplished where it is, then it need not be moved.

And this is another reason she is reluctant to leave the City, though she wonders how much of that is an excuse. She has willingly taken upon this burden, this responsibility, but in truth, she is not the only one capable of such. If an imminent attack were known, they'd also not leave her alone to thwart it. She is surely not the most adept person at fighting those unearthly beings and their horrible powers.

She stands there, now, left arm held over her belly, right bent at the elbow, her eyes on the book. Her thoughts stray, taking up force of their own. Her eyes lose focus, and she thinks of him.

SWORD OF THE BUTTERFLY

A part of her wants to abandon everything else and just be his, just fall into him completely. Another part of her fears this, and not just for how it might compromise her individuality, her independence, but she still lets that gnawing doubt dance at the edges of her consciousness – what if he hurts her emotionally? Her only experience with a serious relationship ended in great psychological pain.

"Lilja?"

She looks over to the delicate-sounding bid to see Marcel standing there.

"Sorry." She smiles pleasantly. "I was lost in my thoughts."

"I could tell. I was just saying that I'm about done for the day. Mind if I head out a bit early?"

"Oh, not at all. Go ahead. Thanks for your help." She keeps up the warm expression, and he gives a short jerk of his head, a sort of simple bow and nod, then turns and heads out.

After he has gone, she looks at the clock, seeing that his 'early' departure is all of twenty minutes. She exhales a single chuckle, lips smirking a touch. She'll have to get him to relax. Even though he spent that time in the general library as a volunteer, he seems anxious now that he is formally employed, and in this respected department, no less. Their business is serious, but there is no reason for it to be stuffy.

She checks the security on the book, noting that, as usual, all is well and in place. She supposes she ought to also relax. Even though she just glanced at the clock, she does so again, thinking that in a short time, she will be at the townhouse, with him. It is his home, he owns it, but she thinks of it as theirs.

Maybe she ought to give up her lease on the apartment. Maybe she doesn't need the crutch of a ready escape plan.

She'll think about it.

*****

If things did not feel so serious, he might crack his usual smile and make one of his disarming, yet acute, remarks. As though in accordance with this singularity, he does not wear his sunglasses, though doing so in a dark room such as this would surely draw unwanted attention. This bar is quite nice, surely not the most exclusive or expensive but more than adequate. He wonders if perhaps the people who have summoned him here think of it as 'common'. He almost lets a smirk touch his lips at this thought. He also manages to keep himself from smoking, though he feels like he could use a cigarette. A glass of good brandy sits before him, barely touched, as he waits.

And as if he had denied his usual nature so much as to leave the cliché meter empty, something happens to quickly fill it.

"Inspector Gaspare Duilio of Interpol," says a voice from behind him, "Good evening."

The accent is polished, deliberate, what some would call Transatlantic, making the place of origin somewhat difficult to peg.

"Good eve-," Duilio begins to return, his own obvious Italian accent emerging within his cultured tone.

"No, do not turn around," says the voice, adding further to the cliché, as if that once thirsty meter will now overflow with gluttony.

Duilio managed to peripherally spy the form of the seated man, obviously wearing a nice suit, dark, hidden mostly in shadow, before turning back forward. It makes no difference if he sees him or not, the inspector decides. He has seen and learned too much in the recent months, and he is far more at risk than he had ever imagined. He chooses, instead, to have more of his drink.

"Thank you for coming," the man continues, and it seems they will have a nice, polite conversation, just positioned further from one another than usual and one looking at the other's back. "We are to assume that you have opened your mind to what we have shown you, what you, yourself, saw last year?"

Duilio nods, ponderously, his hand still about the glass, and he now thinks he should have ordered a double.

He also thinks back on the event at Gnegon's compound. He did not realize what all he had even borne witness to at the time, but now, he knows.

"Si," he admits, exhaling.

"We have need of your talents."

It takes a moment for these words to sink in.

SWORD OF THE BUTTERFLY

"What? How can I help you?" he asks, not a bid, but a sincere question.

"Your humility is not needed, Inspector."

"I am not being humble."

"Ah, well, then if you are unaware of your own abilities, you may not prove useful to us for long. As much as you may find that possibility attractive, let me assure you, it is not."

Duilio looks forward, eyes moving within a series of blinks. He feels like he is drowning. He has always prided himself on possessing a modicum of control in all situations. Such hearkens back to a discussion he once had with some compatriots about this all being a game, like poker, and how to read people and play properly. He thought he was fairly good at the game, and now he finds that for all this time, he was falling for the bluff.

"There is someone out there we wish to find," the man continues, "Information will be provided to you. You have your own resources and contacts, and you will have some use of ours. We expect you to help us to find this ... individual."

"Do I detain him when I find him?"

"Ah, confidence," the voice says.

Duilio hears a very low chuckle. He finds it unnerving.

"*No*," the man resumes, "You will not be able to do that. If you find him, you will let us know, *immediately*, and we will handle it."

Duilio nods.

"We do not necessarily even expect you to succeed, but you may help us to narrow down possibilities."

"I am to assume, then, that this ... *individual* is one of the 'special' entities you've told me about?"

"A very good deduction, Inspector."

Duilio manages to show no response, or he, at least, thinks he controls himself well enough. Though when the other person appears, he does dart his eyes up a bit too furtively, like a cornered animal. He allows himself some relief that the speaker behind him has not seen.

The man who approaches is dressed quite nicely, like a waiter, or perhaps even a butler, though as far as Duilio knows, there is no such person employed here. The man even holds a small tray, upon which awaits another serving of brandy and a small, thin object that looks all the world like an overly-large, though very nice, cigarette case.

The man stops, bending forward from the waist, proffering the tray.

"Uh, thank you," the inspector finally manages, taking the drink and item.

The man dips his head once, a very slight gesture, very cultured, professional, and without a word, he exits the isolated area.

Duilio has another sip of the liquor, a good one, before he reaches for the case, depressing the small button on the side which allows it to open. It possesses some papers, obviously of a custom size, bearing of neatly spaced text, some photographs, and there is also a data key held in a precise compartment on the right side. He gives the information a cursory examination.

"You want me to go to America?"

"Possibly," the voice answers, "You have sufficient information there to begin your investigation. If you think your direct presence is needed at the point of origin, then so be it."

"Do you have reason to think the suspect is no longer there?"

"He is not a 'suspect', Inspector Duilio," the man retorts, "He has entered our world, uninvited, and has already amassed a body count of over a dozen, even killing a Hunter in the process."

Duilio swallows, finding it difficult to do so, so he picks up his glass, drinking more of the brandy. He really needs a cigarette. He has not been told to not smoke, but he feels, for some reason, that he must wait until this appointment is over before he does.

"And now we shall hunt him … wherever that takes us."

So, he is to be a beater for their falconry, he realizes. Very well. He will do his best to avoid the talons.

*****

Courses had continued through the summer, though attendance had been lessened in the already somewhat irregular turnout. There had been a short break, for the instructor had been abroad, but now the self-defense classes have resumed. Therese is here again, showing a greater dedication than she had with her original attempt.

SWORD OF THE BUTTERFLY

The hacker is learning, and she watches closely as Lilja demonstrates various moves, especially how to use them on a larger opponent. Her partner for this is again, as usual, Miranda, the large woman suitable for these examples.

"Learn self-defense for your protection," Lilja begins, readying to execute the motions, "In a fight, size *does* matter. Those who say it doesn't haven't ever fought a bigger opponent. Bigger opponent has more mass, more power, more reach. Well, the number one option is always to get away, but assuming that is not possible and you are facing the bigger opponent, you need to bridge that gap between you and their reach and not give them room to act.

"Become a hard target," and so said, and with a subtle indication of readiness from the instructor, Miranda launches an 'attack'.

The tall woman rushes toward her teacher, hands extended on outstretched arms, and the more petite woman lunges into it, reaching forward with her own arms, using her speed to meet the assault. Her hands go inside Miranda's reach, confusing at her face, then pushing in and out to spread the attacker's arms even as the shorter woman continues with forward momentum, turning herself and her opponent, using the right arm. A knee shoots up to the now bending woman's sternum, then Lilja moves behind, hands on the back, up near the shoulders, a sharp, downward kick to behind the knee, taking her opponent down, her own knee placed over the head as she looks about, then moves away.

They go through a few such scenarios, demonstrating the various ways someone may suddenly attack, and Lilja moves through the motions smoothly, efficiently, coming close to but never fully striking Miranda, giving occasional quick explanations, but mainly just showing the actions for now.

"Alright, I am now going to demonstrate what happens in the case your attacker has managed to get you on the ground, and they are on top of you," she informs.

She then lies on her back, knees up, feet flat on the ground as Miranda moves in, leaning over. Lilja shoots her arms up, pressing back on the larger woman's shoulders, and the other reaches around, placing both her hands about the instructor's neck, as though to choke her. Lilja moves her arms, placing them over Miranda's, crossing them and grabbing her attacker, her thumbs atop her student's wrists, not around them. She then presses down, trying to break the hold, which the larger woman resists.

Making another quick effort, LIlja raises her hips up as high as they can go and brings them down with force, pressing downwards with elbows onto the choking arms at the same time, adding power from the abdomen into the movement. Miranda's arms bend from this, and the pressure from the choke is released. Lilja then slips sideways, using a foot for leverage, until her other foot is also against her opponent's hip. She then shoves hard, sliding the larger woman away, even as Miranda tries to maintain her grip about her 'victim's' neck. She rises up, giving an opening for multiple, fast kicks from Lilja.

Once they have gone quite quickly through the initial show, the teacher gets to her feet, facing the class in preparation for pairing up and slowly going through the various motions in greater detail and tutelage.

Lilja always iterates that the main goal is to escape any threatening situation in which one finds one's self, mitigating risk proactively. Just disable or thwart the attack as best as possible, then run away. Therese is adept at gleaning information, but not so much when it is directly from talking to a person. It has taken time to not only build trust but to also come more out of her own shell. Still, she has learned more of the generally taciturn and private instructor in the ensuing time.

Lilja is an accomplished practitioner of martial arts and a certified instructor, though she does not presently teach that. This is not a mere understanding and practice of self-defense, though, and the woman's level of skill is quite apparent if one watches closely. She does not generally participate in competitions, though she has some experience with helping to train others for that. She thinks that the martial arts are better suited for the benefits of health, confidence, and real world applications. This last part intrigues Therese the most.

She doesn't possess enough information to make an outright accusation. She sometimes ponders just coming out and flatly asking, but then she shies off, thinking even that such would be very ungrateful and rude, considering the vigilante saved her twice last year. Besides, if Lilja

SWORD OF THE BUTTERFLY

is the vigilante, which Therese suspects more and more, why would she admit it?

The young hacker and fledgling detective has generated timelines, and though there was some lagging period, she had been contacted through the usual 'shadow' channels about her cyber skills after she had initially taken the self-defense classes here. That may not prove anything more than coincidence, but the opposite seems more likely to potentially disprove. She is taking that approach – trying to find reasons to strike the name of Lilja Perhonen from her very short list of vigilante suspects.

And then there is this trip abroad and the period of quiet from her contact.

Again, it could be coincidence, and interaction with her contact is not on any set pattern, but there has been an awful lot of quiet for some time, though scant communication has now resumed. She had baited, holding on to some juicier tidbits about the developing situation in the city, thinking that might lure a response. It had worked, and though it had come before Lilja's resuming of classes, she doesn't know exactly when the woman returned or what access she may have had while away.

Lilja takes a short shower, now alone in the gymnasium, having done her own exercises after everyone had left. She knows the risk with Therese, but coming up with some sincere reason why the girl should not attend her class would be even more suspicious. The best way to alleviate curiosity is to continue as though everything is 'normal', perhaps even boring, and most definitely *mundane*.

Her life, which already held a rather exciting secret, has gone so far from mundane as to make her time as the masked vigilante seem child's play in comparison. She continues with that. Tremendous changes have arisen, but there is still crime in this city and that of a sort she will fight as long as she is able. As it had been explained to her so many months ago, the negative energies generated by the human trafficking and sexual slavery had also coupled with the blood sacrifices of the mounting number of dead girls, leading to the opening of the gateway to the other realm, the one they call the Infernal. So, if anything, her new knowledge of this, and her new training as a Hunter of those very demonic creatures, is tied to her double life as the vigilante. Stopping the crimes may help to stem the influx of those monsters. So now she leads a … *triple* life?

She also thinks of him, and a gentle smile takes her lips. They have now been a couple for a year. She can tell he wants more from her, and he generally takes her hesitancy with some display of patience. She is not as free in expressing her emotions as is he, and she does not have his courage in the approach of such intimacies and bonds. She is clearly growing more attached to him, though, having felt herself to fall into him quite quickly, almost frightening herself into putting distance between them. As she thinks back on it, now, she is glad she did not.

Her hands move over her fit, lithe body, a soapy slickness having been generated by her showering. Her fingertips brush very near to her pubis, completely shaved as she has done so for some time, though he had told her to keep it so once they had grown far enough along in their relationship. She enjoys the Rules, along with the continued and increasing BDSM aspect of their union. Another Rule, one which had also developed later in their time together, would be that she would not touch her genitalia in an erotic manner unless she had his permission. She likes that one, too, as though having given a part of her sexuality to him. She knows that some might misinterpret this as his undue control over her, but what they both know is that she is giving it to him, freely, and what more power might one evince? This is what both of them want, and she could certainly stop it anytime.

She lets more stimulating thoughts of him run through her mind, running slick hands over her toned thighs, passing very near her pussy then along her belly and up to her breasts, massaging them, clutching, her nipples perking with arousal. She has kept up with her missions after all this time, namely his task, another standing Rule, that she take some time out of every work day and masturbate and think of him. She is allowed, of course, to touch herself directly during these times, but she had already done her mission earlier today. She will tell him of this when they talk this evening, and she suspects he will like it. She also thinks of how he might react, what he might desire of her, what he might do to her, and this excites her further. She emits a light moan, then she stops, blinking, looking around, a flush rising to her pale skin. Of course, she is alone, and now that the spell is broken, she completes what had originally intended to be a "short" shower, smiling to herself as she thinks of finishing up and getting home to him.

SWORD OF THE BUTTERFLY

*****

They have been partners for many years. They've learned much of each other in that time, and so it does not surprise Quain when he sees the burly man standing there in the park along the route he often uses to jog. What does surprise him is why he has chosen to meet with him this way.

"Hey, Alec," he greets, stopping near the other, shortness of breath evident in him as well as the sheen of sweat on his dark flesh.

"Quain," the other says, eyes taking careful study of the more athletic man.

"What brings you out here?"

Quain places his hands on his waist, taking deeper, more calming breaths, keeping his gaze on Alec, noting the signs of stress, maybe even fear. There is something in the eyes he does not like.

"What's going on?" he pushes.

"I met with the new boss."

Quain nods, still working on gaining a more relaxed respiration. He waits a moment, then realizes his partner has again lapsed into some odd, contemplative silence. He pulls in a much deeper breath, through parted lips, then closes them, holding it before releasing through his nostrils.

"And?" he tries, feeling suddenly like a dentist, "How was it? What's he like?"

"Kazimir Volkov. That's his name."

Quain nods, agreeably, though they both know he did not ask that.

"He scared me."

Quain wrinkles his brow, then blinks it away after a moment of pontification.

"New guy trying to impress people?" he guesses.

"No, no, it ... it wasn't like that," the big man dismisses, and Quain spies a motion of the other's hand as it reaches into his jacket, not to go for a gun, but heading to where he usually keeps his flask.

Alec does produce the metal object, but he just holds it in both hands, fingertips of his right moving slowly over it as though it were some good luck charm that might gently milk it for all it is worth. The index finger teases over the cap, brushing it.

"The whole time I was there, I felt like I might be killed at any moment," he adds, looking away, as though plumbing the annals of his memory, then his eyes snick to his partner, an even greater degree of intensity to his already serious tone. "He's a dangerous man, Quain."

"Gnegon was dangerous, too."

"Yes, yes," and again comes the dismissive aspect, "But with Gnegon, even when we butted heads, I felt like I knew where I stood. When things were calm, or even when I didn't back down as quickly as I should have, I never felt like my life was in jeopardy, or if I was pushing him that hard, he'd take his finger off the trigger when things relaxed, you know?"

Quain nods.

"But this guy … it-it-it's." The stammering alarms Quain for he cannot recall a single time he had heard it from his partner. "It's like any breath could be your last. He wasn't even that obviously threatening. He even *insulted* me, and you know how I usually get when someone does that to me …"

And again come the nods, for Quain knows far too well this behavior on the part of his colleague.

"But I didn't get angry. I was *scared*, and I tried to placate him. I really thought I was pleading for my life. I was *relieved* when I got out of there."

"Then don't work for him," comes the flat assessment.

A somewhat snorted chuckle is the response, incredulity laden in the brief expression.

"We've been doing this for so long that we began to think we *had* to," Quain elaborates, "My eyes were opened after what happened. I'm out. Why don't you get out, too?"

Alec begins to shake his head, a weight to it, before the other's short sentence is even complete.

"No, no. I have no choice."

"There's *always* a choice, Alec."

And another of the single, exhaled chuckles retorts.

The more athletic man looks away, the right side of his mouth curling towards an obvious expression of disappointment.

"You will be happy to know, I think, that he seems to have no issue with you."

Those eyes cut back over, looking sidelong.

"That's good to know," comes the guarded response.

"He respects that you made a choice."

Quain just adds another nod, his thoughts careening with what this all may mean, but he does not show it.

"So, you haven't?"

"I have now."

A larger exhale comes through the nostrils, and then more nods, slow, ponderous.

"I guess we ought to put in a transfer request, or one of us, at least."

"I like working with you, Quain," Alec replies, and his eyes again stare, almost as if boring, as if pleading for a solution that works to keep them together as compatriots.

"I like working with you too, man." Quain grins. "Even if you are a pain in the ass."

And this gets a good-natured chuckle.

"You've saved my fat ass more than once," Alec admits.

"Hey, we're partners."

Alec shrugs his beefy shoulders. "Not anymore, huh?" he finally speaks.

Another audible exhale emerges, this one lengthening into what might pass for a sigh. "Maybe not, but we don't have to become enemies, do we?"

"No," Alec agrees, a twist going to his lips, a short, near silent chuckle, "You'd kick my ass."

"I don't know, man," Quain jokes, beginning to bounce lightly, like a boxer, "You're pretty tough, and you've got me out-weighed."

"You're funny," Alec remarks, "You're the one who jogs." He extends his right arm to somewhat encompass the park with a gesturing hand. "It winded me to take my time just walking here to try to catch you."

"Well, hey, if it makes you feel better, we can be workout buddies if we can't be partners, anymore." Quain gives an encouraging grin.

"As I said, you're funny."

And both share a moment of what closely passes for sincere laughter.

"Don't worry about it, Alec," Quain says, then takes on a caring tone, "I'll put in for a move to another department. You just stay where you are. I'll cause the wrinkles."

"Well …"

"And until it comes through, we'll just figure it out," Quain continues, oblivious to what his partner might have been about to say.

"Okay," Alec says, not sure at all if things will be 'okay', anymore.

CHAPTER THREE

The body of Konrád Michael Wentreck, a journalist and blogger, was found outside the Troika district in a somewhat isolated area, making it easy enough to spot the corpse once the sun had risen. No effort to hide it had been made, and though the removal of the hands, feet, and head may indicate some effort to thwart identification of the body, their all being found less than five hundred meters away suggests otherwise. He had been stripped, and ligature marks suggest he had been bound before being killed and mutilated.

'Michi', as he was affectionately called, had reportedly been investigating a child prostitution ring in the city, and postings on his blog appeared to indicate the nearness of a real, supportable discovery. Local and international media groups have demanded of authorities to commence a concentrated and thorough investigation. The murdered man's wife had been quoted to remark about the commonality of killings in the City, but this one stands out in its brutality, implying her husband had indeed hit on something. It appeared he was being made an example of and a warning.

A more creative member of the local investigatory squad of the police had noted the placement of the head, hands, and feet, realizing that they might mark the points on a pentagram, the main part of the corpse positioned in the center. This had been left out of official reports as well as any announcements to the press. What could not be avoided was Michi's known willingness to tangle with corrupt officials, having exposed more than one in his day as he consolidated his reputation as a stubborn, courageous, if not overly risky, independent journalist.

Even if the ritualistic nature of the murder, still very much under speculation, had been omitted, its brazenness could not be denied. The killer, or killers, wanted everyone to know the identity of the victim, uncaring of what repercussions this might cause. The detectives assigned to the case would have to avoid jumping to conclusions that were already fomenting.

What else would also not be brought forth, the evidence of such already shadowy and now being thoroughly dispersed, was the journalist's connection to that secretive network that gathers and feeds information to the vigilante. He had been tangentially involved, exchanging data with another person as opposed to having any direct line to the main contact, but his death would be felt deeply. The danger was again rising, and all involved would need to be wary or else get away while they still had the chance.

*****

Lilja is not sure how he has procured their use of this expanse of remote land outside the city, but with the resources at his disposal, she is not surprised. They spend some time just walking around, enjoying each other's company, talking, as well as inspecting the grounds for safety and seclusion. They are in no hurry, and this is meant to be part of practice and training. Once they feel confident and comfortable with the area, they walk to the vehicle – an olive green Jeep Renegade.

They take their time setting up the targets, Skot following along as Lilja uses the range finder to set the thick wood and cardboard silhouettes at 200, 300, and 500 meters. The ground seems well suited for this, and she gives some thought to Skot's scouting of it, letting a very gentle curl take her lips for a moment. She gazes out, noting how the land slopes somewhat downward then rises up to a gentle hill, which will serve as a land block for the shooting exercise.

She glances back to see him looking at her, and she blinks her eyes wider from where she had been narrowing them in distant focus.

"Good?" he asks.

"Good." She nods once, and they head back.

They then set up the shooting area, though as with the way things proceed here, she takes care of it. Skot mostly observes and helps a bit. A blanket is laid out not far from the vehicle, upon which is placed a

SWORD OF THE BUTTERFLY

plastic box of ammunition, containing .338 Lapua Magnum cartridges. She then retrieves the encased rifle, having field stripped and given it a thorough cleaning and lubricating before coming here to the range, checking the components for any visible cracks or breakages during that time as well as running it through a bench test.

She now brings forth the black Sako TRG-42, the barrel pointed in the direction of the targets, not at either of them, giving the weapon a short look over before setting it down gently. She glances up at Skot from her kneeling position, noting that in the interim, he has put on his ear protection and retrieved the small pair of binoculars. Lilja gives him a little smile, putting on her own muffs, adjusting them to a comfortable fit, then adding the yellow-tinged shooting glasses. The bipod is then deployed, and she goes prone, checking the sights, locating a mark, and chambering a round.

"Target at 200 meters. Furthest left ... taking a shot," she declares.

The report is easily heard, despite the ear protection, but certainly not enough to potentially cause any damage. Skot watches through the binoculars, noting the slight delay between the sound and when the bullet hits the distant target, the cold bore shot scoring an off-center body strike, somewhat toward the left shoulder region. She adjusts the sights.

"Same target ... second shot."

This one hits near dead center.

She goes through nearly the whole box of ammunition, taking her time, scoring many hits, adjusting the sights on occasion, but it is clear to him that she possesses a marksman's level of ability. He is, of course, familiar with how well she aims and fares in combat situations, but seeing this is still no less impressive. And as if to underscore her ability, as she is finishing up -

"Same target," she says, shooting at the furthest, "Last shot."

He watches, the delay between firing and the hit filled with expectation, and the shot strikes between the eyes. The binoculars are lowered, and he looks down to see her peering up at him.

"Nicely done."

"Thanks."

Afterwards, with the rifle and ammo put away, they have a meal of the food they've brought with them – sandwiches, fruit, and, of course, water.

"You had said once before that the Felcrafts and Malkuths might share a common ancestor," and then she takes another taste of her smoked salmon sandwich.

He has noticed in their time together that she possesses quite a memory. He'd not go so far as to call it photographic, but she will do things like this, where she manages to snatch something from so long ago, as though having mental access to a file, and just mention it in a casual manner. He also understands that this is her way, sometimes, of trying to subtly ask questions or initiate conversation. He knows that in her cultural upbringing, too-pointed inquiries of certain topics are considered rude, so you wait until the other person brings it up, or you broach it in an oblique, polite method.

"Well, that is *suggested* but it is not sufficiently *known*," he replies, her eyes on him as she continues working through her food, munching on a carrot in between bites of the thick sandwich, "Do you mind if I relate some legend to you, something that is considered myth or folklore by some but quite true by others?"

She nods, swallowing, reaching for the bottle of water. "Like religion?"

He perks his eyebrows, then continues, "Exactly, and as much of this is steeped in religion, that may be more fitting than you realize."

She allows her own slight rise to her sculpted eyebrows, belying her curiosity.

"We've spoken, somewhat, about what we consider the genetic potential or predisposition to being able to wield the various skills we do, the Hunter Genes, as we colloquially call them."

She nods to this, scooting closer, listening intently.

"This might seem to suggest a similar ancestry, though the credibility of that could be argued, much the same as arguing a common ancestor for all humans. What we do know, though, is that there is something within us, something that does seem to have a scientific basis, that allows us to do as we do, and it is possible that it has come from a common source.

SWORD OF THE BUTTERFLY

"Have you ever heard of the Grigori or the Nephilim?"

She ponders for a moment, and he just watches as she ruminates. He begins to wonder if he has perhaps lost her to her thoughts, but then she finally speaks.

"Name is familiar, but I haven't really heard anything else." "The Grigori were a group of angels sent by God to watch over humans. They are sometimes called the Watchers. They were also told, by God, to not 'lie with the daughters of Men', so basically, no sexual union with humans."

She proceeds with her second sandwich, looking at him as he pauses to also have some of his own. She is content to wait, silently and patiently, for him to continue.

"Their half-breed offspring were the Nephilim. They were sometimes referred to as giants, other times as cannibals, biters, or even drinkers of blood."

Her brow furrows as she takes this in, holding a water bottle poised for a sip. A question may be on her lips, but instead, she takes that drink, still working on her food and paying attention to his words.

"Goliath from the tale of David and Goliath was thought to perhaps be a Nephilim or a descendent of one."

She looks at him. "So, there would be an obvious genetic component to this, though it would arguably be diminished with each generation."

He smiles, lips still together, nodding lightly.

"Depending on one's interpretation, the Flood from Noah's time was meant to wipe the earth clean of whatever seed remained of those bloodlines.

"So," he continues, "it would seem the Nephilim were these mixed offspring that may have had supernatural attributes. They'd have been rare in the world, and it seems they were malevolent or perhaps remembered that way because they were *different*, and 'normal' humans feared and hunted them."

A short moment passes as she ponders this, her eyes off into the distance.

"Humankind have always hunted, degraded, or even demonized things that are different, especially western and Christian society," she speaks, her tone almost one of musing, then she blinks her eyes to him.

69

"That would mean that any extant genetic component in today's population would be very rare."

She nods to this, her head moving smoothly in time to her chewing, but then she stops, forehead wrinkling in further thought, and she swallows, looking at him.

"The Hunters are the Nephilim?"

"That is a piece of mythology, well, *our* mythology, as it were, not amongst the general populace. As I said, some attribute more truth to it than others. But this is where the concept arises of their perhaps being a common ancestry or 'source' to the two families."

"And all Hunters end up in one or the other?"

"Most."

"What about those who don't? Do they work alone, or are there smaller groups or families out there?"

"Well," Skot begins, shifting in place, carefully weighing his words, "it's difficult to know."

Lilja gives him a calm, open look, one asking without words.

"The Malkuths do not accept the independence of someone with the Hunter genes."

"And the Felcrafts?"

"We do have a record of a Hunter about two hundred years ago. He gained knowledge of some of these secrets on his own, so he was not in the usual nascent stages we encounter. We're still not sure exactly how, but given enough time, it will happen. He did not lose his mind, nor was he consumed by any demons. He was approached by the Family, and everything was explained to him, how he'd be hunted by the Infernal and the Malkuths if he chose to remain independent, and he chose that. We respect that decision, but we know what the Malkuths do."

She nods, pondering further, thinking of all that happened last year.

"How is Ernst doing?" she throws out.

Skot smiles warmly, having grown used to the sometimes chaotic-seeming cadence of her thoughts. The question not only shows the quick logic of her mind but also her sense of caring.

"According to the last news I received, he is alright, doing better, but he will need some more time of care and therapy before he is healthy enough to be given his own recognizance. And yes, he is an example of a

SWORD OF THE BUTTERFLY

person who seems to possess this genetic potential but did not end up in either of the families. It does seem somewhat prideful to say, if not even a bit callous, but due to the ... rivalry and differing moral approaches, we both go after all potentials quite intently. Part of that is because of what the Malkuths do to people like Ernst."

A moment of silence grows, almost as though a short period of respect for the unfortunate young man who had been possessed of great mathematical and artistic ability as well as his sensitivity toward the supernatural realm. The Malkuths had found him and used him in a torturous, perverted way, driving him to the brink of insanity for their own gain, and had it not been for the timely intervention of Lilja and Skot, Ernst would have been summarily executed once he had expended his usefulness.

"What is the other part?" she finally asks.

"Well, we need numbers, of course. Those who may become Hunters are *extremely* rare, and frankly, we'd rather be the ones to come out on top. The Malkuths' vision of human society is less ... free than ours."

She nods, recalling their discussion regarding the ethics of the rival family.

"How do people decide which family to join?"

"They just do." He shrugs. "It's quite interesting, really, and it does sometimes make me wonder about morality and how we come about it, but it just seems it is a simple examination of where one fits. The philosopher in me rebels against the idea of it being so black and white, but the two choices encompass enough flexibility that a way is found to fit in one or the other. We don't have traitors or spies or anything like that," he shows another casual shrug, "We also respect the individual's choice."

"Romeo and Juliet?" she pitches.

He nods. "There have been such cases, yes. And it makes a certain amount of sense. As I've mentioned to you before, we do seem somehow drawn to those with whom we would be genetically compatible, so it would be quite probable that a member of one family would find themselves attracted to someone from the other."

"And their children?"

"Ah, well." He exhales. "That can be difficult."

He pauses, collecting his thoughts, and she waits, eyes on him, her expression calm, open.

"Some parents might want to exert undue control over their child's development. It is quite easy to say that an individual should be allowed the freedom of their own choices, but that may be tested when it is someone very close to you, and especially if they seem to be veering from what you may think is 'right'."

Lilja nods, listening.

"The idea is to aid in the healthy growth of the children, then, when they are ready, they are allowed to make their own choice."

"When are they ready?"

"That is also difficult. I'm no child psychologist, and there is a lot of unknown in that field. Who can say? We just try to do the best we can. And I am hesitant to make these things sound like Fate, but it usually just sort of comes down to a decision known all along, and we just had to come to that realization."

She appears accepting of this, those sparkling blue eyes still set on him.

"So, if I may return to the legend and the Grigori," he leads, "Depending on one's source, those angels fell, becoming devils, and their number also varies. Information has been found, along with various interpretations, that some within our world believe that Lucifer fell this way, too, not due to wanting to take God's Throne, as it were, but he did so prior to the fall of the Watchers.

"I've mentioned that there are two general classes of the Infernal, and we refer to them as Devils and Demons, the Devils being far more powerful and much more rare," he carries on, gaining further, slight nods and intent glances from her, "Some think that the Devils are those fallen angels, a very finite number, and their ability to reproduce, as it were, is also very limited."

"Okay?" she finally speaks into the lengthening silence.

"There are some schools of biological thought that say a life form is imbued with a strive toward immortality, survival, if you want to call it that. This is achieved either through the individual or the species. The more long-lived or stalwart a being is, the less need there is for reproduction. That may make sense from a biological standpoint, but there is also competition, war. Imagine if an army of Devils awaited, ready to attack this plane the first chance they get to engineer a proper passage?"

Her eyes appear to freeze, not widening so much as indicating her fall into the depth of this consideration. She blinks once, still stuck in those thoughts, then her eyes slowly move back to him.

"That would be very bad."

He nods, ponderously. "It would."

"But ...," she begins, a knitting of the brow showing her own attempts to grasp and collect a response, "If the legends are true, they *were* here before. They bred with us. They ... Are you saying that Hunters are part devil?"

"Well," he answers, smiling a bit sheepishly, "Those who subscribe to this school of thought tend to think that Hunters, if they are indeed remnants of the Nephilim, are part *angel*. The timing is delicate, but there is the optimistic approach that the first unions were before the angels fell."

"And then what?"

"Well, then God passed sentence and evicted them from Heaven and earth, throwing them into Hell," he tells, putting forth a small shrug at the end.

"Do you believe that?" she asks, boldly, no accusation or judgment in her tone, merely a sincere bid to know if that is, indeed, what he thinks.

"No," he says, then he emits a slow exhale through his nose, "I don't know, really. There is obviously more out there than our world and that of which we are aware, and we Hunters are able to do things that seem supernatural, magickal, but from where does it all arise? I don't know. What are those things we fight? Are they fallen angels, demons from Hell, aliens, some other sort of supernatural or transdimensional being? I don't know."

She nods to this, the motion so slight as to almost elude notice.

"What we do know is that these creatures, the Demons and Devils, operate differently than we do, and they are rather more resistant to harmful efforts than the average human. We are not sure if the 'killing' of a Demon really is its mortal end, or if we're just somehow forcing some part of it to return to its home dimension. When they come here, are they bringing physical matter from their plane, or are they somehow using the material of this world to give themselves form?"

"That's all very confusing," she comments.

"It is, but in keeping with the biological concept I mentioned earlier, their strength of mortality may keep them from being prolific breeders, like humans."

"We have numbers on our side," she concludes.

"We do, but it all goes back to reproduction. If you just look at the basis of the tale of the Grigori, ignoring the religion and morality, it could have just been an effort to find a way to create offspring."

"I don't suppose they expected to produce their worst enemies," she says, flatly.

He smirks, emitting a single, exhaled chuckle through his nose.

"No, I don't suppose they did."

She stands then, stretching. He watches the movement of her form, a smile growing on his lips. These motions come easily to her, such is her flexibility. She finally notices his observation, and she returns his expression.

"It's getting warmer," she observes.

"It is."

She fixes a look on him, her grin taking on a subtle shift in tone. She then pulls her t-shirt over her head, bypassing the high ponytail with ease, dropping the garment to the blanket. He drinks in the sight of her, the sport bra clinging tightly over her enticing bosom. She is not often this forward, but he likes it very much when she is.

Using that flexibility, she bends over, undoing the laces of her combat boots, then slipping them off deftly. She shimmies out of the somewhat dark cargo pants, finally standing before him in just the bra and tanga. She goes to him then, and thoughts of their conversation are gone for a sudden, spiking need.

*****

SWORD OF THE BUTTERFLY

Her fingers move rapidly over the sleek laptop's keyboard. She holds her hands atop it, poised, no movement for a moment save her eyes as they scan the various, small windows on the screen, picking at the information as though searching an orchard for ripe fruit. Her fingers go to work again, a deft economy of motion. She finds something of interest, using the small pad to move the pointer, clicking it open and then larger, eyes moving more intently now.

Absently, her right hand reaches for the nearby mug, and she drinks of its cooling coffee. It is still strong, bitter, and that is all she cares about. As usual, she plays with the left hoop of her snakebites, the tip of her tongue like a dowser of her thoughts, pressing at the jewelry as one might try to caress fortune from a crystal ball.

She scans over information regarding the recently murdered journalist, Michi. Like her, he had been an investigator, a private detective of sorts. Like her, he had found himself in a life-threatening situation, but his luck had gone sour. Twice the vigilante had saved her from what would have presumably been her own murder at the hands of the city's criminals. She wonders why this man was not rescued, but then, the vigilante is only one person, incapable of stopping all crimes in this large, eclectic metropolis.

She is part of the complex network that feeds information to other contacts, which eventually finds its way to the crime fighter. She suspects her contact *is* the vigilante, and she also has her very strong suspicions as to whom that is. She knows the vigilante is a woman, she is sure of it, and that is limiting enough. She thinks the crusader is her self-defense instructor, Lilja Perhonen, and if one were to think she is merely grasping at the straws in front of her face, she only became part of this network after she first met the woman.

There is a child prostitution ring in the city, and that sickens her. She is trying to find information on it at the behest of her contact, hoping to feed good intel to the vigilante, so that much more able person can proceed to do the job in trying to thwart it. She had also been obliquely working with the now dead blogger, and she shakes her head, quietly cursing Michi for not staying out of it and letting others handle the more dangerous tasks.

And yet, she ended up caught two times last year.

SCOTT CARRUBA

She sighs heavily, still holding the mug in her propped right hand, her elbow tucked into her lap as she sits here in her 'office', the tiny kitchen area of her small apartment. She is taking the self-defense classes much more seriously now, and she feels much better accomplished now that she has been at it with some regularity for several months. Still, she will do her best to henceforth stay out of the risky situations.

She noisily scoots the chair back, deciding to make more coffee, glancing at the clock as she does, and just then, there is a knock at her door. She narrows her eyes, suspicion instantly in her aspect, looking again at the clock. Of course, no time has passed, but now she wonders at who might be calling on her at this hour. She pads over on her bare feet, black-painted toe nails like a shiny beacon in their reflection.

"Who is it?" she demands, forcing the words out in a bit of a gruff, deeper tone, the same she has been taught in those self-defense courses.

"Akua, Therese. Open the door."

She blinks, rapidly, then unlocks the various mechanisms to find her girlfriend standing there.

"Hey, pale and creepy." The dark-skinned girl smiles. "Long time, no see."

She leans in, going for a kiss, but Therese instinctively pulls back. Akua smirks, noting the movement, which happens to create an opening, so she takes it, walking in.

"When's the last time you went outside?" she asks as Therese closes and locks the door, "Seen the sun much at all lately?"

The hacker folds her arms over her modest chest, her eyes narrowing as she leans back against the door, looking at the other slim woman.

"What brings you by, 'Kua?"

"You do." She lets the smirk hint toward seductive, but she still keeps her distance.

The two are girlfriends, lovers, but it is very much an unconventional arrangement. Days, weeks more often, may go by where they hardly speak, if at all. Not because they may be upset with one another, but merely because that is how they are. They each have their own lives, and they occasionally intersect, almost always by will. Akua might like more regularity, more commitment, but she knows how Therese is.

"You could've texted or emailed me."

"I could've." Akua keeps up that playful grinning.

"Why did you bring a bag?" Therese asks, noticing the item Akua totes over one shoulder in addition to her normal purse.

"You, Therese, dear, need to get out. You've been stuck in this cave too long, so I have come to rescue you. Let's go clubbing."

Therese snarls a bit, lip curling. "I don't want to."

"Shut it, brat," Akua is quick to say, then she sets the bag down, retrieving a dark red dress, simple, short, tight, one she knows Therese likes, then, as she begins to also set out a small, clear plastic bag of makeup, "Well? Go get in the shower, stinky."

"Where are we going?" Therese asks once she is done with her wash, hair still wet, in a disarray that will likely not change much before heading out.

She cranes her head upwards, letting Akua apply the heavy eyeliner, some dark eye shadow. Therese is not much for makeup, usually leaving it off or going for something messy of the goth or punk variety. Akua likes to give her a more polished look, and she allows it sometimes, so long as it remains dark.

"Where do you think?" she retorts, dabbing on a few finishing touches.

The other girl scoots away then, finding a pair of impossibly tight black jeans to struggle into, adding to this a matching black t-shirt, heavy black boots, and finally reaching for her leather jacket.

"It's not cold out, Therese, and could you maybe add more black? Why do you hate that color so much?"

Akua gives yet another smirk, adding a little jaunting shift of her hip, her own lithe body looking quite the contrast with her mocha skin and the feminine red dress accentuating her curves. Therese gives her a dry expression, but she leaves the weighty jacket on its hanger, instead opting for a black hoodie, which she makes a point of zipping up nearly all the way, eyeballing Akua the whole time.

"Where are we going?" she persists.

"Collections. Where else?"

Collections is a mainstay of the subculture, making it something of an irony in its own right. Many nightclubs have come and gone, and the more underground scenes like to throw raves that shift from place to place, sometimes only announcing that hours before the event, but this one has been around long enough to make it immortal in relativity.

It is not a very nice one, being mainly comprised of a large, open warehouse-like space, but that is just how its clientele likes it. There are a few smaller chambers adjoining the main area, even a partial second floor and small outside section. A couple of billiard tables hold court off to one side, though the majority of the place is just a large, slick floor that may be as easily used for dancing as loitering. There is also a decent stage, which is generally used for live music, though some other types of performances have seen display on the black-painted wood surface.

It's still somewhat early when they arrive, but they don't concern their selves too much with trying to be fashionably late. Therese doesn't care much about "fashionably" anything. She gives a quick blink, a sidelong glance of surprise, but she doesn't pull away when Akua takes her hand, especially as the other girl releases it once they get up to the bar.

"Hey, Jaska," Akua greets the bartender, smiling brightly.

The young man looks to be in his late twenties or early thirties, tall, lanky, his blond hair spiked out every which way, giving him the look of a hedgehog. He smiles readily in return.

"Hey, 'Kua, Therese," he greets them both, "What can I get you? The usual?"

Therese opens her mouth as though to say something, but Akua leaps with an eager affirmative. The other girl sort of rolls her eyes, slitting them, looking away to the right, as the bartender sets out four glasses, pouring them their 'usual' cocktails along with two shots, all based in cheap vodka. Therese is not really in the mood to get drunk, and the hangover from the swill here can be pretty brutal. Judging from the twinkle in Akua's eye, she is eager for a lot this evening.

The drinks don't last long, as time moves at something like a blurry crawl. Therese just feels like she cannot get into the mood of the evening, and though this causes it to drag, the lights and music and

SWORD OF THE BUTTERFLY

people still make everything seem somewhat surreal. Her thoughts are also a culprit.

She and Akua talk to some friends, well, it is more Akua doing the talking. Therese finds herself sort of sizing people up, especially male strangers, wondering if she could take them in a fight. She then corrects herself, just wondering if she could escape them if a threatening situation arose. She then thinks of Lilja, and a tiny curl dances at her lips, unnoticed by herself and others, as she figures the instructor could easily handle the guys in here.

She sees one in particular, a rather large metalhead, wearing lots of leather, denim, spikes, and he looks to carry himself with that same inflated self-importance that is often on those who are trying to compensate for something. She finds herself feeling aggressive toward him, wanting to go over and subtly start something, just to test herself, to maybe prove something to herself, even to Lilja. She then blinks, holding her eyes closed for moment, shaking her head. Why is she taken with such thoughts?

"Come on, Therese." She feels herself being pulled. "Let's get ano-," and then Akua stops, peering, leaning forward. "Why are you drinking so slow? Drink up, girl!"

"I'm fine," Therese practically growls, and though the dry, almost challenging aspect would put off most, there is a reason Akua is as close as she is.

The taller, darker girl just chuckles to herself, then grabs her partner's free hand, pulling her back toward the bar. Therese refuses another round, but Akua is insistent, even to the point of grabbing the half-finished cocktail in her date's hand and downing its contents, then turning to a grinning Jaska to order more. Grins all around as Akua turns a satisfied, lustful and happy one upon Therese, unleashing its full force. Therese responds with held closed eyes, lips parted, a shaking of the head, and then the release of a pent-up exhale. Akua just keeps grinning, sauntering closer, leaning in.

"Come on, Therese," she bids, whispering, her need practically emanating from her. She draws out her voice, her plump lips so very close to the flesh of Therese's jaw and ear, "Relax."

She pulls away, though, before making any contact, leaning on her elbows on the bartop as she watches Jaska finishing up. Therese looks aside for a moment, noticing the metalhead guy not too far away. Did he follow them over here to this part of the expansive club? He moves in place, grooving on a heavier tune that blasts through the myriad speakers. She then peers, eyes narrowing. Is he staring right at her? A blink resolves focus, and now it looks like he is back to his general observance.

He's putting up a front, and she knows that well. She does it, too. She tries to come off as gruff, cynical, tough, ready to spring into action at a moment's notice, but she has seen her limitations. She knows that much of her persona is from fear. She thinks again on Lilja, realizing that the woman possesses a strength which she finds worthy of envy. If Lilja were here, she'd not be worried about Mister Metalhead maybe coming over and trying to force himself on her. Of course, there are many other people here, including security, so why is she still stuck on such thoughts?

She looks back over to see an expectant expression on Akua, the young woman staring at her with a Cheshire grin, holding up two shots.

"This is it for me, 'Kua," she declares, accepting the shot.

"Santé," Akua practically purrs, clinking the small glass against the other, her eyes holding Therese's.

"Cheers," Therese manages, dryly, then also downs hers, wincing.

"Ha-ha, Therese! You can do better than that." She laughs, taking the empty glass and setting both on the bar near the larger cocktails.

She slides those two over, nestling them on the edge of the countertop, somewhat obscuring the glasses between the two of them, then she roots around in her small handbag. Therese takes a moment to notice this, more intent on her thoughts, but she finally watches her girlfriend with some curiosity. It dawns on her what is happening just as the other retrieves her right hand, holding it open, two, tiny white pills resting in contrast on the dark skin.

"No, thanks," she mumbles, grabbing her drink and moving it away before Akua can drop the pill in it.

"Therese," she pouts, that boisterous grin finally having disappeared for the first time this evening, "What's the matter? You've never turned down drugs before. Is something wrong?"

"No, everything's fine. I just don't feel like it," Therese quips, then brings the drink up, gazing away as she sips, finally looking back to see expectant eyes on her. "What?"

Akua just continues staring, then shrugs and drops both pills in her drink, the tablets beginning to dissolve quite quickly. Therese almost says something, but then opts for her usual emotionless gaze, watching as the other girl gulps down a decent portion of the drink. She wonders if this has turned from Akua just wanting to hang out and probably have sex to her now trying to get a rise out of her due to concern at her reckless behavior. Therese won't bite on that.

They end up heading home before the place closes, which is just fine with Therese, and though it doesn't seem fine with Akua, the other girl decides to turn her remaining energy back to seducing her friend. They are barely inside the small apartment when she kicks off her shoes and slinks easily out of the dress, displaying herself in bra and panties to Therese.

"'Kua," she begins, readying a protest, and the other girl steps over, draping arms over her shoulders, leaning in for a kiss.

This goes on for a short time before Akua pulls back, trying to focus, head perching forward.

"Therese, what's *wrong*?" she asks, exasperation in her voice, and when little more than a blank stare results, she drops her arm away, stepping back.

Silence descends, spreading like a haze. Akua finally turns, reaching for her things.

"Well, if you aren't in the mood, I'll just head home," she says.

Therese watches her back, noting the telltale signs of the continued high. They aren't amateurs when it comes to illicit consumption, but those two pills and all the drinks will take time to work through the system. She figures Akua could make it home just fine, but there is still something vulnerable about her state, especially with her back shown like that, and just as she is shaking her dress out to step into it, Therese moves in, grabbing the other girl's left wrist, gripping it tightly, forcing her to turn with a pull.

Akua blinks, reeling back a bit, and in that moment, Therese grabs her other wrist, then shoves both arms behind and up, effectively pinning the girl, stepping in close, their bodies mashing together as she presses in for an aggressive kiss. Akua emits a stifled noise of surprise, then melts into the exchange, feeling the powerful aggression of her partner. Therese then breaks from the kiss, her face an expression of forceful dominance, which seals in the lust shown in open surprise on Akua. Using her hold on the girl's slender wrist, she turns her again, then pushes her toward the bed, controlling her movements, bending her. Akua reaches out with her free left hand, propping herself up somewhat, but Therese forces her down, her face burying against the duvet, even as the other girl uses her sudden eagerness to grab at the hips and raise the girl's rear into prominence atop bent knees. She then veritably rips off the panties, a breathy gasp escaping lips, and she proceeds to give Akua the sex she wanted, though in a decidedly different fashion than she may have had in mind.

Throughout the interaction, Therese uses precise holds and force, continuing to think to herself and wonder – *is this how Lilja would do it? Is this how Lilja would do it?*

*****

There are three kinds of officers on the force, in general. Firstly, there are the rookies, or those still new enough they are establishing themselves. After that, they mostly develop into those that are good and those that are bad. This is not to imply an evaluation of their job performance but a measure of corruption. Save for those who are so poor at walking the less than legal path that they get arrested, the ones who play the game well enough to stay free are still known amongst their peers. The two sides, though possibly not directly opposing, just do not often mix, nor do they mix well. It is also another unwritten rule that once you choose a side, you usually stay there.

SWORD OF THE BUTTERFLY

Detective Quain Contee experiences this a lot of late, and though it makes his life more difficult, he faces it, knowing he got himself here. He will do what he can to rectify the situation.

He bids Detectives Marek and Graner goodbye with a gentle tilt of his head and a slight raise of his coffee cup, gaining a similar aspect from them. The short interaction had been professional, courteous, and awkward. They have been assigned to the dead blogger case, and they are firmly in the 'good' camp, and they had evinced a veneer of defensiveness when Quain had wandered over to talk to them. It is subtle, but they *are* investigators. He doesn't blame them.

He also has something of an ulterior motive, but where he used to be on the payroll of the local mob, he is now trying to earn his way back into the good graces of the 'right' side, as it were, by feeding information to the vigilante. The vigilante, no doubt, knows who he is, and it is not like he's been approached at night by a sudden dark figure perched next to his bed. Quain is trying to use the shadow network that provides intel to the crime fighter, and he is hoping to gain trust and entry there. He doesn't necessarily expect this to grant legitimacy to his change of heart, but he does have to live with that organ pumping in his own chest. He is trying to appease his own awakened conscience. He does this for himself as well as for others.

He's had some mysterious exchanges of information, though again, he doesn't think he is talking directly with the crime fighter. He could be half a dozen times removed from the source, and that is how it will have to be. He knows enough to know that the child prostitution operation is growing in the city, and though he has no concrete proof, he strongly suspects it to be at the orchestration of the new boss, Kazimir Volkov. He had considered trying to get something from Alec, but he doesn't want to fracture the already strained relations between them. It could even get one or both of them killed.

He'd put in a transfer to his superiors, and they, of course had challenged him and what he might be after. He fobbed it off as a desire for keeping things new and a way to enhance his training and experience as well as possibilities for promotion, wanting to move from the Organized Crime department into the one concentrating on offenses against children. That department usually held openings, as it was not considered the most attractive, but it had been able to prove a good political path to advancement for others. He doesn't really care about that, some of his cynicism creeping in, but he now finds himself imbued with a very real desire to help.

He had turned a blind eye to the way Gnegon and his outfit had treated the victims they brought into the city, but he cannot do so any longer. Now, with it being more blatantly persons of less years, he feels even more compelled to seek his redemption. He doesn't even much think of the danger. Some may consider him reckless for his choice of profession and then deciding to become corrupt, but he's always kept what he hopes is a careful measure of such things. From what Alec tells him, this new boss is much worse than Gnegon, but it's not like Gnegon was afraid to spill blood. Alec says Volkov has a beef with law enforcement, though, instead of the attitude of it being more necessary but not desired bedfellows. Still, a rash of police murders has not arisen in the city, and he'd be surprised if it does. That often proves a great way to get one's self stamped out. These "Thieves" may not like the police, but law enforcement has very real power.

He is going to continue to exploit that, using his contacts, his experience, the resources available to him, some clean, some maybe less so, but he is going to now try to do what is "right".

*****

The climate somewhat reminds him of home, but that is largely where any similarities cease. The town, or small city, if one prefers, boasts a population a bit north of 100,000. It is growing, especially due to its relative proximity to other major metropolitan areas, and even the rare and bad news of late will not hamper that.

Duilio drank down a rather horrid cup of coffee, deciding against a second even though it had not been nearly strong enough, and he crushes out his cigarette, noting the prominently displayed sign that the building he is about to enter is a 'tobacco-free facility'. He has not been to the USA in a long time, and his last visit had been to New York City. He takes in a breath, steeling himself, then he walks through the glass double-doors, entering the local police department.

SWORD OF THE BUTTERFLY

He moves slowly, though not so much so as to draw undue attention to himself. He takes stock of the place. He sees a small waiting room, and he is somewhat impressed. A man sits there, looking like a typical resident, quite slender, blond hair cut very short and noticeable beneath the well-worn ball cap, goatee looking as though it could use a trim. Duilio casts his eyes down to the man's wrists, half expecting to see cuffs there. The man sits somewhat forward, elbows bent upon knees, and of course, there are no such bonds.

Duilio moves further in, the report of his fine leather shoes quite loud in the sterile environment, but the desk officer does not look up. *Odd*, Duilio thinks, but so be it, and he politely clears his throat.

"Yes?" The cop looks up, and Duilio notices the hesitation and slight narrowing of eyes as the receptionist immediately registers that this man is not from around here. "May I help you?"

He speaks with a noticeable Southern American accent for this region, though in truth, Duilio does not have the ear for distinguishing the subtleties of such. The man could be from Mississippi for all he knows.

"Yes, thank you. I am Agent Gaspare Duilio of Interpol," he announces, speaking with some measure of aplomb, showing his identification, but the man just sort of looks at him, confusion mixed with what the visitor might think of as unnecessary defensiveness. "I have an appointment."

The eyes narrow, then the man consults his computer.

"Here it is," he says, and Duilio's disarming smile moves up a touch, "You're to meet with Captain Shinberg. He's just down the hall that way, on the left, his name is on the door."

Duilio nods once, thinking this also a bit different, but he gives a courteous 'thank you' and moves on.

He continues to take his time, looking about as he walks deeper into the innards of the department. He did not notice any signs of upset in the foreparts, nor does he see any here, but mechanical messes are easier repaired than others. He thinks that the number of people is scarce for the population, but he has nothing against which to adequately gauge that. He also sees some further looks of suspicion set upon him, but again, is this normal, or is it paranoia from the attack? It feels as though the officers are on edge.

He finds the room, and the way is open, the transparent door leading into the man's office.

"Inspector Duilio," he greets, standing, "I'm Captain John Shinberg. Good to meet you."

"The pleasure is mine," Duilio returns, shaking the offered hand.

The man looks more refined than his colleague at the desk, , prominent nose and ears on his long face, his white shirt pressed and tucked into his dark trousers.

"Have a seat," he offers, gesturing to one of two available chairs.

"Thank you, Captain." The guest takes the one to the left.

"Would you like some coffee?"

"Uh, no," Duilio puts on a sheepish smile, "but thank you."

"I suspect our coffee here wouldn't suit your Italian tastes," he says, the comment not laden with the prejudice or even subtle insult one could expect, "We do have Starbuck's, though. We're not some backwater little hick-town."

"Yes, I stopped there before coming here."

"Ah, good." The man nods, then pulls in a breath, eyes setting more seriously upon his visitor. "We might as well get to it."

The silence stretches, eventually making Duilio feel a touch uncomfortable. He is about to inquire when the man continues.

"We don't often get official visits from Interpol agents," he says, then raises his chin, fixing a more pointed stare, "In fact, I don't recall us ever having one. Honestly, I can't say as we're too keen on much of anyone coming here. We like to handle things ourselves. We don't much even like the State Police coming around. We don't really roll out the warm welcome to the F.B.I., and Lord knows, they love to get involved around here."

"Yes, you are close to Quantico," Duilio notes, and the other man nods, ponderously.

"But … in this case, I'll tell you, I'm glad you called."

"Oh?"

"We've never had anything like this, Inspector, and in my experience, most mass murderers end up dead or caught at the end of

SWORD OF THE BUTTERFLY

their spree. This makes us look bad, not to mention how it's weakened us, so I can't say as it caused too much surprise when we received word from your office that this guy had done it before and was wanted in other countries."

Duilio nods, slowly, but the man does not carry on, so he speaks, "Yes, yes, it is a very serious matter. We must find and bring this killer to justice, hmm?"

"You'd think someone this evil would have been found by now. How does he even manage to cross an ocean?"

"There are ways, Captain." Duilio spreads his hands from where they had been clasped together in his lap. "Though I assume such a person would take a boat and not an airplane."

Another weighty silence has its way with the moment, and though the agent's comment had been made with a touch of humor, as though trying to placate, the seriousness of the situation supersedes. The host nods, thoughtfully, hands brought together, steepled, fingertips barely touching his lips. He then exhales audibly through his nose.

"This is a bad one, Inspector."

Duilio nods, giving his sympathy as well as agreement in the manner of the gesture.

"Well, of course you know that," the captain adds, hands moving away from his face, and he appears to escape the vines of his dark thoughts, though the smile that comes to his lips is short-lived and a bit awkward.

He reaches for a drawer, retrieving information, and though it is not presented in the customized, very precise and slick way as that given him by the Malkuths, it receives eager reception all the same. Duilio does note, though, that the brown string and button envelope is sealed, the broad band of tape also bearing red letters.

"I am sure you know the need of keeping this confined to official channels," the captain relays, and Duilio nods, remaining back in his chair, not lunging forward for the file, "I'll have you sign a release to get this, and it will discuss the need for confidentiality. I'm sure you boys at Interpol understand the handling of sensitive information."

"Indeed we do, Captain. We often deal with the delicacies of just that."

"Of course, you do. I don't mean to offend … it's just that this … well, this is bad."

"Yes, sir," Duilio dips his head once, then he speaks further, "I think I'd like that coffee, after all, if you do not mind, Captain?"

"Of course, let me just get someone-."

"Oh, please." He raises his right hand from its place on the wooden arm of the dated chair. "Do not go to that trouble. I'll fetch it for myself. I wouldn't mind seeing your facility, anyway, if that is not too much to ask? I am curious." He lets his polite, disarming smile take his lips now as he waits for the officer to reply.

"That's fine."

Duilio receives a short tour, given some basic information from his host. Captain Shinberg is knowledgeable of his own department, but he is something of a dry tour guide. It doesn't matter to Duilio. He looks at the people, taking note of their demeanor. He suspects the "classified" information in the folder will not help him all that much. This is the bare beginning of the investigation, and he is searching, fishing, hoping to find something that will help. They are all little parts that come together to form the bigger picture.

The coffee here is even worse than what he had at breakfast, but he does not show it. He, instead, displays gratitude, and the two veterans resolve easily into talk of their respective understanding of their careers. Both are guarded but for different reasons. Duilio sees no reason to dislike the man. He seems sincere, if not stuffy, but he will be of no further use.

When he finally leaves, after signing the papers and taking custodianship of the file and its contents, he notices that the man from earlier is still in the lobby, and he gives the departing visitor a short look with his pale eyes, hints of blue and green washing away to the underlying color. As the inspector emerges from the building, he also sees a patrolman outside, lingering in the growing heat. Duilio reaches, instinctively, for his sunglasses, retrieving them from his inner jacket pocket and slipping them on.

"Good morning," he greets, noticing that the cop is looking at him.

"Inspector?"

"Yes?" Duilio leads, gauging quite easily that the young man is nervous, his eyes casting about, blinking, fingers and hands not quite resting.

"I know why you're here."

Duilio nods, still as though trying to lead the obviously uncomfortable officer.

"I'd ... I'd like to talk to you about it."

"Okay." Duilio continues nodding, then he perks his thick eyebrows when the other does not elaborate.

"Not here, though."

"What is your name?"

"Gonzales. Arturo Gonzales. I've only been on the force for a couple of years."

"And I ... have not," Duilio announces, affecting a chuckle after this, in which the other haltingly joins.

"Right, right. You ... you have a car, don't you?"

"Of course. This is America. How else would I get around?"

"Right, right," is repeated, along with deep nods, "If ... if you don't mind, would you like to follow me? I can show you a place that has good breakfast and good coffee."

"Oh, well that sounds *wonderful*, Officer Gonzales. Grazie."

"De nada," comes the smooth response.

It proves easy enough, as Duilio is experienced in such things, and he pulls away in his rented white Volkswagen Jetta onto the nearby street, driving quite slow, keeping an eye out. The patrol car emerges soon enough, and he spies Gonzales behind the wheel. The cop pulls around, and Duilio follows.

The place ends up being off the main road, and driving around and into the dusty parking area, Duilio spies the small structure, tucked away in the lot, a few wooden tables set up for outside dining. It is a taquería, and other than the small truck positioned behind the place of business, only two other vehicles are here at this late morning hour. He parks next to the patrol car, walking over to see Gonzales already engaged in easy conversation with the proprietor. Two men, also of obvious Mexican descent, hold place at one table, and where they had given congenial nods to the cop, they gaze at Duilio with open suspicion. He gives them a nod of greeting.

"Buenos días," he says, neither giving a response in kind.

He wanders up to the counter, the woman behind talking with Gonzales, the two speaking Spanish, and Duilio hears of himself, mentioning that he is from Italy and needs a 'good, strong' cup of coffee. A meal is ordered, then the officer turns.

"Would you like some breakfast?"

"No, no, muchas gracias."

"Oh," the young man blinks, "You speak Spanish?"

"Sí, un poco." Duilio gives a slight smile, then he pulls forth his pack of cigarettes.

He flares one up as he waits, looking around, catching the man behind the counter staring, so he gives him a single nod.

"You'd find more further south," Gonzales says, walking over, holding two paper cups of steaming coffee.

"Coffee?" Duilio asks, blinking.

"Oh, no." Gonzales chuckles. "Mexicans."

"Ah, of course." Duilio nods, taking the proffered cup. "Gracias."

"De nada. Cream? Sugar?"

Duilio nods, doctoring his drink to his liking, and he sips, noticing quite quickly that this is by far the best he has had this morning. He looks over, the pair behind the counter watching, and he raises the cup. "Muy bien!"

They both smile at this, the woman more so, giving their thanks. It does not take long before the meal is complete in its preparation, and they find a table, sitting beneath a broad, colorful umbrella to protect them from the sun.

"Thank you for showing me this, Officer," Duilio says as the other dives into his food, perhaps as a defense or distraction, though he pauses long enough to look at the speaker, nodding. "If I am delayed long in this city, I will become a regular here."

"I am sorry to say this, but I hope you're not."

"I completely understand." Duilio nods, having another deep drink of his coffee, swallowing the strong, sweetened brew. "You hope the man suspected of this is no longer here."

SWORD OF THE BUTTERFLY

"Man ...," he murmurs, chewing.

"Hmm?" Duilio snags, pulling on the line, eyebrows rising.

Gonzales looks at him, leaning back, chewing intently, downing the food with his own swallow of coffee, then he wipes his mouth with a napkin.

"Maybe I shouldn't say this, but I hope he'll get gunned down, but ..."

"But?" Duilio continues, slowly reeling, coaxing the unsure fish.

"Well, they say he was shot a whole bunch of times, but it didn't do anything to him. I mean ... how does a person survive that? How does a person just keep going?"

"*They* ... say?"

"Not everyone that was at the station that night was killed, and some saw enough of what happened."

"Were you one of them?"

"No," the young officer is quick to inform, shaking his head, "I'd probably be dead if I had been there."

Duilio picks up on much from this, but he just continues looking. He brings his cup to his mouth, sipping slowly, eyes staying on the man.

"Most of the Christians in this country are Protestants," the cop begins, and Duilio narrows his eyes behind the obscuring shades of his sunglasses, still just silently listening and watching. "You may easily guess that I'm not. My family is Roman Catholic. My parents, though, are much more devout. I've ... lost some of my faith. I still go to church every Sunday, for my wife and kids. My grandmother used to tell me stories. They were scary stories, then they just seemed more fascinating. Then, when I was grown, they seemed like a waste of time."

"What kind of stories?" Duilio asks.

"About the Devil ... and demons."

Duilio chuckles softly, apologetically. "What sort of grandmother tells such tales to her grandchildren?"

"I know," Gonzales huffs out a stunted chuckle within a sheepish grin, then he looks as serious as ever. "I guess it's meant to scare you straight, sí?"

"You wear a badge now, so it worked." Duilio smiles, and another brief chuckle is exchanged, and again, it is gone as quickly, traded for that fearful intensity the young officer shows unable to shake.

"I am trained and given authority and powers to hunt criminals. *Human* criminals."

"What exactly are you trying to tell me, Officer Gonzales?"

The cop looks around, his eyes barely stuttering in their assessment, as he has seated himself to have a good view of the area, then he exhales at length, leaning in close. Duilio comes in, too, trying to encourage and reassure the man.

"That *thing* that killed all of my co-workers, my *friends*, slaughtered them … *slaughtered*. It was *not* human."

"Homicidal psychosis can lead to savage, horrible behavior that we do not think of as being typically human."

"I appreciate what you're trying to say, Inspector, and I'm not stupid. I went to college for two years before joining the force. I'm saying that this … *thing* is not human. It withstood a firing squad. It was in leg shackles. Shackles, Inspector, and cuffed, and it broke free. I don't know what the report the captain gave you will say, if it addresses that at all, but it broke out, then it broke the steel door that goes into the interrogation room.

"That thing ... is not human," the officer concludes, eyes drilling into Duilio.

"Then what is it?" he finally asks into the increasing silence.

"A demon."

"A demon?" Duilio retorts, brow furrowing, as he leans back, and he does his best to hide his true reaction. "Come now, Officer, I know the situation is stressful but-."

"You're from Italy," Gonzales carries on, "From Interpol. Fine. You were vetted. You know that. You work for Interpol, but you are also from Italy. The Vatican is also in Italy."

"Yes …?" Duilio agrees, guardedly.

"I'm not asking for verification. I know how this sort of thing works. This *demon* appears, slaughters a bunch of people, citizens *and* cops, then it just disappears, and then you show up here … from Italy," the officer assesses, and Duilio does not correct him that he did not come

SWORD OF THE BUTTERFLY

directly from Italy. "I think you work for the Vatican, or some secret organization that works for the Vatican or whatever. It's like exorcism. The Church won't acknowledge it, but it's in the Bible, and priests are trained to do it. I understand why it's better for the general public to not literally believe in demons like that. But you're here, and I bet you're not just working for Interpol. You're here to hunt a demon."

The man gives his eyes to Duilio for a moment as though extra evidence to his conclusion, then he raises his fork, not having ceased his hold on the utensil this entire time, making ready to resume his meal.

"Officer Gonzales," Duilio begins, hands coming up.

"No, no," the cop replies, chewing fast, swallowing. "Don't confirm or deny. It doesn't matter. I hope you find and *kill* this thing soon. I hope you do before it kills anyone else. It's unholy, and it needs to die."

Gonzales quickly finishes his meal, leaving Duilio there smoking in contemplative silence, the two deciding it is best if their cars do not leave the lot at the same time. Of course, anyone could have seen them sitting and talking together, but Duilio acquiesces to the young officer's wish. He decides he might as well have another cup of the fine coffee, and when he rises and turns to head back, he sees the man there.

He is white, so he already stands out from the others, but it is clear he is the slender man Duilio spied in the waiting area of the local police station - the man with the gray eyes. He is also smoking, leaning up against the front of a dirty, black Chevrolet Silverado. He does not look away when Duilio sees him, instead casually walking over, boots kicking up some dust from the parking surface. If he were wearing a cowboy hat instead of the ball cap, and if the truck were a horse, it would complete the picture all the better.

"Good morning, Signor," he greets.

"Good morning," Duilio guardedly replies, noticing the man has used Italian, or he is mispronouncing Spanish. Still the subtle correctness of it makes him think it is on purpose.

"How do you like the coffee here?" he asks, eyes moving down to the empty vessel then back up.

"It is excellent."

"Good, let me buy you a cup."

93

"That won't be-," Duilio tries, but the man is on his way, walking up to the counter.

"Dos más cafés, por favor," he orders, then turns back, eyes squinting at Duilio, despite the brim of the cap.

Duilio waits, deciding to play this out for now, getting the coffee with a 'thanks', and once the two are done with their mixings, they return to the table. The man likes a lot of sugar in his. He sips, blinking rapidly, then shakes his head.

"That *is* good," he agrees.

"Who are you?" Duilio asks.

"Oh, I'm sorry," the man says, speaking with the touch of a rural accent of his own, though his is less detectable than the general 'natives' of the area, "Pardon my manners." He extends a hand across the table. "I'm David Felcraft."

"Felcraft?" Duilio replies, barely managing to not stutter, then takes the proffered hand after a very short, awkward delay, shaking.

"Yes." David nods once, then steels his eyes. "And you are?"

"Oh, of course." Duilio exhales into a stunted chuckle. "Gaspare Duilio."

"Pleased to meetcha, Signor Duilio."

"Oh, Gaspare is fine."

David just sets a thin grin on him, then goes back to his coffee when the hands are released, taking a lengthy taste, swallowing.

"You've heard of my family."

Duilio almost sputters over his own drink.

"I … It's just a curious … uh, *interesting* name."

"So's Duilio. So's *Malkuth*."

Duilio blinks rapidly, his lips parting. He swallows, then brings up his coffee cup, the eyes of the other not ever stopping in their observance. Duilio drinks down more of the brew, then he coughs lightly, nodding.

"Yes, another interesting name."

"You work for them," David states.

"I work for Interpol," Duilio rejoinders.

SWORD OF THE BUTTERFLY

"Oh," David responds, his pale eyebrows going up, lips pursing a bit, and he nods slowly. "I bet that's exciting, but ... not as exciting as this."

"I don't know what you-."

"Okay, so I look like I could pass for a local here, though I'm not. And though you might understand the Mexicans, you're obviously not one of them. How many Italians do you think choose this as their vacation destination when coming to America, hmm?" He raises those eyebrows again, his lips curled into a smile within the healthy goatee.

"I am not here on vacation."

"Of course not," David gives, "And I saw you in the police station, and you saw me. You weren't there to report a purse stolen. You're here because of the murders."

"Yes, I am."

"And you're not a Malkuth; you just work for them."

Duilio prepares another round of protests, but again, he is cut off.

"Okay, so here's the situation." David pushes his empty cup aside, having quickly polished off the coffee, and he fishes out a cigarette from the pack of Marlboros. After lighting it, he holds out the zippo, offering the flame. Duilio blinks, face rising up a quick tick, then he pulls out one of his own, Gauloise, holding it between his lips and partaking of the ignition with a muttered thanks before David closes it and continues. "We encountered the Demon first, and we sent word to the Malkuths. We lost one of our own to it. Did they tell you that?"

"No." Duilio blinks, realizing he has just confessed.

"That doesn't surprise me. You're in over your head, Signor," David says, leaning aside to tuck the lighter back into the pocket of his jeans, peering sidelong at Duilio with those eyes again squinted, then he settles back, exhaling smoke. "So, we know they're going to be out here, hunting, and my cousin sent me to try to pick up the trail, so I see someone like you in the police station, and I figure you're working for them. I know enough of the Malkuths to know them. Just like they know me.

"I also know this is a bad one we're hunting," David adds, leaning closer, "One of the worst in a long time. Worst I've ever known about, and they send *you*. I don't mean this as an insult, Signor, but you are not equipped for this."

Duilio sighs, parting his lips in thought, eyes moving away then back to those of the other man. He takes a deep drag of his cigarette, nodding as he exhales.

"I know, I know," he agrees, "But I am here to do a job, and I will do it."

David nods once, firmly. "I respect that. They told you to look for signs of it, find the trail, right? Then what?"

"Notify them."

"Well, good, at least there's that. I'm supposed to do that, too."

Duilio crinkles his forehead.

"There are several of us in the area, hunting, but there are never that many of us. My cousin wanted me at ground zero, so I'm here, and I'll pick up the trail. Maybe the Malkuths just stuck you out here as bait. Maybe they want you watching me and sending back reports."

"I … they did not say anything to me about anyone like you being here."

"Of course, they didn't, but you're going to tell them now, aren't you?"

Duilio's spine slowly stiffens as he rises up, realization dawning on him.

"Look, I'm not here to try to get you to quit them and join us, but this is how they operate. They are very cold with their resources, and everything is 'need to know'."

Duilio nods.

"They will keep you in the dark forever, and they will use you as they like, and a lot of that, you won't even know about. That's just it. That's just their way."

"And the Felcrafts are different?" Duilio pitches, somewhat challenging, though he just as quickly does not know why he would defend the Malkuths; perhaps he is just trying to defend himself and his lot in life.

"Yes," David flatly answers.

Some time passes, the two in quiet thought, smoking.

"We can work together," David then says.

SWORD OF THE BUTTERFLY

"How? I thought you two were rivals."

"We are, but we've got a common enemy. You understand that? We're just like two opposing teams in a race to get across the River Styx but Cerberus is there, trying to stop all of us. We'd better work together to kill him, then we can get back to the race."

"Interesting symbolism," Duilio comments, wondering how truly apt it is.

"We *told* them about this one."

"So you said."

"Ask them when you talk to them next time. They're not that stupid to think we wouldn't have anyone here. Of course, I didn't have to approach you, but I did."

Another moment stretches, more time to ponder.

"I think we ought to work together," David suggests, "You let them know that, too. It'll be better for you, anyway, because if you do find that thing, you will die." Those three words emerge with a cold finality unlike the simmering geniality of the man's usual tone. "I don't know if you'd have time to get off a message, and that's all they care about. They don't care if it slaughters you. But if you are with me, well, if we find it, then you turn and run as fast as you can, then you can send them a message."

"And what would you be doing?"

"I'd be trying to kill it."

"How gracious of you," Duilio speaks slowly, his words dripping with sarcasm.

"If you want to take this as me trying to sell you something, then fine, I guess I am, in a way. But I am also trying to help you."

"Why?"

"Because I'm a Felcraft, and that's *our* way," he says, then gives a little nod and a grin, dropping his cigarette butt in the coffee cup before grabbing it and rising to leave.

"How would I contact you?" Duilio asks, though he suspects he knows the answer.

"Oh, I can find you easily enough. I figure I'd give you a chance to talk to them about this. I'll look you up soon." And with that, he meanders past the trash can to throw in his cup, climbing into his pickup and driving away.

CHAPTER FOUR

Another dark, somewhat dilapidated building, but this one is not a warehouse. Its height shows five stories, the windows of the first suggesting that floor holds more space, while those above hint at the limits to the top access. The architecture is not terribly old, the colors looking bled, if there had been much at all to begin with. This place had been cheap housing when it was originally built, and now it is assumed to be for the very poor. Its true control and use is much more nefarious.

Lilja holds place at a decent distance, standing in the darkness cast by two other structures. It is night, but light needs to be avoided. She wears her dark clothing, but without the gear and head covering, she looks almost passable as a 'normal' person.

She watches through the small binoculars, noting the traffic of the building. There is not much, but there is some activity. She sometimes spies movement in the windows, but the vast majority of them look to be obscured in some manner, not so easily willing to give up the secrets of what goes on inside. The night is quiet, and she pulls her left foot back almost casually, the sole of the jika-tabi creating an inordinately loud scrape against the ground.

The place and its goings-on have been tracked from the train station and a quite popular shopping mall. Those inside against their will have not all been procured via the methods one might expect, some of those overly risky or sadistic, and it makes her wonder of this new crime boss. He is not just after illicit sources of income.

Last year, Skot had told her that the blood sacrifices along with the mounting, coalescing negative energies had produced a gateway for the Demons. She had seen it. She had been there when it had been closed. She had been aware, without realizing it, of the efforts that were underway to unwittingly cause that to happen. Evil was begetting evil. And now she sees it potentially happening again, and quite possibly, in a worse way.

The city is befouled with bad fortune, but she knows that is not just due to chance. Skot had also explained something of ley lines to her, a topic she is not unfamiliar with. The City sits atop a potent intersection, making it a good site for just such 'supernatural' activities. She is no longer just fighting the prevalent crime that appears to find this area so attractive but also the underlying, darker energies of the Infernal. The two intertwine.

Even with the information she has at her disposal, she would normally feel that this operation is not ready. She is not as secure as she'd like in various facets of intel. What is the true scope of the defense? How many guards? What is their weaponry? What sort of sensors or alarms or other security systems? The place is somewhat exposed, boasting, of course, a certain amount of armed sentries, but other than that, she is not sure. Is there really such a lack, or has she just not yet found it?

Still, she does know there are children being held inside and used in horrible ways, and she feels she can wait no longer. After some more minutes of surveillance, she moves back to the hidden area that houses her motorcycle, a black Kawasaki Ninja ZX-6R, customized to be quieter and driven in such a way that is much stealthier than usual, and her gear. She retrieves what she needs from the bag, outfitting herself for the operation, having chosen her FN P90 for this, though unlike her and Skot's descent into the underground, she now uses the subsonic ammunition and suppressor. The rounds are also obviously not the special ones used to hunt Demons. She has had quite the training lately to face these more dangerous, inhuman opponents, but those inside the building are still deadly. She checks her outfitting one last time before applying the black face paint, then cleaning her hands and donning the balaclava and tactical gloves. She then engages her motorcycle's theft deterrence and heads out.

She finds her way inside rather easily, and again, she wonders at the lax security. She avoids a few guards armed with the typical submachine guns – Steyr TMP's, Skorpions, even some KBP PP-90's. She does not

SWORD OF THE BUTTERFLY

notice any of them carrying stunners, and only one looked to be equipped with a radio. She has been somewhat short in her recent attentions to her duties as the vigilante, but she's still kept an eye on the flow of information, executing a few small missions that were likely too clandestine to have been noticed. This will be her first more overt operation in a while.

The ground floor had been partially opened up, making some sort of receiving area. She also spied a small, makeshift bar, which perhaps served as much for the security as the customers. She did not spend long there, not even seeing someone behind the counter.

Floor after floor, door after door, creeping along methodically, slowly, quietly, and yet, there proves little to no sign of anyone or any activity. She continues moving up, not liking the implied lack of her own safety this entails, but she is here now, and she knows there are children somewhere inside. She encounters her first fight as she waits to proceed to the fourth floor, one of the sentries walking out to the landing as she lurks in the shadows. He had been about to miss her, moving on past on his way down, but his lighter had not cooperated as he tried to flare up a cigarette, so he turned, moving more into the corner to perhaps avoid a draft, and the sudden illumination reveals a dark figure.

He startles, emitting a grunting noise of surprise, eyes going wide, freshly lit cigarette faltering, hindered in its descent by his lower lip then dropping free. Before it reaches the ground, she moves, lightning-quick, coming in as he grips his weapon, trying to aim. She dodges to his right, further away from the current trajectory of the barrel, reaching in to grab his hand, trying to keep him from pulling the trigger and raising the alarm.

She grabs his wrist, still moving, using her momentum to apply force, turning the guard. He tries to punch with his left hand, aiming for her face, but the strike is easily seen and avoided. Once she has him shifted, his right arm twisted and pushed up, she shoves him into the nearby wall. He cries out, a grunting noise more of anger than anything else, and she uses her left hand to pull out her stunner, giving it life with a press of a button, pressing the electrified prongs against him. His grunts become stuttered and strained emissions, his body taunt. She releases the button, quickly holstering the device and zip-tying the guard, pushing him down to his knees and using tape to rapidly wind a gag over his mouth.

It all happens very fast, but it is not silent, and she tenses, looking right as she hears a masculine voice calling out a name, likely trying to check on this very sentry. She pulls back, dragging the supine man with her, his eyes partially opened as he emits some weak protests or mere attempts to regain some focus on the moment. She gets back into the dark corner just as the other guard appears. He is wearing a tan beanie, eyes narrowed, trying to better see in the dim illumination, the barrel of his SMG also pointed. He hisses out another insistent call of his comrade's name, then his eyes go wide. He sees a portion of a boot sticking out from the darkness, and just at that moment, Lilja also notices, springing forth from the shadow in ambush.

The guard cries out, backpedaling, turning, fleeing. Lilja curses silently, knowing this will undoubtedly raise a response. She catches the man quickly, twisting and sending out a low kick that trips him. He clambers to the ground with a loud racket, hoping to turn and use his weapon to fire on his attacker now that he is unable to escape, but she jumps on top of him, flattening him with a painful grunt. She looks up, another sharp movement of her covered head, as rapid footsteps reveal two more guards entering the hallway, both emerging from the same room, both raising their weapons and planting themselves in obvious readiness to fire. A quick glance at her near surroundings reveals, of course, closed doors. Are they locked? She has to make a decision, so she springs left, hands reaching out for the doorknob, turning it and barreling through just as the gunshots blare out in the hall. The guard on the ground yells, curling up and covering his head, though his protests are eclipsed by the spray of bullets. She gives a portion of her thoughts to whether or not he will end up shot, but bullets tearing into the doorjamb and causing a storm of wood splinters gives her more concern.

She slams the door closed, looking quickly for the locking mechanism, but there is not one. She backs away, aiming with her P90, holding herself low and steady, waiting. She hears noises outside the door, raised voices. She prepares to fire, but she also quickly takes stock of the room, and there is another doorway. She moves to it, fast and quiet, barrel of the P90 still pointed at the other door, and soon she is

SWORD OF THE BUTTERFLY

inside a very cramped bathroom. She turns, pointing outside the wash closet, waiting, and that is when the other door is banged open and a relentless barrage of bullets is unleashed into the room.

The firing stops after causing a great deal of damage. She can only imagine that the alarm has now been raised over the entire building and more guards must be convening on the area. These three would be smart to back off and wait or use grenades, if they have them. It seems they have neither small explosives nor sufficient intelligence, for after the sounds of reloading, they proceed somewhat carefully into the room.

They do at least fire up a torch, beaming the light into the room. She sees the carnage caused by the bullets, but a portion of the room goes left, having been spared, as has the bathroom. She waits, quietly, crouched low. Voices rise up, obviously noticing there is no corpse or even blood, and she wonders that they don't fire again or vacate the small chamber. She hears the telltale sound of running, one of them obviously heading off for whatever reason.

Another comes into view then, having traversed the short distance from the doorway to being in the room proper, and just as she sees this movement, she fires, the weapon coughing out its suppressed rounds, and the man jitters, yelling, his legs hit several times. She moves slowly and smoothly forward, aim held steady, and though she hears and sees a reactionary fire from the other, he misses completely. She does not, and soon both are on the ground, whining and moaning and cursing, bleeding from multiple wounds in their legs. She does not stick around to bind their wrists or wounds.

She is back in the hallway, moving quicker, though still steady and careful, barrel of the P90 pointing the way. She doesn't hear anyone. Either the guards are still en route, or they are waiting. She wonders why she hears no sounds of the children. The silence bothers her. And then, the loud crack of a gunshot reaches her ears, then shortly thereafter, another. These are not being fired at her, and she can tell they are coming from further down the hall and to the right, muffled somewhat by the walls. She picks up the pace, running now, heading to the source of the noise. Before she reaches the door, she hears the cries and screams, and she knows what is happening. She does not focus on it, does not let it claim too much of her attention or drive, else she might dissolve into anguish. But she knows.

The door, as with the other, is unlocked, and she opens it to yet another report of gunfire, and she emerges unto a scene of horror.

The room is dark, dank, a holding area for the children. The lights that illuminate the place are naked incandescent bulbs, low wattage, casting out in limited areas, giving contrast and shadow to others. The obvious remnants of meager bedding and thin, worn pillows occupy some space of the floor, the only consideration given to provide comfort for whatever sleep may be found within this nightmare.

Lying there are the bodies of the children, at least four of them, all freshly murdered when bound and gagged. Two guards are inside, one nearer to the door. The other, the executioner, is further away, a pistol in his hand. They both look like the other guards she has encountered; neither showing any sort of sign of sadistic enjoyment, but their grim determination tells her much.

The killing one sees her first, and he turns, shouting, raising the handgun. She fires, P90 sputtering out several bullets, and they rip into his torso, center mass. He falls without firing another shot. The other begins raising his submachine gun. Instead of shooting, she lunges toward him, a flare of anger rising in her eyes.

She kicks the gun aside. It is ripped from his hands, the unused strap dangling below it now wrapping about the weapon as it clatters to the ground some feet away. He lunges out with his right fist, but she power blocks it along with a dodging motion, turning her fist to open fingers and grabbing his wrist, moving, creating an arm-bar. She then delivers a sharp punch to the elbow, snapping it in its hyper-extended state. The guard cries out, yelling in pain. Still holding the now broken arm, she turns quickly, using her low center of gravity, smashing the man against the nearby wall, face first, adding extra force by pressing his head with her other hand at the moment of collision.

He emits more stunted protests, blood emerging from his face. She stabs out a sharp, quick kick to the back of his knee, producing another yell of pain, shoving him to the ground, forcing him to land on his back, getting over him and repeatedly pounding into his face with her fist. Each rapid, powerful jab is accompanied by a nigh animalistic grunt on her part, lips parted and clenched teeth borne behind the covering, until she cries out loudly on the last.

She then gets up, aiming the P90 at his bloody face, the guard barely conscious, struggling with respiration. She holds her intent, torqued to this one moment, gloved finger on the trigger, then she realizes what is happening.

A blink, a barely noticeable tremble, and she is past it, finger moved away from its deadly place. She turns, rapidly, pointing the barrel at the door, and she listens. She now hears the approach of others, many, rushing down the hall in this direction. She imagines the other staircase is also being used, or is watched. She glances at the covered windows and decides on another option.

The furnace nearby is bolted. Good. The window is easily unlocked and quickly cranked open. She unzips the pouch at the back of her combat harness, retrieving the tactical rope, pulling the loop to the side to unravel the length. She attaches the end to the furnace, then affixes the lead to her belt, throwing the bulk of it out into the night, then hurriedly getting through and rappelling down. She moves with experience, going out and down several meters before coming back, booted feet connecting gently with the building's surface before flexing her legs and pushing back out to drop further, being sure to bypass the other windows as she goes. She aids the travel with her left hand, fist gripped about the rope, moving it out and in to control the pace of her descent.

She is on the ground in seconds, unhooking, looking up. She hears raised voices. They have seen her, or at least seem to know how she has escaped. They do not fire any careless bullets down at her. She leaves the rope, of course, moving away and into nearby shadows, watching, waiting. She will not give them long, just passing a moment to process and assess the situation. She knows where her transportation awaits, on the other side of the building and a short distance away. She looks about, eyes bright within the black paint and balaclava covering her head and face. She sees a decent enough path, and she is off, moving quickly, returning to her motorcycle with no further impediment.

The mission has been a failure. It is very likely not a coincidence that those poor children were killed when she was there. There is much to process, and unlike formal operatives, she has to handle the debriefing herself as best she can. She fires up her bike, knowing she needs to get home safe before she has to face what she has encountered this night.

*****

"You are right, Mister Felcraft. My employers do know you."

"It's David, Signor. Just David."

"And I am Gaspare."

The two share a friendly smirk, and David raises his paper cup in response to the same from Duilio. They are sitting at the same place where they 'met', though the open lot is now shrouded in gloaming. David had indeed contacted him, surprising Duilio with a phone call to his motel room. In retrospect, it should have not been unexpected. The Interpol man had agreed to meet for some coffee and further talk.

"The Demon's no longer here," David informs after a couple of swallows from his brew.

Duilio is noticing in their very limited time together that the man is not only a fan of sugar but also goes quite quickly through coffee and cigarettes. He had offered Duilio a small, brightly wrapped chocolate, possessed of a pocketful of the candies. Duilio had declined, merely watching as the man munches through them.

He is slender, so it does not seem that his choice of consumptions is causing him to gain weight, but who knows in what else such habits may result? Duilio glimpses the notable signs of strength, firm, lean muscle of the forearms revealed by the rolled up shirt sleeves, in addition to which is the obvious experience and steel in his eyes and hands.

He just nods to the statement, figuring it is true, and there would be little reason to lie to him.

"What have you found out?" he asks, raising his chin a bit, looking out at the Italian beneath the brim of a different, though equally well-worn ball cap.

"Not much, I am afraid. I have done the usual thing, asking around, checking the police files."

"And?" David leads.

"They do not paint the complete picture."

The other man nods, slowly.

SWORD OF THE BUTTERFLY

"The people are scared. They know something very bad happened, but they don't fully understand what that was," Duilio muses, reaching into his jacket pocket for his pack of cigarettes, though he just sets them on the wooden tabletop, then he fixes his eyes on his companion. "They are not used to such things here."

"Who is?" David snorts out a short string of chuckles.

"I had thought *you* might be ... well, *hoped*, really."

David gives the man another smirk. "Not as much as you might reckon," he says, then unwraps another chocolate, cellophane crinkling, before he pops it in his mouth, chewing. "I've got a decent amount of experience hunting them, relatively speaking, but we're glad they aren't overrunning our world enough for us to be bagging too many of them, know what I mean?"

"I do. Yes."

David chases the morsel with the rest of his coffee, then sets the empty cup on the table, throwing the few wrappers in it before finding a cigarette for himself. He lights up, again offering his flame to Duilio, who accepts. The two sit in silence, smoking.

"I'll be leaving soon."

"Oh?" Duilio peers at the man, neither wearing their sunglasses as the dark continues creeping over the dwindling sky. "May I ask when?"

"Maybe tonight," David answers, looking around, as though assessing the situation, "Tomorrow morning at the latest."

"Tonight?"

"Maybe. It's not here, but I've found the trail. I don't want it to get cold. I'm really only sticking around for you."

Duilio blinks at this, healthy eyebrows rising even higher.

"Me? Why me?"

David exhales a thick stream of smoke. "To see if we're working together or not."

A moment passes.

"And what if we are not?"

David looks at the other for a short time, then slowly tucks his shoulders up in a shrug. "Then I'd kindly warn you away. Not as a threat from me but for your own safety. You'll either be on the wrong trail, and it won't matter to me, *and* you'll have to deal with disappointing the

Malkuths on your own," he levels, his casual tone belying the implicit risk of such as that, "Or if you are on the trail, you'll be near me, and I'd rather you be working with me instead of getting in the way."

"I am not trying to hinder you, Mister Fel-," he begins, and the other perks eyebrows, "*David.*"

"Oh, I know, Gaspare, I know, but I *am* trying to look out for your safety."

"Thank you." Duilio smiles a touch more, emitting a light chuckle.

"I'd just as soon you be out of here, entirely. It'd be better for you, but you *do* work for the Malkuths."

Duilio waits, thinking more is coming. He looks at David, the man content to gaze away and up into the colorful sky, enjoying his cigarette. Duilio wonders what all is implied by the statement. He supposes it may intend as a reminder of not only who he works for but what it may also suggest of him to have such an employer.

"So," David resumes, "If you're going to be here, doing your *job*, then we might as well benefit from each other."

"I suspect you will be on the short end of that stick, no?"

"Maybe, maybe not," David answers, beginning it as though with humor but quickly turning it to something serious, "You're the Interpol man. I'm a Hunter. I've dealt with people, but I don't have the … savvy or sensitivity that someone like yourself does, capisce?"

Duilio nods, noting irony there. "I think I do, but how much talking with people do you think this will involve? And you are probably more trustworthy to the locals, hmm?"

"Maybe, but like I said, unless you're planning to go in another direction and report failure back to the Malkuths, I'd rather us work together. I'd make me feel a lot better, and whether or not you realize it, it'd make you feel a lot better, too."

David turns, leaning forward, drilling his gaze into the other man, inhaling deeply on his cigarette, lips pressing inward. Duilio is drawn to the flaring tip, watching as it burns down until the other pulls it from his mouth, depositing it in the empty cup.

"I think it would make me feel better, too, and ...," he adds, "I was … uhm … *encouraged* to do so by my employer."

"Well, that's a plus for them," David easily assesses, then stands, stretching. "I think I'll head out tonight, then. Will you be keeping that rental?"

"Yes?"

"Does it have four wheel drive?"

"No, it does not."

"Well, we'll make do."

"Why do you ask?" Duilio finally pitches.

"Well… our quarry isn't driving, and I don't expect it to stick to roads. We could easily end up in some rough terrain before this is all over."

"Ahhh," Duilio muses, nodding.

"It's going to be tough," David carries on, gaining Duilio's full attention, "This thing may look human, but it's not, you understand that? It could use that to get you to underestimate it, like those cops back at the station. Doesn't matter how big or mean some guy may look, if you have a loaded shotgun leveled at him, you might feel safer, stronger, but don't make that mistake here, Gaspare."

"I … don't have a loaded shotgun, but I understand you."

David nods, slowly, a curl touching his lips.

"Like I said, we'll make do."

*****

He sits in his private dormitory room, accompanied only by the flickering flame of the single candle, a scribbling noise coming from the pen as it scratches over the blank paper. He is bent to the task, his large form awkward in the too-small chair, his proximity to the parchment implying he may have some difficulty in seeing.

Some students have private rooms such as this, though they do not come cheap. Others prefer to have a roommate, but he eschews such interaction and companionship. Classes have just begun, but he is not here to make friends. He is here to acquire knowledge.

He pauses, sitting up, though still with somewhat hunched shoulders. His accelerated growth and unusual height has left him with poor posture. His brain, though, is abuzz, and he ponders. An observer might think him merely sitting, as though in some meditative pose, for he does not show any movement of his ecru-hued eyes nor any furrowing of his rather prominent brow. He comes to something, though, as he bends back to his task, using his free hand to tuck a thick, stray lock of his oily, dark hair behind a large ear before resuming his writing.

The scrawl fills the pages of the journal. He has kept many of these in his time, feeling somewhat compelled to spill the contents of his mind. It is not necessarily a labor of love so much as a necessity of survival. He has not been raised in a manner normal, and he has become his own companion, given quasi-independence by this birth upon paper.

The one class in which he held such hope has proven, indeed, to be the jewel. It is one meant to be a broad, basic study of Mythology, Folklore, and Literature. Such a collection of topics might appear very ambitious for one semester, but the Professor, Ernest Edwards, is up to the task. The senior instructor managed to offend a few students the first day by making a very controversial remark, saying this serves as a gauge of how the content might progress, and if any found such too unsavory, then they ought to drop the course.

He had experienced a stab of thrill when he heard the words, but he outwardly showed no such thing, save craning his head up to better see from his place in the back row. Though he has very little experience interacting with people, he knows enough to sit behind everyone.

Once it proved no one was leaving, or at least that no one had the guts to get up and walk out right then, the Professor had gone down the short list of attendance. It calmed the suddenly turbulent waters, as he made little remarks to each student, displaying some of the obviously vast knowledge of his in how he might pluck a random fact or piece of information from here or there based on their surname.

At first the odd student had followed it with some degree of curiosity, interested to see the interplay as well as the display of knowledge and how each morsel somehow fit, but then it dawned on him that soon his own name would be called.

"Wilbraham?" came the inevitable summons, the professor moving his head around as though in search of whom this may be, though nearly all of the small body of the class had by now been announced.

"Here, sir," he finally spoke, his voice an odd mixture of deep, gruff, but with a scratch of break, as though of pubescence or merely suffering from some chronic allergy.

The teacher leaned forward on the meager bookstand at the front of the class, staring unabashedly at the odd looking lad.

"That is a good, old name from England," Professor Edwards remarked with utmost sincerity, then consulting his list, looking back up, "Pothos? That's your first name?"

Pothos nodded, slowly, almost laboriously.

"Your parents must also be students of mythology to give you a great name like that," the instructor carried on, letting his dark, bushy eyebrows rise as though throwing a question mark onto the supposition.

Pothos has said nothing, and the professor had plunged forward, completing attendance, then letting them all know that their grade for the session would consist of two papers and only two papers. They would determine the topic one-on-one, but it had to, of course, be something related to the coursework. He assured them he would be very liberal in this assessment. The first paper would be turned in by mid-term, the second by the time of finals.

Pothos paused in his recollection, his large, left hand still set on the page, writing again halted, and a shadow seemed to touch his thin lips. One might find it difficult to discern if this was merely the play of candlelight or if he had been set on actually affecting a grin.

*****

"They were all shot in the back of the head," intones the voice, clinical but not without some vestigial touch of repressed emotion, "Marks on the body indicate they had been restrained and gagged prior to death. Much of the rest of the condition ... of the bodies is due to the manner of disposal."

They had been shortly found in a garbage dump, all four of them, very little effort having been made to hide them or obscure efforts at their identification. As it is, records are being scoured, avenues explored, to determine the names of the dead children. Then families will be notified.

Quain stands here with his new partner, Maria Kahler, a rather no-nonsense woman of Germanic lineage, her hair a dark blond, cropped rather short, giving it a lighter appearance against her pale flesh. She listens intently to the other generally no-nonsense woman here, Medical Examiner and Coroner Harriet McNeese, the somewhat overweight lady covered in her usual white coat, a pale yellow dress glimpsed beneath it.

"Their ages range from ten to fifteen, as best I can tell," McNeese continues, "They've been cleaned up." She raises her head, not looking at the shrouded figures out of an act of sheer will, even as her words and the general attitude of all here suggest an air of reverence. "Digital photographs are in the file to be used to also aid in identification."

"Thank you, Doctor," Kahler says, "I can't imagine this has been a pleasant task."

"No," McNeese replies, staring at the other woman, evincing no manner of sensitivity.

She had been rocked last year by the disappearance of Detective Pasztor, a man with whom she had been formerly involved. Their relationship had not lasted, and they generally treated one another with a sort of simmering conflict, but it did not take a psychologist to tell that was because they still harbored feelings for one another. To this day, no other information has been found regarding the sudden absence of the man and his partner, both assumed, but not officially designated, as victims of the serial killer of the time period, who also just up and suddenly disappeared shortly thereafter. Popular opinion is that the two cops found him, were killed, and possibly gave the killer a reason to leave. Interpol is helping, of course, to keep an eye out for similar murders, but nothing ever came up to think the murderer had fled and was operating elsewhere.

All of that had been on the heels of a rash of deaths of young women, some minors. It had been the sort of thing to make her rethink her choice of career. The ensuing time had generally been normal, at least in regards to how she might gauge such a thing, but then the arrival of these executed children had tested her. She wonders if another rash of horrible killings is upon them. She wonders how much more of this she can take.

SWORD OF THE BUTTERFLY

Kahler doesn't like it any more than the coroner does, but what also deeply concerns her is her new partner. They leave the office with their information, heading to the car.

"Child prostitutes."

"What?" she asks, looking over at him.

"That's what I think this is," Quain explains, "I think these kids were held against their will, prostituted out, and then killed, for whatever reason. Maybe they were thought of as baggage, meat past expiration."

"That's a terrible thing to say."

"I know." He nods, his words laced with sympathy below the force of hard pragmatism.

"So, you think they were sex slaves?"

"This city has had them before."

"Yes, it has," she says, steeling a scowling look on him. "You know that. You've seen it. How do you know that is what is going on here?"

He does not step back under her gaze, one which nearly meets him at eye level, such is her height and the few inches added by her shoes, but he knows the point she is making.

"I don't," he acquiesces, "I have a hunch. We use information networks. You know that. We use criminal informants. That's just the way it is-."

"Yes, I know this ," she cuts him off, the expression on her face tightening. "We sometimes use criminals for information. Of course, we do, but *we* are *not* the criminals. I don't know why you put in for your transfer, but I will tell you why I am in this department – for *that*." She points back in the direction of the morgue. "I *hate* seeing that. I hate the horrible things that people do to *children*."

She pauses a moment, drilling her light colored eyes into him. He just waits, taking it, knowing he deserves it.

"You are here for your reasons. Fine. But I will tell you something, Detective Contee, if I feel you are at all doing anything that may threaten the children, I will take you down with whatever force is at my disposal. Do you understand me?"

"I do." He nods slowly, as though placating a mad gunman.

"Good." She turns, heels reporting on the concrete as they reach their car, she going for the driver's side. "I am the lead here," she continues once they are in, "You follow my instruction. Help me, help the children, and everything will be fine."

"Yes, ma'am," he says with utmost sincerity.

He very much desires to positively assist and contribute. He knows he has to prove himself. He also feels confident that these recent victims are from the child prostitution ring. It shocks him to know what has happened, and he feels the need for friendly courtesy between himself and Alec can go right out the window if it has come to this sort of horrible crime now in the city.

Alec had recently quit the department, which, in retrospect, should not have been a surprise to him. Alec had told him that the new crime boss was forcing a choice. It upsets him that his former partner seems to now be content to so thoroughly ensconce himself in that life, but then he decides he is a hypocrite to judge so. He had lied to himself for too long that being a corrupt cop was better than being an overt member of organized crime. What's the difference, he had concluded. Being a corrupt insider who is supposed to uphold the law and protect the citizens, well, that may make him even worse.

He sits quietly as they drive. They have work to do, and yes, he will bow to the lead of his new and more senior partner, but he has other avenues he'll be exploring on his own.

*****

The intensity of her focus might give an observer to think she is paying close attention to the instructor, as well she should. Certainly, it is possible to be too narrow in such, which may cause one to miss things, but her aspect does indicate an unerring study. She watches, listens, goes through the motions, sweat and exhaustion building in her body. She even executes a few of the moves so well as to gain a quick tap from her partner and a notice and nod, even a few words of positive assessment from the teacher.

It all seems to be as one might intend and expect from such a self-defense class. To put an even finer point on it, what one might desire.

Yet in her mind, her thoughts are on other things.

SWORD OF THE BUTTERFLY

She watches as Lilja carries through the class in her usual manner, displaying her obvious skill with a casual efficiency. Therese knows the woman is good, has been doing this for years. She knows that the petite redhead is capable of so much more than the mere running of a self-defense class. There is a strength in her, a great potential, and Therese looks upon her now with a seething disappointment, a simmering, even, of disgust.

She watches, closely, her thoughts often going to 'why?', and she does not even realize what this means of her. She does the exercises with hardly any mind to them, a sign of her own increasing ability. She carries an aspect of determination. She has been thinking of this a lot recently, and the more she watches as Lilja displays her skill, the more is Therese driven further. The time for watching is over.

"Can I talk to you?"

Lilja looks up from nearly being done with putting away the training items to see Therese standing there. The young woman is highlighted with a gleam of perspiration, hands on her waist. Lilja stops what she is doing, rising to fully face her student, suppressing any rising sense of alarm.

"How may I help you, Therese?"

"I know about the murdered children," the hacker flatly states.

Nothing changes in Lilja's outward demeanor, but she feels a sudden shocking stab of anxiety.

"What murdered children?"

"The ones that were found recently by the police," Therese replies, her eyes narrowing, "Come on, Lilja, you don't have to play that with me."

"Play what?" comes the reply, and the redhead stands there, very calm.

Therese just looks at her, then releases a pent-up breath, noisily exhaling through her nostrils.

"Those kids were part of the child prostitution ring, and they were *slaughtered*, just ... *killed* ... in cold blood. They were *children*," Therese continues, her emotion bubbling forth.

Lilja maintains her even appearance, though her blue eyes appear to be shrouded in darkness.

115

"That's *horrible*," Therese adds, losing her limited patience with Lilja's continued silence.

"It is."

"You knew about it," Therese says, throwing out the words like an accusation, accenting them with a fling of her left hand. "I know you knew about it. You *had* to. So-." She steels her eyes on her instructor, her head shaking from side to side, yet barely moving. "So, why didn't you stop it? Why didn't you save those kids?"

Lilja exerts a great effort to limit her reaction. This is thin ice, very thin. She almost feels as though she stands there, at the center of the frozen water, bored into by the silent reproach of the eyes of the dead children, the tears and blood-stained gazes of all the victims she could have saved.

"What?" she finally speaks, though it sounds a touch more desperate than defensive, "How was I supposed to save them?"

"I don't know! You're the one with all the ... *abilities*."

"I'm just one person, Therese," Lilja flatly responds, "I'm not 'super woman'. I can't save everyone."

"You could have saved them, though," the student retorts, though now she sounds more saddened than angry, almost as though defeated by disappointment. She has somewhat turned away, hunching slightly, and she turns her eyes back to the teacher.

Lilja just stands there, seeming as cold as the very ice upon which she treads. It pains her to see that look on the other woman. It pains her to think of those dead children. It pains her to think of all the terrible things that wait out there, large and small, and how could she ever hope to stave that roiling, destructive wave? But she says nothing, displays none of her inner turmoil.

"You saved me ," Therese finally breaks the brewing silence, her voice sounding small, strained. "Twice," then she swallows, blinking, straightening her spine, turning to fully face the other , "Why didn't you save them?"

"I don't know what you're talking about," Lilja forces, "or exactly what you are trying to say. What happened to those children is horrible, and I wish I had saved them ..." Her voice trails off, and though she feels

SWORD OF THE BUTTERFLY

a tremble, like a deep rumbling that may remind one of small fractures, she maintains her appearance.

The emotions warring on Therese are difficult to bear. Lilja sees anger there, sadness, frustration, disappointment, but she cannot give in.

"What's the point of all this, then, huh?"

"I'm trying to make you all stronger," Lilja replies, "so you can help yourselves. I can't be everywhere all the time."

"Self-reliance." Therese nods, shakily, inhaling sharply, tension showing in her jawline and throat. "Inner strength. Right."

Lilja just observes.

"What's all of this going to do for me if I am bound and gagged and shot in the back of the head?" Therese throws out, then she turns and leaves, grabbing her bag, not bothering to head to the showers, just exiting the building.

Lilja stands there for a while, unmoving, just holding place. Her eyes stare off toward the door through which her student has passed. She then shows motion of an increased respiration, taking in a deep, lengthy breath, chest rising with it, then she tenses, turning, crying out and unleashing a powerful strike to the nearby punching bag. This is followed by another, another, and another, all punctuated with loud cries. She does not stop until her knuckles are bloody and the gleam of suppressed tears shines from her eyes.

CHAPTER FIVE

The dark liquid in the bone white demitasse cup is so inky that it looks like a black mirror. It sits on the small, similarly colored saucer, a nearby modest dish with sugar cubes and tiny tongs remains untouched. The hand that finally reaches forth to delicately take the narrow handle of the mug shows some tattoos, the fingernails short, well-manicured. The man wears a pressed, off white shirt, tailored black suit, his hair slicked back. He sips somewhat noisily of the espresso, enjoying the dark, bitter drink.

He has listened patiently to the words of some of those here with him, and once spoken, a certain amount of trepidation seeps up from the others as they wait for him to respond. He holds the tiny mug, seeming to look at nothing of his surroundings, perhaps focused inward, then he sips again. He finally returns the demitasse cup to its saucer, then leans back, inhaling a breath.

"We've not heard from vigilante for so long, I began to worry he might have retired or been killed," Volkov finally speaks.

The men stare, some eyes manage to blink, others look around. Perhaps it is not what they expected. The boss folds his marked hands in his lap, taking in another breath, holding it a bit before exhaling, nodding as though to himself.

"Good, good," he murmurs, then looks up, as though remembering that others are indeed here with him. "So, four dead, unh? That is not so bad. We have many more, yes?"

Some of the men emit low, stunted chuckles, unsure if this is a joke, for the boss does indeed now wear a thin, cold smile on his usually straight lips. They continue to glance about, seeking some sort of reassurance from their comrades.

"Some of the men were not happy about the order, though," one of the others reiterates.

Volkov slits his eyes over, and any lingering chuckling or smiles quickly dissipate. "Of course," Volkov utters, his gaze and manner remaining steeled on his lieutenant, "Killing children is not easy for most." This gets some meager nods, almost as if a sense of relief dawns. "We need sterner men," he adds, choking that embryonic ease, "The ones who object, watch them closely. They will not advance, and if they falter, kill them."

"Yes, boss."

"The children serve their purpose, as children do," Volkov speaks in a somewhat musing tone, and he reaches forward, gingerly placing the fingertips of his right hand about the rim of the mug, turning it, producing a light, scraping noise. "There is demand for everything in this world ... and supply. Children possess vibrant energy."

The silence stretches, and it is clear the others thought more would be coming in this spontaneous lecture, but the man has gone quiet.

"What should we do about the vigilante?" one of them finally dares.

Volkov moves his eyes to the speaker, studying him calmly for a short time, then he replies, "Capture him."

More looks are exchanged, more indecisiveness.

"You don't want us to kill him?"

"Not if you can help it," Volkov answers, "and I will be disappointed if that is result."

This carries more weight, though it is added as if an afterthought.

"I know vigilante is slippery one. He gave my predecessor much trouble, no?" Again some unsure chuckles boil up, though the boss does not even smile, and the brewing noise fails to take hold. "He was killed," the man adds, then he raises his left hand extending the fore and little fingers, then he turns it and presses the digits against the flesh of his own neck, the gesture meant to accentuate the mentioning of Gnegon's death. "But new head rises in place of old. We are not exactly hydra, as I am only one head to replace loss, but we will see how things may go differently. Regardless, we will show vigilante and city that we do not die so easily, mmh?"

This proves much clearer to the men, and they give hearty returns, some raising their glasses.

"Now, get out of here," Volkov says, waving his right hand, a somewhat casual flare of his fingers, and the men rise, nodding, showing other signs of obsequiousness, as they are dismissed.

All save one. The large man hangs back, standing there, just looking at his new boss, quietly.

"It is shame to end the lives of children like that," Volkov resumes the earlier topic, his voice gone back to that slower cadence, "There is great promise in early life, and it may be used, but now, it has been quenched in those."

The other man just continues to stand, watching, listening, a frown on his face.

"Still, that energy manages to retain some memory of origin, and that can be useful."

"Is this all just bait, boss?"

Volkov stops toying with the demitasse, his hand held poised.

"That is not your concern, ex-*Detective* Sladky," the man speaks, "You do only as told and nothing more."

*****

Lilja moves with a smooth grace, a practiced ease as though like water shaping rock, following currents and motions, pathways and energies, focusing and harnessing as well as giving in to that flow. She wears white gi pants and a form-fitting sport top, bare of foot, her hair in a single braid. She engages in practice with her katana.

The room is spacious, the ceilings tall. The coloring of the walls is a somewhat dark, soothing beige, the hue of the ceiling a shade lighter. One wall is covered with mirrors. The opposite side of the room displays some equipment – a rack with a pull-up bar, bench press, and the gleaming array of some free weights. A heavy punching bag also occupies a corner, a grappling dummy showing itself ready for use.

She cuts air as she strikes out, no noises coming from her throat, naught but a very grim determination on her features. Her expression may seem calm to those who do not know her well, but there is something simmering, brewing beneath that controlled exterior. The very effort being exerted to maintain the appearance belies the turmoil.

The polished sword drawn free from having been returned to its scabbard, striking in one single move, executing the iaijutsu flawlessly

She sees the bodies of the dead children, sees the grotesque, obscene flow of thick blood pouring from their head wounds, sees those lifeless lumps, the fire that once animated them gone out. If she had been quicker, faster, better, they'd still be alive.

Striking down from over her head, right foot forward, blade paused briefly at chest height only to rise and swipe out in a second cut, body turning, pivoting on that foot until perpendicular to its prior orientation

She sees the bodies of the dead women from last year, how they mounted and mounted, eventually giving way to the nightmare she witnessed in the compound's basement. She wonders if she is capable of facing such things. Yet, she did. She did more than survive. She does more even now, but is it enough?

Blade brought in and pointing downward over bent, raised arms, sharp edge out, like a block, rising up to the balls of her feet, then leading out with the right foot, lowering the center of gravity, right arm extended behind, blade out, as the focus is forward, anticipating

She considers the last mission a disaster. She blames herself for going through with it as she did.

Not enough intel, not enough planning.

Moving again, weight on the left foot, bringing the right up off the floor, blade brought around and above the head, arms again raised, bent, poised, as she launches into the air

Way too much of relying on luck rather than anything else.

*Coming down as the body twists from momentum, facing now in the opposite direction, bending the knees, force applied to a strong, downward strike*She was fortunate the door in the corridor was not locked. Sure, the many others she had checked had not been secured, so it was a reasonable assumption, but what if she had not been able to get through that one? She was lucky she did not get shot. She was lucky the guards didn't decide to just shoot through the wall into the bathroom.

She let the children die …

121

Rising up, only to swing the arms in a strong, fluid motion in another strike, then looking back and bringing up the left leg, pivoting the hip and right foot and delivering a quick kick

She killed a guard. She lost control, almost killed another …

She whirls, arms following the motive force of her body, both hands on the sword's hilt, striking out with a strong cut, then holding that place. She spies a figure off to the side of the training room as she turns, but she knows who it is. There is no reason to fear, no reason to halt her practice. She is almost done.

She continues, her movements like a methodical dance, the pace of which is controlled through deliberate intensity of muscle, tendon, nerves, channeled from her knowledge and practice until it all works together in a unified expression. It is purposeful and without thought.

When done, she walks over to the place on the far side of the room where her things await, the sword in its black, lacquered saya, tucked into her belt. She'll tend to its cleaning and return to its storage soon. For now, she takes up the large glass, gulping water, then using the small, white towel to wipe at her face.

"Very well done, Lily," Skot says, a light smile on his lips as he walks to her.

She glances at him, giving a very shallow smile in return. "Thanks."

His eyes narrow, brow furrowing as he looks at her. She goes back to her water, having more, lost in thought.

"What's wrong?"

She blinks, looking up, then moves to better face him, staring. He looks into the depths of her brilliant blue eyes, noticing how dark they look. He wants to wrap her in his arms, but he doesn't, instead returning her gaze, knowing something is bothering her, and he tries to be patient, waiting for her to respond.

"I'm okay. Sorry," she says, her lips curling at the edges as though some evidence of her words.

She reaches, picking up the glass of water, the towel thrown over her shoulder. She begins heading away.

"Lily."

She stops, looking back. "Yeah?"

"Something is wrong. What is it?"

SWORD OF THE BUTTERFLY

"Nothing. I don't know. Sorry," she manages, and as she says this, her head tucks down a bit, shoulders coming up, eyes glancing cautiously at him, then away.

"Lily," he says, his voice laden with concern, walking over to her, and now he does wrap her in his arms. "I can tell something is bothering you."

She accepts the embrace, though she only returns it lightly. He releases her after a nice snug, looking at her with a gentle smile.

"Sorry I apologize so much about so many things. I'm not trying to irritate you. Sorry if I do." She gives him another hesitant look.

"It's okay," he tries to soothe, "It doesn't bother me at all." He places his hand on her left arm, petting down. "What's wrong, Lily?"

She keeps her eyes averted, the silence lengthening. He wants to speak further, wants his words and actions to be what she needs to help her feel better and open up. He knows, though, that only goes so far and could even perhaps create undue pressure or dependency, so he again waits, leaving her to her own strength and will.

She finally moves her eyes up to him, looking, and he can see the tension on her. It makes him feel anxious, but he tries not to show it.

"I'm an emotional wreck," she finally says.

"What's bothering you, Sweetheart?"

"I'm not good enough," she says, and the pained look that suddenly takes her feels like a tear to his heart. "I'm afraid I'm going to disappoint you and everyone."

"Lily." He takes her in his arms again, and to his great relief, he feels her accept it, leaning into him. "You're an amazing, strong woman. Why do you say you're not good enough?"

She remains against him for a short time, head lying sideways against his chest, then she also pulls back, eyes moving once again up to his. He sees a shimmering there, a growing wrinkle to her brow. He wonders if she is about to cry, and he wishes she would. It would be a release, but she does not.

"I let those children die."

"Lily! You did not kill them. You are not responsible for their deaths. You are a brave person. Look what you did do. Look what you *have* done. That takes *courage*. Those men murdered those children. *They* are the cowards."

She emits a weak nod, and he is not convinced by it.

"Sorry," she says, her voice very quiet.

He sighs, deeply, bringing his arms up to wrap her in another tight hug. She moves her hands as best she can, returning it.

"Sorry," she says, again, murmuring, "I didn't mean to make you feel bad."

"Oh, Lily," he breathes, clinging tighter, "I don't feel bad because of you."

So much more clambers in his mind, so much more wanting to pour forth from his mouth, but he holds himself. That is his way, how he communicates, but that is not her way. He has to help her in a way she will understand. He feels her pulling back, and he relaxes his hold.

"I'm going to clean and put away my sword then take a quick shower. If that's okay?"

He smiles pleasantly, rubbing slowly up and down her arms, nodding. "Of course, it is."

She smiles thinly, the expression very brief, gone before she breaks contact and turns away. He watches as she leaves the chamber.

He stands there for a moment, and he wants to cry out in anger, sadness, exasperation, and even his own fear. He wants to pummel the punching bag, but he figures that would bring Lilja in here, curious, concerned. He knows that will not help, so he restrains himself. His eyes close, tightly, and he lets some heavy breaths pass through him. These slow, deepening, and he begins to feel calmer.

He is trying not to let his own worries get the better of him, but for all his demeanor, for all his responsibility, he struggles with worry and anxiety quite often. He is worried about the message sent to him from the Infernal. Is there really such a thing as they claim? Is that the reason for his father's curious illness? Is he infected? Is someone else?

He greatly admires his father for how he endured through that. He doubts he'd be so stalwart. He sometimes wonders how it is even possible to live up to that legacy, that example. How can he do his father and family proud?

SWORD OF THE BUTTERFLY

He wonders if he has sent David off to his death. He knows they are in the midst of a war, and there have been casualties, and there will be more, but it does not mitigate the feelings. If anything, since the more powerful creature appeared and the discovery of Charles' body, Skothiam's confidence has been shaken. Sometimes he makes the mistake of letting himself think they are doing so well they are invulnerable, untouchable. That is foolish. It is not something he carries like some bravado, but after enough time with no serious repercussions, it does creep into him with a sense of unwarranted security.

He worries also of her. Not only the situation she has faced and just opened up to him, but he feels some concern for her in general. He is somewhat used to risk, and so is she, and he hopes this does not make them complacent. He frets over her possibly suffering injury in her outings as the vigilante as well as the even greater danger to which he now exposes her. He knows that will not stop. She is who she is, and he holds great admiration and respect for that, but he feels the walls cracking.

That is what they want. He knows that, and he has to be strong. Just like she has to be strong. But there must be a relief to that mounting pressure. They must support and help each other.

He finally breaks from his reverie, moving from the room. He hears the sounds of the shower. He knows she is in there. He ponders going to her, but he falters. And just as this happens, he questions it. He does not like this feeling of insecurity. They both must possess a certain fortitude.

Still, he wonders, what should he do? What should he do?

*****

Just as David promised, their trek has taken them off the beaten path. A camp has been pitched here in the forest, a large clearing occupied near to the rising slope of a gentle mountain. Others have also joined them. Several tents dot the area, surrounding a central fire pit that has been further cleared and encircled with rocks.

Once the trail had been picked up outside of its point of origin, these others had gathered. Duilio had been surprised by the arrival of a couple of members of the Malkuth family. Though just as with David's contacting him at his motel, the inspector figures these sorts of things ought not be unexpected. Three Felcrafts had also convened on the area, and now the entire group of seven works more overtly in tandem.

David had explained to Duilio that the others were 'lesser' members of their respective families. Like the Felcrafts, the Malkuths have a Head of the House, so to speak, and the more powerful of the network are closer either in relation, ability, or both, to the Head.

"How is the Head determined?" he asks as they recline in two reasonably comfortable plastic and canvas chairs near the fire, relaxing now that the camp has been pitched, supper consumed.

The two of them sit somewhat isolated, the others self-segregating by family, engaging a somewhat begrudging civility. Some did not bother with this at all, going off to wander, check the perimeter, other defenses and sensors, gather fire wood, or any number of other 'chores' that might be done.

"Depends on which Family," David answers, taking a sip from a metal mug of campfire coffee.

Duilio senses tension, and he wonders if it is due to the people here being rivals or a potential proximity of their quarry.

"Yours?"

"It's a bit complicated, but you could think of it sort of like a practical form of democracy, or maybe more like a republic, because not everyone gets a say, but basically there are many factors that go into it, and I assure you it's not just how good a Hunter you are." David sort of pulls up and in on one side of his mouth, nodding slowly, and Duilio wonders what underlying commentary this implies. "But we balance out the requirements, and then we know the candidates. Then, we have a kind of council that votes, if it needs to."

"If it needs to?"

"Yeah, it usually doesn't, or the vote is usually unanimous."

"More like a formality," the other suggests.

"Yeah, like that, since, generally, we all know who it ought to be."

"There is never any doubt? Never any ... competition?" He perks his eyebrows.

David throws on a more obvious smirk, glancing sidelong at his partner in conversation.

SWORD OF THE BUTTERFLY

"Good-natured. Discussion, more, really." David takes further sips from his mug, swallowing, parting his lips and pressing his teeth together. "Call us pragmatists. We know what we want, and we're usually able to evaluate and make a good case as to who'll best lead us in that direction. We're not always right, and it may not always be smooth as glass, but it works out."

"And the Malkuths?" Duilio leads.

"Well, you might think I'm being biased."

"Please. I know you are both rivals, but I am still interested to hear."

"Alright, then." David nods, pursing out his bottom lip. "They're more sophist and social Darwinist."

"I presume you mean sophistry in the disparaging way," Duilio does not quite ask.

"I do, though the irony of it is that they don't. They're Machiavellian. They encourage internal conflict, thinking that the best will rise above, victorious, and take the reins ... you know, that kind of bullshit."

"Is it ... bullshit?" Duilio advocates, "You mention Darwin. That technique is based on evolution. The strong adapt and conquer."

"Sure, sure, and militaries aren't a democracy, and in times of strife, martial law may be declared. I know all that, but think about it, Gaspare." David looks back over, tilting his head away so that he sort of gazes at Duilio mostly with his left eye, squinting. "Nature is programming. That's the basics, the survival, the *mindless*. Once a species advances enough to become sapient, doesn't it rise above its programming to become something more? How far will a society get if it's all 'caveman' and just club everyone and take what you want?"

"True," Duilio gives, "But is that how the Malkuths operate? Sophistry and social Darwinism are not tools of animals."

"Sure they are. Look at chimps," David says, and the two chuckle, "But I get your point. It's how those tools are used. The Malkuths aren't offing each other in duels for leadership, but they hurt themselves sometimes in how they treat each other ... and their people."

"Well, good for you, then, since you are their rivals."

"Yeah." David smirks. "Good for us."

127

The conversation dwindles from serious topics as some of the others begin gathering, and as the crescent moon rises, they eventually retire, leaving two on watch, along with the electronic and other forms of surveillance.

Pèire, a Malkuth who married into the family, and, as tradition generally dictates in both, changed his surname, wakes some short hours into his slumber. He rises onto an elbow, pushing his long, black hair away from his face and checks the time, then listens, hearing the sounds he might expect from within his tent. He lies there, staring up at the canopy before he realizes he shan't be returning to sleep anytime soon, so he decides to get up. He slips on his hiking boots, having been only wearing some cotton pajama pants, and leaves his tent.

He walks somewhat quietly to a nearby tree, relieving himself, casting his eyes about slowly as he does so, ignoring the sound and smell of his urine as he keeps his senses more attuned outward. Finished, he moves away, taking a slow stroll about the boundary of this side of the camp. Though the senior Hunter, David, had not particularly enforced this arrangement, the Malkuths are on one side, the Felcrafts on the other. He knows his side is not only less in number but also weakened by the presence of Duilio, but he doesn't think a fight between them will ensue.

"Anika?" he whispers into the darkness, wondering where his kin is, the younger woman drawing guard duty for their side during the first half of the night.

He gets no answer, but that doesn't surprise him. She might be a few meters away, silent, watching, not inclined to reveal her presence. She may be younger than he by several years, but she is the more accomplished Hunter. He is not incapable, but he is no match for her. When they had arrived, the twenty-something lady had exchanged rather laser-pointed looks with a young lady of the Felcraft camp, a somewhat dark-seeming girl named Zoe. It had been a bit uncanny, since they are both slender, about average height, possessed of short, dark hair – Anika's brown whereas Zoe's is dyed black, both pale of skin, but the similarities had ended there, as the Malkuth appears more posh whereas Zoe's style hints toward dark punk.

SWORD OF THE BUTTERFLY

"Anika? It's Pèire," he tries again, pitching the sound of his whisper higher.

He pauses, taking in a sniff, then a much deeper one, and he experiences some alarm. He has a keen sense of smell, and he has caught the coppery tang of blood. He bends his knees, cursing himself for not bringing a weapon or light. He turns, focusing on the source of the odor, shifting left, then he proceeds cautiously, somewhat dragging his steps just above the ground, slow, deliberate, mainly using the balls of his feet.

He is not three paces in that route before he feels the object on the forest's floor. He crouches, touching it, peering intently, and he can tell it is Anika's weapon, a Heckler & Koch MP5A3. He knows she'd not just leave it lying here, so he picks it up, very anxious now, feeling that the magazine is in place, and he racks the slide, an unfired round flying out as another is loaded. He then turns on the tactical light, quickly locating her.

She is unconscious or dead, her head lulled as she sits there on her rear end, back against a tree, legs splayed out as though she were hit there and slumped down along the trunk. Her head and torso are covered in the dark sheen of blood, much of the clothing of her upper body in disarray or outright torn away. It appears she has a chest wound, but he can't be sure. He rushes to her, grabbing her right arm, fingers over the inside of her wrist, and he finally feels it – a faint pulse.

"Wake up! Wake up!" he shouts, running back into the camp, the gun slung over his torso, and he experiences a very sharp, short moment of fright before anyone responds, wondering if the powerful demon has left only him untouched, perhaps as some sadistic game.

"What's going on?" David asks, rising up from his tent, looking not at all as though he has just wakened, holding a Smith & Wesson Model 500 revolver, loaded and ready, finger near the trigger, the eight inch barrel pointed down.

He casts a wary eye on Pèire, especially as the man shifts his gun to a more ready hold.

"It's Anika," he informs, some measure of alarm in his voice, "She's been attacked, seriously wounded. She needs medical attention."

"Shit," David replies, speaking in a much calmer tone than one might expect.

Duilio has risen, too, his own sidearm in his hand, held with the practiced assurance of a veteran, though he does not possess the proper ammunition for hunting the Infernal.

"That's not going to do you any good, Inspector," David says, noticing the gun, then he looks around, seeing as the others emerge from their tents, "Where's Jeff?"

They all look around, but it's clear the man is not coming.

"Zoe, stop!" David commands as the young Huntress had been shoving cartridges into her Remington 870 MCS, strap dangling, then used the foregrip to load the first round and make to go search for their relative. She gives him a scowl, so he amends, "Alright, go look, but take Uncle Owen with you. Don't be long. Get back here quick. Shout if there's trouble."

The older man nods, hefting his own similar make and model shotgun, shells showing in the side saddle holder. His looks more conventional, with a short stock, longer barrel, and pistol grip, and he flicks on the integrated light, following in the other's rapidly dissipating wake.

"What ...," Duilio tries, speaking very low, looking around with wary curiosity at the area and the remaining two Hunters here with him. "What's going on?"

"The Demon is here," David says.

"What about Anika?" Pèire pushes.

David does not acknowledge the question, just continuing to keep watchful and ready.

"It's *here*?" Duilio finally chokes out.

"Gaspare?"

The inspector's eyes have gone wide, and he points the barrel of his black Beretta 8000. There is a noticeable shake to it.

"Gaspare?" comes the voice again, speaking firmly, yet calmly, and Duilio finally looks over at David. "That gun is only going to hurt you or one of us. I'm not going to tell you to put it away, but be very careful. Zoe and Owen are out there, and I'd hate f-," and he stops, for just then, a ruckus erupts off in the general vicinity the two Hunters went moments ago.

SWORD OF THE BUTTERFLY

All three level their weapons in that direction, and when David turns that way, Duilio manages to spy two daggers held criss-cross in a custom sheath at the man's lower back. They look broad of blade, though short in length, the handles thick.

Gunshots ring out.

"Mierda!" Pèire curses, then lopes toward it.

"Pèire!" David shouts, the force of his voice bringing the man to a halt, "You stay here and guard the inspector. He's here for *your* family. I'll go check on Anika."

"David, but ...," Duilio begins, but the Hunter is gone, having grabbed a small, leather bag which presumably contains first aid gear.

The inspector continues to stare after the man's departure, hearing more sounds of battle. His eyes go wider, head jerking over into that direction, as though trying to will the ability to see whatever is going on. Even the bright moments of gunfire do not bring him any clarity, the flash at barrels, the occasional amber-tinged traces of the enhanced rounds, only adding to the chaos. He finally glances over at Pèire, noting the man's near look of disgust.

"Qué?" Duilio asks.

"Estás muy cerca del Felcraft," Pèire notes, his words heavy.

"Will you protect me if the Demon comes here?" Duilio asks, forcefully.

Pèire just smirks at him.

The expression is dropped instantly as a louder noise arises, much closer. Pèire turns fully in that direction, tensing, raising the rifle, knees lightly bent. He steps towards it, moving slowly, carefully, much as he did when trying to find Anika earlier. Duilio glances about, his eyes and aspect showing his continuing fear. He glances at Pèire, then in the direction the Malkuth peers, trying to add his own aid to the effort, but he sees nothing. He hears sounds of the others, insistent questions, unsure answers, hisses of pain, but those noises have lessened. He looks back at the Hunter just as it happens.

The figure comes out of the darkness, rising forth as though emerging from thin air. It looks human but not entirely so, something of the shade of its skin, its feral aspect, and the eyes. The eyes alight with a red luminescence, and they look right at Duilio as the Demon closes the short distance, claiming Pèire at the man's throat, teeth bared for the kill.

.. if we find it, then you turn and run as fast as you can...

David's words reverberate in his memory as adrenalin spikes through him, and Duilio whirls in the opposite direction and sprints away.

His breath is ragged, heavy, loud, no thought given to the fact that he is moving at full speed through a forest at night. He could easily twist an ankle, break a leg, collide with something and go unconscious, but he just runs. The night is not pitch black, so he is able to discern some of his surroundings. The further he moves from the camp, the less he is able to do so. Still, the monster is back there, perhaps chasing him even now, so he runs.

His noisy breaths rush out into the air, his loud, careening steps adding to the cacophony. He would certainly not be proving difficult prey to pursue. He pounds out further, feeling the burn in his leg muscles. He is not in bad shape, but he doesn't really spend a lot of time exercising. He feels a pressure in his chest.

He spies a rising thicket of scrub brush next to some trees, and he practically dives into it, pushing his back against the woodland sentinels, taking his pistol in both hands and pointing in the direction from which he has come. He tries to catch his breath, hold his aim steady, and listen.

He hears nothing.

How can that be?

He figures if the Demon has not pursued him, then he ought to hear sounds of fighting off back toward the campsite. How far did he run? He feels panic teasing just at the edges of his perception, and he fights it back. He continues to try to catch his breath, and it settles. He opens his mouth, using it for quieter respiration, keeping his gun pointed, straining to see and hear.

Moments pass, drawn out, his ears straining for any sound, his eyes doing the same for sight. He does not want that hideous thing to find him, but he doesn't want to be lost out here by himself. He supposes he could wait until sunrise, but that seems a silly notion.

SWORD OF THE BUTTERFLY

There is a snap, and he jerks his aim in that direction, trying not to tremble too much, giving away his position. He hears another, and he fires off two quick shots.

"Gaspare?"

"David?" Duilio replies, then curses silently, "Did I hit you?"

"Nah, I'm fine," comes the reply, and a light is flicked on, pointed toward the hiding Inspector. "Come on out."

Duilio does, trying to look the man over.

"Are you alright?"

"I'm fine. Let's get back."

Once they return, Duilio sees that the wounded Malkuth Huntress has been moved to camp, and she looks to be in critical condition. David heads over, quickly, grabbing up more from the first aid kit and moving to resume assistance. Duilio follows, noticing the large amount of blood, gazing at the woman with grave concern, then looking about with a different sort of wariness. He spies the crumbled and rent corpse of Pèire. Even if the man had not been trying to protect Duilio, he gave his life, so the inspector might get away.

"Where are the others?" Duilio dares to ask.

"I found Owen out there," David comments as he works on the rival Huntress, "He's dead. I didn't find Zoe ... She's gone."

"And the ... demon?"

David keeps working, intent on the stabilization and field dressing. He shakes his head without looking at the other.

"I don't know."

The Italian stares at the Hunter's back, as though willful of different news, then, when none is forthcoming, he glances back around, raising his weapon.

"I told you that would only hurt you or us," David remarks, still tending to the other.

"Forgive me," Duilio quips, "Old habits."

David stands, placing his hands at his waist, pulling in a deep breath, eyes on the Interpol man.

"Ask your people for some enhanced ammunition, once we get out of this."

"Once we get out of this, yes." Duilio nods, eyes still looking out into the night, fear still etched on his features.

"We need to pack up. Anika needs better medical attention. We need to dispose of the bodies, get the important gear and get out of here."

"Dispose of the bodies …?" Duilio peers, this point piercing his trepidation.

"We can't leave behind that sort of evidence to be found by others."

"Are we going to bury them?" the man sincerely asks, brow furrowing from the deepening confusion.

"No. Leave it to me. I need you to start packing up. Quick. Mainly the technical gear, weapons, and ammo."

Duilio looks at the man, not moving to do as he has been bid. Shock still has its way with him.

"Gaspare?" David tries, more firmly, yet still not shouting.

"S-sì?" He looks up, slowly raising his chin.

"The Demon, as you noted, is still out there. I think it's done with us for now, but we need to pack up and get Anika to an emergency room. Are you with me?"

"Yes, yes." He nods, blinking rapidly, fighting to collect himself. "I will help."

"It's me - Zoe! Don't shoot!" calls out a female voice from the darkness, and all eyes turn.

The youthful Huntress walks in, her form taking more solid shape as she nears the camp, moving steadily on booted feet. Her shotgun is strapped to her back, and she holds a black kukri-styled, curved machete in her right hand, the twenty inch blade angled outward, dripping a black ichor that also shows to be stained quite abundantly on the young lady.

"My God," Duilio mutters, eyes wide, "Are you hurt?"

"I'm fine," she says to the man she perceives as not only a potential enemy but also an outsider, her tone somewhat cutting, then she looks back over, her eyes giving a very brief, cold appraisal of the wounded Huntress before settling on her relative. "It's gone."

David nods once. "We need to pack up, and get out of here. Anika needs a doctor."

Duilio notes a slight rise of the top lip on Zoe, and he suspects it is beneficial to the Malkuth that David is in charge.

SWORD OF THE BUTTERFLY

"How do you know it is gone?" the inspector demands, but he only gets those cutting eyes as a response.

"Gaspare, it's dark out there," David speaks, "The trail is difficult to see, but some of us are very good at seeing in the dark. Zoe is one of those. If she says the Demon's gone, then it's gone."

"I've never seen anything like it," she says as they proceed to packing, "I think Owen got it before it got him. I know I hit it once with my shotgun, and all this blood on me is from a good slice I gave it with my sword, but it didn't let up. It sounded more like it was just chuckling at us the whole time, then it just ... took off. I tried to trail it, but it's gone."

"Chuckling?" Duilio murmurs, but he is overshadowed by the other's response.

"Let's finish up and get out of here," David assesses.

The three proceed to more packing, Anika still unconscious, though somewhat stable. Zoe wipes off her blade and sheathes it, having gathered up other weapons. She then grabs a curious-seeming phial from a zipped up leather bag.

"I'll deal with the bodies," she somberly volunteers, then heads out after an affirming nod from David.

Duilio wants to ask, but something in the other's aspect prohibits this. Instead he does as he is told and continues helping to pack up what is necessary and before long, they are on the road, Zoe and Anika following in their own vehicle, the third car left behind to be picked up later, if at all.

"It was toying with us," David says to Duilio in the truck, breaking the tense silence, having reached paved road now and in hurried search of a place to take Anika. "It took out our guards, didn't trip any sensors. We were all asleep. It could have killed all of us. It was waiting for us to wake up, waiting for us to go searching for it."

Duilio looks at the man, staring, the dim glow from the dashboard casting an eerie illumination.

"This is worse than I expected. I'm going to report back to the Family, as soon as I get a chance, and you need to do the same with the Malkuths. They need to know."

"Are we giving up?"

Duilio barely notes the shaking of the head in the darkness.

"No, but that Demon just took out nearly half of us, and I think it was holding back. We need to approach this differently."

"Why would it be holding back?"

"It's just how they are. They're sadistic. It's not fun to just slaughter all of us in our sleep," then David pauses, taking in a breath, trying not to think too much on the slain , "We need to keep on its trail, but we need to be better prepared. We'll get Anika fixed up, and we'll find a place to get some good, safe rest, and we'll move on."

"Are we taking her to a local emergency clinic?"

"Yeah." David nods, peering about, some lights in the distance showing that they will soon arrive at a town. "We'll use one of these small, less-used places. We can make up something about an animal attack, and we'll be able to handle any records or information they try to pass on."

"I suppose you've done this before."

David cuts his eyes to his passenger, looking for a bit, then he just nods, re-focusing on the road.

"This is a bad one, a bad one …" he says, his voice trailing in volume, "We'll get it, eventually. I just …" He pauses, and though Duilio hangs on his words, he begins to think David has ceased, but then the rest finally rises, like brittle petals on a warm, coiling breeze , "I just wish I knew why it was here."

*****

He's been contacted.

The person who has done so has proven themselves by sharing information they ought not know, some of it similar to that he has given the network that feeds the vigilante. He'd then offered to prove himself, which the person scoffed off, for it seems they'd satisfied themselves before approaching.

He sits in his car, waiting, occupying a space in the middle level of a parking complex, one that he was told to go to. This structure typically services the more modern, surrounding office buildings, so it is mostly deserted at this late hour. He's taken a ticket from the machine to get in,

SWORD OF THE BUTTERFLY

and he knows there are cameras, so there will be some record of his having come here. Still, he figures he ought to be forthright if he is now on the 'right' side of the law.

The car's engine lies dormant, lights off, and he just waits. He spies a few other vehicles in the general vicinity, none too close, and none have arrived or departed in the short time he has been here. He takes occasional sips from the bottle of water. He's a cop, so he's done stakeouts before. He's not here with his new partner, though, and he figures she'd not be too happy with this. Still, maybe she'd not mind, as this is just the gathering of information. Investigating, as it were.

He's learned that she is a single mother, though she's not very forthcoming with her personal life. Still, they *are* detectives. She has a young daughter who's giving her some trouble, skipping school, getting into fights, and it seems poised to get worse rather than better. He figures that is part of why she is so intense regarding her job – she's trying to make up for the lack with her daughter by protecting *all* the children. He pities her, though he knows she doesn't want it. He thinks she ought to focus more on what she even has a chance of affecting. No one person can save everyone.

His raises the bottle again, and he pauses, his action and thoughts interrupted by the sight of a flicker off in a dark corner. That's the sign, so he gets out of his car and walks over.

The form is smaller than he had expected, but then, what did he expect? He was contacted, and the individual doing so had proven they were part of the vigilante's network. He realizes he is hoping it is the vigilante, but that's more of his unreal expectation. He pauses a decent distance away, not too far, not too close, understanding the clandestine nature of the rendezvous.

The lighter's flame had been closed out before he got all the way here, but he spied enough to note that the person is small-framed, wearing dark clothes, a dark hoodie, and when the voice chimes forth, he is surprised to realize it is female.

"We need to do something to keep more children from being killed," she says, "and to stop the prostitution, the sex slavery."

She speaks with a cold cadence, as though almost uncaring of the very shocking things she wants to thwart.

137

"Yeah, I'm on the case. We're processing leads, working on ID'ing the bodies-"

"I know all that," she cuts him off, and he senses a rise there.

He wonders if it is from exasperation, or if he has somehow offended her.

"Alright, it's clear you're well-informed," he acquiesces, then tries, "You're receiving lots of intel from all over the city."

"If I know where the kids are being held and prostituted, then so should you. What are the police prepared to do?" she demands.

"We," he begins, then pauses, perplexed, "We're going to do all we can … *within* the law." He sees the expected scoff. "Look, we follow process, you know that. That's why the vigilante is so important. He doesn't have to."

He glimpses the hints of another reaction there on the face shrouded by the hood. He is not sure what it means though.

"The vigilante is one person. How much can one person do? Doesn't it help if you police get the information? Does it need to be gift-wrapped?"

"That wouldn't hurt," he tries, smiling a touch.

It doesn't work. He can feel the frown growing on the person.

"Are you taking this seriously?" she pushes.

"Yes, yes I am," he is quick to say, putting on a tone to match.

"We may not be able to rely on the vigilante for this."

"Why? What's happened?" he pitches, but it seems his requests for information are being ignored.

"There are things I can do, but if the police would actually just do *something*, that would fix everything."

He senses the cynicism in her. She doesn't want to be here, doing this. She doesn't trust him. For some reason, she's desperate.

"What do you want us to do?"

"These people are breaking the law, in a very organized fashion. Find them and stop them."

"It's not that easy," he says.

"Why not? I can tell you where this is happening. Go … do what it is you do."

And again, the exasperation.

SWORD OF THE BUTTERFLY

"I'll take all the help I can get. We often work on leads provided by civilian witnesses and informants. The question is going to arise though, who you are and how you came by this information."

"Why does that matter? These kids have been kidnapped, held against their will, used for prostitution. They are being raped, tortured, and some murdered. More lives will be lost. Is that what you want?"

"You know I don't."

"Then prove it. Do something."

"I am," he says, his own frustration brewing, then he changes his tone, sighing, realizing the complications of his own situation is largely his doing.

He moves his eyes to the obscured figure, not anticipating any sympathy. She does not disappoint that expectation.

"It just takes time," he says, feeling the silent drilling of her attention.

"While those children are raped and may be killed." She throws acid on the fire.

"Then *you* do something," he challenges, his anxiety again trying to get the better of him.

She raises her chin, and he sees a bit more of her, noticing a glimmer at the edges of her lips.

"I am," she grates out, "And if you don't want to help, then why the fuck am I here?"

"Sorry," he says, holding out his hands, placatingly.

"You're the fucking police. What good are you?"

"Alright, alright," he says, "I *do* want to help, okay? Maybe more so than a lot of others in the department. I'll keep providing information, and I'll take what you can give me. I'm not going to rely on the vigilante to take care of all of this, but … I'll take that help if I can get it."

"It's not for you," she points out.

"I know. The children," he says, trying to sound sincere and not peeved, "We want to help them. I got it."

"Good," she emits after a moment of just looking at him, "I really hope so. This is serious."

"I know," he repeats, a touch of defensiveness to his words, "So, what now?"

"You keep feeding information to the network. I'll send stuff to you, too, but you've got a badge, so feel free to make some arrests and save some of these kids."

He exhales through his nose, fighting to not shake his head. He doesn't like her tone or accusation, but he understands. He *is* an officer of the law. The purpose of that institution is to protect people and to arrest violators. She is doing no more than expecting him to do his job. In fact, she *is* doing more, she is trying to help him do it.

"Thanks," he mutters.

"For what?"

"For helping."

She eventually gives out a single, begrudging nod to this.

"Are we done, then?" he asks, delicately.

"Yes."

"Do you …?" He looks around, then back. "Did you drive here?"

"We're done."

"Okay, got it." He holds up his hands again, then he turns and walks back to his car.

Therese watches Detective Quain Contee until he has driven away. Her right hand never left the pocket of her hoodie the entire time, holding onto a can of very potent pepper spray, ready to use on him and run if need be. She wants to trust him, but she feels like she needs to stop being so stupid in some of her endeavors.

She thinks further on Lilja. She had not exactly denied being the vigilante, but her attitude makes Therese question if maybe she is wrong. She knows she *wants* Lilja to be the vigilante, and she realizes she had put her on a pedestal, maybe still is, and she thinks she ought to be a superhero, saving all the children. It hurts her to think less of the woman, to do this and try to make progress on her own, but still, this is about helping the victims, stopping the criminals. It's not about that cop or the vigilante or even Therese.

She can't escape the feeling that she is disappointed in Lilja, or the vigilante, and she still holds onto hope that maybe the vigilante will come through. Maybe Lilja will end up all she expects her to be.

*****

SWORD OF THE BUTTERFLY

Marcel is busy cleaning books in a back room, so she walks to the front when she hears the unobtrusive, electronic noise that announces someone has entered the main area of the library's Rare Books Collection, the chamber being open for access some hours of the weekdays during academic semesters. The person standing there is a sight to behold, though she displays no untoward reaction. He is looking about, having bent to peer more closely at some of the shelved tomes, but he turns to set his gaze on Lilja as she comes forward.

He is very tall, and as he moves, she notices his lack of a well-defined chin, his lips somewhat protuberant, thick, a rather wide mouth. Dark, coarse-looking fuzz has sprung up about the lower half of the face, more like the beginnings of a pre-pubescent boy than a day or two's growth of beard on a man. His nose is firm, though a bit bulbous along its bridge, and his ears appear almost elongated. She cannot escape the feeling of general oddity that permeates as he sets his dark eyes upon her, not in the least bereft of a focused acuity, though he does look awkward.

"E-excuse me," he begins, clearing his throat, as his voice breaks, and he looks away, then back, eyes moving over the diminutive woman who waits patiently, looking up at him. "I ... I've come for a book."

Lilja smiles politely, holding her hands together at her belly, left hand cupped over the curled fingers of her right.

"How may I help you?" she finally bids after the silence merely continues to lengthen.

"I'm working on an assignment ... for a class," he expounds, "Folklore and mythology."

"Ah, that sounds very interesting." Lilja nods, her smile increasing a touch, and this encourages him.

"Yes, it is. It's about the connections of many tales and how they permeate many cultures, having developed commonalities that span societies and civilizations that had no known way of communicating with one another."

"Fascinating," she remarks, "Is there a particular source you are seeking, then?"

"Oh, yes." He nods his head in a pendulum-like fashion, and then he utters the name of a book, *the* Book, and she freezes. "I was told by my

Professor that it was here in this collection. He referred me to it as a good source for this project."

He had begun rooting about in the drab satchel he carries over a shoulder, so he does not notice any response from her. He then comes forth with a piece of paper that looks worse for wear for having been in his bag, and he extends it to her. She does not reach for it.

"I'm sorry. You are a student here?"

"Yes." He nods, looking confused.

"What's your name?"

"Oh." He blinks, the action taking longer than usual, as though like an amphibian. "Pothos Wilbraham."

She nods, pulling in a deep breath, still not taking the offering. "Mr. Wilbraham, that is one of the most rare and valuable books in our collection. It is not just made available like other books."

He blinks again, his arm still somewhat outstretched, hand still clutching that piece of paper, and his brow furrows. "But this is a library. I thought you lent out books to the students?"

His tone is one of utter confusion, not a drop of challenge in it.

"Well, we do, of course. The books in the general library above are available under the common guidelines, but those here in the Rare Books Collection are subject to more stringent restrictions, especially certain ones of utmost value."

He just looks at her.

"Which this one is," she adds.

The quiet again grows as they both look at each other. Lilja is stalwart, though polite, now hiding any anxiety she may be experiencing due to the request. Pothos falters under more stupefaction.

"This …," he tries, then he licks his lips, "I … but my Professor told me of the book and has given me permission." He moves his hand, again trying to get her to take the paper. "We came up with the assignment together, and because of the nature of the folklore and cosmology, he recommended I use this book."

She again fights to not reveal anything, but the word he has chosen, 'cosmology', shakes her. It is certainly not so rare a word as to go unheard, but she learned of its meaning that time when Skot was here studying this very book. It may prove nothing, but she cannot shake the feeling that she needs be now more a guardian than a librarian.

"I am sorry, but it is restricted," she rebuffs, "Arrangements may be made, of course, for supervised access, but I am not aware of that having been put in place."

"Supervised access?" he asks, his broad forehead wrinkling more, and he slowly puts the paper back into his satchel, closing the flap.

She nods, eyebrows rising, head moving with the expression as though leading, trying to force the understanding of the obvious or inquire if such an apparent thing has somehow been missed.

"I can't just ... borrow the book?" he tries.

"No."

"But this is a library." He tries again, confused.

"Yes, and this is the Rare Books Collection of the library. Some of these books never leave the building except under very controlled circumstances, and that would not be under the custodianship of a student."

He looks at her, the moment lengthening, then he blinks, and she imagines she can hear the wetness of it. He then turns, somewhat upset along with the near abject confusion. He reaches for the door handle, then he pauses, and it suddenly reminds her of the time Denman Malkuth came to see her, looking for the same thing. The student turns, staring back at her.

"I'm sorry," he says with a cold lack of sincerity, then mumbling as he turns back, opening and ducking through the doorway, "I'm supposed to say that, aren't I? I'm sorry?"

CHAPTER SIX

Skot sits at the table where he has spent much time studying *the* Book. He sips occasionally from the cup of water, the late hour of the workday lending itself to that rather than coffee.

Such evil sorceries I have done, facing demons that possess no human shape, he reads, translating the words in his mind as needed. He has come to a part that reads something like a melodramatic journal, and it takes him a few pages to realize the words are meant to be taken at face value. It is but another of the somewhat jarring changes in the tone of the tome, moving from depthful, flowing poetry to dry, expository lengths as of a textbook thence to fiery warnings.

The author purports to have been trained in the occult, making mention of a somewhat formal education, becoming a mage, a warlock, and enduring the pursuit of "unmentionable orders" that worked to capture, torture, and burn him. Words tell of explorations that part the veil unto the hidden world that may harbor the fog of confusion as the Infernal and this plane mingle.

And even beyond, traveling to a planet that orbits binary, greenish suns, the blighted landscape of bones upon bones, piled high into hills, implying that Demons have used this place to discard the leavings of their victims. The remains picked clean by the armies of scurrying, rodent-sized insect, whilst glimpses of enormous worms disrupt the distance.

Skot is not sure what all to make of it. There is ample evidence that the Books were not written by only one person, but this section, this journal, if that is indeed what it is, suggests this person lived for hundreds of years. There is mention of a "special heritage", and he wonders if this ties to the folklore of the Hunters being descended from

SWORD OF THE BUTTERFLY

the Grigori. Is this, indeed, the recitations of a Nephilim? There seems no way to prove this, and the inconsistent nature of the very contents of the tome gives skepticism to all of it. He knows it was written thusly on purpose. Merely finding the book is but the first of many steps in solving the mystery.He pauses, leaning back, stretching his arms up, letting the information sift about in his mind.

Lilja mentioned the curious student who had come in, asking about the Book. She had done a check on him, the quite interestingly named Pothos Wilbraham, finding some information on his age, upbringing, and the accomplishments he demonstrated to gain admittance. She had also followed up, via e-mail, with his Professor, not wanting to draw attention to the situation by reacting too alarmed. The student's story does check out. Still, something of the entire thing does not feel so innocuous. She and Skot discussed it, and they know they have good systems of defense in place, so they shall remain watchful.

It does trouble him, though, that he is scheduled to board a flight this evening to head back to the United States. He has decided to return for a short time due to the concerns with the hunt for the powerful Demon and the newly slain. This is a serious issue that does demand his attention, and though he could arguably give that attention remotely, he has elected to make the trip. He is also experiencing some somewhat subtle pressure from members of the Family to be there in person.

He looks up as she comes over, touching his left arm up near the shoulder, her hand turning as she moves, retaining the contact as she slips into the nearby chair, smiling lightly at him. He leans closer, and she moves in to the kiss.

"It's getting late," she notes, her assistant having been dismissed some time ago.

"I know," he speaks, sounding reluctant.

"You don't want to miss your plane," she comments, "Do you?"

"I will confess that I don't want to go."

"They need you there, Skot," she says, placing her hand atop his, there on the surface of the table, very close to the open book.

"I know. The news *is* tragic, but I'm not going to join the hunt."

"We could, you know," she tries, having brought this up before.

145

"I know, but we won't. It's too risky for you, and you have your duties here, especially now that the Fall Semester has started."

He sees a look in her eyes, and he wonders if his comment about it being too risky for her has affected her negatively. She does not seem to become overtly upset, but he sees something there, a slight tightening of the flesh of her forehead, eyes moving fractionally, as though looking at him a bit differently, then they slowly move away.

"I want to be here with *you*," he says, moving his other hand to clasp atop hers.

She nods, looking back, and he smiles at her, getting a similar response.

"I want that, too, but this is important."

"It is," he agrees, then he sighs, "Three deaths, so close together, not to mention the Malkuth that has been added to the tally."

"And the civilians and police," she reminds.

He nods, solemnly. "Yes, this is very bad. We need to get this one and put a stop to it."

"If I can help, please let me," she all but pleads, and he senses it in her, not a desire to be complimented or assessed for her worth, but a very real drive to just want to provide aid.

"You do a great deal for me, Lily, and you help much more than you may know by being a guardian to the Book. That is a very serious responsibility."

She smiles at him, openly. It is a lure to him, and he leans in, kissing her, pressing into it, making it turn to something hinting at more passion. He moves his hand up along her arm, grasping at her bicep, continuing the kiss, parting his lips, gaining a similar response from her. He sends his tongue into her mouth, receiving a soft reciprocation from hers. They move together lightly, almost languidly, exploring. He finally parts it, staying close, noting the rise of a blush to her pale skin, and he leans in near her ear.

"Don't forget to do your secret mission while I'm gone. I'll want to hear all about it," he whispers, reminding her of something she no doubt remembers, though the point of bringing it up is to flirt and subtly assert dominance.

"I'll miss you," she breathes, after nodding to his words.

SWORD OF THE BUTTERFLY

"I'll miss you," he adds, and they just stare into one another's eyes for a moment before he speaks again, "We'll have the Ball to attend when I get back."

She smiles further at that, the blush rising more as she coquettishly averts her eyes, then blinks them back.

"You are so alluring."

"Thank you," she murmurs, still bashful after all this time, and he very much likes it.

He feels a stab of worry, something with which he often struggles, but he refrains from saying anything. Besides, she can take care of herself. He wonders why it makes him feel better to vocalize such or to give out warnings like some nagging mother. Does it imply that she would not have thought of these things if he had not reminded her? He won't marginalize her that way, or he'll do his best to contain such.

He doesn't want to leave, because of that worry. He knows she struggles with the deaths of the children and how poorly her last vigilante mission went. He, honestly, would rather her not do any of that while he is away, but again there is that false sense of security and unneeded fretting. True, he'd be closer if she did need him, but what difference would he really make if he were here? She got along fine before he came along. She'll be alright. He needs to offer support, not exacerbate under the guise of concern.

And so their remaining time together this evening is well spent, and then she sees him to a car, and he is off for the airport, promising to call during his one layover en route to America. She misses him even as she watches the car pull away, but she does not linger, needing to get to the gymnasium to teach her self-defense class.

Therese is there, and though Lilja experiences a note of anxiety and awkwardness, she doesn't show it. Nor does the young hacker, it seems, as she comports herself in her usual taciturn, somewhat brooding, but serious and attentive manner, almost as though nothing had passed between the two women. The lessons are carried out, many thoughts lying in wait to consume Lilja's own concern, but during the time of the class, she is focused.

Therese is not without her own concerns, ever-watchful and mindful of Lilja without making it obvious. She wonders about approaching

147

Quain, thinking back on her endeavors last year that landed her twice in the predicament of being caught by criminals. All of this is in effort to improve her abilities when in the real world, as she still feels much more comfortable behind a computer. She sometimes wonders at her social justice attitude, trying to pinpoint exactly when she decided to so undertake the cause, sticking her neck out from the shadows, as it were. It is exhilarating, but it is also risky. She'd not mind at all if the vigilante somehow managed to thoroughly clean up the city.

She does understand, though, how unfair that is. It will take more than one person to handle all the problems out there, and she is sure there are more than she even realizes. And, ultimately, they are treating symptoms, not the cause.The class ends, and she showers and gathers up her things, walking slowly out to her bike, concerns still careening in her mind. She straddles the café racer, having picked up another after her Mac Peashooter "disappeared" when she was abducted that second time, and she loses herself in thought.

"Everything okay, ma'am?"

She blinks, looking over to see a security guard inquiring of her. He looks young, sincere enough, and there is even a sense of harmlessness about him, despite his uniform and the display of non-lethal deterrents on his belt. She also notes the small, rectangular name patch at his breast, which says "Billy", not even Bill or Wilhelm, but the more boyish nomenclature.

"Yeah, I'm fine," she says, speaking with her usual, guarded cadence, but as he continues staring at her, she allows a slight curl to her lips as though to reassure him and get him on his way.

"I noticed you came out of the gym over there. I guess you're in Miss Perhonen's self-defense class? Not too many others out around here this time of night." He throws out his own little smile, though his is more sheepish, almost as though apologizing for continuing to talk to her.

"Yeah." Therese continues looking at him, then she reaches for her helmet, holding it as though about to put it on. She's still got those thoughts running around in her head, but maybe this will clue the guy into leaving.

"She's something else." His tone is musing, and she narrows her eyes in confusion, though he doesn't take note. "I guess it's a comfort to

SWORD OF THE BUTTERFLY

know she's helping more people. I don't have to worry so much when a lady is out alone around the campus at night ... Unless she needs help," he quickly amends, taking her cold-seeming exterior as perhaps distaste to his remarks, "That's why we're here ... you know?"

She begins wondering how Billy would have fared against those criminals she faced. Probably not well at all. Then something else dawns on her, as he stands there, that boyish grin hinting at a shyness of another kind. He has a crush on Lilja. Therese is not surprised, for not only is the redhead quite physically attractive, but she has a sort of casual confidence that becomes its own charisma.

"Do you know Miss Perhonen well?" Therese asks, shifting on the seat of her bike, the low creak of metal announcing the movement.

"Oh." He blinks, then sort of chuckle-exhales through a brief grin. "No, no, nothing like that," he explains, telling her more of how he feels without realizing it, "I mean, we've both been on staff here a few years, but we don't really cross paths that much."

Therese nods, remaining the stoic to his effusive display.

"If she offered self-defense classes for guys or just some sort of general karate, I'd be the first to sign up," he announces.

"She's capable enough to do that," Therese appears to casually remark, but she is trying to subtly lead the guard.

"Oh, definitely." Billy brightens, showing the hacker further evidence of her suspicions. "I heard they once formally approached her to teach a style of self-defense that is more suited to police than civilians, but she turned it down."

"I wonder why."

"Who knows?" He shrugs. "She's pretty busy." He slips his hands in his pockets, looking back toward the gym as though they may see the woman in question walking out at this moment.

"She is?"

"Well, yeah, I guess. I don't know," he alters, "Maybe it's because she just usually seems so business-like."

"You think she's cold?"

"No!" Billy's hands come out of his pockets, held up. "I don't mean that. She's just ... I don't know ... focused, driven ... uh ... *disciplined*!"

Therese looks at him, noting how he sort of falters under her steady gaze.

"She sure is," she finally concedes.

"How long have you been taking the class?"

"For a while now," she answers, which doesn't tell him much, but his emphatic nodding indicates he is quite satisfied with this.

"I guess you like it, then, and I bet you've gotten pretty good at handling yourself, huh?"

"I guess," she says.

She yet has much more to learn, but the months of training have done more for her than she realizes. How odd that it takes a casual remark from this stranger to open her own eyes, and here she was thinking to learn something from him, but it was certainly not that.

"Well, you take care," Billy offers, putting on another of his youthful-seeming smiles, raising his right hand in a sort of half-wave, then moving on.

She doesn't say anything in return, just watching as he leaves, more thoughts moving through her head. She then dons her helmet, firing up the motorcycle and heads out.

*****

Quain gives the barest glance and expression of disgust as the other man, Alec, picks up the rigid paper dish containing the bratwurst and sauerkraut. The portly man mixes it up with the plastic fork as he walks to a nearby table, causing the sauce to somewhat disappear into the gooey mess. They take a seat, and Alec picks up the knife, trying to slice through the sausage.

"Damn things are worthless," he comments, though he does manage to get a decent sized piece, adding some of the side dish and filling his mouth, chewing mightily.

Quain just watches, having ordered nothing from the small food outlet. He isn't admitting it to himself, but his upset at the recent goings-on have him less tolerant of his ex-partner's aspect and diet. Alec picks up on this, knowing what a health nut the other is, and he speaks through a not quite empty mouth.

SWORD OF THE BUTTERFLY

"Hey, at least I passed on the beer."

"That you did." Quain nods, eyebrows perked.

Alec swallows, using his fork to scoop more of the sour cabbage, holding up the utensil, pieces dangling from the tines. He sees the other looking at him.

"Sauerkraut is good for you."

"Some of it is," Quain agrees, passing unspoken judgment on the quality of this serving.

"I was surprised to hear from you," Alec remarks, reaching to the rear of his belt, somewhat obscured by his jacket, to produce a short lockblade, using it to cut the sausage, eyes moving up to Quain as he saws more effectively at the meat, continuing to tackle his meal with gusto.

Quain watches, returning the gaze, steeling himself, though he shows nothing but fortitude, trying to remain calm. He's had to do many things that weren't very savory in the course of his career.

"I wanted to talk to you about the child prostitution in the city, particularly those murdered children."

Quain keeps his eyes steady on the man; he is not sure if it comforts him that Alec seems to have no reaction.

"Why?" he finally asks, using the convenience of his open mouth to feed more food into it.

"I know it has something to do with your new boss."

Alec just stares, setting down his knife and fork, chewing, getting it all good and done before swallowing, wiping his mouth with a paper napkin, never moving his eyes from the other man.

"You trying to get killed?"

"Not if I can help it."

"Are you trying to get *me* killed?"

"Same answer, Alec," Quain says, then leans closer to the tabletop, shortening the distance between them, "This is bad stuff, man. Prostituting and killing kids. Come on. What have you gotten yourself into? It was bad enough with Gnegon, but this? Come on."

"Come on, what?" Alec demands, taking up the utensils, but barely lifting them, growing agitated.

151

"Why stay mixed up in this? Doesn't it bother you what he's doing?"

Alec doesn't answer, just finally moving his hands, more cutting of meat, gathering of food, chewing, as he looks at the detective. Quain waits, watching, never figuring he'd be using interrogation techniques on his former coworker. The silence stretches, becoming weightier as Alex swallows but doesn't hide behind another mouthful.

"Yes, it does," he finally admits, "I don't like any of this." He gestures with the blade, swirling it somewhat in his hand. "I told you that when I first met the guy."

"Then why work for him?"

"I already answered that, too, Quain," he says, brow furrowing, and he has more food, slicing up the sausage with some suggestion of anger.

The cop sighs, air passing through his nostrils.

"We have history. I like you," and this gets a perk of eyebrows from the other, "I'm being serious, if you hadn't noticed. This shit has to stop, with the child prostitution and the executions. Seriously, Alec. Kids being shot in the head in cold blood. What kind of fucked up shit is that? It's going to stop."

"So, Detective Contee," Alec says, wiping his mouth again, then the blade, folding it and putting the knife away, shifting in place as though about to leave, "is this a professional warning or a threat?"

"Both," he says, and this causes the other to freeze in place, eyes again just set on the man across the table, as though he is taking new and newer stock of him. "This is not my personal crusade, Alec, so if your boss thinks taking me out will stop it, it won't. This is bad. You're in a position to help. You can help us, help yourself, or you can go down with the ship."

Alec purses his lips to one side, then sucks in his ample cheek there, then slowly nods.

"I see. Well, thank you for the courtesy."

He stands, looking around. Quain does not get up, but he does closely watch the other man who finally gazes back down at him.

"You know my address, so let me know if anything more comes up … and I know yours."

Quain nods, slowly. "That you do."

SWORD OF THE BUTTERFLY

"Maybe you ought to change it," Alec suggests, then he turns and walks away.

*****

When the noise finally enters her slumber, pulling her to consciousness, she somewhat blindly reaches for the snooze of her alarm. Disorientation lulls her, and it takes her a moment of pressing the button to realize the sound is not stopping. Her breaths come slow, somewhat noisy, through parted lips, her brain still fighting, a collision of fatigue and focus. Then it hits her, eyes blinking to wide, and she feels a jolt in her spine.

It's not her alarm to wake her for the start of her workday. This is the sound of the security at the library being breached; someone is trying to get the Book.

Lilja springs from the bed, already having gone to sleep later than usual and fighting some unrest at being alone, and she rushes to her computer. There is a delay, though not a very long one, before local law enforcement will be notified. She can override this, if need be, but she has to get there in time. She sees then what has been tripped, and she gasps.

She takes brief, anxious moments to pull her long, red hair into a ponytail, slipping into combat boots and a black hoodie over her pajamas. Grabbing her weapon, she heads out.

She opts for her car, the black 1989 BMW M3, hoping she doesn't get pulled over, but she figures it's too risky to take the motorcycle. This is not vigilante business, so she avoids that quicker, stealthier mode of transport. The drive to the campus is a short one, but her tensing nerves make it seem overly long. She chances one vacant intersection, going through it as the light has barely turned to red, hoping that no cops are nearby. She gets lucky. She knows she'll chastise herself later, but for now, she'll take the good fortune.

She screeches into a parking place right out front, barely taking time to close and lock the door of her car. The library is not open at this time. There will be a record of her after hour's entry, but she isn't going to worry about that. Not yet. She shoves the Glock 19 into the pocket of her hoodie and rushes in, turning off the general security of the building, realizing this has not been triggered. She spares a moment in hope that the alarm in the Rare Books Collection room is a false positive, but she doubts it.

Her booted feet resound rapidly off the steps as she rushes down to the place that is so often her office. The door to the rare books room is open, that alarm having been bypassed. She'll have to figure out how the thief did it, but for now, she has to stop them from taking the Book.

She doesn't slow her pace until she is almost there, both hands now holding the loaded and ready pistol, finger near the trigger, the weapon held close to her chest, pointing out. She hears a noise, labored breath, and she pauses just around the way from it, near a tall, heavy shelf of books. She listens, the respiration coming with some sound of moisture, some grunts, a sound as though a slogging movement of something heavy. She tries to calm her breathing, and she pulls in a slow inhale, then peeks.

She sees a large form there on the floor. It appears human, but Skot had told her some of the protection put in place would only trigger for Infernal attacks. He had assured her. She sees some dark, shiny stains of what must be blood. The figure is trying to move, one long leg dragging behind the effort, useless. She walks fully into the area, pointing the gun.

"Stop," she commands.

The figure grunts in alarm and a spike of anger, jerking its head about, and there is now no mistaking that this is Pothos Wilbraham, the odd-looking student who had come seeking to borrow the Book. She is somewhat stunned, eyes going wide, and he grimaces, baring his teeth, raising his right arm, and she sees the flaring to life of outré light there, like a strangely colored flame taking his clawed hand. He unfurls it, lashing out at her, and she manages to dodge most of it, feeling a sharp spike of pain in her side as the magick bolt partially collides with her.

With this, he forgets her. He gets to the rarest of the rare books, pulling himself up, his hand now aglow with a different color as he tries to force his way through the rigid plastic, pounding it with his gigantic fist.

"Stop!" she tries again, now on one knee, aiming better, ignoring the pain in her side.

SWORD OF THE BUTTERFLY

He does not, and when the manmade substance does not give, he flexes his fingers outward, that preternatural light rising, preparing to focus the use of his supernatural abilities on the enclosure.

"Stop, or I will shoot," she declares.

Another growl from him, his red-tinged eyes slitting over to her, and the color about his hand changes to what it was moments before. He is preparing another attack. With the cool assurance of a veteran of much practice and experience, she fires.

The bullets fly out with the amber-tinged hue of that special preparation done to give them enhanced lethality to the Infernal, and Pothos spasms as he is hit by all three of the quickly delivered shots. He is struck on the right side of his torso, and the force stuns him, and he falls forward. His hand collides with the cabinet housing the book, and the transparent face protecting it fractures. This sets off another defense, another poised to only arise if breached by magick, and this one is far deadlier than the one already triggered.

She watches, her gun still aimed, but it becomes quickly apparent such will likely not be needed. A swirling force, a white luminosity, spirals up from nowhere, going about the intruder. His eyes gaze at it wildly, then it spikes with a brilliance, closing in on him. Lilja does not know if it is heat or what it may be doing, knows little to nothing of it, in truth, but it seems to be causing him terrible pain.

He howls with an ululation that threatens to curdle her resolve, but she remains poised, watching, waiting. He rises up some, of his own accord or from the supernatural power, she knows not, but the tension in his large form is apparent. He begins to spasm and quiver, then his appendages flail more openly. He remains contained in that spiraling light, and finally, when she is about to have to completely close her eyes to the brightness, it stops, and he crumbles.

She waits, still holding her aim. Seconds pass. There is no movement from him to indicate respiration or life of any kind. She finally dares to move closer, arms still out, pistol still pointed. The attack has rent him, body and clothing, and what she sees defies explanation. She is somewhat bulwarked by her limited experiences with the Infernal, but his grotesquery is still a challenge for her senses. Not just in what she sees, but also in the smell as his ichor leaks out.

The dark, coarse hair covers his upper torso like a matted, uneven carpet, some areas of his pallid flesh showing through completely, but as her eyes travel down, she sees that his semblance to humanity falters. The flesh becomes dryer, harder seeming, as of a carapace, giving way finally to a rash of tentacles as though the fat and stunted lengths of an anemone. These cover his belly, following his shape in a way that offsets the location of his ribcage, beginning short and growing longer the further down they go. The remnants of his clothing, his wounds, and the lack of light spare her much of it, and for that, she is grateful. He appears dead, and she is not entirely inclined to check for a pulse, but, holding the Glock ready in her right hand, she does finally press to the inside of a wrist. She feels nothing. She experiences no guilt at the sense of relief this brings her.

Is he a skin wearer, she thinks, recalling the discussion back at Felcraft manor, *is this the one they're hunting in America?* Her mind reels with the possibility, with confusion, and she shakes her head sharply, realizing all of that can wait.

She steps back then, knowing what she must now do. She has been left very specific instructions of how to handle something like this, and she goes for her phone, setting that in motion.

*****

They have now been tracking their target for many days and hundreds of miles. Nothing further has happened as substantial as the attack on their camp, though there have been two more killings, both of civilians. One was in a small town as they passed State lines, the other in a more rural location. Neither looked as though they'd be found anytime soon by anyone else, seeming to have been chosen as a taunt to the pursuers.

It upsets David, as well as all of them, but he makes the decision to delay a call to local authorities just in case such proves problematic to their hunt. When more time has passed, hopefully, when this is soon done, then they'll make the reports if the victims have not already been found by then. For now, they need to keep on the trail and stop the monster doing this.

SWORD OF THE BUTTERFLY

The hunting party is now a trio, being comprised of David, Duilio, and Zoe. Anika had been left in medical care, her family informed. It had been close, but as far as they could tell, she'd survive. She had suffered a rather nasty wound at her chest, as though the Demon had been trying to get to her heart. For whatever reason, either its impatience or her fortitude, it had not succeeded. She would have died of blood loss from that wound and the one at her skull, but they'd done enough, gotten her to the emergency clinic in time to save her.

There have been no further updates, and none of them expect any. She is the concern of the Malkuths, and they certainly are not inclined to share. Duilio would not even be getting that information, largely told to continue providing status reports and stay close to the Felcrafts.

The comment that Pèire had lobbed at him moments before his death, observing that the inspector appeared to be getting quite close to the Felcraft Hunter, holds somewhat true. Duilio is experienced enough to understand this. He respects the younger man, and their time together in this crucible is also forging a bond. Such does not take a licensed psychologist to realize. He cannot quite say the same for Zoe, though, the Huntress generally keeping to herself, giving him little more than cold stares if not the occasional sneer. It is clear, though, that she respects and defers to David, and it is obvious the elder Hunter acknowledges her tracking abilities.

Duilio wonders if they'd have been able to maintain this pursuit at all without the young woman, feeling fortunate that she was not slain in the attack. He does not fully understand her supernatural abilities, so for all he knows, there are others who possess similar skills, but he is glad she is here. He senses a chip on her shoulder, though, and not just due to his being affiliated with their rivals. He suspects her youth, gender, and general personality may lead to her being discounted by others. Duilio does not do so, and he'll happily let her lead any charge to confront the Demon, if and when they finally corner it.

"Why do you suppose it has come down here?" Duilio posits, peering over at David, Zoe off out ahead some ways as a scout.

It is muggy, hot, both of them covered in a sheen of sweat. They are beneath the earth, traversing the pathways of a long derelict coal mine, the fires of which still burn further within. They bear head-mounted lamps on adjustable, canvas straps, their mouths and noses covered by mask or cloth to avoid the potentially toxic fumes.

David glances back at Duilio. He would have rather left the man on the surface, but he knows that would have been riskier, just leaving the inexperienced agent alone as a veritable offering to the monster. Zoe had mentioned some difficulty in discerning the trail here, but they feel confident the beast has gone into the subterrene pathways. Confident enough to pursue, but not enough to leave Duilio behind.

"You think it's cornering itself?" David finally speaks, keeping an eye out, both of them holding loaded weapons at the ready.

Duilio looks over, peering, the Beretta held in his hands. David's large caliber revolver is in a holster at his hip, the twin blades also sheathed and ready at his lower back. He holds a customized M4 Carbine, one hand on the fore grip, ACOG scope and tactical light rounding out the system. They have other rifles, too, and they could have loaned one to Duilio, but all they have done thus far is provide him with some rounds of the enhanced ammunition. David had received reassurance from Skothiam that this was alright, while at the same time letting the Malkuths know and garnering a sort of promissory of payment. It is all part of the sometimes intricate diplomatic dealings between the two Families. The Felcrafts do not seek an exact tally of bullets used so that their rivals will repay in kind. They just want them to know what has been done, building up a potential debt to be properly repaid at another time and in another fashion. They both do it, sharing a lengthy historical precedent of such methods.

"Maybe?" Duilio tries, finding his potential resolve already quaking under the experienced Hunter's query.

"And maybe it's luring us into a trap."

The beam from the light shows more of the dark walls, some portions looking veined, others almost rugose, trails and tales of the insistent water that had run through here in the past.

Duilio shifts his eyes about, as with a newfound cautiousness, though what he has already seen of the Demon fills him with trepidation. He is now better armed, but he has still been advised by David to flee in the event of encountering the creature, then send alarm to the Malkuths as quickly as possible.

SWORD OF THE BUTTERFLY

The place also worries him, the eerie illumination of the very deep and incessant smoldering of the coal leaking somewhat into the passages giving the place an unearthly feel, as if the heat and noxious fumes were not enough of a hazard. As they further descend, moving slowly, casting their attention about in a careful, methodical way, it begins to feel more and more overwhelming, even as the glow grows. Before long, they don't need the lights they have brought, save for shining into precise locations, for there is still the contrast and shadow cast throughout the tunnels.

Duilio blinks, freezing in place. He stares, willing his eyes to remain open. The heat is oppressive, the fetid air unpleasant, and he has to give in, blinking again. He swears something has changed. He remains in place, looking, and then he thinks he sees something on his periphery, so he moves his eyes left. He does see it again, something that looks like the reflection of featureless eyes, somewhat large, wide set, very round, not human. It is not the beam hitting some small, shiny metallic deposits in the landscape. The motionlessness is uncanny, haunting, but he is beginning to realize they are being watched.

"David?" he whispers, still looking in the direction of the objects.

The Hunter stops, sensing the urgency in the tone, peering over. He sees that the inspector is frozen in place, staring, so he looks in the same direction. He then points his barrel, shining the tactical light, and when he does, they see the blink of movement.

"Shit! Get down," David commands, rushing nearer, and Duilio does, crouching low.

The sounds then arise, something like a scurrying, a dull tap and drag to it, despite the rapidity, like a staccato drumming with soft-headed sticks on a solid surface. David jerks his gun in that direction. Duilio ducks instinctively, though the barrel of the carbine does not come near to pointing at him. He sees another glimpse of movement, more of the sounds, and David fires three quick shots.

And more noises, more of the movement but also sounds that come from throats - screeches, low growls, labored breaths, as though the entire bouquet of terrible tumult had been there all along, very close, only now revealing itself to their ears. Duilio turns about more, twisting up his legs some, feet shifting on the hard earth to try to keep up, and he sees now more of those paired reflections. The possessors of them have now revealed themselves, and though they are not the original quarry, they are Demons all the same.

The beasts are small, like a human toddler, though weightier, bodies hairless, comprised of pale, wrinkled skin. Their overly large heads connect directly on their paunchy torsos, no visible neck, though they prove capable of independently moving them, one in particular turning to focus directly on the inspector, its lipless maw hanging open, slack, in a misshapen oval, displaying large, uneven, chisel-like teeth, blunted at the tips but still promising pain. There appear no noses, the place for an ear being a useless pucker, like a sphincter. The bodies hold no visible genitalia, nor are there digits of any kind on the ends of the four limbs.

At least half a dozen have come out of hiding, and they stare, emitting that terrible, throaty hiss, like a threatening passage of air. They move well enough over the rock, unperturbed by lack of claws or fingers as well as any expected obeisance to gravity. As they slowly creep, appearing to be taking stock of potential prey, some others appear, and soon the small group has increased in number and threat.

"David?" Duilio asks, eyes shifting to the man, then back to the creatures.

He does not answer, eyes moving about as he assesses the situation.

"David?" Duilio tries again, speaking slower, pitch rising at the end.

"Stay down," David iterates, bending his own legs more, readying for the fight.

Duilio wishes these were just some strange but mundane subterranean creature that he happened to never learn about, but he knows they are unnatural, demonic. He doesn't know how they'll keep them all at bay, and he experiences a rising horripilation at the thought.

"Duilio?"

"Yes?" he replies, quickly, as though David's voice is a life preserver thrown to a man in the middle of the ocean.

The Hunter speaks slowly, but emphatically, "Keep your head down and prepare to fire."

A somewhat shaky nod, even as the beasts seem to sense something. Several of them bring their exposed teeth closer together to emit a keener

SWORD OF THE BUTTERFLY

hiss. Bodies move as the slender appendages flex, an obvious preparation of movement.

"Fire!" David shouts.

A cacophony erupts, bullets flying from the carbine and Duilio's handgun, the enigmatic light tracing the trajectory of their specially treated ammunition looking quite at home in the electric vermilion environ created by the deep, undying fires. Duilio stays down, noting that David whirls about rapidly, shooting in many directions, the barrel of his rifle passing over the other's head from time to time. Several hits are scored, the loathsome beasts crying out as the dark ichor spews from their bodies, but not enough are stopped, and they prove difficult to strike as they rush about.

Duilio quickly reloads, chambering a round, then starts rightwards, looking further left to see that David has shot one out of mid-air as it leapt for them.

"Conserve ammo," he says, "Shoot them when they get close. If they stay back, we don't care. *Zoe!*"

The inspector realizes the wisdom of this. Whether the beasts are so strategic is unknown, but they may indeed be hanging back, trying to get them to waste all their ammunition before rushing in to swarm them. Just then, he sees one peek up from a hiding place, then dart back down, only to rush out, moving zigzag along the sloped wall, heading across it, not toward them. It seems they are indeed attempting to get them to use up all their bullets.

Duilio's eyes widen as one appears from below, rising up through a barely noticeable access, keeping itself low to the ground and moving very effectively on all fours, teeth bared, mouth slavering. He wastes three bullets before it reaches him, launching itself the remaining short distance, latching its teeth about his shod left foot. He cries out, the thing's nubby-tipped appendages moving in a frantic near-blur.

David glances down, having changed out his own magazine. He sees the thing attached to the inspector, noting that its teeth may have barely made it through the leather of the man's shoe as it moves its mouth, trying to bore deeper.

"Shoot the fucking thing!" he orders, then continues his own firing.

Duilio nods, the expression almost more of a tremble, then he aims, the barrel mere inches from the target's bulbous head, and he pulls the trigger. The dark vitae that powers them bursts out, and the creature slumps, relinquishing its hold.

"Duilio!" David snaps, and the inspector looks up to see several of them gathering in front of them, but as he aims, he hears something he did not expect, "Hold your fire."

He blinks, looking up at the Hunter then back at the cohort of seething creatures. He wonders why they are waiting. He senses movement in the far left periphery, and he turns just in time to hear the loud report. He cringes as several of the beasts are blown aside, some killed, others wounded, and then Zoe racks her shotgun again, quickly, unleashing another load of buckshot, repeating this several times as David adds to it with his carbine. Duilio finally rejoins, and within moments, their precarious situation resolves to seeming safety.

Duilio works to catch his breath, eyes still somewhat held wide, lips parted. He looks at the other two, who take little notice of him. He then stares at the bodies of the things that attacked, lying in pale lumps, leaking a contrasting dark fluid from their crumbled and rent forms. He notices that the slide on his gun is locked open, empty again, and he has no more ammunition on him. He presses the button, closing it, then puts it away.

"Decoys."

His eyes move up to the Huntress, curiosity on his features, but she is speaking to her relative. Her goggled eyes are hidden, her voice, like theirs, slightly muffled. David nods, thinking.

"Our Demon isn't here, is it?"

Duilio knows he is not being addressed, but he follows the conversation as though rapt in the most intense tennis match. Zoe shakes her head.

"Is that what took you so long to get back here?"

The young lady nods.

"I went pretty deep, following hints, but ..." She purses her lips, gesturing with a rather casual hand toward the dead ones.

"This place is a Gateway," David says, and when Duilio looks back, it seems the man is speaking to him, so he perks his eyebrows.

SWORD OF THE BUTTERFLY

"A ... gateway?"

David nods. "A semi-permanent way for them to get in. I'll bet there's even mention of it in our records somewhere. It also means that the sort of signs we've been following, that Zoe's been seeing, well, this place would be littered with them, obscuring the real trail."

"And these ... things?" he dares to ask.

"Rats."

"Rats?"

"Vermin of the Infernal, numerous, weak, easy to move through portals like the one here."

"Did our Demon use this way to get to this world?"

David peers, cocking an eyebrow. "I see more of why the Malkuths chose you."

Duilio assumes this is a compliment, but he cannot be entirely sure.

"Let's get out of here," the Hunter then says, turning to head back, Zoe in quick follow.

"So," Duilio says after they are shortly on their way, beginning the exhausting trek back to the surface, "The one we hunt is not down here?"

David does not answer, but he gives a barely noticeable glance to his fellow.

"No," Zoe says, her tone giving defiance to any further question in this regard.

"Then we ...?"

"Got led on a wild-goose chase," David says, still moving, "You got that saying in Italy?"

"Yes," Duilio answers, weightily.

"We've been duped. I told you it was toying with us. It's been leaving just enough of a trail to keep us on it but not make it too easy."

Duilio continues moving behind the other two, his lungs burning, wishing to be home there and ready for some secure rest. He also wishes, though, that this were over. He had been nervous to confront this beast, worried for his own life, of course, but he had also been excited. He had wanted to succeed.

"Are we giving up?"

"You asked me that before," David comments, then emits a bit of a grunt as he moves up a relatively steep area, getting over some large rocks. "Watch your step there. We're not giving up, but we need to consider this. Just like before, we're going to report back and see what's the next step, but the Demon just gave us the slip, after leading us around for all this time. Don't you wonder why?"

CHAPTER SEVEN

It has been a hectic few days.

Skothiam had flown to America to deal with things there. True, the planned trip had been short, but it had been cut even further when Lilja had notified him of what had happened back in the City. It had bothered him greatly, though he was comforted to hear her voice telling him of what had happened and that she was alright. So, he had changed his itinerary and acquired a return flight for sooner than anticipated.

Then, after the initial report and examination of the body, he had called Nicole, and now she has joined them. If that were not enough, they had shortly received the update from David regarding the hunt.

"It is related."

Lilja glances over at Nicole, the woman still as stately and ethereal as always. She then moves her eyes to Skot, next to whom she sits in this comfortable room in the town house. Nicole had spent a good deal of her time today alone in the presence of the corpse before returning here for this 'debriefing'.

"Are you certain?"

Nicole takes a moment to react, and Lilja wonders if the woman is somehow offended by her brother's requested affirmation. Then, she gives a single, slow nod. Skot exhales through his nose, eyes moving aside as though in pondering, then frustration. Lilja places a hand on his right thigh, which he acknowledges by moving his own atop. She turns hers, moving her fingers to interlace with his, grasping him more intently.

He finally looks over, and she offers him an encouraging smile. He returns it, albeit weakly. When she moves her eyes back to his sister, Nicole is staring at them. Lilja blinks, blushing slightly, unsure if the woman merely waits or is somehow displeased with this display. Skot reciprocates that depthful observance.

"They have acquired a breeder," she finally informs, as though her brother has mentally bade her to give her report.

Lilja is confused, and when she looks at Skot, she sees he has closed his eyes. He takes in a slow breath, finally opening them, looking at her.

"The Infernal are obsessed with reproduction," he says, and she nods, recalling their conversation that alluded to such. "Their abilities in that vein are also very restricted, but just as I mentioned the legend of the Nephilim, what truth may be inferred from it is that it *is* possible for them to find some humans that are … compatible with them and may be used to produce progeny.""So …," she begins, eyes blinking to a narrower focus, brow knitting, "they *mate* with humans?"

He nods further, the motion still slow, as though careful to introduce acknowledgement of this reality. "This is something about which we know. This is not just conjecture. It's rare for them to find a suitable person, but when they do-."

"When they do," Nicole interrupts, taking up the thread, her cadence less gentle, though her voice is not harsh, more like the trained voice of an orator or singer, "it is akin to a coup, or a potential one. This allows them to learn more of us, to more easily introduce themselves into our population. This one bypassed notice and some of the security measures *because* it was part human."

"It also translates into their being able to produce more offspring," Skot adds.

"But …," Lilja pauses, again wrinkling her brow, "How many children can a woman produce, even if … even if it's forced on her as often as possible."

"It could also be a male," Nicole intones.

"Oh."

"It also requires members of the Infernal that are fertile, many of which are not. We are not entirely sure of their gestational periods or other such basic biological understanding. Many of them have no apparent sex, some seem to be fluid of gender, or even hermaphroditic, but our chances to scientifically study them have been a bit … limited."

SWORD OF THE BUTTERFLY

She nods, slowly, taking this in, then she glances at Nicole. "Is there no way to know if the human was the mother or father?"

Skot blinks, eyes moving to his sister. This is another of Lilja's astute questions, and not just in the asking, but of whom she asks. He marvels at the potential in her.

"I am not certain, but it *feels* to me as if the mother is human," Nicole gives.

More concern and empathy etches itself on Lilja's features, and she looks back to Skot, then down and away

"It's horrible," he all but whispers.

"It is *unnatural*," Nicole continues, gaining both their attentions, "The progeny was no more than a few years old."

"A few ...?" Lilja retorts, then blinks rapidly, closing her lips, perhaps surprised at herself, and she turns her eyes to see Skot looking at her, giving a short, encouraging nod, so she continues, "I looked up his records of admission, and he was listed as young for university, but his age said he was sixteen."

"That is incorrect," Nicole flatly states, "Part of the deception. They chose an age they knew we'd find acceptable without it being overly suspicious. If he is more than three years old, I'd be *very* surprised."

"But ...," and she again looks back at Skot, "How?"

"As Nicole said, 'unnatural'."

"So they ... bred this ... child," Lilja continues, "specifically to infiltrate the school and get the Book?"

"That seems unlikely," Skot answers, "Finding a breeder is very rare and valuable to them, so they would keep him or her hidden, and they would also keep the offspring hidden, unleashing them for only an important task ... such as this. It also seems they did not know of the Book's being here last year."

"But the gateway?" she posits.

"Yes. That appears as a possible set-up for trying to get the Book, but it seemed misdirected were that the intent. This city is not accidentally the site of so much supernatural activity. It's possible that the reason for the gateway *and* the Book finding their ways here may be similar in nature but not interdependent."

"But now they do know."

They both look over to Skot's sister.

"True," Skot is forced to agree, then he squeezes Lilja's hand, getting her to look at him, and he casts a more open, genuine smile on her. "Good thing we have such a capable guardian in place."

She is stunned for a split second, then her eyes go through three rapid blinks, the edges of her lovely lips curling, and she looks down, her pale flesh beginning to flush.

"No, I …," she tries to say, "I just … the traps, the magick." She looks up, using her eyes to gesture to Nicole, then Skot. "That your family set up. That stopped him. I didn't do much."

"You were hit with the Dark Claw of Botis."

Lilja looks at Nicole, confused, then back at Skot.

"The magick the intruder used on you."

"Oh. Is that … is that bad? I'm okay," she says, and Skot is again impressed, because she says the last as a statement.

"It *is* bad, quite powerful, and it tells us much of its wielder … and of you," he adds, putting a light curve to his lips.

"Wh-why?"

"Most would not come through such a strike unscathed," Nicole says, "and you are, as you say, okay."

Lilja notes the cast of the woman's eyes, and it seems Nicole may have used her unique talents whilst here to do more than just examine the corpse.

"The spell is not just one of a force but it is also toxic, yet you are having no residual effects," Nicole adds, and were it not for the woman's matter-of-fact tone, Lilja may be inclined to be worried. "As if you are possessed of not only great fortitude but perhaps even immunity."

"What … what does that mean?"

He continues to give her that light, warm smile, and now, he adds a shrug of his shoulders.

"We're not exactly certain, but you're tough, that's for sure." He perks his eyebrows, and she grins more openly, even blushing further.

"It is fortunate," Nicole says, but she does not give voice to something else that carries through her mind, for she wonders if it is coincidence at all that Lilja serves as Head Custodian to the collection in which the Book has found itself.

SWORD OF THE BUTTERFLY

"You said they were related, though," Lilja reminds, eyes flitting from Nicole to Skot and back.

The awkwardness spikes, for no answer proves forthcoming, the older woman merely looking back at the younger. Skot also remains silent, as though merely waiting for whether or not his sister will answer. Lilja's spine stiffens slowly, almost imperceptibly, but the tension is finally released.

"I did," Nicole says, and a curl touches her lips. "Skot, would you mind leaving us alone for a moment?"

Lilja is confused, but Skot does not react at all as though curious. He merely nods, then gives Lilja a very warm smile and flex of the fingers entwined with her own before smoothly rising and exiting the room. She watches him go, silently bidding him to not leave, eventually sending her eyes back to the other woman. Nicole rises, slowly, again that ethereal, almost inhuman aspect to her motions and appearance, though her smile has grown and looks genuine enough. She steps over, seemingly gliding in the long dress she wears. She sits besides Lilja, taking her hands in her own, uninvited, to be sure, but in an undeniably casual way, as though they were the best of friends. Lilja feels a squeeze, though it is nothing too intense, her hands mainly resting in those of the other woman. She fights to return that calm gaze, fights to keep too much blush rising to her flesh.

"You are very special."

Lilja doesn't know how to respond, so she says nothing.

"Very strong," Nicole speaks, still settling that pleasant smile and stare upon her, which Lilja still finds uncomfortable. "Even though he gives you much praise, Skot is not even fully aware of it all."

Lilja finally blinks, but Nicole's eyes remain in their repose, cat-like in their calm focus.

"Thank you," she finally says.

"Oh, you need not thank me," Nicole replies, releasing the hold, and Lilja breathes a sigh of relief. "I am merely observing, granting nothing."

The younger woman shifts in place, still not sure what to make of this, and though Nicole broke the physical connection, she still holds her in that observing gaze.

"It is obvious he is very fond of you. If there is anything you need, do not hesitate to ask me – woman to woman."

"Okay," Lilja replies, fighting to keep the end of the word from rising up as though a question. "Thank you."

"You're welcome. I'll let Skot know we're done."

Done, Lilja ponders, *done with what?* But she keeps such thoughts to herself.

*****

"Okay, I'll help you, but you need to pay me, and I don't think you have a lot of money. So, what can we trade?"

Therese looks at the guy on the other side of the desk, his smug expression causing a simmer to her anger, but she suppresses it. She wants his help. She won't give "anything" for it, but she wants it. She's prepared to walk away from the table at any moment, but now is not yet the time.

He wears a little smirk on his decently-fleshed lips, the edges angling up to rather sharp points within the subtle, hinting grin. His brown eyes peer at her beneath dark, thick eyebrows, the edges becoming more scant and tapering as they follow the bone. His hair is cut very short, nearly non-existent, revealing a slightly bumped top to his somewhat narrow head. His ears almost seem pointed, also longish like his face, the left pierced twice, one a black gauge of relatively small measurement, the other a silver hoop with captive bead. His complexion is olive-toned, though relatively light, his build somewhat slender. He is not a bad looking man at all, but his demeanor strikes her as generally creepy.

"Look, Macar. I'm not going to fuck you," Therese bluntly states, which hardly fazes him.

She is wearing a black hoodie, zipped up all the way, her dark jeans not the usual tightness most of her choices usually display. She also wears her clunky, black boots. She knew the conversation would go this way, and hiding her thin body has done nothing to discourage him.

He parts his hands, their having been casually interlaced in his lap as he just looks at her like a salesman fully confident in closing the deal. He purses out his lower lip, eyebrows perking a bit, as though he is giving her the most eloquent rebuttal without uttering a word. It is all a sort of shrug, as though to say that there is one price, and if that is not paid, then no sale.

"I'd like your help," she continues, *forces* herself to continue.

She did not want to come here at all, but when she went to her other private investigation contact last year for help, it did not pan out. It seems her plans are still risky for the more professional, less dangerous approach taken by the only other one she trusts enough with this. Macar may be a lech, but he is good at his job, has many of his own contacts and resources.

"And I can help *you*," she adds.

"Oh?" He perks his eyebrows more, almost as though patronizing, as though he cannot fathom what she could do for him.

"You know I'm good with cyber-work. That's how we met. I could work for you more, help you with other cases, even help with your network security, maybe even help you get data you aren't supposed to have."

"I know what you do, Therese," he says, speaking calmly, his accent barely betraying the combined influences of his heritage and environment, "But wouldn't it be a lot easier for you to just … give me some of what nature gave you?" He turns up the intensity of his little grin, just a touch, but enough to add to the heat of his flame.

Not only is he not a bad looking man, but he is quite charming. Therese wonders if it is general protection that he is often so smarmy and prurient, otherwise he might be seriously dangerous.

"That's not going to happen," she mutters, "I won't be your sex toy."

"Well." He affects that subtle shrug again. "Who is to say I want your other … talents? Yes, you've done some good work for me in the past, and if I need that, I'll contact you, pay you real money, but I did not ask you here. You came here wanting something from me."

"Macar, listen." She actually scoots a tad closer, and though there is a desk between them, she is sure he picks up on it. Therese is quite sincere in her bid and also quite sincere in setting the boundaries she is unwilling to cross to get it. "This is also *good* work, okay? I want help in stopping child prostitution. This could be good for you, too."

"And how is that?" he retorts, his demeanor becoming a shade more serious, "You want me to stir up organized criminals *and* the police?"

"I'm not going after corrupt cops here."

"Come on, Therese, don't be so naïve. If this sort of thing is brought to light, it makes the police look bad, because they were either in on it or too dumb to know it was happening and put a stop to it."

"Okay, okay, but what if I told you I have a contact in the department, and we can feed everything to them, and they'll make the hard moves, the real bust."

"Hmmm …" It seems he is about to say more, but he stops, and she sees that look she wants to see, the one that means his veneer of trying to score has been punctured, and now the real curiosity and drive has been hooked.

She knows there is a reason he is successful at what he does, that he is willing to take on risky, even questionably legal work. Beneath it all, there is some good to the man. He ruminates for a brief moment, then his dark eyes snap back to her.

"*Are* you telling me this?"

She nods.

"Alright, hmmm. You … hmmm. If I do this, and you choose your currency to pay me, then I will need a lot of work from you. Not just your help on this but many other things."

"How much?"

"I'll let you know." He shifts back to that grin.

"No, unh-uh." She shakes her head slowly, eyes drilled into his. "I won't become your indentured servant, either, then you'll just end up trying to coerce me into some early buy-out with sex."

"Therese," he says, his voice drawing on the word, "Would it be so bad? Why are you so against it? I'm not bad at it, mmm?"

"It's nothing personal, Macar," she somewhat lies, but she hopes there is enough truth and sincerity to sell it, "I'm just not interested, especially not like that. It's too much like prostitution."

He narrows his eyes, flesh crinkling, as though he thinks she may indeed be lying, or he just can't believe what he hears.

"Against your moral code? Is that it?"

"I *do* have one, Macar, and so do you."

"Eh," and the hands part again, "I guess you're right."

A moment passes, both sizing each other up, neither willing to budge at this point, and he finally speaks.

"What do you propose, then?"

"You've paid me before, so we've negotiated a rate. I'll work for you to pay back whatever your bill would be for the work you do for me."

"Ah, well, yes, I guess that makes sense."

"All documented and legitimate," she pushes.

He unfurls a full-on smirk at this.

"You *are* serious." He looks upon her steadily, and she nods. "Alright, then, full rates, nothing held back. You will get a tab as if you are a rich client, and then you will pay me back … in full."

"Okay."

"Good," he says after a moment, "I'll have something drawn up, then."

She blinks.

"You said all documented and legit, didn't you?"

She nods.

"Then it will be, and if you don't pay me back, I'll just go through the legal system."

"It's not going to come to that, Macar," she quips.

She knows he has hit her in a weak spot, for she has had trouble in the past, and though things have been alright for a while, she wouldn't want the system to feel like they need to pay undue attention to her. He knows some of that, too, so he is telling her what might lie in store if she tries to take advantage of him. She has no intent to do that, but she won't be taken advantage of, either.

"Good," he speaks, tasting the word, "Now, tell me your plan. What is it you want to do?"

*****

The venue is a large warehouse, cleaned up sufficiently, decorated, and furnished for the event. Darkness and light both serve to accentuate and hide, giving suggestive hints to the imagination. The place occupies many cubic meters, the ceilings in most areas quite high, though the main room boasts the most open space, along with a large dance floor, the surface sparsely interrupted by small, raised areas for the more adventurous or exhibitionist. All in all, there are three main 'rooms', connected by throughways and some short passages, along with two other smaller chambers. One of the smaller rooms is a VIP area, one which garners access through purchase or being granted such privilege. They have the benefit of such use, though thus far they have only passed through it to see what it holds, spending little time there as the evening has developed.

They have gone through some drinks, he slowing his pace due to her own general savoring of spirits, but he has spent most of the evening drinking in the site of her. She wears a black latex dress, one that is very short, cut low across her bosom, the bra beneath doing more to give tantalizing glimpse of her cleavage. Her arms are bare, as are her legs, going down into the black, quite tall, spike heels, the platform shoe entirely covering her toes and heel, a single strap about the ankle to add to the fit and appearance. She also wears a thin collar, black leather, simple, elegant and well made, customized for her, the inside of it baring a soft, comfortable lining, the O-ring dangling in front not overly large, the silver metal polished and gleaming, resting like an invitation over the crook of her collarbone.

They stand very close to each other, and he slowly glides a curled index finger down along her arm, completing the touch by turning his hand and gripping it about her slender wrist. She smiles at him, bashfully, but not overly so, the expression also coquettish. Even after all this time, she is not entirely comfortable in this skin, but then, they do not get out to events like this very often. She wants this, but there is still an anxiousness to it. She does it for them both, but were it not for his behest, it would not happen at all.

He wears all black, bespoke button-down shirt over tailored pants. The cufflinks in his shirt are of black onyx, the oval-shaped jewels a shimmering invitation to mirrored depths surrounded by intricately-patterned white gold. He does not wear tie or jacket, though he does carry a length of very delicate chain, the links quite small, though the integrity of the metal is above reproach. For now, the item hides away in his pocket, awaiting use.

He leans in, kissing her neck, just above the collar, her vibrant red hair out in all its glory, given extra flair with wave and curl, and he gently nudges it aside with his attentions, lips pressing slowly, savoring over that delicate flesh. He moves up beside the nape, then toward her ear, before pulling back, gazing upon her. She returns it, the smile still on her elegant lips, painted a rich, dark red for this evening's outing. Her pale flesh is flushed somewhat, and he relishes the sight of it on her, relishes their proximity. She moves a bit, adjusting herself, causing a light, creaking noise of the material of her very tight dress.

There are many here at the Ball. The various modes of dress range from those in very fine suit and tie and quite elegant cocktail gowns to those in more daring, brightly colored outfits that show an exuberant flair even in this environ. Some even harken to something more futuristic or fey. The purpose of the gathering is a celebration of the fetish and BDSM subcultures, and thus does the myriad of clothing choices and displays reflect that sumptuous and exotic buffet.

"Are you ready, Pet?" Skothiam asks.

Lilja's expression changes by miniscule degrees, but he notices it. She experiences fear at the thought. He knows she has courage, though, in many ways that go well beyond anything anyone else at this ball ever has to face, but this does test her. He is gracious that she seeks so within herself for them both. She nods, and the manner of the subtle expression is a sizzling lure to him.

"If you want," she says.

"I do," he states with even measure, returning her gaze, letting the moment linger, and he notices the taut poise of her anticipation.

He then brings forth the chain, one end a clasp, the other a finely-crafted, leather strap, and he attaches it to the O-ring at her collar, then slipping the fingers of his right hand through the hooped material, holding the end of the leash with a casual assurance. He does not pull the metal, does nothing to overtly humiliate her, just holds the connection which now exists in physical manifestation between them.

He continues watching her, noticing an increase to the rise and fall of her chest, a deepening of the lovely flush to her skin. He waits, letting her experience this. She looks about, but her eyes always return to him. He notices as she averts them, looking down, still reeling under the experience of being leashed in public in this manner, then she blinks them back up to him.

The assortment of winking lights and sultrier, ambient illuminations catch in those eyes. He could drown in them, such are their depths, openness, and the nigh crystalline variations in the colors. It all appears subtle, but one need only study them to see how remarkable they are, how they may so transparently show her soul.

"If it becomes too much, you need only say the word, and I will unlatch the leash," he says, his tone one of care, not taunting.

She nods. "I know."

"Good. It's important that you know."

A shuddering breath passes through her, a sensation of strength and pleasure that comes from the realization of what transpires between them, what they grant one another, and what they help each other understand of themselves.

"Skot," she all but whispers, "you make me feel sexy."

He grins at this, the curve of his pleasant expression rising a few degrees, and she returns it with yet another shy smile, as though somewhat embarrassed at what she has felt and revealed to him. He brings his face closer, whispering in her ear.

"I find you highly desirable."

She feels another warming wave cascade through her, remaining almost perfectly still as he has come so close from an already near position. Her eyes flick over to him as he pulls back, her lips held in a straight line, her aspect one of openness and trust along with a barely concealed excitement. What will he now do with her?

Take a walk, it seems, and he begins to slowly move away. The distance increases, the chain quickly losing its slack. There is anxious thought that she may not move, but finally she does, going somewhat rapidly to catch up. He keeps his pace slow, a meandering, casually exploratory gait. She is shorter than he, and the foot wear, though elegant

SWORD OF THE BUTTERFLY

and enticing in aesthetic, is not something she is used to, but she manages very well.

They cut across the main floor, and for a short moment of illogical panic, she thinks he might be leading her to dance. She enjoys dancing, has had some formal training in it, but not under these circumstances. She just as quickly thinks that he might just hold her close as they move, and she finds this a nice idea, but his continued heading shows he does not intend to stop here.

They pass by a couple of tables set back away from the main area. These are being used as a small market of sorts, wares displayed in as elegant a way as possible under such temporary arrangements. She sees that he glances briefly that way, but they still do not pause. They turn left and enter a large hallway, one that is not as well lit, painted black. The end of it may be spied none too far away, an opening heading into the adjoining chamber. Two doors hold place on the right side.

Once a few paces inside, he stops, turning to face her. She looks up at him, eyes curious but still open, patient, trusting. He gently guides her the short distance to the wall, placing her back to it, but he does not press her up against that surface. He keeps the contact, one hand on her upper arm, the other still holding the end of the leash, and he leans in, turning his head to place a deep kiss upon her lips.

She pulls in a breath, almost as though drawing him closer with it, even as it displays her sense of rising excitement. Their mouths meet, the yielding flesh pressing together, warm breath exchanged, and she feels his tongue seeking into her mouth with a direct insistence. She responds, though more passively, subservient, offering herself in a way she thinks he desires. She feels as his hand grips slowly tighter about her arm, and she experiences a heightening of arousal within herself, a warming.

He eventually pulls back, still holding that languid pace, and their eyes lock. His expression is one of calm, though very pointed arousal, confident. She returns it, holding the gaze, though that hot creep of blushing rises up along her neck, jaw, and to her ears. She pulls another breath in through her nose, blinking. He finds her expression so honest and charming. Then he turns, resuming their traverse of the hallway, and she follows.

"Skot?"

He pauses, glancing at her, eyebrows perking slightly. He sees her eyes move right to those doors then back to him.

"May I use the restroom? I'll be back soon. Is that okay?"

"Of course." He unhooks the latch, and she gives another of her beautiful, little smiles and heads inside.

He knows that though there are two doors, either visibly indicated for a gender, the adherence and enforcement to such at events like this is fairly relaxed. He would be fine escorting her into the ladies' room, even daring enough to go with her into the stall, but he knows she is not comfortable with that, so he awaits her here.

As though to prove his point, two males walk out after some minutes have passed. They share smirks, and he is left to wonder what they may be talking about, what they may have been up to in the ladies' water closet. They are both rather young, one quite bulky with short hair, and the other is slighter of build and height, wearing his hair long. They give him no notice, moving on to other areas of the building.

He begins to feel worry as he waits. He knows he is being anxious, and there are others obviously inside. He also knows that Lilja is well capable of taking care of herself, but each passing minute leads him to debate with himself if he ought to go in and check on her.

When she finally emerges, he experiences a very noticeable relaxation and relief, a stark awareness of how tense he had become. He smiles at her, and she walks up to him, stopping before him, chin raised, dutifully waiting to be hooked, but he notices something seems tense in her. He pauses as he raises his hand to affix the latch.

"Is everything alright?"

"Yes," she says after snapping her eyes back to his, but he knows, and the cast of his eyes presents the further inquiry. "There were two guys in there kind of bothering someone. They were giving her crap."

"What?" His own worry spikes again, but this time for a different reason. "I'm surprised that happened here."

She screws up her lips, shaking her head slightly, and she continues, "It wasn't physical, but it was obvious. She was trying to ignore it, but I could tell it bothered her. I was pondering intervening, but they left."

"Two guys," he says, "One taller, bigger, had short, dark hair? The other had long, blondish hair in a ponytail?"

"Yeah. You saw them?"

"Yes, and ... well," he starts, pausing, and she gives him a look of concern. "They didn't seem 'right', like two guys joking with each other as they leave a crime scene, though that's horribly judgmental of me to say, but I got a little anxious about you."

"Aww." She moves in closer, slipping her arms about his waist, and he returns the embrace as she snugs in, then tilts her face up, and they exchange a quick kiss. "I'm sorry to make you worry."

"You didn't."

"Well," she adds, a devilish grin taking her lush lips, "If they had been screwing with me, they would have regretted it."

"Lily," he playfully chides.

"What?" she jokes back, "I wouldn't have hurt them *too* bad, just some pain to their prides."

"Right." Skot smirks.

He then moves away the barest bit, bringing up the clasp in hand, showing it to her, and she acquiesces, moving her hair out of the way as sign of this, though it is hardly a real obstruction. He reattaches the leash, and her demeanor changes, as though she has shifted back into that submissive role they both desire. He smiles, then turns, leading her through the hallway and into the next room.

There is another bar off in the corner, the small area surrounding by a dense crowd of people, leaving the remainder of the room relatively spacious. It may give one to think that the tiny locale around the serving area is its own microcosm, a very different and pressing experience compared to that which is only a few meters away. There is also an area obviously intended for dancing, though at present the people upon it are giving a somewhat artistically choreographed display of some basic BDSM activities. Some of the scantily-clad bodies are bound, some of those receiving the attention of spanking or other devices. Lights gleam off the tight, shiny coverings of latex, giving hints of the vibrancy that the general lack of illumination enshrouds, almost as though the people wear candy shells.

There are various seating offerings along much of the wall, some couches, and even some booths, and he spies one that is vacant, somewhat close to the bar but not of such a proximity as to perhaps warrant avoidance due to the smattering of people. He walks her into the partially enclosed section, sitting in the middle of the bench. She remains standing, looking down at him, and he is pleased with her behavior. He glances down, and she sits on the floor at his feet, nuzzling in close to him. He begins to pet gently over her luxurious hair, also touching of her neck and shoulder.

She enjoys the attention, losing herself in it, feeling a dissolving of the anxiety that had been rising in her. They are isolated enough within this booth that they have mayhap entered their own universe. She wonders at the worlds built within this place, various sections and divisions to suit the varied tastes and imaginations.

And then the spell is broken.

She senses it, opening her eyes, not even sure if she realized they had closed, and she feels a slowing of his attentions, knowing that he has also noticed it. The two young men from the bathroom stand nearby, cavorting in that same manner. Sniggering to themselves and at others, undertaking a general show of disrespect.

Their attention veers toward the bar, and she leans forward, peering, and she sees the very same person from the bathroom. It appears the two have decided to continue their insulting treatment. Skot registers that the person they are making fun of appears to be a cross dresser or a male to female transsexual. He also notices that others at the bar do not seem very appreciative of the behavior of the two, but no one says or does anything.

Then some words are exchanged, the victim stepping closer, obviously very agitated, and delivers some sharp retort, a renunciation of their behavior. Skot hears sounds, but they are too far, the music too loud, for him to make out the details. He notes that one of the two puts on an act of being scared, evincing his immaturity all the more, while the other gives a somewhat worrisome smirk as though eager for violence.

Before anything further happens, the other person turns and goes back to the bar, disappearing in the throng of people. Some of them even appear to be now acting as quasi-guardians, having turned to face the two men, giving stern, reproachful looks. All this does is perhaps deter them from pursuit, but they continue their giggling. The shorter, slim one nudges his friend, and Skot thinks they are turning to leave, but then, when he points, somewhat subtly but obvious enough, at them, he realizes it is not over. The other alights his eyes on them, then follows as his friend takes a few steps nearer.

He glances down at Lilja, his hand placed protectively on her neck and shoulder, as if she were needful of such, then he moves his eyes back up to the duo. They do not come too close, but near enough, and their focus is now obviously on them. The one with the longer hair points, hiding his mouth as he speaks to his friend, who nods, slowly, then the other laughs. Then there are words that reach them, though still not entirely legible, but a remark is made regarding Lilja being in her proper place.

"Skot?"

He looks down, his adrenalin spiking, tension rising, but she looks rather controlled, his name having been uttered rather calmly.

"Yes?"

"Would you please unhook the leash?"

He does so, and once done, she stands, going toward the pair. Skot immediately notices the relative height disparity, and he realizes she has slipped off her shoes.

The ponytailed one widens his eyes, mocking her, reeling back, and again putting on the display of mock fear, acting as though he is going to hide behind his larger friend. She walks in front of the pair, facing them with a strict and freezing stare.

"You have ten seconds to leave us alone."

"Or what?" the larger one replies, arms now folded.

"Or I will break your fucking arm and throw you out myself," she answers, her tone sharp and cold, that steely, icy gaze not faltering in the least.

She has already sized them up, determining that neither has any formal training in fighting based on how they stand, imbalanced, unprepared for any real threat. They obviously do not think of her as one, either, for the smaller guy goes through his now common routine, eyes widening, the afraid act, then he loses himself in a bout of semi-stifled laughter. The larger one just continues to give out that awkward smirk.

Skot wonders if he ought to stand up. He worries of it, though. The two may not be inclined at all to physically harm a woman, but if he engages the situation, he provides them with a male adversary. He is also unhappy with their behavior, and he thinks his inaction as somewhat condoning it. They are also being very disrespectful to her and to him. This may not still warrant a physical response, but they should be stopped.

He breathes an inaudible sigh of relief when two rather large, black-garbed men show up, both security here, their somewhat tight t-shirts identifying them as such along with the ear piece sported by one. The two other guys turn, looking like kids caught with their hand in the cookie jar, but then the larger one speaks.

"She threatened to break my arm."

But before anything else may happen, a swell of people from the bar comes forward, all but delivering an onslaught of words to the guards, the prior person of their attention at the vanguard. By the time two more security show up, the situation is diffused and determined, and a small smattering of applause results as the two young men are escorted out.

Lilja returns, having exchanged a few brief words with one of the guards, and she sits back at his feet, turning and offering the ring of her collar as though nothing untoward or stressful had just passed. Skot blinks, exhaling through his nose, and he reattaches the leash. He looks at her for a bit, but she seems to be focused elsewhere, and when she leans her head against the outside of his right thigh, he goes back to petting her.

Their drive home later that evening is uneventful.

They have engaged in some fun and play on their way home many a night out, some being more casual flirting, some evolving into full blown sexual activity. He steals glances at her as they make their way to the townhouse, feeling a mingling of worry and enticement at her aspect and appearance. She does not appear upset, but some distance now shows. A placement of his hand on her leg, gets him a short glance and smile, but nothing more. He tries further, moving his touch up along her slender, well-toned thigh. She gives him another very light smile, and she lays her own hand atop his, squeezing, and effectively holding it there. He does not try more.

Once home, he is taken by that sense of conflict and confusion. He is aroused by her, brought along that wave almost as though against his

SWORD OF THE BUTTERFLY

will, and he wants to take her, be with her. They walk inside, the sound of her heels resounding off the hardwood floors. The reports slow, then go quiet. He stops behind her, gazing upon her form.

"I'm sorry," she says, not facing him.

"Why, Lily?" Skot moves in, placing his hands high up on her arms.

She turns, shifting her eyes to his, seeming to have to force the connection.

"For the trouble I caused at the Ball."

"You didn't cause any trouble," he is quick to reply, smiling at her warmly.

"I should have ignored those guys. I ruined the evening."

"No, Lily." He embraces her. "You did not ruin anything, and the evening is not yet over."

They remain like that for a time, then he feels her pulling back. It worries him, but he sees that she pulls in a breath then drops to her knees and nuzzles into his crotch. He is taken by it, a bit startled, though he shows none of this. There is also an undeniable surge at his loins. He watches her, and she turns those eyes back up to his, and there is an altogether different appearance to them now.

"I was a bad Pet. I'm sorry."

"You are not a bad Pet."

"We went there to have fun," she continues, still nuzzling, and he feels her chin moving along the growing length of his organ, "And I got too upset by those guys. It could have been bad. I was bad. I ought to be punished."

He reaches down with his right hand, caressing the side of her face, and she presses into that touch, turning to kiss his palm.

"Are you mine, Pet?"

She nods, then kisses his thumb, turning her head to slip her lips about it, suckling the length, looking back up at him as she nods again. "Mmhmm."

"Good," he intones, the pace of his voice smooth and slow, "Then I will punish you, but not for what you did at the Ball, just *because*."

She nods again, still pulling on his thumb with the suction of her alluring mouth.

183

He places gentle pressure on her jaw. "Get up now, and I want you to go to the bedroom and take off all your clothes, except your shoes, turn to face the bed, and wait there."

She nods again, rising, and he watches the shift and tease of what little light there is as it plays over her latex dress, suggesting along her curves. He does not wait long before he follows, but he does try to give her enough time.

When he enters the room, she has done as told, standing nude save for her high heels, facing the bed. He drinks in the sight of her spectacular body, noting the accentuations as found by the dim illumination emanating from outside the room. He takes his time, letting her ponder, and he moves to the nightstand, removing two items, one of which is a lighter. Soon enough, he has brought a few candles to flame to add to the ambience, hoping to increase the warmth of their sharing.

He then moves to stand behind her, very close. He can hear her breathing. He inhales her scent, then uses his free hand to collect her hair, holding it somewhat tightly, and he moves it aside, pulling, and her head tilts in that direction. He then leans in, placing kisses on her nape, increasing the intensity of the affections as he does until he is using his teeth. Her breath pulls in quicker than before, more audible, then follows with a slightly stunted exhale as he applies the most pressure yet. He then stops, letting go of her hair and stepping back.

"Get on the bed, Pet, on your hand and knees."

He watches as she does so, continuing to look over her enticing form. She glances over, briefly, then lowers her head, causing an arch to her back and a greater prominence to her rear end.

She starts when she feels the first spank, the first sharp touch of the black leather paddle. A grunted exhalation is released on the second which quickly follows, then a third, and more, and before long she is emitting short, sharp whimpers. He does not stop until he has delivered a dozen at least, taking his time between each, savoring it, noticing the subtle change of color to her flesh. Lilja feels the tingling burn as her skin flushes, taking on a pink shade atop its usual pale.

He stops, setting the paddle atop the bed, and he gently caresses her behind, rubbing and squeezing, and she emits a light sound of pleasure, moving her hips as he does so. He lets his fingertips move teasingly

SWORD OF THE BUTTERFLY

close to her pussy, but he does not directly touch. He bends at the waist, adding some gentle kisses to her skin, and another humming response emerges from her throat.

He picks up the paddle, and he sees as she stiffens in anticipation. A shudder, almost imperceptible, courses through her lithe form as he sets the paddle against her right butt cheek. He does not resume the spanking, instead rubbing over her with the instrument. He pulls away then, letting her again expect and wonder, but again, he does not spank. He walks away, and she visibly relaxes. He ponders blindfolding her, but she does not overly follow him with her eyes.

When next he stands behind her, he holds the black flog. She takes in another, short breath when the ends of the lengths touch and caress over her back, that intake turning to a pleasant hum. She has felt the sting of this one before, too, many times, and she has some idea what to expect. He spends some more moments just moving the tentacle-like strands over her back and rear end, and she begins writhing with it, moving her body sinuously.

Then the whipping continues, and she gasps, taken unawares as he has lulled her. The sound of the flog is quite different than that of the paddle, and the sensation it delivers is also different, deceptive, sometimes giving one a sense of ease as though there will be no intense pain. After some time, though, of the rippling strikes, that changes. Her whimpers rise to cries, even moans, and soon that pink shade to her lovely skin has spread. He pauses many times to tease at her flesh with the lengths, giving way to a riotous array of sensations.

When he stops, her breathing has increased. She holds herself taut, eyes closed, all but trembling, and he experiences his own surge of arousal to see her thusly. He feels his erection pushing at his trousers, wanting to be released. He wonders where she is, mentally, if she has retreated into a more private space of her own, riding and reeling over the many feelings.

He takes his time disrobing, his eyes kept on her the whole time. He sees her from the side, bent there on the bed, still catching her breath, still with her head down on the covered mattress, the duvet showing signs of having been pulled by her grasping hands. Her eyes open when the sound of his zipper interrupts the other noises, and though she does not raise her head, he sees the gleam in her eyes, and she tugs at her bottom lip with her teeth.

"Turn onto your back, Pet."

She gives a very brief nod, doing as told, and he sees the rise and fall of her pert breasts, the nipples quite firm and pointed atop that soft flesh. He reaches forward, hands sliding under and grabbing her slender thighs, and he tugs her down so that she is on the edge. He slowly removes her shoes, depositing them on the floor.

Her legs stay spread, held up and apart by her more than capable muscles. He glances at her naked pubis, then back up to her, and she smiles shyly. He then takes his stiff cock in hand and nudges in, pressing it against her delicate lips, pushing forward with his hips to glide it along the length of her pussy, massaging her with it.

She gasps, and he is inclined to agree. He can feel the wetness there, the deep, nigh undeniable invitation. He wants to be inside her, but he manages to refrain. He feels a throbbing as her hips gyrate slowly, then shudder somewhat as he travels again over the rising bud of her clit.

"Oh, Skot, I want you inside me," she pleads.

He can take no more, so he now guides the swollen crown of his cock into her wet depths, finding her open, eager, and receptive. He slides his length within, delving until he can go no further. She emits another sharp gasp, and he responds with a lower, more forceful exhalation. He moves his hands to her thighs, holding her legs down, using her flexibility as he pushes his weight upon her, thrusting himself in and out of her moist channel.

She clutches about him as he penetrates her, replying to his drive with presses of her pelvis and flexing of her muscles. She knows he likes this, though it generally results in a quicker conclusion to their lovemaking. She does not mind, wanting this more for him than herself. She knows he is attentive to her, sometimes almost obsessively insistent, but she feels it is important to please him right now.

She holds her arms up, slid under the many pillows, grabbing at them, then finding the top of the covers, discerning that they provide greater resistance, so she pulls and tugs at them, writhing and gyrating, feeling the surges of pleasure, but mainly hoping he likes what he sees.

SWORD OF THE BUTTERFLY

She feels him release her thighs and lean forward, groping and fondling of her breasts, and she moves her legs about him, grabbing of him as she crosses her ankles, using her strength to hold him tight and pull him closer. He falls more forward, though still held back by his feet being on the ground, and he kisses her chest and neck, then finds her mouth. They gasp and moan together, their hips thrusting as they exchange the meeting of lips and tongue, speaking in a universal language of need and love.

She wants this, though she is still often taken with the doubt that she does not know truly what it is or how to attain it. She trusts in him, wants to make him happy, and she knows he cares deeply for her. And the pleasure, they do bring each other pleasure, and as her thoughts return more to the now, she can tell he is close.

"Please cum for me, Skot, *please*," she begs.

"I will, Pet, for you."

She holds him even tighter, arms and legs about him, and he thrusts harder, harder, but it does not take much, and soon he expends himself inside her, his noises louder now, his back taut, legs also strained, as he feels his orgasm take him.

They remain in their close embrace, catching their breaths, feeling the warm, sweaty flesh, experiencing the headiness they have created. After a time, he moves, kissing her, which she returns, then he moves from atop her, and he reaches for a nearby nightstand, retrieving a folded towel from one drawer.

"Do you need this?" he asks her.

"No, thank you," she murmurs, barely shaking her head, then she shifts to something more comfortable, pulling herself up to rest on a pillow, curling into a quasi-fetal position, her back now to him.

He moves closer to her, placing a hand on her, touching of her gently.

"That's nice," she finally comments, her voice an airy whisper.

"Lily?"

"Yes?"

"What's wrong?"

It takes a moment, but she finally turns onto her back, looking up at the ceiling. He continues to softly caress her with his one hand, looking upon her with obvious concern.

"Those two guys … back at the Ball …"

He nods, stifling his own urge to give voice, letting her speak. "I was very angry with them, too angry, and I was staring at them, ready … and I was half-expecting their eyes to glow red."

"What?" he says, brow furrowing, "You thought they might be demons?"

"No." She exhales noisily. "Of course not, but … I was so taken by anger, even a sort of fear and paranoia, I guess, and I was almost willing it, like thinking, 'show yourself, so I can deal with you'."

He pulls in a slow breath, so many things there on the edge of his lips, but he remains quiet, thinking. She seems to be doing the same. Instead of speaking further, he helps to pull the covers back, then settles himself in close to her, both of them now fully on their sides. He slips his arms about her, cuddling into her backside, kissing her gently.

They both eventually fall asleep.

*****

He sits in the secluded booth, the sense of isolation more delivered via the fact that there is more space around him than most of the others in here. The place is a somewhat nice drinking establishment, and judging from the décor and most of those inside, it sprang up to provide service to a particular subset of the multicultural city.

The bar offers many choices, but most of the bottles are various brands of vodka, some reasonably well known, others imported at some cost in order to satisfy the particular and varied palates of its clientele. Local vodkas are to Russia what local beers are to Germany, and many of those who have expatriated here like the taste of home.

Though the place does not exclusively serve those who may make their living outside the laws and norms of the Establishment, it generally seems that a good portion of the customers are indeed of that ilk. Even so, they all know who he is or know enough of how he is treated that they give him a wide berth.

SWORD OF THE BUTTERFLY

The music is a sort of dark, pop rock, not to his liking, but he has it removed from his focus. It is also not turned up too loud. He presently sits alone, a short glass before him, empty, though close examination would show the vestiges of moisture indicating he has recently drank. The bottle of vodka also on the table is about three quarters full. His tattooed hands hold a small, leather bound book, one that happens to be a diary, and he carefully turns one page, showing a delicateness and care that some might be disinclined to expect from him.

His eyes move, imbibing the words on the page, and as though without thinking, he reaches for the bottle, pouring a decent measure of the clear liquid into the glass. He brings it to his lips, eyes angling to stay on the pages as he tilts his head back enough to drink nearly the entire serving. He returns the glass to the surface of the table, his fingers not breaking contact with it. He reads.

Once he completes these pages, he finishes the drink, but as he prepares to continue, his peace is interrupted. One of the nearby sentries, a large man who wears a dark suit much like that of his employer, steps nearer, waiting. The man's eyes settle on the guard.

"Boss?"

Volkov perks his eyebrows as if his focus ought to be permission enough.

"Azim is here."

He nods, bringing up the thin length of fabric attached to the book and using it to mark his page before setting the journal aside.

A man is admitted to the vicinity. He has dark hair, thick, the suggestion of a tight waviness, and the obvious signs of it not being too well cared for. He also has a prominent, hooked nose, and a scraggly growth of beard. He slips into a chair opposite the softer, more comfortable bench that makes up the booth, eyes glancing about furtively, then upon Volkov.

The crime boss just looks back at him, waiting, so the man produces a small pouch, setting it on the tabletop and untying the coarse rope that threads about its neck. Though it is subtle, the nearby sentries pay close attention. Nothing dangerous comes out, instead the man produces a rather large, gleaming, dark red gem, and he sets it atop the small satchel, then gestures toward it with both hands as a sort of presentation. He then sits back.

Volkov looks at the stone, silently studying it for a moment, then back at Azim. He reaches forward, sliding the sack and the rock upon it to himself. He peruses it more closely.

"What is this?" asks an accented, female voice.

The woman who stands there is well-dressed, though not without an obvious intent to display her body. She wears a dark, clinging dress, a bold swathe of color coiling about, tapered just below her right breast and broadening as it curves around to eventually meet the hem. Her coltish legs are displayed from upper thigh to ankle, where the stylish and quite tall heels completely encase her feet. Her hair is a shocking blonde, obviously fake, but all part of the look she cultivates. She holds a drink in one hand, leaning onto the bench, one foot still on the ground, obviously quite permitted and comfortable to be this close to Volkov.

"I am trying to determine that," the boss utters, paying her little mind.

"It is the stone you asked me to procure," Azim announces, desperation creeping into his tone, "It is the Orac-"

His voice stops as the boss holds up a hand in an obvious command to cease. Volkov goes closer, staring into the remarkable looking jewel's depths. The woman also leans in, one hand slipping over the man's shoulders.

"It is beautiful," she intones after some time of relative quiet.

Volkov's concentration broken, he looks up at her from his studying position. He does not look upset, but the cold stare he gives her is the sort that might cause fright in any number of people in his employ. She just looks back at him, also calm. He turns his face to more fully point at her, then raises his chin, and she leans in close. Words are exchanged, the two speaking in Russian, and then she saunters away, returning to other ladies gathered at the bar, all of a similarly stylistic bent. She is greeted boisterously, her name coming from their painted lips - Yelena.

The boss goes back to studying the gem, eventually pouring himself another vodka. He downs it, somewhat slowly, then sets the empty glass on the tabletop just as his eyes settle on the man across from him.

"It is the stone," Azim reiterates.

SWORD OF THE BUTTERFLY

"You will be paid," Volkov states, his voice somewhat deep, gravelly, "You brought me object I asked for, so you will be paid, but I will determine if it is particular stone I seek."

His eyes cut away, and the sentry returns, none too subtly encouraging the visitor to rise from his chair and leave the area.

After he has placed the jewel back into its pouch, put it away and is pouring another drink, Yelena returns, slipping fully into the bench and Volkov's lap. He holds out his glass, a look of chastisement on his features. She smirks, then leans in, stealing a very quick kiss from his lips.

"Will stone be present for me?" she asks, speaking again in Russian.

"No," he flatly answers.

Her smirks grows, and she snorts a short exhale. Yelena sips of her drink, something darkly colorful in a martini glass, snugging her bottom more firmly into his lap.

"I *am* working," he tries.

"Pah," she slits her eyes at him, lips pursing, continuing in the Slavic language, "You are reading book, drinking vodka, then buying beautiful stone. We are at bar, Kazimir."

"And I am working at bar."

"Just because you pour own drink does not mean you work here."

He narrows his eyes at her, and she leans in close, whispering, "Do you wish to draw blood tonight?"

She pulls back, and he continues to look fully at her, again giving that almost unreadable stare that in nearly anyone else would cause fright. In her, it causes a nearly ubiquitous smirk.

"I might," he says, and then he glances over to see some other men approaching; he pushes on her, obviously wanting her to again leave.

She stands, making a show of it, looking back at him, perking her rear out a bit. He takes in that sight, and she grins, walking away just as others of his organization arrive at the table. His demeanor changes as he hears their reports.

"Nothing," he comments, summing up the information presented to him.

"Sorry, boss," one of them dares to speak, and Volkov's eyes snick over.

191

"Are you vigilante?"

The man's eyes widen, and he leans back in his chair. "No," he says, obviously confused and scared, eyes then looking about.

"Then do not apologize."

The man breathes a sigh of relief.

"Vigilante wants to continue to operate on his terms," Volkov speaks, pouring more out of the bottle, sloshing a smaller than usual portion into the glass. "That needs to change, so, we will offer bait."

Once said, his eyes move over and settle on Alec before the vodka is drained.

*****

The place is in the City's limits, but it is right on the edge, in a reasonably isolated area, as if specially chosen. It has taken them a good half hour to get here. Quain thinks this locale is not the only thing on the edge, noting some tension in his partner.

"Are you alright, Kahler?" he asks as they are pulling up to the small hovel of a makeshift building, other cars already here, the area being cordoned.

She applies the auto's parking brake with likely more force than is necessary, casting a sidelong glance at him.

"Yes," she offers the clipped response, then exits the vehicle.

Quain follows, standing up and leaning onto the roof of the sedan. Kahler peers at him.

"We're detectives, you know?" he says as the silence stretches.

"Yes, and we have a job to do in there."

"Have you ever built a house?"

"No," she says, then does a quick check of herself, making sure she has all she needs, but when she looks back, her new partner is still just standing there, leaning on the car. "What?"

"Without a good foundation, it doesn't matter how well you build the rest. It's all going to crumble sooner or later."

"Thank you, I'll keep that in mind when I change careers." She heads toward the structure.

He catches up with her easily, despite her determined pace.

"It's a metaphor," he persists.

She glances up at him as they walk. "I'm not the most subtle person."

"No shit."

He sees her try to suppress it, but the grin takes on her lips. She pushes her tongue into the lower part of her mouth, looking down, slowly shaking her head. Then she stops, turning to face him, squinting against the sunlight.

"Okay, Contee. No, I'm not okay. My daughter got in trouble in school for fighting, and this is not the first time. I've seen enough of this shit to tell that it's probably not going to get better anytime soon."

"Oh, come on," he chides, leaning back from the waist, arms crossed, "I doubt she's a hardened criminal. She's probably just acting out for attention."

"I'm not a home builder, and you're not a child psychologist," she says, some of her levity drained.

"Right, fine, gotcha."

They resume heading to the derelict-looking building.

"I appreciate the concern," she offers, forced, more polite than sincere, "I've got a job to do, both as a detective and a mother, and both are hard, and both will get done."

"Right. But if you need anything, even just to talk or vent, or hell ... do you box?"

She pauses again, giving him an askance look.

"Why?"

"I do some fitness boxing, nothing fancy. I thought you might like a chance to beat up on your new, annoying partner."

"I've had training in Krav Maga and kick boxing. Do you want to rescind that offer now?" she announces, moving again.

"Nope," he says, grinning.

She lets another curl touch her lips, again looking down as though to somewhat obscure it, but both their expressions disappear as they turn and confront the awaiting scene.

It had registered on a seeming subconscious level, but the smell of cinnamon, though strong, is overpowered by the stench of blood and death. The place is basically a room, four sides, a shoddy roof, mostly made of wood, save for the rickety garage door that has been put in one side to act as a strangely accessible door. It faces away from the approach, and is open, presumably to let some air in, but it is also letting the same out.

"Detectives," speaks a voice, and both look over to see a bespectacled man from Forensics addressing them.

Quain wonders at how quickly this guy must have gotten here, but he doesn't voice it. The scene is far too over-bearing to worry about such things. The man begins giving them a briefing, but Quain feels a sense of anger and even some brooding shock, despite his experience, and he takes it all in with very little active reception.

The smell of cinnamon and other spices is almost cloying. There are some plastic cups strewn about, the empty vessels stained with what looks to be wine, especially judging from the voided bottles. There are candles, but they have been burnt down or blown out. The body hanging suspended from the ropes is that of a child, no more than preteen, if that, though the condition of the corpse makes any such precise determination difficult at this point.

The victim also seems to be male, but again, condition of the body, along with presumed age and thus lack of development, prohibits a real conclusion. The Crime Scene Investigator mentions that exact cause of death is unknown at this time, but it is obvious the victim has been split open vertically from neck to pelvis, much of the viscera hanging or emptied in a congealing, dark mess.

They let the man go about his tasks, handling some of their own business as quickly as possible in order to get the body down and taken away. It affects them both, though they do their best to contain it, standing back, thinking out loud.

"It could be the same people who killed those other kids."

"It could," she agrees, "But that's a bit premature."

"Yeah, I know." He studies the grisly scene. "It's ritualistic."

"Like a serial killer's fucked up fantasy?"

"Maybe like the murder of that journalist … what was his name?"

"Who?" She turns to look at him, her own brow now furrowing like his.

"The blogger. The one who was investigating the child prostitution."

SWORD OF THE BUTTERFLY

"Wentreck?"

"Yes, that one."

"Too soon."

"I know, I know," he continues, nodding, then exhales, looking at the scene, making a face of disgust, then looking back at her, "This is messed up, though. Too much of this already here. We've got to stop it."

"Yes, that's our job, and I plan to do it."

"What if ...," he begins, and she is still mainly focused on the horrible scene, jotting information in her small notebook. "What if we could get help?"

"We have help. We've got Forensics here, and we have the resources of the department. We can check with Marek and Graner, if you want, see if it does match up with anything in their case," she names the two detectives investigating the death of Wentreck.

"No," he says, and she looks up at him, curious. "I mean, well, sure, that's worth checking out, but I mean ... what if we could get help from *outside* the department?"

"You mean like informants?" she asks, now more confused and suspicious.

"Yes," he is quick to say, "Well, sort of."

"Sort of?"

He leans in close, whispering, "The vigilante."

She just stares. He has moved away, going back to ostensibly studying the scene, acting like he has not uttered a word.

"Are you serious?" she finally asks.

"Yep." He nods, once, still looking forward, as if they were two clandestine agents trying to have a secret conversation whilst under surveillance.

"Contee!" she insists, turning more to him, and he looks at her. "Are you *serious*?"

"I am, yes. I mean, it's not like I know the guy, but he has access to some pretty good intel. What if I might could get one of his informants to be an informant for us?"

"Wha-? Are you ser-?"

"Yes!" he all but shouts, chuckling a bit to relieve the tension, then he steps away, beckoning her to follow, which she does, and he continues, pitching his voice low, "Look, I was contacted by someone who claims to be an informant for the vigilante, and that really doesn't matter. What matters is that I think they have some good stuff on this child prostitution ring. That could help."

"Okay, okay. It *could*, *if* it is legitimate, and of course it matters. The vigilante is breaking the law, and anyone directly associating with his actions is also breaking the law."

"Right. You're right, and I'm not on task to bring in the vigilante. I want to bring in the mother fuckers who did *that*."

A short moment passes, his eyes drilling into her, not accusatory but demonstrative.

"Okay." She exhales, then nods. "Okay," she says more firmly, "I want that, too. Frankly ... the vigilante is also not on my radar of law enforcement," and her pause makes him realize she has amended what she had planned to say, "If you have something that could help us, then great, but ... Let's be adults here - you know your reputation in the department, and I am not asking you to defend yourself, but you do need to prove yourself with me."

He scowls.

"Hey, tough shit if you don't like that," she pushes, and he mellows, realizing he deserves it, and she sees the change, nodding once. "Good. Let's get some good, legitimate, preferably *legal* information on this, and then yes, let's get the mother fuckers who did it."

CHAPTER EIGHT

Lilja is a bit surprised when she is told someone is here to see her. Barring the recent developments, her job is largely calm, some might even think it boring, and she rarely gets unscheduled visitors that are not a student or part of faculty. The woman waiting for her in the lobby makes her think of the time she met Skothiam, though he, of course, had an appointment. She is seated in one of the few chairs, the furnishings scarce since hardly anyone ever really uses the lobby, and she rises as Lilja approaches.

She is young, likely of similar age as Lilja, and dressed very nicely, smartly, looking all too refined for this place. Her dark dress is quite form-fitting, along with the tight necklace of pearls. She places a light, thin smile on her lips, curling them up just enough to affect the polite expression. Her jaw is rather pronounced, strong, and it presses into further definition, as if the woman grinds her teeth together as opposed to really smiling. Her eyes are a striking grayish-blue, and her dark hair is short, slicked down and parted on the left, tapering down in its severe style, going toward her right ear. Lilja thinks she glimpses something there, as though the intent is to hide a portion of the woman's brow, but she cannot be sure.

"Good morning," she greets, extending her hand, which Lilja accepts. "Anika Malkuth. Thank you for seeing me."

There is a very brief pause from Lilja when she hears the name, and she stares, openly, contemplatively, retrieving her hand.

"Why are you here?" she finally asks.

That smile touches up, hinting at a smirk.

"I would like to see the Book and that it is well secure."

"It is," Lilja intones, still unmoving, just looking back at the woman.

That polite smile never falters, and Lilja begins to find it insulting, annoying.

"I would very much like to see for myself. Please?" she adds, perking her sculpted eyebrows just enough to subtly accentuate the word.

Lilja knows this is part of the deal. Skot explained it to her, and she was even asked if she would accept it. She knows they did not necessarily have to gain her acquiescence to many aspects of the negotiation, and she is thankful and appreciative to Skot that he made that so. These two powerful, wealthy families did not need the approval of a librarian, even if she is Head Curator of the Rare Books Collection. They could have gone over her, using their considerable influence on those higher up in the university's power structure, or they could have undertaken any number of less than legal options to procure the tome. One of the points insisted upon by the Malkuths had been that they would be allowed a reasonable number of unscheduled visits, to not only check on the Book's security, but also see it still resides in this more public venue instead of disappearing into a Felcraft vault.

"Follow me, please," Lilja says, her tone rather cold, and she turns, walking away, the Malkuth in tow.

Anika manages to get beside her rather smoothly.

"There is no reason for this to be unpleasant, you know?"

Lilja briefly glances sidelong at her unexpected visitor, continuing down the stairs.

"A scheduled appointment would have been more pleasant."

"There is a purpose to 'surprise' inspections."

Lilja stops, her hand on the door to the collection's room, turning and looking fully at Anika.

"You imply a lack of trust," she says, "So, how *pleasant* do you expect this to be?" Before the other may answer, she opens the door, moving inside.

She does not bother with the sort of general tour she might with another type of visitor, instead giving a short glance to Marcel, politely dismissing him, and he gets a studied observation from Anika. Lilja proceeds to the rear, halting beside the display, turning to face the other woman, gesturing with her left hand to the book, then clasping them in her usual fashion.

SWORD OF THE BUTTERFLY

"There it is."

Anika flexes her jaw, and again that forced-seeming smile shadows toward a smirk, then she turns her focus to the tome, going in close. She raises a hand, well-manicured fingernails getting close to the transparent, plastic cover. She turns her eyes to Lilja.

"May I touch it?"

Lilja just looks at her.

"Will anything harmful happen to me if I do?" she amends.

"Not from a light touch, no. The security measures are more stringent when no one is here."

"Is that so?" the woman remarks, and her nails click on the rigid material, gliding over it, "But when someone *is* here ...?" She looks back at the woman who is both curator and guardian.

"If you were to attempt to gain entry, alarms would go off. It is not *unprotected* when we are here, only that some of the stricter securities are disengaged."

Anika rights herself, turning to face Lilja, nodding, slowly, thoughtfully. She looks about.

"Impressive," she seems to casually remark, "I assume there are many measures in place, but I note few of them."

She speaks with a detectable accent that possibly indicates she hails from somewhere much closer to here than does Lilja. It is obvious the woman is fluent with English, the intonation changing as though fluid, giving her to sometimes sound like a native speaker from America.

"The Malkuths have been apprised of the exact security in place, both mundane and extraordinary. If you wish, I can provide you with a copy of the details."

"That sounds rehearsed. Someone breached the defenses. Well, some*thing*, I suppose," she amends, though Lilja does not break the ensuing, baited silence. "But you did come right away and kill it, didn't you? Or ... did Skothiam help?"

Lilja assumes the Malkuths have since been given a report of the break-in. She does not know how much Skot chose to reveal of the details, so she elects to be careful.

"Of course, he did," she says, "I did not put all these defenses in place, just as I did not put in the basic alarms and cameras. This is a combined effort."

And now the lips of the other drop some pretense, pulling up to one side in a more obvious smirk.

"I meant that night, when it happened. Was he here?"

Lilja wonders why she is being asked such a pointed question, and she hesitates on how to answer, wondering if she ought to just refuse to talk of it, but she elects for a minimal, honest response.

"No."

Anika perks her eyebrows.

"You did good to stop the attempted thievery." The polished woman seems to give compliment, but Lilja does no more than look at her. "Though I suppose it was more the supernatural traps that really did the job."

Just as with the shallow praise, the librarian does not outwardly react.

"Well, the attempt was thwarted. Good. But that does mean they now know it is here."

Lilja says nothing to this.

"It is possible they may unleash a more open, concentrated attack."

More silence stretches, and Lilja finally gives a brief nod. "That is possible."

"Does that not worry you?"

"Is this part of the inspection?" Lilja returns, after another short moment of quiet thought.

"You are part of the security here, are you not?" Anika gives right back, speaking with a sharp undertone, that lingering curl gone from her lips.

"Are you here, then, to evaluate me?" Lilja shows she is not unwilling to engage, also portraying a cold, strong aspect.

"In some respects, I may be."

"I will make available to you all necessary information regarding the security systems in place, even down to detailed specifications, if you wish," Lilja informs, "You may ask any question you want of me, but I will not answer any question you ask. If I feel it is pertinent to your *inspection*, then I will answer. If you are unhappy with my not answering, or any of my answers, then I invite you to follow the proper channels in whatever way you see fit."

The little grin does not leave the other woman's lips. She steps closer, her heels resounding off the resilient flooring. She interlaces her fingers, holding her hands before her on bent arms. She stops, closer to Lilja, though not an improper or dangerous proximity, letting her hands fall loosely to her sides.

"My, my," she comments, "It seems the Felcrafts have chosen a worthy custodian. Good for them." She raises her chin, angling a somewhat downward gaze at the shorter woman, as though waiting for a response.

Lilja says nothing, just maintaining her observance.

Anika exhales through her nose, enough force to make it quite audible, and as she does, her face is lowered, the grin creeping more onto it.

"Denman has shared some information of you," she reveals, "I especially found interesting the part about you two helping Skothiam to close the Gateway."

"Did he mention about me holding my sword to his throat?"

Anika's eyes narrow, her lips pulling up more on one side, as she gives the petite woman a studied look. "No," she finally says, going back to the more polished, professional attitude, re-clasping her hands with the interlaced fingers, stepping away. "Though he did say that you project a cold exterior that is part professionalism, part challenge, and part defense. I see that is true, and just as he says, that exterior, as strong as it appears, may be quite easily chipped." She turns, pausing, fixing her eyes fully on the other. "If not cracked."

Lilja seethes a bit, but she fights to not show it, for she knows she has been chipped. The woman is indeed testing her, and she let her get under her skin. Part of that is because of Lilja's distaste for Denman, but it does not excuse her lapse. She takes some slow, deep breaths.

"I'd like to examine the Book," Anika states, still sounding polite, though the request comes off rather bluntly.

"Of course," Lilja replies, having regained her professionalism, "When I see the appointment has come through the proper channels, you will have the same sort of supervised access as others have been granted."

This does not faze Anika at all, almost as if she has thrown it out as an offering.

"Well, I doubt that will happen, but it would be interesting to see what all the fuss is about."

Lilja has seen and heard enough to now realize that the woman and Denman are indeed cut from the same cloth, though the elder man is obviously more experienced. Both of them are possessed of a certain culture and charm that would grant them easy access to people and places. Were the gatekeeper more susceptible and naïve, such would happen here. She realizes this is all part of the test, though if this woman and her family truly are aware of what all Denman did last year, then the futility of this attempt should be known to them.

Superfluous testing, perhaps, but then, one may hide more subtle scratches within.

"Thank you for your time, Miss Perhonen," Anika finally speaks into the growing silence, "I'll show myself out."

Lilja follows, keeping a wary eye on the woman. She fully expects her to pause, door handle in hand, to deliver some parting question or barb or some such, but she does not. She merely leaves.

*****

Therese stares at the slim screen of her laptop, eyes not even reading the information. There is an abundance of it, many windows of various sizes all over the monitor, a seeming chaos. One holds the most available real estate, emblazoned with an undeniable bid for attention.

"How could you let this keep happening?"

The whispered words fall from her lips, going into no other ears than her own. It is as if they had to be vocalized, given birth in sound to add weight, to reflect the intensity of what she feels.

"How could you!" she cries out, suddenly clenching her fists, bents arms rising up with a surge of motion.

She lowers her chin, eyes now clamped shut, trying to fight off a further expression of emotion. She pulls in a slow breath, her chest rising

SWORD OF THE BUTTERFLY

within it beneath the well-worn white tank top. After a time, she raises her face, again looking at the screen, and the shine of tears may be seen at the bottoms of her eyes. A scowl then slowly traces over her lips, and with a quick, deft movement of her right hand, she puts the computer into sleep mode.

She stands, slowly, and pauses to take in another slow breath, head still hanging somewhat. She grabs the coffee mug, glancing inside, reminding herself it is nearly empty, so she walks the near distance to the kitchen counter, emptying the cooled contents into the sink. She adds fresh water, shoving the cup into the microwave and turning it on.

She has a way with gadgets, contraptions, electronics, and the virtual pathways and codes used within them. She is not so good with people. She thought she had left behind such emotions as she now feels. She had become about as cold and unfeeling as the very machines with which she so often interfaces. She's hardly spoken to Akua of late, and though they might often go a good length of time without seeing each other, they have never gone this long without engaging in some form of communication.

Even then, she was never that deep into it. It was for fun, more like friends with benefits, if she has anything that comes close to the normal social concept of a friend.

But now, she experiences these annoying, unexpected sensations, like water seeping into the long-dried cracks of a desert landscape, one that has thirsted so long, it has forgotten it even possessed such a craving. She *feels*.

Therese is not comfortable in her own skin. She prefers her online persona of the Sparrow, hacker and data gatherer extraordinaire, yet she now finds herself caring. She cares what is happening to these children, but this is not just some awakened sense of social responsibility and justice, no, she also realizes she cares quite deeply for one person in particular.

And that person is disappointing her.

She pulls the ceramic cup out of the microwave, absently spooning some instant coffee into the now hot water, stirring, then adding some sweetener, mixing it all together before bringing it up and having a taste.

It does not prove pleasant, but she doesn't care. She's gone through cases of this particular coffee. It's cheap and simple.

Her computer beeps back to life, and she pads over, sitting and nigh robotically executing the commands to see what is asking for her attention. More information pops up, and she scans it quickly, the mug still held in one hand.

"No shit," Therese mutters, "I already know about this."

She scans through the entire message from Macar, then sends him a very short reply, eloquently expounding her knowledge and abilities in very few words. She supposes he is doing this as a show of good faith in their deal, but she is the cyber expert. He needs to more concern himself with finding things on the ground, as it were. Maybe he is testing her, or reminding her just how valuable she is, or is not, to him.

She's working on a report that details some of the financials of the local criminal organization responsible for the child prostitution. It has not been the easiest to discern, Not due to any state-of-the-art defenses or fancy financial techniques, but because it is quite old-fashioned. They seem to be mainly dealing in cash, and then their efforts to launder it are more difficult to find. Well, the points of origin are more difficult to find. She's located a few, changed some tactics, and the greater picture is beginning to take a more focused shape.

She still ponders what to do once the report is ready. This is the sort of thing that could cause a lot of trouble, and she'd prefer that not come back to bite her. She's hoping the police, or the vigilante, stop them sooner. She's hoping that Macar might even come up with something good to give to the cops, and then she won't have to go after the criminals' money. She'll be ready if worse comes to worse. As she ponders this, she again becomes more upset.

She goes to one of her myriad email accounts, composing a rather terse, demanding missive to the contact whom she presumes is the vigilante.

She rises from the chair, stepping away from her work station, sipping of the coffee. She meanders to the small kitchen window, the one that is marred and stained and shows little to nothing of the outside world. Even if it were spotless, Therese would have a great view of the mundane wall of the neighboring building and little else.

SWORD OF THE BUTTERFLY

She gazes into and through the window all the same, thoughts wandering.

*****

The message is received, but it is not the motivation.

She is out, having found the time to analyze the data, and this proves a suitable place to strike. It's small, somewhat out of the concentration of other operations, and it is a one story building. She feels better prepared.

A part of he wonders if this place has been left so as a sort of trap. The other potential areas of activity have been in dense parts of the city, those used by other criminals, not often frequented by the police outside of specific calls. They have been under heavy guard and generally in large, partially abandoned structures or operating out of places working as fronts.

None of them have been easy to find, but she took her time vetting this one, and it has proven to be good intel and a good place for a mission. She is not sure of the exact number of guards, but her other surveillance and reports suggest around a half dozen. She also is not exactly sure of the number of children inside, but she does know that the place has been built-out into very small rooms, basically packaging the small, young humans into cells. She's seen at least three different children during her observance, and she assumes there are more. She feels confident enough to say she knows there are more, but she then checks herself, not wanting to fall to any mistakes of assumption. She's not intending to abscond with them, anyway. She plans to neutralize the guards, secure the area, and call the police - her general modus operandi.

She crouches in the dark on the southeastern side of the building, the face of it here somewhat small, comparatively. She holds the FN P90, suppressor affixed, the fifty-round magazine loaded with subsonic ammunition. She casts her eyes about, hoping she is not somehow spotted by some random person, upsetting the entire mission. She needs to get inside. There is a window here, and she has her center punch tool amongst her gear, but she knows from prior reconnaissance that the windows are all boarded up. She could still get through, but she'd need more time. And such would increase the chance of an alarm being raised.

She keeps watch around the corner, peering at the main entryway, the smallest bit of her that she can manage being exposed. There would not show much more of her than a dark figure, a deep blue eye peering out from beneath the black-painted brow. Finally, it happens. A client shows up, knocking on the door, and after a short exchange with the intercom, the door is unlocked.

Time for speed now. She covers the distance with a rapid walk that grows into a jog, barrel of the P90 pointed downward, held close to her chest, ready to be raised and used in an instant. She keeps herself low to the ground, following the man through the door in such a way that he does not realize it, using him as concealment. She then grabs the customer, and she kicks him in the back of the knee, pushing his head on the doorframe, then leaping over his quickly crumbling form in order to get inside.

Her eyes sweep quickly, taking in the scene as she has been taught to do. There is a raised area, forming something of a counter, behind which stands the 'host', a young man with scraggly, dark hair. He has already begun walking out, a knowing smirk on his lips in greeting for what must be a regular customer. That expression drops instantly, covered in shock and fright. He does not immediately appear to be armed. The other two men in here are, and they level their weapons at her.

She continues moving toward the receptionist, her weapon pointed, diminutive frame held low, and she fires quickly, barrel adjusting after the first pair, delivering two more coughing shots, and both sentries go down, hit in the upper arm, one also in the right side of his chest near his shoulder.

When she turns her attention back, the host has dived behind the counter, whimpering and calling out in fear. There must be a panic button, and she needs to keep him from pressing it. She glances up and notices the camera and realizes she has likely already been seen. The children are already in danger. She hears rapidly approaching footsteps, and she gets behind the bar, readying herself. The young guy cries out in fright, trying to curl up in more of a ball, hoping to push himself into the wall and be as far from the intruder as possible.

SWORD OF THE BUTTERFLY

    The other three guards come barreling up through the center hallway, uncaring or ignorant of basic tactics, as this routes them into a limited area and makes them easy targets. They fire wantonly, one holding a submachine gun, the other two unloading their noisy shotguns. The receptionist cries out as a projectiles gets through the meager wood of the counter, hitting him in the leg. Beneath the ruckus, she fires her weapon with much more care and precision, and soon the other three are in a crumbled heap like their comrades, some semi-conscious, others moaning, cursing, all of them bleeding from painful wounds.

    She turns to the man with her behind this area of concealment, and he whimpers in pain, holding tight to his leg. He finally notices her attention, and he raises his hands in a warding gesture.

    "No, no! Don't kill me! Please don't kill me!" he cries out, cringing from the wound, moving his hand back down in a flash to cover the area.

    Without a word of response, she quickly zip-ties his wrists and ankles, also ignoring his further protests and shouts of pain. She is not sure if this is all the resistance. She feels fairly confident that no other clients are here, since no one had arrived during her lengthy surveillance before beginning the mission. She moves out, weapon ready, barrel moving from man to man, assessing if there are any threats. One is meekly trying to aim a pistol, his hands shaky, and the P90 coughs out, and he slumps, not dead, but out of the fight. She is more careful now, moving slowly, listening, wishing the receptionist would shut up. She hears cries from some of the children. She quickly zip-ties the guards, the customer she followed, then heads further in.

    All of the doors are locked from the outside, easily opened from the hallway, and within, she finds them. Some are frightened of her, of course, some are in a state more akin to near catatonia. She speaks to them in a calm tone, trying to reassure, trying to let them know they will soon be rescued, that she is here to help and more help is on its way.

    Then, in one of the rooms, she sees the explosives.

    She rushes about, alarm gripping her, and she sees that other rooms are also wired, and she runs back to the foyer.

    The receptionist cries out as he is grabbed, hurt, pain purposely applied. Lilja does not take care in handling him, wanting it rough.

"You're going to blow this place up, aren't you? You're going to kill the children? I won't let you!"

His protestations go unheard or ignored as she holds him by the neck, jerking forth her Glock to point it at his head.

"I won't let you!" she yells, her voice a force of its own, drowning out his continued cries.

She spies movement in her peripheral vision, and she angles her gun in that direction, pointing it with the unerring precision of one who has spent many hours in practice. The child screams, freezing in place.

Her eyes are held open, just like those of the young girl, just like those of the bound young man, both of them looking at her with abject fear. She blinks, pulling in a sharp, stunted breath, and she releases the man, realizing he had not been moving at all as though to trigger the explosives or call for more help. She re-holsters the pistol, holding her hands out, fingers splayed. The young girl is crying.

"It's okay. It's okay. Help is coming," Lilja tries to sooth, but as she steps nearer, the child emits a strangled sounding whimper from within her throat, and she turns and runs back to her cell.

Lilja takes several deep breaths, then pulls forth the disposable mobile phone, calling the police, letting them know the number of perpetrators, how they are armed, their condition, the number of children, and informs of the explosives. When the operator demands to know who she is, to know how she knows all of this, she calmly sets the phone on the top of the reception counter, not disconnecting the call.

She stands there, trying to regain herself, and she waits. She steps through the front door, and she hears the sirens in the distance. She then leaves.

When the emergency services have arrived and secured the area, they know this is the vigilante's work, but they also note the increased violence. Though the vigilante has not been as active for some time, they know that guards are usually subdued through non-lethal means. These have all been shot, some in spots quite close to vital areas, requiring critical, emergency care. They wonder what this might portend. Is this a war?

Is this personal?

SWORD OF THE BUTTERFLY

*****

The meeting consists of more people than are in the hotel suite, the room having been acquired partially for this purpose. The place is not the kind David would usually choose, but he'd been directed here. He knows how to follow instructions.

He and Duilio sit in comfortable chairs about the small, circular wooden table. The entire room is warm, composed of soothing colors and conventional, if not a bit modern, décor. The sizable, high definition flat screen monitor is split in half, showing images of the two other people in obvious attendance – Skothiam, the Head of House Felcraft, and Asenath, the Head of House Malkuth. They are also able to see each other from their respective locations as well as the two in the hotel room. Zoe is in her own room, ruminating. It did not please her to fail to receive an invitation, but David has promised to talk to her afterwards.

"How is Anika?" Duilio carefully intones, his first vocalization since the appointment began, a slight pause in his cadence, as though he is somewhat intimidated by this whole thing.

"She is fine," Asenath smoothly speaks, the voice silken and polite, yet still managing to convey being bothered by this inquiry.

"Then why isn't she here?" David adds, his eyes moving minutely from the woman in charge of the rival family to his cousin and back. "No offense to Inspector Duilio, who did great under the circumstances, but shouldn't a more … direct representative of the Malkuths be here?"

"I am not direct enough?"

Skot manages to suppress anymore reaction to Asenath's words than closing his eyes briefly and pulling a slow breath in through his nose.

"I meant one of yours that was actually on the hunt."

Some time passes, and they begin to wonder if Asenath will merely refuse to reply, but she finally speaks, "This was a Felcraft hunt. We were just there to assist."

David's eyes shoot back to his cousin, realizing the implication of this.

"Thank you for saving her instead of leaving her there to die."

The experienced Hunter looks back over, his eyes narrowing slowly.

"You're welcome," he finally manages, begrudgingly.

209

"She *is* fine now, thanks to you, and as far as why she is not in attendance … ask your cousin."

Both men seem confused by this, both pairs of eyes looking at the other person on the monitor.

"Skot?" David finally nudges as more silence ensues.

"We'll talk about it in private, David. This is a joint debriefing of the hunt. The hunt is over. When the Demon makes itself known again, a new hunt will begin."

David finally gives forth a short nod, also realizing the implications of this. After a time, he finally sighs.

"It was a wild goose chase, just like I told Duilio. Even though we had Zoe, I think that thing could have lost us anytime it wanted to. It took us all over, for *miles*, then it finally led us into that mine. And though they would have been happy to kill all of us, its real goal then was to finally elude us," he continues, eyes again moving between the two figures on the screen. "What happened?"

"Something *has* happened," Skot finally admits, "But as of now, it's conjecture as to whether or not it's related. We're still looking into it."

"So," David presses, obviously displeased, "we have no idea where the Demon is?"

"We are no happier than you to know such a creature is walking this earth," Asenath interjects, "but if it just walks the earth, then there is no threat. Once it does something, we'll know."

David does not manage to conceal all signs of his seething, but he does no more than glare at the woman. He is not stupid. He knows this. He also knows that the Demon could do things, very terrible things, without their knowing it.

"That monster was one of the most powerful I've ever seen. It's amazing that any of us survived, and I only think we did because it let us."

"Come now," Asenath quickly says, "you're a better Hunter than that."

"You lost one." David steels a narrowed gaze at her, not bothering to hide his brewing anger. "Almost two. We *did* lose two. That Demon could have had us all. I already told you how it bypassed our defenses. It's killed at least a dozen people, probably more, and now it just

SWORD OF THE BUTTERFLY

disappears? No. One that strong doesn't get out that often. They're planning something."

"Of course, they are," Skot says, noting that he has kept Asenath from speaking, though she closes her rouged lips, waiting. "But as I said, this is a debriefing from *that* hunt."

Asenath gives a very subtle smirk. Of course they all have their ideas as to why this powerful skin wearer is here and why it made itself known as it did, then disappeared. Skot is trying to get his cousin to shut up about that since he does not wish to discuss such in mixed company.

"David is very driven," she observes, "I would assume he just wishes to continue the hunt and kill this Demon."

David and Duilio see Skot's eyes shift a bit, and this is from him moving his focus to the image of his rival on his own computer screen.

"I'll handle the affairs of my Family."

"Of course."

There is more talk of what happened. More questions asked by both Heads of the Families, and eventually the meeting ends.

Skot disconnects, then sits for a moment, collecting himself. He takes in some breaths, then reaches for the stout glass of vodka and soda just as she walks in.

"You witnessed the whole thing?" he asks of his sister.

The woman nods once. Skot turns in his chair, taking a decent swallow of the cocktail, noting the stark hit of the fresh lime.

"What do you think?"

"David is correct in his assessment," she replies.

Skot looks at her, his hand and wrist moving lightly, doing so to somewhat further mix the drink. He takes another taste, eyes on his sibling.

"They *are* related," she expounds, "The Demon is a piece on the chess board - a powerful one, and it was used to distract us from the half-breed. There is no way Lilja would have recognized it. How many of us have even ever seen one?"

"So, now what? Is the Demon going to try to get the Book?"

She notes the concern laden in his voice, and she wonders if he is more worried for the rare, powerful tome or its guardian.

"I am not sure, but the Infernal will try for the Book again."

211

He nods, contemplatively, looking away as he ponders. "Skot?"

A short moment passes, and he looks up. "Yes?"

"We must find the breeder."

He sighs, nodding. "I know, but we also have to be concerned for the safety of the Book."

"Can we not come up with some reason to temporarily remove it from the collection?"

"Probably, but it would not be easy, and it would take time. We left it there, because we accepted it to be safe."

"Then it is safe," Nicole iterates, gaining a look from him that might as well be the beacon of a lighthouse for all it tells her. She files this away for later thought and possible discussion. "We must find the breeder."

Skot emits another exhale, this one louder, more forceful, and he stands.

"You're right. They can do too much damage with a breeder, and I cannot imagine the state of the poor person. We need to find and rescue them."

"Or put them out of their misery."

"As I said," Skot states, "rescue them."

She merely looks at him, that half-lidded, calm gaze that rarely changes. They know one another on many levels, though as with any other individuals, not entirely. They at least have an understanding with this.

"How do we find them, though? Do you have anything?"

"I might," she says, and he knows what that means, "Would you like me to speak to David about it?"

He considers this, then nods. "Yes, that may help. He was very agitated to have not gotten this one."

"Or would you rather he come here?"

Skot angles his eyes at her.

"Why would I want that?"

"It seems prudent to assume and prepare for the Infernal to try again for the Book. It might also be a safe assumption that the skin wearer will

SWORD OF THE BUTTERFLY

come here for that purpose. We might increase our defenses and conclude the hunt to our satisfaction at the same time."

"Our awareness of that helps, of course, but speak to him, anyway, about what you know."

She nods, taking her leave. Skot picks up his drink, preparing to head to the bedroom, where the woman he loves awaits.

At that same time, Duilio makes it into his own hotel room, and he is quite startled, for he did not expect anyone to be awaiting him.

"Inspector," the culture voice intones.

"Dammit, Denman." Duilio takes in a breath, trying to ease the tension of being so surprised. "Why do you do this *espionage* thing? Can't you just call me and tell me you want to meet?"

"Of course, I can." Denman smirks.

Duilio turns to fully face the seated man, hands going to his hips, and he presses his lips together, nodding slowly.

"Fine, then," he accepts, returning to his small tasks of depositing the contents of his pockets onto the counter, removing his jacket, and making a drink for himself. He does not offer one to his unexpected visitor.

He sits on the side of the large, plush bed, drinking quite generously of the whiskey he has poured himself.

"Well, what do you want?"

"You didn't think all was said and divulged in that little debriefing, did you?"

"I'm tired, Denman, and I did all that you *Malkuths* asked. Please say what you want to say or ask what you want to ask and let me get some sleep."

Denman's smirk increases.

"Do you hear the way you said that? The way you said my family name?"

"Uh?" Duilio replies, glass tilted up to his mouth, eyes on the other as he drinks more.

"You don't like us," Denman continues, leaning forward, a certain sound of amusement coating his words, "The corrupt career Interpol agent does not like the Malkuths."

Duilio fixes a narrowed stare on his visitor.

213

"Oh, please," Denman finally speaks, "Don't try to intimidate me."

"I was not," Duilio says, "but you *are* pissing me off. What is the point?"

"Ah, yes, well, I suppose there is no point to that," Denman admits, giving his own casual wave of one hand, before bringing it to its partner, holding them loosely together in his lap. "I have come to warn you, Inspector. We saw potential in you, so we recruited you. The Felcrafts did not. I don't care how well you and David may have gotten along. You are with us. You are not *one* of us, make no mistake, but you are now *with* us. You are an *asset* of ours. We do not lightly lose the assets we have so carefully chosen."

"You were rather flippant toward my safety in this first assignment."

"Our work is dangerous by its very nature. I don't suppose all of your dealings with Interpol … and other parties, were some glistening examples of safety."

A moment stretches, both men studying one another. Duilio's drink seems forgotten.

"Did you come here to threaten me?"

Denman perks his eyebrows, that ubiquitous smirk still on his handsome lips. "I thought I just did."

"Good. Consider me threatened. Now, may I please get some sleep?"

"Very good, Inspector. You will be happy to know that you passed the test." Denman rises.

Duilio looks up, still sitting on the side of the bed. "What test?"

Denman's grin increases, and the Italian does not like it one bit.

"The one where you get to live or die," he says, speaking in a casual, charming tone, "Though I am assuming you *want* to live."

"I *want* you to get out of my room. *Now*."

"Oh, I'll leave when I'm ready." Denman steps closer, looming. "And do not forget who is paying for this, so one may consider it more my room than yours, hmm?"

Duilio does not reply, his grip tightening on the glass, his eyes piercing into the other.

"There really is no point for you to get upset. You chose your life." Denman meanders away. "You did a fine job, too."

SWORD OF THE BUTTERFLY

He looks back over, angling a smile at the agent that causes more inner seething, and then, as quickly, the expression is gone for a very serious look.

"We'll be watching you, and we'll be in touch."

And then he leaves.

Duilio breathes a sigh of relief, realizing just how tense Denman man has made him. He looks into his glass, as though scrying of its contents. He then does make a prediction, his words a muttered leak.

"I hope there is enough booze in my room."

*****

In the midst of the warm-up, she feels a light tap on her shoulder. She looks at Miranda, a slight perk of her eyebrows an unspoken query. The tall, well-fleshed woman points a thumb toward the entrance.

"Looks like a new student."

Lilja looks over, her usual calm, open expression dissolves immediately as she sees Anika Malkuth nearing. The woman is obviously dressed to exercise in her form-fitting, black athletic shirt, sweat pants, and bare feet. Lilja meets her before she breaches the chosen area of the classes.

"What are you doing here?" she demands, voice low.

The light grin on the woman's lips does not falter.

"Good evening, Lilja. I noticed your classes are open to any woman eighteen years of age or older. Well, I qualify, so I thought I might attend."

"You want self-defense training?" Lilja presses, and she can sense in her side vision that some of her students are taking notice of the exchange.

"I'd like some from *you*, yes," Anika replies.

Lilja ponders this for a split second, getting the underlying meaning, and she nods once, a brief, economical gesture.

"Fine," she gives, then turning and going back to her class.

Everyone gathers around, then, though it is obvious some of the more regular students note that something seems off. They see a strange

215

tension in their teacher, and they rightly attribute it to the arrival of the new woman.

She goes easily into the warm-up routine, something like this not cracking the near subconscious knowledge of her moves and exercises, not after so much training of her own. She watches Anika. The woman is obviously fit, flexible, experienced.

"Class," she begins, once the warm-up is complete, and she has their collective attention, "We have a new student with us today – Anika."

This gets some smiles and greetings, which Anika returns with the characteristic Malkuth charm. Lilja notices, though, that Miranda, though polite, is very watchful, almost as if protective of her teacher and curious of what passed between the two. Lilja proceeds with a very abridged form of her usual speech for new arrivals. She expects, perhaps, a cynical reaction, but all Anika does is pay close attention.

"Anika, have you done any martial arts before?"

The open-ended question gets a further curl to her mouth, then she nods once, arms held easily at her sides as she speaks.

"I've had some combat training, and I have seen some combat," she informs, which gets some reaction from the others.

Lilja nods, trying to be more precise, "Only close combat training or some formal martial arts, too?"

"Yes."

Silence stretches out as the two look at each other. It is obvious Lilja wants more information, but Anika proves unwilling to elaborate.

"Any particular style?"

"No. I had a private teacher growing up."

This gets some further reaction from the others.

"Alright, then, let's continue while we're still warm," the petite redhead announces, clapping her hands together once.

Lilja proceeds to explain some new moves, adding to some basic instructions, then lets the students pair up. She is still not sure of Anika's abilities, though it is obvious the woman is far from a beginner, so she has one of her more experienced pupils work with her.

It is not long into the drill when the shout is heard, and everyone stops to look over and see that Anika has executed a wrist lock throw and hold, resulting in her partner tapping out. She releases the woman,

SWORD OF THE BUTTERFLY

helping her stand, as the others gather. Lilja hears appraising comments, some remarking how cool the move was, adding other praise in words, expression, and body language. One turns to her.

"Can you teach us that?" she asks.

Lilja remains quiet for a moment, noting the satisfied grin on Anika's mouth. The students are supposed to be practicing other moves, but one thing Lilja prides herself on is having interactive self-defense classes. Even though she senses this is a flagrant display and manipulation by the Malkuth, she will not ignore her student's requests.

"Okay," she gives in, trying to resume control of the situation. "For those who didn't see, our new student showed a good example of how to utilize a technique in a changing situation. Miranda, would you come here for a moment?"

The larger woman gives a single, curt nod, moving quickly to her long-time teacher's call, and Lilja proceeds to demonstrate and breakdown the move Anika has just performed. Soon enough, they are paired up again, practicing the lock and throw. She keeps a close eye on Anika, but the woman is at least now content enough to stay within the lesson, one she shaped and introduced.

The class proceeds with no further unexpected changes, though Anika continues to demonstrate a technique and charm that earns her fast credit with the others. She holds a fine balance between being accomplished but deferential, confident and polite, and it shows in how quickly she endears herself to most of them. Lilja keeps more than an impartial portion of focus on the Malkuth, and she catches the woman looking back at her from time to time.

Soon enough, the class ends, and Lilja feels an unusual relief. She proceeds to picking up as the others make their way to the locker room or exit, some having lingered to exchange more positive words with Anika. She somewhat loses herself in thought, figuring she knows why the woman came here but still curious, also somewhat upset to have been approached this way. The classes are something of a haven for her, even as their purpose is to be aware of and adaptive to risks and threats.

"So ..."

She looks up to see the very woman standing there, still in her workout clothes. The two of them are now alone, and the Malkuth wears the challenging smirk more openly on her lips.

Lilja rises from where she had been putting away more of the equipment, facing Anika fully, just looking at her.

"It's very nice. What you're doing here."

Lilja continues to look, remaining silent.

"How about a sparring match?" Anika pitches, seeming at the spur of the moment, but Lilja doubts much of anything the woman does is not calculated.

"No, the class is already dismissed."

Anika's head tilts a small fraction, almost as if she is surprised. She then proceeds to pull her shirt over her head, leaving herself in a dark sports bra. Lilja notes not only the obvious tone and development of the woman's abdominal muscles but also what looks like the crooked lines of a scar that disappears behind the garment, heading in the region of her heart. She is curious of it, but such is not a real concern at the moment.

"One sparring match won't hurt anyone," Anika states, and Lilja notes the subtle, sure movements of a practiced fighter as the woman goes into a combat stance.

She looks at the one she has challenged, waiting a brief moment. Lilja just returns the stare, not speaking, and Anika proceeds, moving closer. She does not run or launch an attack, but her intent is clear enough. Lilja has sparred many times, so she is no stranger to it. She makes no outward response, does not go into a fighting stance, but she is ready when the other woman finally nears enough and goes onto the offensive.

Lilja is not struck, but she is immediately surprised at how quick and strong Anika is, how fast and precise the kicks she launches. First comes a front kick, then a combination of punches, then another quick kick. Lilja dodges away and back, blocking some. Even with the speed and intensity, she knows Anika is testing her. No kicks of this kind were used in the class, of course, so Lilja has no early knowledge of the woman's capabilities in this regard.

Lilja moves aside, not wanting to be backed against the nearby wall, fending off or dodging more of Anika's tireless execution of moves. The

SWORD OF THE BUTTERFLY

woman is accomplished, but Lilja does not feel overly taxed in defending herself. It is a trial, though obviously unleashed with serious intent. Anika had implied as much at their initial meeting, and Lilja knows she is being evaluated. It is somewhat impractical, though, as she does not expect to engage in unarmed hand-to-hand combat with any demons if she can help it. This is more of the Malkuth's manipulation and other of their subtle, nefarious methods.

But she is evaluating Anika, too, and though the woman is good, she is not in Lilja's league.

She then sees the gleam in the other woman's eyes, that mischievous smirk still there amidst all of this, and Lilja decides she is done.

She drops her central gravity, rooting herself to the floor, the retreating over. She sees the next attack coming, mid kick, and she catches the limb, launching herself forward and sweeping the support leg with her own, slamming Anika onto her back, turning and twisting the held ankle, forcing her opponent onto her belly as she performs a backwards knee-lock.

"Aaaahh!" Anika cries out as the lock is pressed, but she does not tap.

Lilja glances toward the woman, angling better to see toward her face. She increases the pressure again.

"Gaaah! Okay, okay," in a breathless voice, and Anika taps out.

Lilja releases the hold, getting up, facing her opponent. She shows obvious signs of exertion, but her focus is calm, ready, her mouth a straight line. Anika rises, collecting herself, eyes assessing the shorter woman. She gives a single nod, as though of approval.

"You're very good," she remarks.

Lilja does not care or want it, so she silently gathers her bag and leaves.

CHAPTER NINE

"Despite the economic situation of the inhabitants of the area, violence of this level is virtually unknown to them, yet this rude awakening met them full force that evening. At least half a dozen casualties resulted from an exchange of gunfire between an intruder and armed guards at the location. Police have been rather quiet about why there were such guards there in the first place.

"One might assume violence between two rival criminal gangs, but information leaked to this station suggests this was an attack from the vigilante. Though there has not been much in the news for some time regarding the night time crusader, this attack is much bloodier than usual.

"I wish I could say that this was highly unusual, but let us not ignore what is happening in our City – prostitution and ritual murder of children."

The two people at the table in the somewhat darkly lit pub turn their attention away from the broadcast on the screen hanging over the bar. The man perks his eyebrows at the young woman. She seems more interested in the steaming cup of coffee in front of her, bent over it as if in reverence or an attempt to block out everything else. If the latter, it doesn't work, as she turns her eyes up to see him.

"What?" Therese demands of Detective Contee.

"Information leak …?" Quain pushes, his fingertips held against the pint glass of tomato juice.

"Not from me. It makes … the vigilante look bad, and I'm not trying to do that."

SWORD OF THE BUTTERFLY

He notes the slightest hesitation in her speech, and he wonders if she might have almost slipped and let out something about the vigilante that she is trying to hide.

"But you're holding him to task aren't you?"

Therese's face pinches up a bit, her default defensive state, but it almost as quickly fades, and something more forlorn creeps unto her. She nods slowly, lost in thought for a short time. Quain studies her intently.

"The vigilante is a tool," she finally resumes, looking up at him, bringing her cup off the table as though in preparation for a taste, "There's more than one tool for this problem."

"Right," he says, and as she turns her own piercing gaze further on him, he adds more sincerely, "Right. We're on it, too. There were kids there, and none of them were hurt in the attack."

Therese nods, still that slow, contemplative gesture, as though she is not being given any new data but is still processing and analyzing what she can.

"Good."

He watches as she finally partakes of her coffee, one he offered to buy for her, but she declined. She doesn't look at him, going inward, ignoring the editorial news, the few others in the tavern.

"You gave him the information instead of giving it to us," Quain finally speaks, trying to get her back into the focus.

She shakes her head, taking another sip.

"Some, yeah, but not nearly enough. I'm not the only tool the vigilante uses, either."

"Right. So what do you have going on?"

She does not react with her normal barriers to this inquiry as the two of them have further communicated since the initial rendezvous, and they have agreed to such exchanges.

"My P.I. is still looking into things on the ground. I've found some … interesting information on the 'net, but I'm still verifying and compiling it."

"I doubt it's confessions and addresses of operations," he says, picking up his glass for a decent intake of the thick juice.

221

"I'd really rather finish the analysis before saying more," she states, seeing through his none too subtle attempt to glean the details.

"Fair enough, but we go on leads all the time, and a lot of them turn out to be false positives. Investigation is pounding the pavement, you know? We play the numbers. Check and check and check some more."

"Yeah."

"So, when do I get to meet this P.I. of yours?"

She shrugs, thin shoulders rising within the thick leather jacket. "I don't know. Maybe never. That's more up to him. Besides, he's working for me. He's also good. He'll find something, give it me, then I'll deliver it to you."

"Actionable intelligence?" Quain perks his dark brow.

"Whatever you want to call it. I really don't care."

"Well, I hope something good breaks for us soon," he admits, and his manner gets more attention from her, "This is getting really bad. It's already really bad. So, it's just getting worse."

He pauses, looking away, and she just stares, her eyes seeming magnetized to him.

"Frankly," he resumes, looking back at her, "I'm worried about him."

"Him?"

"The vigilante," he elaborates, and though she gives no more reaction, he believes he's gotten a small morsel, "There was the one attack that left those kids dead, and we're pretty sure the other case I'm on was a reprisal or bait. And now this. Those guards weren't killed, but they were all shot. One will take months, if not years, to recover."

"So?" she demands, and he can see it in her, how much this affects her and what she thinks of those involved.

"Look, I'm not defending these guys, but the vigilante somehow managed to be less … bloody, in the past. It looks like they're openly declaring war on each other."

"Yeah, well, the criminals will take it personally, but the vigilante … shouldn't." Again a brief pause that makes him wonder what may have been altered in her speech or what it may mean of her personal investment in all of this.

"Okay, but how?"

SWORD OF THE BUTTERFLY

"What?" Her eyes dart back to him.

"How do you not take this personally? Think about it. This guy decides to put himself at very serious risk to take care of some business that he obviously thinks the police can't or won't do on their own. And now, these criminals may be executing kids to send him a message? Shit, I mean ... well, it would take a lot of fortitude to not take all this personally."

She just looks at him, letting some moments pass. He returns the gaze, waiting. He sees a small movement in her jaw, a curl to her upper lip.

"Yes, it's tough. I just hope the vigilante is up to the challenge," she finally says.

*****

Lilja comes in from having spent many hours out, jogging, walking, rock climbing, trying to sort things in her mind through this combination of physical activity and the embrace of nature. It is, perhaps, a distillation, a way to reduce the chaotic components into something more palatable, something more comprehensible. She has not come to a conclusion, but it allows her to better see and focus on the problem.

Skot looks up from his laptop as she walks in, doing more of his work, whether further study on the Book or communiques to oversee the various family or business interests, she is not sure. He brightens as she enters, a smile taking his lips.

"Lily," he greets, quickly saving his work and preparing to push back from the computer.

"Hi," she says, her hand moving a bit in a sort of half-formed wave, "Sorry I was out so long. I'm going to take a quick shower."

"Okay," he says, concern already leaking into him like a virus.

He has missed her, of course, though she did text him a few times during the hours-long jaunt. Upon seeing her, he just wanted to jump up and wrap her in his arms, exchanging kisses, but it seems she had not been interested in that. It only adds to his worry.

He tries to get back to his work, but this is only more caution. The infrastructure of their family and the myriad financial ventures is well in place, and he needs not really deal with any of the multitudinous day-to-day maintenance. He likes to read over reports, of course, but the machine works without micro-management. He is involved in bigger things, such as the continued lack of any information regarding the skin wearer, study of the Book, and its protection. All signs point at the Infernal making another try for the tome, and why would they not?

Though he has much with which to occupy himself, he finds it difficult to focus, and the time of her 'quick' shower takes too long for him. He hears her return, moving about in the kitchen. He picks up his large glass, downing the remaining water in it, and heads to her.

She looks up to see him there. "I'm making some coffee. Would you like some?"

"Sure." Skot smiles.

He looks at the play of her wet locks over her back as she moves. How it hangs as she bends to get some of what she needs, then falling back. She is in a simple t-shirt and sweatpants, and he finds her enticing. He knows, though, that she is not in such a mood, so he represses his own feelings of arousal.

"How was your time out?" he tries.

"It was okay."

She adds water to the machine, turning it on. He waits, hoping she will now give him more attention, give more of herself, now that her task is complete. She just stands there, hands held on the countertop, as though she is supported by it, just staring at the coffee maker.

"Lilja?" he begins, stepping closer, placing a hand lightly on her upper back, letting it glide down slowly in a soft, hopefully comforting motion, and she turns to look at him. "Is everything okay?"

She moves in closer slipping her arms about him, and he returns the embrace with an almost physical sense of relief, holding her tight. He feels as her own hold increases in strength.

"I did a lot of thinking while I was out."

He nods, still holding her, knowing that is something of her way. When she is troubled, she heads into nature or exercise or both, but she needs some time to herself to sort things. He is one to want to talk things out, to try to use words and communication to drive to a conclusion. She is not.

SWORD OF THE BUTTERFLY

"Did you want to share any of that with me?" he gently tries.

The moment stretches, and he can all but feel the turmoil inside her. Not only is she torn by her own inner demons, but she experiences difficulty in deciding if she will even speak of it with him.

"Okay," she finally agrees, stepping back.

She goes to preparing the coffee, knowing how he likes his just as he knows how she likes hers, and it takes some time before she continues. He thanks her for the brew, the two of them taking the initial tastes. He just watches her, though her eyes stray, more of her collision of thoughts. It is difficult for him to observe and say nothing, but he does so because he believes that is the best way to support her at this time. Despite this knowledge, he feels impatience and concern gaining more of a hold. He is about to give in and prompt her, when she pulls in a breath and speaks.

"Please don't get upset with me," she begins, which puts him more on edge, though he says nothing. "These are just my thoughts, okay?"

"Okay." He nods, calmly, his coffee largely ignored.

"I feel ... overwhelmed, kind of even ... lost," she says, still not looking at him, more traveling in her thoughts and feelings, still trying to make sense of the maelstrom, "Before we met, I thought I had it all figured out, knew who the bad guys were. I know I can't stop them all, but I felt capable enough to handle what I did, even with the obvious risk. Some risks are necessary."

Her voice trickles off, as though even she is not convinced. He just looks at her, remaining silent, hoping she will say more.

"And you showed me a whole new world out there." Then her eyes move quickly to his. "I'm not blaming you, okay? I'm glad you showed me. I want to help, but ..."

And he sees the beginning of pain there, the furrowing of her brow, the tense stare in her remarkable eyes.

"Lily," he says, moving to her, wrapping her again in his arms.

She accepts the hug, for a time, then extricating herself. She stays close to him, but she resumes her coffee. For all that she generally seems so inward and taciturn, she appears now ready to say something, whether to help herself or offer him some insight, or perhaps both, he is not sure, but he is still grateful for her effort.

"Your joining us feels miraculous, though I know it's not coincidence," he says, forgetting so easily how he intended to let her speak, his words tumbling forth like a frothing river, "You have been amazing ... *amazing*." Skot lightly grips her arms, getting her to look him in the eyes. "I have never seen such an impressive acclimation. You are *wonderful*."

"No," she flatly states, looking away, "I'm not."

"Don't be so hard on yourself, Lily."

"I have to be," she forcefully retorts, and the intensity she suddenly wears gives him more concern. "I'm not just playing with my own safety but also them, those children."

"You saved all those kids on your last operation."

"I pointed my gun at one of them," she reveals.

"Oh, Lily." Skot reaches out to comfort her again, but she moves away.

The motion is fluid, easy, so he is not sure if she has deliberately avoided his attempt or just meandered off on her own. She does not go far, but she does put some distance between them, whether intentional or not.

"But you didn't shoot," he says, a statement, not a question. "How did it happen?"

"I ...," she starts, and the tension rises further, one of her fists clenching, "I was ... making sure one of the bad guys was secure, and I saw movement, so I just went on instinct, training, and I pointed my gun at ..."

"Well, that's not so bad," he proceeds, carefully, "You know there is a reason why innocents are told to lie down and be still during a crisis. The responders are there to secure the situation and neutralize threats. You saw movement, you aimed, then you realized it was one of the children, and you didn't pull the trigger. That could happen to anyone."

She just stands there, looking downward, though the tension appears to have left for the time being. Her head finally begins a slow nod.

"I guess so."

"Come on, Lily. You *know* so. The kid was probably in shock, scared, but you know the safest thing for someone like that is to remain in place, down low, and wait."

"Maybe, but I also have an idea of the condition these children are in. I can't expect them to be calm and logical."

"No, but you did not pull the trigger," he reiterates, speaking slowly, emphatically.

"I pulled it a lot on that mission."

He lets a slow breath cycle through him, preparing to speak again, but she carries on.

"The pressure is enormous, and I'm not saying that as some excuse, but I had no idea they'd be so ... *cruel*, even with what I've seen. Cruel and cold. How could they just execute those other children? How can anyone do that?"

She turns her face to him again, and the look he sees pains him, just as it shows her own pain and simmering anger.

"I ... don't know, but it happens."

"So, now I know that they will kill the children I try to rescue. I can't afford mistakes. I can't afford to be as careful as I like."

"Maybe ...," Skot starts, and Lilja jerks her eyes to him, almost as if she had forgotten he was there, "Maybe you just need a break?"

She blinks, brow wrinkling, a light shake of her head. "What? A break?"

"Yes," he answers, still trying to speak slow and calm, "The tension is obviously getting to you."

"So, what then? Just leave those children out there to be prostituted?"

"I-," he tries.

"I won't do that," she persists, the volume of her voice still normal, but the forcefulness of the words is undeniable.

"Lily, you can't spend every moment of every day fighting. You'll burn yourself up." She turns, facing him more, and he sees the tension there, the anxiety. He cares so deeply for her, so he will push, but he fears making her think of him as an obstacle. "We have a lot of resources in the Family. Why don't you let me help? I can take that information of yours and send some teams to rescue those kids, or I could even exert some political pressure, get someone to champion the cause."

"No," she flatly states, "This is mine. I'll do this. Don't come in and try to 'fix' it."

"That's not what I'm trying to do," he says, somewhat exasperated, "I just want to help. Let me help you."

"I don't need help!" She suddenly hits her clenched fist on the countertop, her shoulders rising with the rhythm of her strong breathing as she defiantly stares at him. "I won't lose my independence."

He stares at her, his eyes wide, realizing he is afraid, not of her physically but that he may have gone too far. He never wanted to cause such a reaction in her. He dares not even to breathe, just looking at her.

After a time, her shoulders slump, and she covers her face with her hand, letting out a deep sigh. "Sorry ... I just need some space, some time ... to figure all of this out."

"Okay, that's fine," he says, "That sounds like a good idea."

"But I can't take time." Lilja looks deeply at him, her eyes taking on a shimmer. "The children can't wait."

He sighs, deeply. She looks away. He looks at her.

He takes the few steps to be near her, putting an arm about her shoulders. She leans into it, pressing herself against his chest, tucking her arms in rather than overtly returning the hug. He tries to remove all worry from his mind and just enjoy the feeling of her proximity. He knows there is much mounting, much teetering on the edge, and he must do something to help her to keep it from falling over.

Something must be done.

*****

He sits for a moment on one of the chairs at the heavy, wooden kitchen table. Though he lives alone, he actually enjoys taking meals here as he is able. Though it is not often, he relishes the peaceful passing of time when he cooks and savors the food. He is not an especially good cook, but he still likes it. It is more a luxury, even something of a ritual. This is not one of those times.

He has just hung up the phone, still keeping an old-fashioned land line here, not many of whom know that number. He has been summoned by the boss. He wonders, *fears* what it may be.

Certainly such calls to work have happened before but never like this. The voice is one he recognizes but not one he knows well. Someone

SWORD OF THE BUTTERFLY

closer to the top than he, far closer. He'd been given the opportunity to speak but one word before the single sentence had emerged, ordering him to the appointment, soon.

Instead of a self-prepared meal, the serving space before him shows an empty, clear glass, a bottle of vodka, and a loaded pistol. He ponders his life, wondering how he got to this place where he feels he needs any of those. He has often thought and said that it is too late for him. This is why he has never let himself get too close to any one woman, not that droves of them are throwing themselves at his bulky frame. He has no children he is aware of. There is not much to him now, if there ever was. His eyes nigh unblinking, he stares at the bottle and gun. He's been summoned.

He finally moves, his hands unscrewing the cap and pouring nearly a glassful of the potent liquid. He downs it rather smoothly, his throat working with the swallowing. He then takes up the pistol, standing, and tucks it in his waistband.

Ex-detective Alec Sladky leaves his modest home, fueled to face whatever shall come.

A short drive later, and he is at the park. It had seemed a somewhat strange locale for him, one which might also give him a false sense of safety. It is not nighttime, but they could lead him anywhere, take him anywhere. He rises out of his car, noticing them quite easily. There are a decent number of folk out here, some jogging, others walking or just enjoying the day. He can so easily distinguish between the civilians and the soldiers. He is given a surly head-jerk of a greeting, unspoken permission to pass through the tight knot of guards and go to the man.

"Look at them, Sladky," Volkov says, motioning to the general area, a tattooed hand moving from within the gray encasement of his shirt sleeve.

Alec turns about, not fully putting his back to the man. He is not sure to whom his boss refers.

"See heavy clothing, jackets, trenchcoats," Volkov instructs, and Alec does. "It is still autumn. These weaklings do not know of cold. I know cold."

Alec wonders what the man will say or do next. Unless there is a sniper, or the man will be like Gnegon and do something himself, none of the sentries can approach him without his knowing. Still, even if that happens, he will not jerk forth his pistol and shoot the boss or himself or any such nonsense. He will face his fate, such as it is.

"We are still having trouble. You know this, and not just the vigilante. Police are becoming more of pain," he informs, giving his underling a particular look, "Your friend, Detective Contee is on case, hunting me."

The moment stretches, and though Alec has tried to now only speak to Volkov when asked a direct question, he senses the man wants something.

"Of course he is. That's how it works. He's a cop, so he goes after criminals."

And then he see something he thought he'd never see - a smile forms on Volkov's face, though it does not stick, more like a cut forming on the man, a jagged opening appearing, trying to take hold, more disturbing, frightening, than anything reassuring.

"Good. Good. I am glad you finally understand. And you will go visit your old friend ... and kill him," he orders, the short-lived smile gone, a mayfly having done its duty and now passed into memory.

Alec stands there, and though his immobility and focus may hearken to a statue, his blood pumps rather intently. He suspected this moment would come, and he is incensed. He suddenly wants to defy his own recent resolve and jerk forth his pistol and blow Volkov's head off, then make a hole in his own skull. That seems a beautiful way to end it.

"What will that accomplish?" he opts for instead.

"It will probably make things worse, da?"

"Da," Alec iterates, uttering the word with a dryness.

"It is stupid idea, to assassinate police detective, even if this one used to be corrupt. This will bring more heat to us."

"So, then why do you want me to do it?"

Volkov turns minutely, raising his chin, managing to drill his already focused eyes more deeply into the other.

"It will be message and test."

Alec blinks, brow furrowing.

SWORD OF THE BUTTERFLY

"Message for police," the boss elaborates, though Alec already assumes, "This is war, not *duty*. The police are self-righteous fucks, *yebany suki*."

Alec does not bother asking after a translation of the obvious slur. Volkov merely stews, the coldness of his exterior along with the expletives and obvious tension making him seem all the more serious and deadly.

"Test for you," he adds, composure returned, "but you knew that."

"I don't want to kill him," Alec flatly states.

The other man gives a slight shrug of his shoulders.

"I know," he offers, quite casual, "You don't have to, of course. It is choice, Sladky. But if you do not, then you no longer work for me, and I may give similar order to someone else for you. I doubt they would be reluctant."

"Threatening me is pointless. You threaten everyone who works for you."

"Yes. You *are* insight." He then cocks his head, pondering. "Insight*ful*." His expression somewhat dissolves, leaving the practical. "You are not stupid, Sladky, and being ex-detective is beneficial. I am also not stupid, but I will use tools as I see fit. I am chief."

Alec stares right back at the man, still pondering his actions. He figures Volkov is well aware he might try something dangerous right now. Perhaps there are hidden gunman watching through scopes. The former lawman thinks he could do some damage before they might intervene, but he has decided on another course.

"You are," he agrees.

"Good. I will not believe you, though, until task is done. Go now."

And Alec does.

*****

"She sees demons."

He sets his blue eyes on her. The tilt of his face, the cast of his brow, and without a word, he communicates.

"When there are none there," his sister adds.

She is his junior, by a time period measured better in months than years, but her understanding of the supernatural is beyond his, beyond anyone their meticulous records can recall in recent history. He knows she has ways to see things that are denied to most, but such does not make her infallible.

"Don't we all?" he decides, the fingertips of his right hand moving over the stout glass, it holding a decent measure of whiskey.

"And you are drinking more than your usual."

His eyes again go back to her, and again they mingle challenge within the usual array of his demeanor.

"I am not trying to be Mother," Nicole explains, her usual smooth cadence not interrupted at all in its flow by his reactions, "It is clear there is stress within both of you and between you."

"A feedback loop?"

"Mayhap, but either of you are capable of stopping it, though you are in a better psychological position to do so." She again pauses if for no other reason than effect. "If you do not let the worry consume you."

"You don't have to be melodramatic," he remarks, his fingers again touching along the cool surface of the glass, but as with before, he does not raise it for a drink.

"I am speaking to you in a way I hope you will not only understand but also take as observation and advice offered in good will."

He exhales, nodding slowly. "Yes. Thank you. What else have you observed?"

"I have told you of her powerful potential, but much of that is yet untapped."

"Much?" Skot perks his eyebrows. "She's one of the most adept Hunters I've ever seen. Look how she was before we found her."

"I have."

He waits, for he senses another addition thrown out in her deceptively calm, dramatic method. She merely looks at him.

"So, is she seeing something of the Infernal, maybe even some dark potential in people that might lure the Infernal to them?"

"I have thought of that, and it is possible, but I think she is conflicted and suffering from some paranoia."

He nods, pondering.

SWORD OF THE BUTTERFLY

"It is not unusual, as you well know. We were reared in this environment, but those who are brought into it later in life often go through such, and here she is, going out on missions with the Head of the Family, expected to protect such an important personage."

He narrows his eyes slightly, but he knows it is enough for her to pick up on his reaction.

"You think it's too much for her."

"I am not the only one."

He inhales slowly, trying to fight to not shake his head.

"Skothiam, clearly there is something bothering her. Do not let your love for her make you defensive. We want to help her and help the Family."

"She is a fiercely independent woman. Even if I tell her to stop-."

"Do not *tell* her ," Nicole cuts him off. "Of course she is strong and independent. I doubt you'd have been attracted to her otherwise, but she is vulnerable. Right now, she is troubled, deeply troubled. She needs help."

"We've talked about it some, and I'll see if I can get her to talk about it more. I *am* the Head of the Family, so I can control any formal assignments she receives, but it's not just about that."

Nicole begins to move about the room, her clothing its usual mixture of form-fitting and loose, the sleeves of the light-colored dress flowing with the fluidity of her motion. She gazes down at a trinket on a nearby shelf, her long, straight auburn hair framing her face.

"Of course it is not, and it is not just about her being the vigilante." She then turns to look at him. "Lilja is the type of woman to go out and hunt demons on her own."

He nods, looking away from that piercing gaze, musing, "She wants to make right what she can, even at the toll of what it does to herself."

"And to you."

He looks over, sighing, lips pressing together somewhat. "We know the risks involved."

She closes her eyes, nodding once, slowly, then opening them again as she goes back to wandering about the expansive and warm chamber.

"We do, and we have all paid prices, and further tolls are yet to be collected. She needs further training, and not just in combat. If anything, that is the area where she is least in need."

"She could very well be a trainer to some of our Hunters."

"Indeed, so, we need address the areas where she *does* need help."

"And what areas are those?" he asks, sincere, not pushing.

"I am not yet sure. I would like to spend more time with her, if she is willing. I am not sure if she is delusional in the sense of really seeing things that are not there-."

"I doubt it's that," he interjects.

"As do I, but it is a possibility that must be considered," she presses in her own way, and he nods lightly in acquiescence. "She may, indeed, be possessed of an awakening sensitivity as you mentioned earlier, and if that is the case, we may help her exercise and hone it. It would become a powerful ability."

He nods again, waiting for her to continue.

"Or she may merely be trying to deal with the intense stresses of her life."

"Regardless, she needs help," he states, and his sister is quick to give a slow nod.

"She is stubborn, but not in every way. She also possesses a near child-like inquisitiveness and openness. I do not think she would become defensive and close up if this subject is broached in the manner it deserves."

"Yes, well." Skot exhales, standing, seeming to have forgotten his whiskey. "You don't know her as well as I do."

"I do not," Nicole agrees, eyes slitting a bit.

"What?"

"Do not plant the seeds of resignation or failure."

"I'm ...," he begins, but he stops himself, taking in another slow breath, "She is earnest, a person with great bravery, but she also exhibits signs of paranoia. I don't mean in a clinical sense, but she very much is the kind to retreat, but not necessarily to hide. She would retreat into a fortress, a place of defense."

"That *is* hiding," Nicole observes.

SWORD OF THE BUTTERFLY

"Somewhat, yes, but I think she also retreats and tries to figure things out by herself."

"That is commendable, but there is only so much each of us may accomplish on our own."

"Yes, yes." He nods, the words tumbling out in a musing tone.

"She may have trouble recognizing her own limitations."

"Yes, I would say that is accurate in some cases."

"But she is also a very humble person."

"She is."

"Then she is somewhat prepared to see those barriers. Again, she needs help."

"Do you think she needs therapy?" he asks after a moment of silence.

"No," Nicole resolutely replies, "She just needs a way out of the dark places."

*****

He is not that used to attention from women. He gets it, surely, usually as a direct result of his choice of employment, but his magnetism is unrefined. He takes care of himself in some regards, shaving often enough, keeping his light brown hair cut on a regular basis, the barbershop near his home being one of his favored daytime locales. But the barbers have to sometimes knock on the inside of their own window to get his attention to come on in.

He is not so much negligent as focused, practical. He keeps up some modicum of appearance, because he ought to, but he is not a vain man.

Were one to see him naked, they might think him so due to the physical condition of his body. Again, he is as he is due to the practical needs of his career. His unkempt growth of body hair might clue one in, were one to see him naked.

Yet, the attractive woman sitting less than half a dozen spaces down the bar keeps looking at him.

He had been paying more attention to his beer than to anything else, but he finally looked over, more just a casual, if not even bored, sway of his general focus. She met his eyes, her dark ones finding his paler ones, and she gave him a smile. Unsure how to react, he merely blinked, then went back to his beer. It was not a reaction of bashfulness, merely confusion. Her grin had grown.

She could be a cop, but he did not think so. Besides, though she is good looking enough, she is not some overdone model-type like the boss' new girlfriend and the cohort of elegant, almost uncanny ladies that seem to be around her most of the time. This woman looks 'real'.

He notes this with a few sidelong glances. She notices them, but she does not overtly react, letting him have his secret observance. She wears a tan trench coat, opened. He notes the dark clothing beneath, a dress or a skirt, as he gazes down, noting her bare ankles and the black pumps, not too tall, alluring yet still somewhat sensible. His eyes move back up, and he notes the look of her neck. She is not too young, either. Perhaps she is a mature-enough woman who happens to be single or merely out for some adventure. Who knows?

He does not, so almost as a shrug, he goes back to his beer, tilting up the glass and finishing it.

"May I treat you to your next?"

He looks over to see her there. How very sneaky of her to have gotten off her stool and walked over without his realizing. He finds himself liking that. He still says nothing, just looking at her. The bartender, ever attentive, especially with the amount of people in here being so low, waits.

"You're drinking Saku, no?" she notes, her voice revealing an accent as though her native language may be French.

"I am," he finally speaks, "What are you drinking?"

She smiles, then turns to the barkeep. "Two Sakus, please," she orders, and he nods, preparing the drinks. She looks back, but her flair has not cracked his exterior. "What's your name?"

"Soosaar."

She perks somewhat thick, trimmed eyebrows. "That's an interesting name."

"It's ... it's my last name."

"Ah." She nods, slowly, trying to encourage him. "Is your first name a secret?"

He looks at her for a short moment.

SWORD OF THE BUTTERFLY

"Kalju, but most call me 'Kal' ... or Soosaar."
"Pleased to meet you, Kal, I am Livie Cloutier."
"You're French."

The curve on her lips increases. "I am, and I don't think you're originally from here, either."

He exhales through his nose, his own lips pressing together as though they might curl. "I am Estonian."

"Ah, of course, I should have guessed," she grins, glancing at their beers, and when she takes hers up, gesturing, he proves amiable enough to the toast.

Throughout their time talking, his mind is working. He continues to wonder why she is here, why she is talking to him. She might indeed just be a woman who has come in here for a drink and some possible company, but he holds doubts as to that. She appears quite comfortable and confident, so he thinks she'd not come to a dingy place like this. She wears no wedding ring, but he still wonders. Maybe she is married, or involved, and she is here for a quick, illicit incursion.

She's quite forward, too. Pulling the nearby stool closer, though it is already near enough, and as they spend more time, she often touches him, placing a hand on his shoulder or arm. They go through some more drinks, though they take their time, not downing shots like some young people looking to lose themselves or stir their courage.

"Well," she says, glancing at her watch, "I think it's time for me to leave."

He feels an unexpected stab of disappointment, and he wonders if he ought to ask for her number or some such, but before he can decide, she speaks again.

"Would you like to come with me?" she bids, putting on a rather seductive smile.

He would, but he hesitates.

"Or at the very least, walk me to my car?" she opts, eyebrows perking again.

"Yes, of course," he agrees, rising from the stool, slipping some notes to the bartender, and they depart.

The lot is mostly empty, but she parked on the edge, the meager lights from the space barely reaching one side of her car. A vehicle drives by on the road, but overall, it is relatively subdued on this week night.

"I thought it might get busier," she says, offering her explanation to the obvious, though unspoken inquiry from him.

"If you're worried, you shouldn't park so far from the lights."

"I know," she says, and she takes on a slight expression as though a scolded child, though the obvious intent is to appear alluring.

It works, and he stares at her, feeling that undeniable hunger of which she has reminded him.

"But I like the dark," she adds, sauntering to him, and she places both hands on his chest, guiding and turning him until his back stops against her vehicle.

They kiss passionately, hungrily, all pretext gone. Their hands work on each other, exploring. He begins to feel his excitement growing, a demanding stirring in his loins. As though sensing this, she pushes forward with her hips, pressing against him, all but mounting him right there.

"Excuse me."

The voice intrudes like a barb, and she pulls away from him immediately. Again, his initial thoughts go to it being a cop, and he prepares to growl out some irritated words, but the man wears a suit, and he, just as with the woman, does not give off the vibe of the police. Kalju pauses, staring, brow furrowing. He wonders if this is Livie's man, perhaps having trailed her or more likely determining where she has gone. He seems polite enough, even cultured, but he cannot be happy with what he has found.

Then he reaches into his jacket, and Kal stiffens, but the man pulls forth an identification.

"I'm sorry to have disturbed you, but I'm with the police," he informs, and Kal narrows his eyes, not to further study the presented information, but because he knows the guys does not *feel* like a cop. "I'm in the area asking questions of people. Do you mind?"

Livie looks at Kalju with wide eyes.

"I do mind," Kal grumbles, his words and manner quite clear.

"I'm sorry," the man smoothly carries on, not perturbed in the least, "but I have a job to do."

SWORD OF THE BUTTERFLY

He speaks with a definite German accent, and his lighter toned hair and eyes, well-formed jaw, mark him as potentially of such descent.

"I don't care."

"Kal?" comes her voice, and he turns his attention somewhat to her, "Let's not make a scene. Can't we just answer his questions and be done with it?"

"Thank you, Madam," the self-identified law enforcement officer says, giving a polite smile which does not waver as he sets his eyes back on the other. "Do you know a man named Kazimir Volkov?"

Alarm spikes in Kalju, but he does not show much reaction. Maybe the guy *is* a cop. Maybe he's just one of those fancy Interpol agents. Still, something is not right.

"No," he clips.

The man smiles a bit more.

"Well," he continues, the word punctuated by a breathy exhalation like a patronizing chuckle, "You have been under surveillance for some time, Mr. Soosaar, and I feel quite confident that you do know the man of whom I speak."

Enough is enough, he decides, and he reaches for his pistol, but it is not there.

The other man perks his eyebrows. "Looking for something?" he taunts, and when Kalju returns his gaze, the other glances briefly at the woman.

Kal shoots his eyes over to find that Livie is holding his weapon, looking suddenly like a more experienced handler of guns than men. She has moved further away, turning to face him, holding the pistol in an experienced grip with both hands.

"What the hell is going on?"

She says nothing.

"I am here to ask you questions," the man reminds.

"Fuck you. You're not police."

"No." He gives a grin, almost apologetic. "I'm not." He slips the ID back into his coat, pulling forth a suppressed Glock 17, and before Kalju may much react, two quiet shots are fired.

He drops, hit in his right knee and thigh, the pain excruciating, and he cries out, more of an angry scream than anything, hoping to not only

239

unleash his rage but also get attention from inside the bar. The shooter swoops forward, going down to his victim, angling the barrel at his head. Kal defies his own pain, lashing out with an arm to swipe away at the gun. The man does not lose his hold, but he is deflected, partially losing his balance. Kal uses his other hand to try to attack the man, but his opponent uses the sudden change in situation to slam his elbow into Kalju's face. Bone cracks and blood spurts, and he feels a short stun.

"Livie," the man calls, the word sharp and short, like a command, like familiarity, and the two go to quick work, dragging their prey back around to the other side of the car, the side shrouded in darkness.

She used her real name, Kalju finds himself suddenly and quite oddly noting.

Once done, she again steps back, getting some decent distance and covering with the appropriated firearm.

"Now, I will ask again," the man says, patiently, "and every question I ask will be answered with truth or pain. You will decide."

"Fuck you," Kal manages, blood pooling and running aside his upper lip.

The man huffs out a short chuckle. "I haven't asked anything yet."

Then the interrogation resumes.

CHAPTER TEN

He stands in the shadows of the small arrangement of foliage. The trees were planted here years ago, artificial efforts at natural-seeming beautification. He thinks life does need its efforts at such improvements, even if it is just a charade. The trunks of these are narrow, the bark quite pale in color. He is not sure what kind they are.

He watches the doorway across the distance. He knows the occupant is inside. He had warned the dweller at one time to change his address. He realizes with some measure of satisfaction that the advice was not heeded. Still, this will not be easy. He takes another pull on the flask, the cap off, held in his left hand. He feels the nice burn of it, takes another drink, then puts the flask away. *How does alcohol forge steel?* Perhaps it is all just part of that charade. He feels more compelled by external forces than his own volition. He knows that is empty, an excuse, but he still feels that way. He's made his decisions.

With a noisy huff, he plods over the ground, moving his bulk with no sign of difficulty. He passes through some light from streetlamps, the cone of illumination showing the person, the conflict there. Alec is determined, but he is also troubled. His face gives forth signs of regret, sorrow, but fear has no place in him.

Quain usually sleeps quite deeply. He also adheres to a fairly regular schedule, unforeseen demands of his job notwithstanding. He's finished this day like many others, spending some time at the gym, then coming home, having a decent meal, then heading to bed. Thoughts have coursed through his mind. He wonders about this case, the children, his partner, her life, the vigilante, Therese, and yes, even somewhat of his ex-partner. He wonders how things could have gotten so terrible. When they worked for Gnegon things got bad, bad enough for him to go straight, but now, it just gets worse and worse. Why can't they clean the city thoroughly enough to put a stop to this? What is it about this place that seems to attract so much that is negative, even as it continues to prove a cosmopolitan haven for many good things?

He turns to his other side, trying to cleanse his own mind and reach slumber. He doesn't hear the expert work of the man who enters his apartment.

Alec carefully closes the door behind him, not even bothering to worry if anyone may have seen his illegal entry. He treads quietly on the floor, moving with a quiet grace some might not expect from the large man. He may be loose of tongue sometimes, but he *is* experienced. Sometimes one needs a rolling boulder, an avalanche, and sometimes one needs the silent slip, like a thorn or needle.

He pauses, looking at the living room. He's shared a beer here with his ex-partner. Yes, though Quain is a fiend for fitness, he drinks a beer or two from time to time. Alec tries to recall the detail of the memory, why Quain was having a beer with him, what were they talking about? He can see it in his mind, but he can't hear anything. His recollection narrows, becoming like a pinpoint. Things used to be a lot easier. He wishes for those times again.

He knows what he needs to do, but he just stands there.

Meanwhile, Quain lies in bed, now on his back, unable still to sleep. He thinks about his new partner, Maria. She's a strong woman, that's for sure. He respects her, and not just in her approach to her job but also how she deals with the trials of her own life. He still thinks she sometimes hides behind an occasional self-righteous veneer, but no one is perfect. They've begun to open up and share more, and he knows that she is also into fitness, though not to the same degree as he. She's even told him a bit about her daughter.

The case, though, isn't getting any better. It's been too long since the occurrence of the crime for them to have a lot of hope, except he feels fairly certain it was perpetrated by the same element responsible for the child prostitution. He doesn't think it's some lone person who's fled the area or gone into remission or hiding. There's still work that can be done, and he also holds out hope for the information Therese may provide. He then lets his thoughts flow to the vigilante. He wonders what

SWORD OF THE BUTTERFLY

lengths they are willing to go in their fighting of crime. Does the vigilante already know who is responsible? Has it already been dealt with?

He then hears the noise from inside his apartment.

He sits up, blinking, looking about, as though that would help him discern what may be going on. He doesn't snap on the light or call out. Those are amateur things to do. If no one is there, it won't matter. If there is an intruder, he doesn't want them to know he's heard.

Maybe it's the vigilante, he lets slip almost comically through his mind.

Very quietly, he retrieves his pistol from the nearby nightstand. He knows it may not be the safest course of action to leave a loaded weapon there, but ever since he had that last talk with Alec, he's kept it nearby and ready. He slowly gets out of bed, straining to hear anymore sounds. He doesn't, but he won't let that convince him everything is safe. He'll check the entire apartment. Then, if it's nothing, he'll get back to his inability to sleep.

As soon as he barely cracks open his bedroom door, he knows something is wrong. He sees the light coming from the living room, and he knows he did not leave it on. He walks very carefully, his bare feet making next to no noise as he steps with purpose. He holds the weapon close to his chest, pointing the way. He gets to the end of the hallway, then dares to peek around the edge, bending at the knees, so his head does not emerge where someone might expect it. He is stunned.

"Alec?" he says, walking into the living room, pistol pointed, though it pains him to do so, "What are you doing here?"

The bulky man sits on his couch, the nearby lamp casting its light over him. He just stares ahead. Quain sees no weapons, and his ex-partner sits in a way that he does not have his hands hidden.

"I've been sent to kill you," the man finally utters.

"Is that so?"

Alec just slowly nods.

"Well, I see you got into my flat, but …?" he leads, moving more into view, still pointing his weapon.

"I'm not going to do it," Alec states.

"Thanks?"

Alec then finally angles his eyes to the other.

"Arrest me. Put me in custody ... *safe* custody, and I'll tell you all you need to know."

Some time later, after transport, booking, some arguing, and Quain and Maria have been given permission to question the recent arrestee.

"I'm doing what I can to secure special arrangements. You know how this works, Alec, and I wish I could say that your being an ex-cop was helping, but..." Quain's voice trails off.

"I appreciate it," Alec replies, "and I understand."

He looks over at Quain's new partner. She looks more interested in her coffee, though Alec presumes some of that may just be irritation at having been called in here when she'd probably rather be asleep.

"So?" Quain tries, his brow rising, "Do you want to begin?"

"Sure," Alec says, glancing once at the two cops, then looking down at the surface of the table for a moment, sitting forward in his chair, cuffed hands clasped together. "I was ordered to kill you. *You*, Detective Quain Contee. I was ordered to kill you by Kazimir Volkov."

"We've heard that name before," Maria remarks, still more interested in her drink.

"Sure you have, and I work for him. I can describe him to you, in detail. I can give you distinguishing marks. I can tell you where he spends a lot of his time, and I can tell you about some of his operations."

"Some?" she angles.

"I don't handle everything for him."

"Right," Quain interjects, though, for once, Alec proves the calm one in a potentially brewing situation, "What sort of operations?"

"The usual," the ex-cop begins, "Conspiracy, extortion, racketeering, assault, money laundering. Kidnapping, coercion, human trafficking, forced prostitution of children."

"You witnessed this?" Maria perks up, moving forward in her own chair.

Alec nods, again that weighted feel, as though a pendulum. "Yes, yes I did."

"What about the murders?"

He looks over to see that Quain has asked this, and he is somewhat placated to hear the underlying hesitancy.

SWORD OF THE BUTTERFLY

"No, and I'm not just saying that to save my own ass. I'm completely fucked. I'm done for, but I do know how this works. I won't overstep what I can offer you."

"So, you don't know anything about the child murders?" Maria persists.

"I didn't say that. I didn't *witness* them, but I've been there when he's given the order to execute them, and I've heard him talk about other things," he says, his voice somewhat losing its volume, eyes looking away.

Quain sees it, and he is reminded of their talk those days ago. He knows from experience that not much frightens his ex-partner, and he sees fear in the man.

Maria looks from one to the other, then when the silence stretches too long for her, she speaks, "What other things?"

"It's a sacrifice, a ritual, even the executions," he finally answers, eyes still averted, words so heavy they almost disappear into a consuming silence as soon as they fall from his mouth.

"How?"

Quain looks at his partner, blinking into a confused frown. He had not expected that reaction. Alec knows what she's after, though, as he swivels his head back, so slow, like the workings of a rusted machine.

"It's a transference of energy. Volkov has talked to me, said odd things, but I'm not as stupid as most think."

"What kind of odd things?" she presses.

"About the vitality of children, about their ... *potential*."

The interview and debriefing take some time, but Alec has provided enough to convince them to put him into solitary holding for now. Quain walks slowly toward the exit of the building, his partner with him. He glances at her.

"Thanks for coming."

"It's the job," she comments.

"Yeah, but, well, it's not always convenient."

She sets a smirk on her lips for a moment, then repeats, adding emphasis, "It's the job."

He nods, going through one side of the double doors as she takes the other. He pauses once outside, taking in the night air. They've eaten most of the evening away now. He turns his eyes back to her, finding that she is standing there, looking at him.

"You want to get some coffee?" he bids.

"No," she says, not entirely unexpected, "but I could use a beer."

He grins, eyes opening a bit more, nodding. "Sure. Let's."

They take her car, since heading back is on her way, and he continues in his surprise as she orders a particularly dark, potent brew. His choice of pale ale looks almost meager compared to hers, almost as if it is the shadow of a beer, despite it not being the darker of the two.

"I wonder if this has anything to do with the Soosaar murder," she comments, the high ranking lieutenant in the local criminal organization having been recently found and quite easily identified, no effort made to hinder such.

"Probably," Quain says, tilting up his glass.

"Internal issues?"

"Maybe. I'm sure glad Alec didn't want to go through with that order he was given. Maybe some other guys are having similar problems."

"Even hardened criminals have a conscience?" she pitches.

"Sure. It's one thing to take out another guy who's into the Life, but to execute some innocent kid in cold blood? That's too much for some."

"Not all of them." She samples more of her beer.

He ponders for a moment, both of them content to sit in the quiet of the early morning hours in the nearly desolate pub.

"This could be a huge break, though," he finally announces.

"It could." She nods, then fixes a stare on him. "People will talk, though, since it's your ex-partner."

"So? Let them."

"I appreciate your sentiment, Quain, and you're tough enough, but this may also become political, and politics will play in how the prosecutors handle this."

"Yeah," he agrees, "Okay. So, do I need to take a hands off?"

"Probably." She leans forward, fingers moving along the table top, closer to him. "You brought him in. We did the initial interrogation. It's a good arrest, but you know it's not our sort of case, anyway. When you

SWORD OF THE BUTTERFLY

get into work tomorrow, and it's been assigned to someone else, don't get upset."

"I won't. And tomorrow?" he jokes, "I don't have today off."

She glances at her watch. "Yeah, me, either. Only a few more hours before we start again."

He spends a brief moment looking at her as she muses, eyes away from him.

"It's a good break," he repeats, more sincerity in his tone.

Her eyes go back to his.

"It is, and we have you to thank, so … thanks." She offers a smile.

"Huh? Thank Alec."

"No," she iterates with a shake of her head, "If you two had less of a friendship, he'd have gone through with the order, or tried, so…" She blinks, her smile changing its appearance. "I'm glad you're such good friends, and I'm glad you seem like a good cop."

"Seem like?"

She just keeps giving him that little grin.

His car remains in the department's parking lot. Instead of dropping him off, she takes him to her home.

They move slowly, despite the hunger. And there is hunger, a spectrum of it, from the most base to something more refined, something perhaps even of which they are not fully aware in themselves. Still, what they may lack in self-reflection, they have applied to each other, and it has only given fuel to the thirst.

She places a hand on his chest, feeling the muscle there beneath the fabric of his shirt. He takes this as not only cue but also permission, still keeping that relaxed, controlled motion, and he places his hand on her bosom, as though they were imperfect mirror images.

They take their time, but eventually, they are disrobed. Even in the dim lighting, she may see how refined is his body, how much attention he gives it, the available illumination enhancing the lines and definition of his muscles. She has more superficial flaws, but these do not concern her, nor do they him. They have simmered into a respect of one another, despite obvious misgivings.

They use their hands, their fingers, more than anything else. Eyes show heavy, half-lidded, some mingling of excitement, fatigue, sudden expectation. They both move in a bloom of fortitude, eager for this even as other needs press at them.

When they finally kiss, it is as though a peak has been reached, this union of intimacy, vulnerability. She yields somewhat, also leading with this action, and he follows her to the bed. She exhales a muted gasp through her nose when he enters her. His lips barely part, continuing the quasi-reflection. As they move their bodies together, they continue to take their time, as if owning this action which perhaps neither thought would ever happen, which perhaps both may have worried was a bad idea, regardless of desires. Now that they have consciously decided to dive into one another, they will brook no hesitancy or shyness.

It is savored.

Afterwards, he still finds himself unable to sleep. She shares no such difficulty. He slips quietly out of the sheets, tugging on his boxer shorts and walking to the kitchen. He narrows his dark eyes at the light of the refrigerator, finding that there is some juice in there. He picks up and examines the bottle. Apple is not his favorite, and he suddenly decides that water will do. As he is closing the door, he turns, starting somewhat to see the figure there.

"Hi," he manages.

"Who are you?" the girl asks.

"Uhm." He swallows. "I'm your mother's partner," and just as he says this, he closes his eyes, gritting his teeth, wishing he had chosen other words.

"Oh," she replies, staring at him, then she moves past, gaining a turn from him as he gets out of her way in the none-too-large kitchen.

She opens a cabinet, pulling out two glasses.

"There you go," she says, then opening the fridge to pour herself a glass of milk before going back to her bedroom.

"Thanks," he manages when she is almost gone, then he gets himself that water.

*****

She sits in the university's commons, a sparse meal on the plate before her, attention focused into something she reads on her phone. She has

SWORD OF THE BUTTERFLY

already done her usual and chosen a table somewhat on the edge of this outside area, minimizing angles of approach. It is not empty here, so she also subconsciously adjusts her perception to ignore peripheral movement that is sufficiently distant. When the one figure nears, intention obvious, she looks up.

"Ah, hello there," greets Anika Malkuth, looking polished as ever, her sure stride barely slowing as those vibrant eyes settle upon her.

"What are you doing here?" Lilja all but demands.

"Looking for you," the woman informs, slipping uninvited into an available chair, eyes glancing at the meal. "How do you eat this terrible food? I tried to find something, but it's all so unappealing."

"I usually bring my own."

The dark-haired woman moves her eyes slowly up to the redhead. Calculation, analysis running rapidly behind those orbs.

"Ah, I see. So … today is different. What's bothering you, Lilja?"

Deep blue eyes narrow. She does not like this intrusion. She does not like the Malkuth using her first name in such a familiar manner. Anika merely smirks, the expression dimmed in its potential cliché and immaturity by how subtly it is wielded.

"That's none of your business."

"Of course, it is. If you weren't the *Guardian of the Book*, then it wouldn't be, but you are," she is quick to press, sitting up quite straight in the chair, legs crossed.

"It's nothing."

A moment of weighty silence ensues between them, sounds of the world enveloping in calming tones and expected clatter and conversation.

"Everyone has their ups and downs, hmm?" Anika speaks, eyebrows rising slowly, "But something bad might happen during one of your downs. Some might even be waiting to take advantage of that."

Lilja's eyes again become more like guarded slits.

"If you don't want this responsibility, just say so. I'll be happy to report that," Anika continues within her insufferable tone.

The librarian remains silent, just looking, though it seems this comment may have somewhat gotten under her skin. Anika returns the look.

"You really do have some impressive potential. I wish we had found you first."

And her face moves back a very small amount, spine stiffening as her eyes widen slightly before closing back to that more focused, defensive expression.

"Though I guess it doesn't work that way," Anika admits, "We all have our ... proclivities, yes?"

"I'm a Felcraft."

The posh woman grins, as though having achieved a victory.

"No, you aren't. You aren't in the Family by birth, blood, or bond. Though you did manage to land quite a catch – the wealthy and powerful Head of House Felcraft. Congratulations. Tell me, did you study any archaeology or geology when you were at university?" she taunts.

"No." The word is clipped, dry. "And not everyone is in the Family by blood."

"Ah, you're referring to Jericho, aren't you?"

Lilja does not respond to this, feeling as though she is being trapped, wrangled, and her retorts sound weak, or worse, like evidence of the insufficiency this other woman implies.

"Skothiam and Jericho have known each other nearly all their lives," Anika carries on, "Schoolyard chums. So special, isn't it? I presume they've told you of the lure of our genes. We call to each other, like lodestones. Those two came together as friends and developed a lasting bond. It doesn't have to be romantic. I can feel your allure right now, just sitting here."

So said, she grins again, looking, the tone of her voice there at the end, her expression, all increasing in an obvious flirtatious manner. Lilja does not rise to this bait. She just remains silent.

"Well, regardless, congratulations."

Lilja scoots her chair back, readying to leave.

"Running away again?"

Her eyes snick sharply back to the other woman at these words.

"You obviously did not study poker," Anika observes, almost as an aside, then, "Are you ...? Are you and Skot having troubles? Is that it? Are you going to run away again?"

She just stares, silent, brewing.

"Why did you leave Finland, Lilja?"

And again, her eyes widen somewhat, but she then regains control.

"That's also none of your business," she manages, her tone as one that might cut through ice.

As though proof of this, Anika smirks, almost deliciously.

"Did something bad happen?" she presses, "Something with family, friends, your job? And you ran away?"

The redhead stands, picking up her bag and the plate upon which rests food hardly touched.

"If you leave like that, it will go in my report, and then Skothiam will learn of it. Then he'll come talk to you. You agreed to a certain amount of scrutiny when you also agreed to undertake this very important responsibility."

"I know that, but there are limits."

Anika casually waves a hand, dismissive. "Yes, there are."

After another short, tense moment of silence, Lilja retakes her seat.

"You're ex-military. You understand the idea of pushing limits in training. Do you think the Infernal give a *fuck* about your sensitivities?"

Lilja remains like a statue, staring back, but inside, she experiences a buzz, a war of her own thoughts and feelings.

"Well, of course they do," Anika adds, an afterthought, "They'd love nothing more than to learn of those, to learn your limits, your weak spots, then they would exploit that."

"I'm not the only measure in place to guard the Book."

"True … but you may be the key reasons it's still in the library here."

"Are you suggesting my relationship with Skot is-?"

Anika holds up a hand, stopping the quick retort. "He's not that stupid. It's due to your qualifications, which are quite substantiated. I presume he doesn't think it coincidence that you and the Book ended up together, as it were."

Lilja takes this in, wondering of it, and not for the first time. She also notes the almost casual validation. This woman likes to take her on a roller coaster, a way to test and possibly upset her. She finds the method sophomoric, and she feels she does not deserve it.

"You should have learned something of me in our sparring match," Lilja says.

"Oh?" Anika perks her eyebrows, amused.

"I am well aware of my own abilities. Do not take my silence as fear. It is pointless for me to boast, and even if I did, why would you accept my words as proof? I think this goes beyond a mere *audit* of the security." She peers, drilling Anika with her eyes. "You are trying to crack me. You don't just want to see the defenses or even test them, you want to fracture them, so you Malkuths can make some case for removing the Book. You want it for yourselves."

Anika does not say anything. She does not look perturbed, either, but Lilja takes the reaction as something of a victory.

"In fact," she adds, sounding somewhat casual, "I wonder if that is your charge, or if you are doing it on your own to try to earn favor within your Family. Maybe I ought to give my own report on our interactions."

The Malkuth grins, the expression already hinted at throughout Lilja's speech, now growing in a slow manner, as though the time-lapsed unfurling of petals. "Very good. I like that. Push back. And feel free to tell Skothiam anything you like of me. Maybe it can be pillow talk," she chides.

Lilja smirks right back, staring.

The moment stretches, the surrounding sounds again wrapping them in their embrace, a potential chaos reduced to white noise. Both just stare. The game of silence, though, is one in which Lilja has been raised, and not even as a game, merely as a culture.

"Well," Anika exhales into the word, "Good for you, then. I suppose you may count this as a small victory."

Lilja leans forward, voice pitched low, direct. "It's not the first time I've made you tap out."

She then rises, collecting her things, and leaves.

*****

"This is one bad dude."

Therese moves her eyes up from where she had been looking at information on her laptop. She's at Macar's offices, though they're in something of a break room, sitting at a round table that has seen better days. The coffee, at least, is strong, and both of them partake.

The P.I. is standing, one hand in his pocket. Therese had not much been paying attention, just arrived for this exchange of information, status updates, and she had taken a mug and a seat, preparing her own files. She studies him now, and she notes the difference in his demeanor. For all his bravado, his image, his effortless calm, he's bothered. She thinks he's even afraid.

"He lords over a kidnapping and sexual slavery ring of children," she comments, "Of course he's bad."

She then gets back to her computer.

"Yeah, but …"

She finally looks up after the silence takes on its own volume. He's still just standing there, not even looking at her, not trying any of his usual charms and tricks to get into her panties. He finally moves his arm, almost as if in a dream, taking a sip of the powerful brew.

"What have you found?" she asks.

"A lot," he answers, slipping into the chair across from her.

That's also different. He'd usually take the seat next to her, maybe even sliding it closer, going into his usual, almost thoughtless routine of coming on to her. It's just his nature, and though it is bothersome, she finds its absence to be chilling.

"He's not just into the kidnapping, trafficking, and prostitution."

"I know," she replies, her voice even, though still laden with some of its usual defensiveness.

"And not just the other things you'd expect, like extortion, racketeering, all that." He pauses, taking another slow sip of his coffee.

"Macar?" she summons his slippery focus, "What did you find?"

"This guy's into some weird shit."

She sighs, rolling her eyes. "*I'm* weird shit. What do you mean? What did you find?"

"He has some interesting appetites," he continues, "Extreme bondage and sadism, the occult."

"What?"

"I found some things, during my investigation. This sort of stuff comes up a lot … well, not the bondage and occult shit, but I often end up stumbling onto some personal things, even if I'm not looking for them."

"Stumbling?"

"Yeah." He finally looks at her, his own thin coat of challenge rising. "I'm digging, and people don't hide their secrets near as well as they think."

"Well, regardless of your opinion, none of that is illegal."

"I know that," he retorts, dismissive, "It's just more of the colors on this guy's palette."

"How poetic," she snarks.

They trade further stares.

"Look, that doesn't make him a bad dude, okay?" she speaks, "I told you what was going on when we started this. You took this case, knowing he's a powerful, dangerous crime boss, knowing the kind of shit he's doing to children. But now you find out he's into whips and pentagrams, and you're spooked?"

"It's not just whips and pentagrams," he throws back.

"Then what is it?"

"It's just …," he pauses, licking his lips, eyes moving away then back, "I'm not so sure the people he's doing this to are all into it, and-."

"So, he's also a rapist? That doesn't surprise me," she interrupts.

He just glares for a moment.

"*And*," he continues, "the stuff he *is* doing is generating some bad energy."

She blinks, shaking her head as though having to force her eyes to re-open. "What?"

"You may not buy in to this stuff, but frankly, it doesn't need people's belief to be true."

"What the fuck are you talking about, Macar?" she asks, her voice surprisingly taking on a more casual cadence.

"There's stuff out there, things, powers, and they generate energy, or they change it. I don't fully understand it, but I've seen some things, and I'll tell you, there's bad things out there in the world that most people don't know about. This guy knows about them, and he's bad news."

"Are you talking about the supernatural?"

"I don't know," he quips, his voice raising, "It's just energy, okay? Energy can't be created or destroyed, right, so we're all just gateways for it, catalysts … batteries. Most of us just eat, shit, fuck, and die, so whatever, normal, boring lives, but some people know how to use that energy for themselves in bad ways."

"What … the *fuck*, Macar? Are you saying he's some devil worshiper or warlock or something?"

"No, nothing like that, but he's into some weird shit, generating some bad energy. I felt it."

She shakes her head some more, small noises of frustration emerging, incoherent words belying her own inability to form cogent expression in the face of this revelation.

"Look," she changes tact, turning her laptop to face him, "I've found some things, too. I've been keeping on the trail of their finances. They're sloppy, not normal."

"What's normal?" he thrusts.

"Neither of us are new to this, okay?" she counters, "I've had to do some imaginative digging and hacking before, but with this, I just finally realized they're old-fashioned and sloppy."

"Doesn't make sense."

"Maybe he expects his magic to protect him," she ejects, gaining another glare from him, "I've found some investments, properties, probably efforts to launder money, but one place stood out."

He scoots closer to the edge of the table, his curiosity finally getting through his unusual demeanor.

"It's a flat in a nicer part of town. Not the nicest, but still, many steps up from his usual places," she shows.

"Maybe it's just where he's living."

"You know it isn't."

"Okay, then, just an investment? He flips it, makes some profit, another cog in the chain to distance him from his illegal income."

"I don't think so."

"Why not?" he presses.

"He's had it for a while," she informs.

"What's a while?"

"A few months."

"A few months? That's nothing. Maybe he's just waiting for the right offer."

Quiet descends. The two just look at each other.

"Fine," Macar finally gives in, "I'll check into it."

*****

He exits his vehicle after having been admitted through the gate, parking his rental in some of the limited available space. This is a very nice part of the City and a very nice townhouse, but real estate is still quite sparse here, things somewhat packed, narrow, and rising up instead of out. There is a garage, closed, and he supposes the vehicles owned by the people who live here are inside. Not everyone here feels the need to own an automobile. He does not. He travels so much, uses rentals so often, that owning his own car is pointless.

He is greeted at the door by the man himself. It surprises him, his having thought perhaps a butler or assistant or some such would field the arrival.

"Thank you for coming," Skothiam offers once they have formally exchanged names and a handshake, inviting the agent into his home.

Duilio's grin increases, a brief nod of his head in thanks. "How could I refuse such an invitation?" he asks as he walks in, looking about, turning in the expansive, high-ceilinged foyer to politely await his host. "You have a lovely home."

"Thank you," Skot replies, wearing a pleasant, light smile, "If you please?" He then leads the way into a comfortable sitting room.

A tea service awaits, and again, Duilio is surprised when his host offers to pour it himself. He accepts graciously, then once Skot has his own, they both take seats in the several available and quite comfortable chairs.

"This is very good tea."

"Thank you," Skot replies, still wearing that genteel smile, "I do thank you for coming. You did not have to accept my invitation."

The grin on the other man's face falters, a stunted, breathy chuckle emerges, and he looks down for the duration of it.

SWORD OF THE BUTTERFLY

"Well, as the Malkuths are fond of reminding me – I work for them. I am not *one* of them."

Skot's grin slides up at this, eyes studying the man.

"Oh, we have meetings with them, too, as you well know."

"I would suspect they'd not like one of their ... *assets* having an unsupervised meeting with their rivals."

"Well, if it makes you feel better, you can always tell them about it when we're done."

The two men share a quiet grin.

"This is a courtesy, of course," Skot continues after a sip of his tea, "But it's also a way to let you know that we're aware of you being back in the City."

Duilio nods, swallowing his own further taste of the mellow drink, hints of some spice tickling his palette but not overwhelmingly so.

"I've tried to relieve myself of expectation when it comes to dealing with ... uhm ... people like the Malkuths and yourselves."

Skot's smile again increases.

"How is that working out?"

"Eh, not so well," the agent admits.

"I would suspect your experience with Interpol has helped."

Duilio looks at his host for a moment, wondering what his words imply, wondering what all he might know.

"I guess my experience helped me to get *noticed*," he says, speaking slowly, carefully.

Silence descends, the two looking at each other, their drinks untouched for the time being. Skot finally breaks the quiet.

"Some might consider it a poor idea to go down the rabbit hole."

Duilio gives forth another of his short, stuttering-seeming exhalations, like an aborted laugh.

"Working for the Malkuths has been ... uh ... interesting," he eventually offers.

"The Malkuths are very Greek tragic."

Duilio blinks his eyes, his little grin gone, traded for confusion. His expression asks for better understanding, but he does not say anything. His host merely looks back, that polite smile still there on his lips, and he also offers nothing further on the subject.

257

"What was your involvement here in the City last year?"

Duilio huffs out a short grin. "Of course, you would know of that. It would be stupid of me to ask how."

Skothiam just looks at him.

"I was not working for the Malkuths, then, if that is what you are after."

"I know that."

"Ahhh." Duilio licks his lips, nodding. "Yes," he mulls, giving himself some time by having another slow taste of his tea. "It really had nothing to do with any of … *this*."

"That is what you thought, initially," Skot expounds, gaining a look from his guest, "There are those who are born into this 'world', Signor Duilio, and all the others who find their way in do so in a manner that necessarily originates from ignorance."

"Yes," comes another of the shallow grins, though the host's has dropped some due to the sudden seriousness of the topic.

"So, whatever it is you were doing, you somehow became exposed to … *this*." Skot offers a light gesture of his hand. "Though if you are uncomfortable telling me more, so be it. My point is that something happened, and I'm sure you know what that is. *And* it gained you notice. Now, after going on a hunt with my cousin, David, you have been sent back here. Does that not strike you as odd?"

Duilio's eyes widen, and he sits up in the chair, shoulders going slowly back.

"Is the Demon here?"

"Not that we know," Skot reveals, and when he sees some relaxation in the other man, he reiterates, "Not that we *know*."

Duilio stares back, noting the piercing gaze beneath somewhat raised eyebrows. He nods his understanding. He then drains his cup as though willing it to have a more potent potable than its current contents.

"Would you like more?" offers the host.

"Ah." Duilio seems lost in thought. "Yes, but do not trouble yourself. I can get it myself … if that is alright with you?"

"Of course." Skot returns to his pleasant smile, sipping much slower of his own drink.

SWORD OF THE BUTTERFLY

He glances more pointedly at his guest when the man's back is to him, thoughts whirling through his mind.

"As you might guess, Mister Felcraft, I was raised as a Catholic," Duilio says, mixing up a fresh tea for himself, "I even spent time as an altar boy."

Skot nods when his guest's eyes find him again.

"But when I outgrew my childish innocence, I found it ... uh ... difficult," he sends out a short-lived grin, continuing, "to maintain my faith. I tried, but it just wouldn't take. My mother was very disappointed."

"I can imagine," the host remarks.

"Yes." Duilio gives another of his brief smiles, almost as though he is somewhat embarrassed or that he may have even spent an instant forgetting anyone was there. "But now, learning that demons are real, all of this ..." he says, moving a hand in a circular fashion, "*business* with the Infernal ... well, it's quite something to process."

"It doesn't mean the Catholic faith is true."

Duilio looks over, eyes widening a bit.

"These are not demons from Hell?"

"We don't know. They are malignant, non-human entities that come from another plane of existence than our own."

"But..." The agent blinks, eyes narrowing, pondering. "Your family does not believe this is proof of the existence of God, Heaven and Hell, Angels and Devils?"

"I do not."

"You said 'I'."

Skot nods once, slowly.

"But you are the Head of the Family. Don't you speak for more than yourself?"

"I do in some things, but the beliefs, the conscience of a person, that is their own personal business."

"Yes, of course," Duilio almost whispers, eyes again lost in thought.

"Why do you think you were sent back here?" Skothiam finally asks after giving the man a moment.

He blinks himself back into focus, looking over. "I don't know. Do you?"

"I'm not sure, but I have some suspicion."

"May I ask what that is?"

"Both of us, the Felcrafts and the Malkuths, have reason to believe the Demon you helped to hunt is going to come to the City, or perhaps may already be here. In addition to this, we think the Infernal may be preparing to launch a force, an attack, to acquire something important we are trying to keep from them.

"Something similar happened last year. There was a confluence of forces, of power, though much of it was not deliberate. It culminated at the well-protected compound of a local crime lord who, incidentally, lost his life that same evening."

Duilio's eyes are locked on Skot, his body betraying a stiffening, a rising tension, though the host gives no reaction, continuing in his speech.

"Many other lives were also lost. It was a tragedy, one which was largely hidden from the public, much of which was also hidden from the local authorities. Unnecessary death, pain, and suffering. All to further the constant attempts of the Infernal to enter this world and subject us. And it was, as I mentioned, mostly unintentional. We worry that now, the efforts are more-."

And his words halt as the fine china teacup falls from the inspector's hand, shattering on the floor.

Duilio starts, blinking rapidly, looking down at the mess then over to his host, preparing, no doubt, to offer apologies, but the seated man is quicker of tongue.

"I forgive you," he says, casually, unperturbed by the lost cup.

"I am ...," Duilio manages, then gives up another of his huffed-out grins, "Ahh, thank you, though I *am* sorry. I don't know what came over me."

"Don't worry about it." Skot gently smiles. "The cup is not important. Other things, though, important things, *will* shatter."

The two share a serious exchange of their eyes.

The host then speaks, "Would you like to help prevent that?"

*****

SWORD OF THE BUTTERFLY

Their flashlights are yet off, but it doesn't seem too much more time is left before they will need such artificial assistance. The place is generally comprised of light colors, the stairs and railing white, the walls a cool teal, though now the vibrancy has faded, dusted in ash, paint peeling. The three curious boys begin to mount the broad steps, noticing the rubble collected in the corners and edges of some, and the available illumination diminishes.

"I heard this place was closed down because of some murders," one of them says.

"We've all heard that," another says, but all three have ceased in their assent.

"Let's go," finally utters the third, plodding onward.

The other two follow.

There are many windows on the ground floor, tall and narrow, and the meager condition or outright absence of any drapery gives full access to the sun. Such apetures prove to be in less abundance on the dingier, darker floor atop the stairs. The three curious teenagers flick on their torches.

The place had once been an orphanage, and it had indeed been shut down. The fine example of architecture and décor of the place had not proven reflective of the manner in which the children were treated. The justification and approval behind such excess in its construction now more lost than the truth of what led to its closure.

There had been murders.

"I read about it," the initial one speaks again.

One beam reverts back to shine on the lagging boy.

"What did you read?" comes forth the demand, as the other continues his exploration, rather stoically focused.

Shoulders are shrugged, resolve disintegrating under the challenge.

"If you want to go back, go ahead," the skeptic offers, then turns to continue.

For those attuned to such, tales wait to be told in the small rooms on this floor. The number of beds yet remaining in them do not always indicate how many occupants tried to find some peaceful hint of home inside. Not all of the workers were bad, some even sincerely cared and tried, but it is regrettably true that such has been eclipsed by the terrible things that did happen. There are shadows here, darkness that no amount of light will dispel.

The stoic feels some of it, scratching at the edges of his awareness like the beginning peel of a migraine's blind spot. His inherent gifts are so miniscule that their traces do not affect him in any conscious way. He has oft been noted for his taciturn study of things, his natural insight. He is too young yet to try to explore it in any real, deep way, if he might ever at all. For him, it is just who he is.

In one room, he notices the shattered remnants of a lamp, some of the pieces on the table against a wall, some on the ground. He picks up a sizeable shard of the ceramic, noting a peculiar straining on the inside of the piece. It is blood, but he cannot be sure of that. Was this the impromptu weapon of an evil orderly or perhaps a desperate attempt by an orphan to escape this place via the only avenue they felt was open to them?

"You find something?"

He looks back over at the skeptic. "Nothing that matters."

He releases the piece, letting it fall the very short distance to the tabletop, joining its brethren. The trio of young explorers moves on.

The residual energies of this place may be a feeding ground. Negative potencies saw cultivation, some grew and were harvested, others, though, remain in a fertile, even feral, state, pulsing like an oily pool hoping to breach its barriers and infect others.

By the time they complete their exploration of this floor, it is full night. Only one of them has received a text from family, trying to check on them. It is ignored. The three have been friends for years, and they often go out and about. They've never had much success in bonding with larger social groups, so they stick together.

"Do you think we ought to head out now?" asks the most timid of the trio, the one who mentioned doing some reading.

There is silence.

"That didn't seem like much," the skeptic offers, somewhat non-committal, but there is a show of relief in his tone.

"There's more," the third mutters.

"What?"

"A basement level."

SWORD OF THE BUTTERFLY

"How do you know that?" the timid one asks, tension evident in his voice.

The stoic one shrugs, then walks away. A look is exchanged, fear in both, though the skeptic hides his somewhat behind a smirk. As they always do, they follow.

The door is found with little searching, as though he is being called. It is not a personal lure, but it is powerful enough to get through his meagerly developed sense. Three beams angle into the downward, narrow staircase. The blackness begins immediately at the edges, no transition, as if lurking there, waiting to feed on the light, add it to the impenetrable darkness.

"We're not going down there, are we?"

Another smirk is given in response, but then the skeptic looks to his other friend, waiting, perhaps hoping the search will now, indeed, be ended. His expression drops as the stoic heads down, his shod feet resounding off the wooden steps with a volume that sounds unnaturally loud. His gait is steady, even, like the report of an announcing gong. The chilling noise becomes shrouded in the irregular, hesitant steps of the other two as they also descend.

The outré-seeming quality of the darkness proves more imagination than reality, retreating as their beams move, enveloping the way through which they came. More dust and debris awaits, along with an unnatural silence. No insects, no spiders or varmints make their home here.

"It's *huge*," the skeptic notices, sending his cone of light out in many directions, shining on shelves, boxes, walls, "It must be as large as the ground floor."

"Larger."

The light is shined on the stoic, challenging questions left to mumble and die behind frightened lips.

"Why would they have a basement like this?" comes the whispered question from within the darkness, uttered by the timid one.

"Hell if I know."

Their footsteps crunch over detritus as they move deeper within. Objects are seen on some of the shelves, layers of dust caking over them as though this place has been abandoned far longer than it truly has.

There are wisps of spider webs, equally devoid of occupants, some empty carapaces clinging with mindless stubbornness.

They round a bend into a larger room at the rear of the expansive level, and they find a water softener, the tank ruptured, angles and bends of metal turning outwardly, a standing pool of liquid on the ground.

"Wow, I wonder what caused that?" the skeptic asks, a grin on his lips.

All three beams shine on the ooze, only inky blackness reflected.

"Weird," the timid one comments, crouching, showing his own bravery in his gaining of proximity to the spill.

He shines his light on it in different ways, turning his head, examining what he sees.

"This doesn't make any-," he begins then looks up, perplexion on his face.

The skeptic had been watching him, and he turns his focus in the same direction. The third, the stoic, is walking to the liquid, his aspect as one under hypnosis. The skeptic furrows his brow.

"Hey, man, what're you doing?" he asks, reaching toward his friend who makes a rather deft dodge, shoulder going down just enough to prevent the physical connection and hinder his movement.

His left foot touches the edge of the spill, a sound of wetness resulting as one might expect. His right foot prepares to settle well within the boundaries of the ooze, but instead of a similar resistance, he drops, disappearing into the liquid as though it were bottomless and devoid of any friction, hardly any ripples occurring on the surface of the black ichor.

"What the fuck!" the skeptic cries out as the timid one just yelps, jerking backwards.

The timid one continues recoiling in fear, but the other recovers himself, making to move in to see what happened to his friend. Perhaps a hole has formed in the ground, though that would not allow the standing pool, nor the odd behavior of his friend and the liquid, but his mind is now reeling. He cannot explain what he has seen; he just wants to find his friend.

"No!" the timid one shouts, dropping his flashlight and lunging forward, all but jumping entirely on the skeptic's back, holding him.

"What the fuck are you doing?" he struggles, his beam angling about wildly, the other torch now rolling on the floor, casting its own unhelpful illumination as the pair fall to the ground.

Both cease their movement quite quickly when they see the shape rising up from the pool.

"Adam?"

The oily liquid clings, giving forth form of what seems a head above shoulders, a figure that could be their friend. The lights shine erratically still, and the skeptic, grumbles in anger, and he pushes himself free from the fearful clinging of the timid one with a jerk of his arms. More flickering and un-aimed flashing of the held torch, and when it goes back, the shape is not that of their friend.

It still looks somewhat humanoid, even beneath the slick, sluicing gelatin-like shell of the liquid, but parts of it move that should not, in ways it should not, were it human. The thing continues rising, coming up as though propelled smoothly from beneath, and the shape of shoulders leads down to arms, or appendages at the very least. One is like a human arm, held at the side, but the other comes free, clinging tendrils of the ooze threaded between the limb and torso. It is too long, possessed of too many joints, and the fingers unfurl, far too many, tipped with hideous claws.

The boys are held in fright, sheer, freezing panic. Their hearts pound, bodies trembling, the light still held on the thing there, two pairs of wide eyes not turning away, even as a third appendage rises from the backside, bent like the arm of a praying mantis, going out, then up, higher than the head, thick, ropey lengths of the goo lazily dripping down.

Eyes then blink open on the face of the creature, and thankfully, there are only two. They do not reveal in unison, though, slitting open with irregular appearance, then, not so thankfully, settling on the two unexpected visitors.

Screams then do come.

The thing had been resting, recuperating, gathering strength. It had travelled some distance, traversing lands unfavorable to it, and such had taken a great deal of energy. This sanctuary had been known, and thus had it been the destination, the rest stop. It had chosen the pool as an obvious place to regenerate, a ready-enough tether to its homeworld, if not a precarious connection. This visit from the three humans would prove a boon, a truly unexpected treat. The one who fell first would provide the juiciest sustenance, but these others would not be neglected, no.

    The skin wearer shall walk again, sooner than expected.

CHAPTER ELEVEN

Skothiam sits there, trying to keep himself occupied, but the object of his worry, so close, yet so far, continues to distract him. He looks over toward the sounds emerging from the kitchen. Lilja is in there, cleaning. He knows that such activity is not amongst her most favored. They even have a maid service that comes in every so often to thoroughly clean the place, but she is in there now, immersing herself in the mundane. He wonders if she is thinking of her issues, or if she is doing this to occupy herself away from them.

He goes back to his notes. He's read the page on his tablet many times, eyes travelling over the words, as though a drone passing over clear lands. He is imbibing none of it. He lets a somewhat noisy breath of exasperation pass through his nostrils, adjusting himself in the couch cushion, trying again.

He hears water as the faucet is turned on in the kitchen. His eyes move in that direction, though he cannot see her from this vantage. He wants her to finish her chore, then maybe she'll come in here, and they can talk. He wants to help her, wants to talk to her, but he still second-guesses. Is this even the correct approach? But he understands the potential disaster if this is not properly handled, sooner than later. He feels a growing tension in his belly.

Negativity. This is how they feed.

He is not succumbing to paranoia. He does not think the Infernal are out there, lurking, haunting, waiting, drinking up these tidbits in anticipation of a greater meal, but he does understand the potential power of negativity. It feeds itself, growing, becoming like a bloated leech threaded throughout one's being, making you think you had never lived without it before and you could not possibly exorcise it without destroying yourself. Doubt, fear – older demons than even those they fight.

He realizes the sounds from the kitchen have ceased. What is she doing now? Just as he is about to put away his work and go find her, she emerges into the living room.

"All done?" he smiles at her.

She nods, a bit weakly, humming, "Mmhmm," then sits herself beside him.

He feels her proximity like a relief, raising his left arm to drape it across her shoulders, gently coaxing. She leans in to him, snuggling before raising her face to place a kiss on his cheek. His smile increases, and he turns to look at her. Her eyes drink in the depths, unquenchable. If they are mirrors, they are so complex as to cause more awe than reflection. He lowers his face to hers, offering another kiss, which she accepts.

He feels her hand as it goes to his arm, moving along it slowly. He manages to set his tablet aside, his other hand now free, and he touches her in return. Their kissing increases in intensity. He feels a great need for this, but he remains largely passive, taking cues from her.

As their interaction continues, her hand moves from his arm to his side, and she presses more into him. He accepts it, pulling her closer. He tentatively cups at her breast, just holding. Her lips linger on his, their warm breath intermingling. He returns it with an increasing hunger, his hands now moving in more inviting motions, exploring, testing.

And then she pulls away, her face more an expression of one intent on other things, if anything at all. She reaches for a nearby copy of a science magazine for which she has a subscription, flipping it open, checking its contents.

"Lily?" he finally speaks.

She looks over to him. "Yes?"

He blinks, brow furrowing, that smile from before gone entirely.

"What …," he begins, finding words difficult, signs of the tumult within him, the war of feelings, "Uhm … I'm a bit confused."

"What about?" she replies, sincere enough, and that also adds to his perplexion.

SWORD OF THE BUTTERFLY

"This," he speaks in a gentle tone, "It seemed to me that we were about to have sex."

"Oh." She blinks once, eyes then held open. "Sorry," she finally opts, looking away, hunching somewhat into herself, a frown taking her lips.

"It's okay," he says, an attempted warm smile showing, and he places a hand on her back, trying to console. "I just want things to be okay between us."

She nods, not looking at him.

"Are you okay?" he presses, his expression now one more of concern than conciliation.

She continues slowly nodding, the motion suggesting more a dowser than a willful person, and a light noise emerges from her lips, a sad sound.

"I want to help," he ventures.

She sets the magazine on the coffee table, turning in place, tucking up a slender leg, facing him. He can sense the sheer force in her, knows she is warring with herself. He sighs.

"I'm sorry, Lily."

"Why?" she asks, "You have nothing to apologize for."

"I want to help you, but maybe the best way to do that is to leave you alone."

Silence. He experiences fear in that moment, doubt eating at him, trying to dislodge him from what he believes to be a helpful path.

"How so?" she finally speaks.

He ponders for a moment, her eyes on him. He wants to seize this moment, to use it to make everything better, or at least, to perhaps fuel a breakthrough.

"I know you're having trouble. I know this whole thing can be very stressful. I know this world, and I want to help you to better understand it," he begins, and though his words come out smoothly, he feels as though he is fumbling, "I know it can be difficult, because we've even told you how they can sometimes possess people or look like people, so maybe you just need some better training in how to really see the threat, how to determine when it's really there."

"There are certain signs," he begins to gain steam, though in the back of his mind, he knows this has been shared with her, "minutiae, ways to detect these small, subtle signals. We can spend more time with you studying those, so you won't think that-."

"I know about this," she snaps, though her voice does not raise in volume, but her anxiety is clear. "Why are you talking to me like I don't know this?"

"I was just ..."

"I know about threat and risk assessment. I teach a class on it," she continues.

"I'm not talking about that."

"Then what are you talking about?"

"You're not yourself," he comments, his own ire threatening to spike, "This isn't rational. What's wrong? You're not like this, Lily." The last is toned down, more sensitive, caring, but for all the attempt at checking himself and trying to be helpful, it backfires.

She rises from the couch, tension heightened, glancing at him, then looking away as she takes steps from him. He fights the urge to spring up and take hold of her. He looks at her as she just stands there, eyes down. He can all but feel the tumult.

"Lily?" he surrenders to his impatience, speaking her name quietly.

"Just give me a second," she says, then leaves the room.

He sits there, as though he is in a mild form of shock. Lines rise on his face, growing pathways marking the way to feeling distraught. He lets himself breathe, slow, deep, controlled, trying to meditate himself into a better place. His love for her is a storm. It careens against him, making him want to go to her, but she has clearly asked to be given a moment. Even as he sits there, motionless, it buffets him.

"Skot?"

He looks up to see she has returned. He had not even realized it. He is not even sure how much time has passed. She stands there, still some space away, looking all the world like a chagrined child.

"I'm sorry," she says, weakly.

"Lily." He rises, going to her, wrapping her in a tight hug. "I'm sorry, too."

"You have nothing to apologize for," she repeats, "You've been so patient and supportive."

He continues to hold her tight, feeling a strong squeeze from her own arms about his waist.

"But," she says.

He pulls back. She looks up, tears welling in her eyes.

"I know something is wrong, and I think I need to go and work on it," she finishes.

"What?"

"I'll come back," she is quick to say, "I promise, and..." She hitches in a breath. "We'll stay in touch. I want to talk to you. I care about you. You are dear to me, but ..."

"Oh, Lily," he speaks, hugging her tight, some irrational hope that such might extract the negative from her.

"I've been trying. I have," she continues, then again moving herself somewhat from his insistent hold, "but I think I need to go back to my apartment for a bit, just find myself, work on this in my own way. Okay? Please don't be upset with me."

He manages a nod.

"Okay," he says, and they hug again. He experiences a rush of hope from her physical proximity, but in too short a time, it is stopped as she pulls away. "I won't be upset," he says to her, and the shadow of a smile on her lips adds to the encouragement. "I respect your strength. I have faith in you and our relationship."

She nods, silent.

He runs his hands down her arms, looking near to tears of his own.

"I'll ..," she starts, his eyes clicking to her, "I'll go gather my things."

*****

The office shows a degree of décor that might make one think of a museum, a place of memory and manners, a place to be on good behavior and be careful not to touch anything. The colors of it are warm, the walls, the furniture, seeming to lull into a relaxation. And the books, volumes upon volumes, lining two of the walls, going up high enough that one would need a ladder.

"Thank you for welcoming us to your home, Dr. Malkuth," Maria says, stepping forward from her partner, the man still taking in the large chamber.

"It is my pleasure," Denman replies with his cultured voice, a warm smile on his lips. "Detectives ... Kahler and Contee?" he correctly 'guesses', angling his face to each in turn.

She nods, reaching into her short jacket.

"Oh, identification is not necessary," Denman charms, "You two do have an appointment."

"Do you often have appointments with the police?" Quain asks, pitching the question in a veneer of casualness, still looking up and about at the impressive room.

"No." Denman chuckles. "But you did check up on my references, so you know I have done such consultation in the past."

And they did, having decided to seek the help of a professional, once further information began to flow from their very cooperative witness. Alec had begun to feed them knowledge of not only Kazimir Volkov's appearance but also his mannerisms, things he'd say. The case had been given to others, as suspected, but because Alec purported to have direct intel related to the child murders, they were allowed some more time with him. Comparing notes had begun to paint a rather disturbing, chaotic picture of their suspect, so the department had decided to approve time with a professional consultant. How convenient when one such candidate arose.

Dr. Denman Malkuth, psychiatrist, also highly regarded in the fields of folklore, mythology, the occult. One might think that having enough time for so thorough and varied a knowledge would be difficult at best, but his information had checked out.

"You also teach at college," Maria mentions.

"I do," the elegantly-suited man replies, "One class of undergraduates, and a select few seeking post-graduate degrees."

"That's a lot of books," Quain remarks, finally looking over and studying the man they have come to see.

"Do you like books, Detective Contee?"

SWORD OF THE BUTTERFLY

"Not especially," Quain replies, "I just don't know when I have seen so many outside a library or book store."

"I am quite proud of my collection, though there is always room for more," he continues with his polite smile, "Would you two care to sit? I can have coffee or tea brought or whatever else you may desire to drink."

The two share a look of unspoken communication. Such does not go unnoticed by their host.

"No, but thank you," Quain replies, and the two take seats in the high-backed leather chairs facing the man behind the desk.

After a short moment, Maria adjusts herself, moving forward a touch, her lips parting as though she is about to talk.

"So," Denman speaks instead, "how would you like to begin?"

"We're specifically investigating the murder of a child-" Maria starts.

"Just one?" Denman asks, and though it might seem cold, almost rude, his tone and aspect belie his sudden shift to seriousness.

"Is one not enough?"

The host minutely moves his eyes to focus on Quain. "No, not enough to establish a pattern. I understood I might be needed to develop a profile. Such will be limited if there is only one crime."

"There's not only one crime," Maria explains, "We have a suspect. We even have a name, and we have other crimes that are alleged to have been committed by this man, but this particular case might lend more insight."

"Aaah, I see. What will you share with me?" he then asks, eyes moving to a file held by Maria.

She leans forward to deposit the folder atop the heavy, wooden desk. He calmly takes it, slowly flipping through the pages.

"This is related to the children who were killed in that ...," he comments, pausing, looking up, pondering, then to the two before him, "abandoned apartment complex, was it?"

Quain blinks, head moving back, eyes narrowing.

"Yes," Maria answers, "there is information in the file regarding that, though we've obviously left out many of the details."

He looks up, propping the opened folder in his hands as if measuring its weight or lack thereof. "Obviously."

273

"Some of the information has been left out due to-," Maria begins and is again interrupted.

"I understand the protocol," Denman says, exhaling, bringing his hands up to interlace his fingers, "but the more you leave out, the more my profile will be prone to error. This could quite especially be noted if some of the more gruesome details are excised, such as the condition of the bodies, the manner of death, anything that may have been missing, ostensibly taken as a trophy."

"This is an initial interview," Quain says, "We're not even sure how much you might be able to help us."

"Of course." The host puts on a shallow version of his charming smile, staring at the other man. "And you say you have a suspect and a name of said suspect. Why don't you arrest this person?"

"We don't have sufficient information to issue a warrant."

"And you may not even know where this person is," he says, only adding the barest touch of a lilt to the final word, as though making it a question out of politeness.

"That's right," Quain finally speaks in the broadening quiet.

It is like a pebble in a pond, as that same silence envelopes the short sentence. The three sit there, studying one another.

"This ritual killing, even the executions, they seem like sacrifices," Denman pronounces, intruding on the quiet.

"Seem like? Who has told you this?" Quain challenges.

"It's fairly obvious-," he tries to resume.

"Is it?" Maria cuts him off.

Denman stares, the curve of his lips gone, though he appears to be calm, intensely focused, but he does not immediately speak, then, finally, "a sacrifice is a gift, but it is also a transference of energy. Did you know that some cultures thought that birds would carry the soul to the Afterlife?"

The mention of a transference of energy spikes reaction within both detectives, but they hide them fairly well.

"There were no birds or evidence of birds at the crime scenes," Maria offers.

"Of course not."

"But you just said-," she tries.

SWORD OF THE BUTTERFLY

"I did, but the only birds who may have had it right were the carrion eaters."

The two detectives share a look.

"Are we discussing theology now, Doctor?" Quain furrows his brow.

"Forgive me my indulgence." Denman smiles warmly. "I'm quite sure my personal beliefs are not germane to the investigation, but it would be helpful, for a profile, if I had some idea of the mental workings of our killer. It's actually difficult to tell if this is someone comfortable with killing."

"What?" Maria has her turn to wrinkle her forehead, face turning slightly as though literally trying to better hear. "They've killed children in cold blood."

"Yes, but they do it as a sacrifice. They use metaphor and ritual to possibly obscure what they are doing, perhaps even to obscure their own feelings about it."

"What are you saying, Doctor?" Quain pushes.

Denman pulls in a deep breath, sitting up straighter, then leaning back in his own chair. "When killing is a ritual, it takes on new meaning, new depth," he elaborates, "This is not just the physical ending of life. There is a purpose here."

"We want to link these to the suspect, and we want to bring him in and make him pay for this," Quain speaks, his words and tone even a bit of a surprise to himself.

Maria glances at him rather quickly, eyes blinking wider.

Denman almost smirks. "Foregone conclusions will not benefit an investigation, Detective. They might even compromise it."

"What's a profile, then, if not a foregone conclusion?"

Denman just stares at Quain, still calm, focused, and his lips do curve into the hint of that smirk, a shadow beneath a polite grin.

"A profile is usually done to help identify a suspect, to predict when next there may be a victim. Since you have a suspect, I am left to assume this is being done for the latter; otherwise, it might seem I am being manipulated into providing evidence to your foregone conclusion."

Quain stiffens, shoulders going back.

"That's not why we're here," Maria quickly says.

275

Denman moves his eyes quite slowly from Quain to his partner.
"Then why are you here?"
Maria sighs.
"We have little evidence to connect our suspect. We would like this profile as a way to tell if we're on the right track."
"I see," the host remarks, "Well, I will be happy to provide this service."
"Thank you," Maria offers.
"You are welcome, of course."

The appointment concluded, Denman meanders over to a hidden bar, opening to reveal several crystal bottles. He pours himself a decent measure of fine scotch, neat. He takes his time, enjoying its scent, then has a light taste.

It had not taken much to find out the police were looking for outside help on this most difficult case. It had not taken much beyond that to generate the proper credentials and get himself put to the top of their list of potential candidates. All others had proved a pale, distant second at best.

He drinks further of the scotch.

He almost pities the two detectives, for they are in far over their heads. He wonders also of Quain Contee. The man knows not how close he lingers to the edge. Denman ponders, *is the man little more than meat? Is there more worth to him breathing than dead?*

He wonders.

*****

The sound is like a hard slap against dense, wet meat. Another, then another. Voices raised. The two men that form the main focal point wear only the meager wraps over their hands and their dirty and scuffed pants. They are both possessed of lean muscle, looking like they may have been carved from wood. One is slightly taller, and he appears to have the upper hand, taking several hits from his opponent, blocking some, then hitting back with ferocity. The other goes down. The crowd's loud voice goes up in volume.

SWORD OF THE BUTTERFLY

There is no referee. There are rules, but there is no official in the midst of the fight to enforce them. There is no count. If someone is downed, he may stay down, and the fight is lost. If he loses consciousness, the fight is lost. If he wants a chance to win, he must get back up. This one does, none too worse for wear, relatively speaking, as both bear marks of the fight.

The other gives a taunting wave, a 'come on' gesture, and the fight is re-joined.

Volkov watches from a perch, a meager balcony. The entire structure looks somewhat weak, certainly lacking in decent maintenance. The days when it saw more conventional use are long since gone. Its owner had died deep in debt, though not the kind of debt that might show up in a legal credit report. The space had been claimed, then left to rot once anything inside of value had been taken. It had passed through a few hands, and now it has been claimed again.

The crowd roars as the same man is knocked down. The other does not press, as that is generally frowned upon. It is not technically against their rules, such as they are, but it usually does not happen. So, the one doing a better job stands, waiting, dark eyes slit, focused, bouncing in anticipation. The other looks at him, then gets back to his feet.

Bets have been laid on both sides, of course, and the crowd cheers and groans in line with their own perceptions of fortune. From his place on the raised level, he remains passive, uncaring. He has not made any bets, and he will make more money than probably anyone off of this 'event'. He finds it distasteful, but he is not one to shy from such things.

She seems to be enjoying it, though, crying out when a particularly nasty series of blows is landed. She claps her hands, bobbing on her shod toes. She glances over at him, then smirks her deeply painted lips.

"What is matter?" Yelena asks him in Russian.

Volkov looks from the fight to his girlfriend, eyebrows rising.

"Eh, not enough blood," he responds in the same tongue.

Her smirk increases, then she unfurls an open laugh. Some of the nearby guards look over. They have grown used to the sight of the platinum-blond woman, but she still makes them feel unsettled. She certainly stands out, being not only well-dressed and very attractive, but also because she is the only female present.

277

She looks sharply back over when the crowd roars, noticing that the fighter who had been lately twice to the ground has gotten the upper hand, taking the fight to the floor, grappling with more aptitude than his opponent. Yelena cries out her support, pumping one fist into the air. She then looks back, giving her boyfriend more of her delicious smirk.

"You watch. I have made right bet."

"What do I care?" Volkov retorts, then turns and walks away.

Judging from the raucous, the fight has indeed ended as he makes his way to an office of sorts. He is quickly met by some of his men. He sets his eyes on one of them.

"Still no word," the man informs, looking quite reluctant to deliver this news.

The boss sits there, unmoved by this. Tension rises.

"You have checked his home?"

"Yes, boss," the man says.

"No sign of him? No word?" Volkov asks.

"No, boss. Nothing."

"This does not sit well with me." He pauses, coming to a decision. "Filat?" he summons, and another of the men goes more to attention, pleased to have been called. "Ex-Detective Sladky has gone missing. I need you to find out what happened to him. Has he fled city? Has he been arrested? Is he dead? Find out."

Filat nods once, then heads off on his duty. Volkov angles his eyes back to the other. Some moments pass as he just looks at the man.

"You have been replaced," he finally says.

The man looks around, nervous.

"I have had to put Filat on this, as you just saw. Filat has better things to do, but I know he will do this. But you. What can you do for me now?"

"I ..," the man begins, more agitated, "Let me help Filat."

The boss shakes his head.

"You had chance. No, you will go to guard children. If you cannot handle that, then you are useless to me."

He waves a hand, dismissively, and the man wisely leaves.

"Boss? I found something about Soosaar," says another.

"Oh?" Volkov turns to peer at the man.

"Yeah, I was just going through his normal places, and I talked to the bartender at some joint he likes, the Dove."

"Yes, I know place."

"He says he saw Soosaar there, and some lady came up to him and bought him some drinks. They left together."

Volkov blinks a bit, cold eyes narrowing.

"Did you get description?"

"Yeah."

"Good, good," he remarks, "Pass it around. Maybe we find this woman and see what she knows."

The man gives a single nod then heads off. Volkov then gets back to other matters, wanting to finish up with this and get to far more important things.

*****

The scent of coffee permeates the room. It is a somewhat cramped space in this hotel. The accommodations are certainly not the nicest, but that is how they want it. It is not too bad but definitely not too good. They have acquired quarters here in the corner of the floor, quite by design. Though there are beds in the humble suite, they are generally not used. Each of them has independently acquired a safe place to sleep, keeping such locales secret.

The woman, Livie Cloutier, speaks in her native tongue on a cell phone, her tone somewhat quieted. The other three men, one of whom aided Livie in a recent interrogation, discuss business.

"We know he is here. We see signs of his work."

"Of course we know that," another snaps, this one wearing a tie and jacket, his accent decidedly English, his dark hair cut short, his eyes peering out behind somewhat large, rounded spectacles. "We didn't have to find out that intel on our own."

The one who worked with Livie gives the man a patient look, though it speaks volumes of their professional relationship.

"You know we like to be thorough, Eldon. We've verified initial intel before on other jobs."

"I know that, too." Eldon narrows his eyes, hands going to his waist. "This shouldn't be a big deal. We're getting good money on a lot of faith. We need to end this one quickly."

"He inspires too much fear. How do we get people to talk about him?" the other, Tomas, counters.

"We had a good lead on the one lieutenant, and you botched that."

Tomas sighs, still showing signs of his patience.

"He was not going to tell us anything more, and we couldn't leave him alive."

"I don't care about your killing him," Eldon gets closer, his tension rising, "but we felt he had good information."

"I'm sure he did," Tomas responds, "but he was not going to share it with us."

"Everyone has their breaking point. *Everyone*."

"We've been doing this for a while now, Eldon. You know how I work. You've seen the results," Tomas calmly speaks, "I can read people fairly well, and under the circumstances, we would have had to kidnap him, find a place for him, then spend many hours torturing him to get anything."

Eldon huffs, then turns, moving away, going to grab his cup of coffee from the counter, sipping of it with a reaction that seems to belie his distaste with not only the conversation but also the drink.

"How are we doing with the police?" he then asks, and all eyes move over to Livie.

She finally realizes the focus is on her, so she speaks more into the phone, then ends the call.

"Alex is set up. He's going to need a bit of time to get some initial information. He's also working on getting deeper in."

"I wish that paranoid brat would just-," Eldon begins.

"He's good at what he does, and his paranoia is part of it," Livie breaks in, her relationship with their technical specialist going back to prior to the workings of this group.

"What's got you so bent, Eldon?"

The basso voice is thick with a South Slavic accent, and the unshaven man takes a casual taste of his coffee as the challenged eyes of the Brit glare at him.

SWORD OF THE BUTTERFLY

"We've only been here a few days," Tomas interjects, "and you're pressing us much more than usual on this one."

"Our employers are very adamant about this assignment. As I said, we've gotten a nice bonus up front, and the desire on their part is for expediency. You all also know how important reputation is in this business."

All three pairs of eyes look back at him. All three bear experience in their aspects. None say a word to this obvious lecture that is wasted on them.

"We'll find him," Tomas iterates.

"I think the police will be very helpful," Livie adds, shifting her legs as she reaches for her own cup of coffee. "Volkov has been causing them a lot of trouble. They'll have a good file on him. Alex will get access to it."

"The former boss, Gnegon," Tomas brings up, "He had police on his payroll. We'll also try to find some of them, see if they can be useful."

Eldon nods to this, suddenly thoughtful. He has another taste of his drink, his arm moving almost absently. The others again go quiet, watching, waiting.

"What about this vigilante?" the Serbian almost casually interjects.

Eldon actually chuckles briefly, almost silently.

"Yes, that's an interesting thing, isn't it?" he muses, then looks back up at the others. "Livie? Can Alex find out more about that?"

"I'm sure he can."

"To what end?" Tomas asks, speaking quickly on the heels of the woman's statement.

"Intelligence," Eldon replies, a smirk on his thin lips, "Maybe this vigilante knows something helpful about our target."

"You want us to be quick about this?" Tomas continues, "But you also want us to try to find this … individual and then capture and interrogate him?"

Eldon looks like a statue, his gaze and manner showing his displeasure.

"Just see what you can find. These are all potential angles of approach. You blew our best one, so get on it," he orders, then checks his watch and leaves without another word.

"I wonder what deal he agreed to," the Serbian all but growls out.

The others look over, then exchange a glance.

"It does seem out of the ordinary. Nenad?" Tomas summons, and the Serb looks up at him, having already drifted off to whatever takes his mind during such moments. "Do you think some of your contacts might help with finding this vigilante?"

"Maybe." He gives a shrug, holding his shoulders up for a bit within the dark sweatshirt. "I've mainly been casing the city for Volkov's operations."

"Right, but I think Alex's work will prove better for that."

"You want me to alter my task?" Nenad asks, his demeanor not implying any preference one way or the other.

"Just add to it, okay? Just do like our dear Eldon has asked and see what you can find."

Though his eyes do not move from Tomas, Nenad mentally chews on this. They know he is already planning methods. He then nods.

"Okay."

*****

The hooded figure lurks just outside the glow of the streetlamps at the bus stop. This is not to avoid the light but the cameras. There's one hovering there, its unblinking eye grazing over the area where people might wait for the next bus. Another hangs none too far away, but the two are not nearly close enough to overlap in their surveillance. There are many blind spots.

Footsteps. This is not a commuter. Quain has parked around the corner, feeling exposed, but he walks nearer to the bus stop. He has his pistol, his light jacket concealing it. He bears its weight with years of familiarity.

The hidden person sees him, eyes studying him with intensity. He hears the hissed sound when he gets close enough, and he stops, pocketed hands coming out of his coat. He peers into the darkness. He sees the shadowed person there, and he catches a glint of metal. It must be her. And as if to dispel any doubt, Therese steps forward just long

SWORD OF THE BUTTERFLY

enough for him to know, then retreats back as though swallowed by the blackness. He heads over.

"What's going on?" he asks, noting the young woman's agitation.

She jerks a hand, beckoning him further into the darkness. He blinks rapidly, frowning, but he goes deeper into the shadows. He can see her movements, how she sort of jigs in place, probably even unaware of it. Her eyes dart about within the covering of her hoodie.

"Are you on something?"

Her eyes stop on him, as does her motion. She is still, staring.

"No," she answers, defensive.

"Want to tell me why you called me here, then?"

"Something's happened."

"I kind of figured that."

"The P.I. helping me," she continues, and he can feel the effort it takes her to talk. "He's missing."

"Missing?" His brow knits.

She nods, somewhat jerky.

"Yeah. I ... uhm." She licks her lips, the jewelry there again managing to find some remnant of the light, a dancing reflection. "I found a house ... owned by our guy."

He notes her choice of words, as if they dare not mention the name of the person they hope to catch. Something else dawns on him, then.

"When did your P.I. go to check it out?"

"I'm not exactly sure, but I told him about it six days ago."

"Six days! Shit." Quain moves his head in exasperation, hands going to his waist.

Therese just stares at him, looking up from within her head covering.

"Why didn't you give this intel to me?"

"What difference does that make now?" she throws back, but he can sense a change in her usual demeanor – she's nervous, pleading for help in her own way.

"Well, why don't you give me the P.I.'s name? I can run some checks, make sure he's really disappeared or that maybe something else didn't happen that has nothing to do with this."

"What makes you think I haven't already done that?"

"Come on. What does it hurt to give me the guy's name? It will help me to find him."

"Okay," she finally gives after enough time to make him doubt if she would reply at all.

"Alright, and this house, you want me to go check it out?"

"I don't know if you should," she says, stepping closer.

He looks at her, his thoughts interrupted, already gone smoothly to the methods he'll use to check on Macar, the P.I.

"Look, you don't know if your guy even made it there. Let's handle this properly, okay? I'll check for him, and I ought to check into this house."

"You don't ..," she begins, eyes darting away and back, "You don't know if there's anything there to find. Just … just look for Macar."

"Going to that house is part of looking for him."

"Don't go alone," she warns, her voice emphatic.

"What do you think I'm going to find there?" he returns, a bit confused, seriousness warring with an inclination to perhaps patronize.

"I don't know," she grates out, her own continued tension evident.

"Okay, okay. Just try to calm down. Let me do some digging, and I'll get back to you."

"Something bad has happened," she says, and he notices the small, jittering motion again.

"What? What happened?"

"I don't know," she angles back, again going motionless, eyes glaring. "But Macar and I had been in regular communication, okay? We exchanged messages almost daily. I have not heard from him since I told him about the house and he said he was going to check into it. He had … found some things about our guy, things that scared him. He didn't want to go."

Her eyes have now latched onto him, like a deer's staring into a bright light.

She's worried, because she feels it's something of her fault, he deduces.

"No one made him take his job."

SWORD OF THE BUTTERFLY

She rolls her eyes, shaking her head quickly. "Look, it's dangerous. Just don't go alone. You're a cop. Take other cops with you. Take guns, whatever."

"I know procedure. It has to be followed, especially if there's something important or dangerous to be found."

"Okay, good." Her tongue moves inside her mouth, her jewelry again glinting, giving her an oddly contemplative appearance. "Be careful," she adds, each word uttered with weight.

He nods.

CHAPTER TWELVE

Fingers searching for the sure and stable grip, muscles flexing as she pulls herself higher while pushing with the legs. She looks up and to her sides, trying to find the next handhold. She sees something that looks promising and tries to reach it. Muscles tensing, digits outstretched, but she can't touch it, so she returns her hand next to the other. She extends her leg and tries to get a hold on the cool rock. The grip of the sole of her shoe feels sure, so she puts on some weight, reaching again to the possible handhold.

Thoughts mangle through her mind - the kids, being the vigilante, the growing problems between her and Skot. How can she help everyone, even herself? Can she? Is it possible?

Just when her fingers touch the rock, she loses the grip of her foot, slamming against the stone and barely managing to pull her hand back next to the other, hanging in there, fingertips digging, body tense. She keeps herself from falling. After regaining a position for her feet, she closes her eyes, taking in deep breaths, trying to calm herself.

Lilja eventually completes her climbing, finding herself in a familiar area near a large pond. The weather has been very nice today. She revels in it, letting it lull her as she sits in the grass, having ventured somewhat deep into this park area, removing herself from the urban noise of the city proper. One of the many things she misses from her home is the closeness she felt to nature. The population of this country is quite larger than Finland, and she is not used to such metropolitan density. Even after the time she has lived here, she still misses her forays into nearby lands where Mother Nature holds more sway. She tries to keep connected to such as much as possible, especially in times of duress.

SWORD OF THE BUTTERFLY

She feels like she is disappointing Skot. Her mind and emotions are a clamor, like the growing clatter of rusted machines and instruments out of tune fueling a frenetic surge that threatens to overwhelm her. She does not show it, resting here, calm-seeming, amidst the trees, but she certainly feels it. It claws at her, snapping at her from within the shadows in which she has tried to dispel it, tries to ignore it. She knows that does not solve anything, but sometimes, a lost swimmer just treads water.

Her lips edge into the merest of smirks, eyes on the lovely calm of the nearby natural pool. She knows this body of water, knows this spot of it that lies nestled within the trees and rocks of the nearby hillside. It is a privacy, though one that offers no further barriers than the ones she has crossed. This is a cradle to some, a nigh impenetrable border to others. She so desires to be cleansed, to not just tread water, hold her breath, trying to live on false hope, but to do something to fix all of this. She wants this, wants to be *better*.

She imagines what he would say – probably that she should not so berate herself, that such leads to surrender, perhaps even willful martyrdom. She does not want that, but sometimes the lull of it beckons to her with its simplicity. Just lie down, shut off the world, go into shelter.

She has relished the feeling of freedom by being back in her apartment the past few days. But even with that thought, she somewhat chastises herself. Again, the lull, the lure – just run away, hide. She should not feel any freer at her apartment than in the townhome with Skot. She feels like the force of his will and expectation threatens to stifle her, control her in a way she does not want to be controlled. But even as Lilja recognizes this, she again reminds herself that not only is that not his intent, but he is also an imperfect human. As he has said to her so many times – they need to work together.

Still, this has been worthwhile to her. She needs the reflection, the quiet introspection. If she is able to calm her turmoil, even forget it from time to time, then she goes back to it with a renewed perspective, as though hurling herself out from under the pile, seeing the spread pieces, realizing the weight is not so great as she thought, the puzzle not so confounding. She tries to be meditative, clear the mind, then approach the problem later, but she has trouble emptying such thoughts.

She finishes changing into her swimsuit, quite like one a competitive swimmer would don, leaving her clothes and small pack in a tidy arrangement on the side of the pond, and she prepares to take a dip. She pauses, blinking, pondering, and she picks up a small rock, throwing it, disturbing the placid surface of the clean, cool liquid.

"Näkki maalle, minä veteen," she intones, a Finnish folklore, some might say superstition, which is meant to dispel a malevolent water spirit, one intent on drowning.

She waits a moment, then another light smirk takes her lips, a short exhalation through her nose. She steps nearer the pool when she hears the movement, and looking over, she sees a rather large, dark green frog jumping out of the lake and onto the nearby ground, water droplets slipping along its bumpy, mottled back.

She pauses, eyes fixed on the amphibian who seems to pay her no heed. After a moment, she enters the water. She feels the sudden sting at her elbows, glancing down to the scrapes she got earlier when she nearly fell. She knew they were there, but this she had managed to erase from her focus. She'll clean them thoroughly later. Extending her arms, she knifes through the water, going at a slow, relaxing pace, a cooldown after the tense exercise of her rock climbing.

She feels the soft floor of the pond, pushing off of it with one foot as she goes further, gaining depths that allow her more freedom of movement. She swims, feeling the stretch in her muscles, turning to her back to drift for a moment, arms swaying to keep to her heading. She hears the sounds of the myriad life here, knows there are things in the water with her, things out on the shore and in the forest. None of that bothers her as she knows it would bother some.

She treads water, realizing she is not succeeding in clearing her mind. She closes her eyes, takes in a deep breath, then submerges. She floats, moving about, just experiencing the buoyancy of her body held in the fluid. She pushes against the available density, straightening herself expertly, diving out further into the depths. She drifts until her momentum falters, then she kicks, her head breaking the surface. She breathes, hands wiping at the water on her face.

She presently finds the edge again, stepping out, pulling the towel from her pack to dry off and change back into her clothes. She glances at

SWORD OF THE BUTTERFLY

her phone, then at the sky, as if bidding of the angle of the sun's light to affirm what she reads.

It's been longer than she thought. As often happens, she's lost track of time.

She has nowhere to be, but she does wonder. How is he doing? Is he thinking of her? She'll call him later, but for now, she has the trek home ahead of her, so she sets out.

*****

He told her he wouldn't come alone, that he'd follow procedure, but he just said these things to placate her. He has no real cause to investigate this house, especially since Therese's methods of gleaning the information are not exactly legal. There is, of course, an ongoing investigation of the man in alleged ownership of this property, but there is nothing concrete to tie him to it. He'll check it out in his own way, ways of which he learned when he worked less on the side of the law, and then if he finds anything worthwhile, he'll take steps from there.

In much the same manner as Alec gained entry to his apartment, Quain acquires passage into the flat. It is in a nicer part of the city's available residential districts, but it doesn't take up too much space relative to its neighbors. It is actually somewhat sort of hidden, being surrounded on two sides by taller, larger structures, one of the other sides being the edge of the area, thus nestled near a wall, leaving only the one approach.

He suspected security measures, especially in this nice of a part of town, but his initial checks had found nothing registered for this domicile. Somewhat odd, but it would make his job easier. It also makes him wonder, though, if there really will be anything worth finding. He half expects to enter a sparse, clean, barely used place, possibly kept for the address and little else.

At first, it seems that way. The dwelling is very clean, looking more like a model home than one occupied, the décor rather cold, lacking. He notes quality tiling on the foyer, possibly marble. The furniture in the front room is nice, wood and glass, some metal, and just enough to keep the room from feeling too empty. A single, abstract painting hangs over the fire place. He can't make out much of it in the dark, and he doesn't spare any time in contemplation of it.

The kitchen is nice, what one might expect. His cursory peeking into cabinets, flicking on the sleek, small light he has brought, shows him space nearly bereft of anything, and what is there is nothing out of the ordinary. He even opts to look in one box, wondering if something untoward has been placed inside instead of cereal. He sees only the expected flakes.

He takes his time, trying to be thorough. He feels comfortable enough that no one is home. He'd spent time surveilling the place before undertaking the break-in. He'd never seen anyone coming or going, more fuel to his suspicion that this place is not really even used.

He finds the master room, and it is bearing of a very nice bed, the head and foot boards looking strong with the coursing metal cast to look like vines, the duvet a rich color, probably crimson as best he can tell. There is an end table, a dresser, nothing else, all drawers empty. The closest, also large, holds only a few stray hangars. Compared to the rest, this could be a jackpot.

He wonders again if he is wasting his time.

Maybe Therese's P.I., Macar, found nothing, figured the hacker was wasting his time and has not made it any sort of priority to check in with her. Quain doesn't want to discount the girl as being paranoid, but ... no, he stops himself. He even told her to feed him leads, that detective work is following up a lot of stuff that goes nowhere, checking and checking again. It's the job.

He finds himself also wondering about his suspicions of her. He'd first felt that spike, like his cop's hunch flaring into brightness, when they'd initially met – could the vigilante be a woman? Is it her? Is she reaching out for help? The more he's spent time with her, he must confess, the less he's thought of that. He does wonder, though, because some of the information they received about the vigilante makes him think that hunch may still be correct.

When he enters the next room in his check, such considerations leave his mind.

Here's something, for sure. The room is also large, possibly more so than the master bedroom, and though he doesn't see anything

SWORD OF THE BUTTERFLY

immediately illegal, he is given pause. He snaps on his light, angling it about, still standing just a few paces inside.

Whereas the rest of the house looks unused, merely a prop, this room feels rich with ambience and vitality. Amidst the décor on the dark walls, four pieces stand out, one on each, holding sway high up and in the center, marking the four cardinal directions. First he sees the massive head of a lion, and for all he knows, it is indeed such, having been preserved by a taxidermist. Flaring out behind the noble head are two glorious wings, also looking to be those of an actual animal held in similar preservation. He is no expert, but they look as though they have come from a bird of prey, possibly a falcon or eagle.

He next sees another large head, this one having once belonged to a living bear, though it appears rent across much of one side, an open exposure of flesh and bone, its deadly teeth bared, holding bones of their own, as though a final treat offered before its own death. He steps closer, examining, noting that the bones in the mouth look like human ribs. He wonders if he should a sample.

The next is another odd collection of large feline and bird – four leopard heads, placed together in such a way as to give uncomfortable, gruesome implication that they are connected, as though a horrid birth defect has fused together an entire litter. As if to give further evidence, this piece has a neck and shoulders, showing with certainty that it is meant to signify one animal. The wings that lurch out from the backside do not offer any comfort upon viewing.

Quain turns to the rest of the room, the far side being on a raised dais, supporting a powerful-looking pedestal, quite large, spreading across a few meters, its height well above his waist. It shows a sizeable surface, and he imagines it may be a workspace of sorts. Above it, on that far wall, is the fourth piece, and where he could at least recognize the animals in the prior three, this one is a beast of such an alien look he is not sure if it began in life as the others.

Its maw is open, showing lethal teeth, but as Quain steps up to get a closer angle, he can tell they are made of dark metal, polished to a careful smoothness. As if these protrusions were not sufficient, it bares horns along its brow and head, ten in all, bending out in various directions, ending in sharp points. They do not look to be made of the same metal, something more organic. The thing's flesh is dark, showing eyes of a piercing, sickly yellow. It is more a thing of nightmare than nature.

He notes a pair of tiny doors below the head, and he opens one, then the other, revealing a small recess in the wall. It holds items. He finds a chalice and a dagger. Neither appear very ornate, merely made in strict allegiance to form and function. The blade may cut, the cup may hold. There is also a small leather pouch, and a quick inspection finds a dark red gem within. He is no jeweler, but he thinks this stone is worth a fortune. Though it heightens his suspicions, he cannot assume it is stolen or acquired in any other illegal means.

He leaves it, going back to the raised area that looks so much like an altar. Amidst the trappings, he has glimpsed curious sigils and pictographs, the room holding a suggestion of precision, yet seeming like a controlled chaos. This chamber is full of secrets, the hidden, the occult.

He bends sideways at his waist, then crouches, inspecting closely. It is as he suspected. The top of the altar may be removed. It proves to not be terribly heavy, but it resists. When he finally gets it to give, he feels the unmistakable release of a gasket seal, like the front door of a refrigerator. The scent hits him almost immediately.

He reels back. He knows the odor of rotting human flesh. This, then, will be enough to warrant further investigation. He'll just need to arrange a few things to make it all legitimate, but first, he looks inside.

There is indeed a corpse, and from what he can tell, it is likely Macar. The description fits. It is so stuffed inside and contorted that he cannot tell much else, so to spare his nose, he drags the cover back, settling it into its seal. The snick of the connection barely precedes the shotgun blast.

Quain reels back, pain blossoming from his belly. He falls, his mind blurring, adrenalin spiking. He's dropped his light, but he reaches for his gun. He hears footsteps, quick. He tries to be quicker, even as shock threatens to overtake him. He gulps in breaths, and he feels the wrench of pain in his stomach. He's been gut shot, no telling how badly. He knows those don't end well.

He manages, somehow, to get a hand on his pistol, but then he feels another pain as the foot steps down on his arm. The person crouches,

SWORD OF THE BUTTERFLY

pulling the weapon free. A tactical light from the shotgun is shined on him.

"Ah, Detective Contee. I see Sladky did not, in end, do his job."

Volkov then stands, moving away, setting the pistol on top of the altar, as though perhaps an offering, or a prelude to one.

Quain says nothing, merely reeling from the pain, his blood copiously leaking. He curls up somewhat, holding his torn gut, feeling things he should not feel, wondering how this can all be fixed.

"Pardon shotgun," Volkov says, "but I guessed correctly you were armed. I would prefer to have not shot you."

Quain blinks, thinking to murmur an agreement, but what's the point? He grunts instead, teeth clenched. He tries to find his cell phone, desperately wanting to call for help. He can't locate it. He wonders if Volkov also took it. His focus is fading. He fights to remain conscious, panting through his bared teeth. He feels something rigid in his pants pocket. Is that it? He tries to reach for it, his hand sloppy and slippery with his blood and bile. He can't get a grip.

"You have much energy in you," Volkov speaks, again very near, Quain not having registered the return. "You are full of power. Pity I had to use shotgun. Some of you is wasted."

Volkov takes a hold of him, and Quain fights back, trying to hit and strike, digging within himself for vestiges of that very strength. Volkov is hit once, in the face, though it does little more than make a wet slap and spread blood. The crime boss calmly pulls back, then delivers a powerful punch down into the detective's stomach wound.

Quain cries out, the end of it hitching as though becoming a sob. He tries again to curl up, his hands going back to trying to hold his ruined abdomen, as though some blind attempt to repair, or at least to hold in what life remains.

"You are second man who comes uninvited to here. I will need to find leak, plug it."

"No," Quain tries to protest, but it comes out weak, barely vocalized. He pushes harder, fighting the pain and encroaching darkness, the sound rising to a growl of determination.

Volkov remains placid, grabbing Quain's right wrist and slamming the man's own hand back down against his belly. Another howl of pain.

293

"You care about this leak," Volkov notes, perhaps ironically, "Someone you know. Not just some anonymous tip. Hmm. I will find it, but for now, you."

The blade of the dagger slides smoothly across Detective Quain Contee's neck, slicing open flesh and veins so cleanly that the man barely feels it. Blood spurts then rains then spurts again. Volkov holds the wounded, dying man, bending him, trying to direct the flow of rich fluid, trying to catch as much as he is able in the chalice.

This has not been as either intended, but Volkov will not let all this man's power go to waste.

*****

He sits along the gentle rise of the hill, not on the crest, but in a natural cleft made as the side rises to its low peak. There are trees here, too, and brush, and it makes for a fine sniping position. For that is what he hopes to do.

It is night, though early enough into the break from the sun, and he is garbed in all dark clothing, more deep grays than black, not wanting to stand out from being too dark, as though an inky shadow come to life, catching the eye. He doesn't expect to be spotted, but they are not one hundred percent sure of the security. He is sufficiently far away, and they've done some initial intelligence gathering, so they feel reasonably confident. Besides, he is not the only one.

"Nenad?"

"Check," he says back into the comm, peering through the scope of his Heckler & Koch PSG1, watching as very fine automobiles continue to pull up, their equally elegant occupants rising forth to attend the lavish gala.

They use a special application to their smartphones, low-latency, asynchronous communication, the microphones hidden in their clothes, though Nenad does not need such secrecy in his position. The unobtrusive earpieces tuck neatly in the canal, significantly reducing the possibility of being noticed. The frequency is generated by the hardware, thus increasing the security.

SWORD OF THE BUTTERFLY

The couple is already inside, being amongst the earlier guests to arrive, though not the first, as that would have possibly aroused undue attention. The names on their procured invitations and the ones they are using as they are introduced to people are not their real names. "Tomas Schmidt" and "Livie Cloutier" are hidden away this evening. She gives a charming smile to the other couple they are meeting here near one of the bars, allowing Tomas his chance to check in with Nenad.

As is usual with such operations as this, Eldon is not present here or remotely. He merely waits for the results, delegating field command to the more experienced and capable Tomas. Alex is present, and a quick check with him reveals that all is well on his end. The hacker is remote, of course, contributing his invaluable skills from his hiding place in the city.

Their continued efforts had finally produced results. Nenad had found some interesting things about the vigilante, all sorts of stories ranging from the basically believable to the dark avenger being an angry spirit or demon. Tomas had found it quite ironic that criminals would consider someone out to get them to be a demon. What does that say of them?

Information Alex had gleaned through the police had proven much more useful, and they had followed many threads to finally learn of this party. From what they can tell, this is not the man's usual thing, but he had apparently been compelled to throw it, inviting many wealthy people not only from the City but some more distant areas. Tomas wonders of it, thinking such an event does not sit with what he thinks he knows of the man's reputation and ways. Why have this gathering at all?

Still, it has presented itself as a wonderful opportunity for them to do their job, so Nenad sits outside, ready to attack or even serve to protect them if need be. They are inside, mingling, carrying sufficient weapons to do the deed, searching for their prey and the chance to kill him.

Their prey is not yet even there.

"Oh, don't be so grumpy," Yelena speaks in Russian, a seductive smirk on her lips as she ties the man's bowtie.

"I am not interested in this," Volkov says, sounding indeed something like a pouting child.

"I know," she says back, still grinning, looking very attractive and striking in her cocktail dress,

The shimmery, white material clings to her body like a heavy liquid, the hem of the skirt stopping around her knees. This, along with her pale flesh, make-up, and bright blonde hair makes her seem a creature of ice.

"At least," she comments, stepping back, perusing him with a purse to her lips, "You look good."

He gazes back at her, the length of the stare encroaching into the territory of becoming a challenge. He finally blinks, his eyes taking her in within a very brief sweep. She notes it, her lips pressing into a smirk. She knows he finds her desirable, for her being able to not only sense his appetites but also satisfy them is the backbone of their relationship.

"There is honor and power in this," she says, "You will see. Now, come."

He follows her lead, and they take a car to the location. Yelena had found this mansion, procuring it for tonight's soiree. The vast house and property had been left in an estate, no regular occupants desiring it despite its surface charm, so it has been placed on an exclusive market for just such temporary use. The price for one evening had been exorbitant, not to mention the deposits and assurances of liability, but there are more than sufficient resources available here.

Nenad might grow bored with watching the influx of guests, despite the exotic and expensive nature of the automobiles and the fine appearance and dress of those emerging from such. He is not here, though, as some paparazzi or voyeur. He is here to hunt. He is patient, careful, and something about that particular vehicle seizes his attention. If this were not enough, then the reaction of the guards convinces him.

"Possible target," he announces, watching through the scope, the volume and cadence of his voice low and calm.

"Copy," Tomas replies through their comlink, going quiet, waiting.

Darkness surrounds Nenad, such as it should be. The lights at the front of the immaculate mansion prove sufficient. They cause shadow, of course, and things may hide in shadow. The guards cast their eyes about, not overly concerned that anything may actually happen. They are a precaution, and they sense nothing amiss. Darkness hides, and darkness grows.

SWORD OF THE BUTTERFLY

Yelena emerges first, her coltish legs leading the way, gathering a good deal of attention. One of the more caring, or perhaps daring, sentries offers her a hand. She smiles at this, and the remainder of her delivery from the car is made all the easier. Volkov comes out after, no expression on his lips that might speak of amusement. In truth, were that so, the guards might become nervous. They've never seen the man smile. He stands, looking about more openly than his sentries, though he does not sweep for danger. He feels the need to more check his environ to merely gauge it, to determine if there is worth here, or if he is entirely wasting his time.

The guards wait. Yelena waits, though she begins the trek up the broad stairs, seeing someone she knows. The two women exchange kisses of greeting, then she looks back to her man. She smirks, rolling her eyes a bit. Just as she is about to move back down to better guide him along, it happens.

He steps forward of his own volition, joining her. She takes his arm, and the two head inside.

"Nenad?" Tomas summons over the link when he spies the couple.

No response.

"Nenad!" He ducks his head down, turning away from the majority of the guests, still whispering, but more demanding.

Still nothing.

"Alex?"

"Here," comes the thickly accented voice.

"Is something wrong with Nenad's connection? Is he there?"

The words are almost instantly repeated in French, Livie translating.

"The connection is fine," she informs, once Alex checks and gives his answer.

"Why didn't he take the shot?" Tomas muses, brow furrowing, "Nenad? Check in."

There comes the same reply as before – only dead air.

Scheiße, he curses silently in his mind.

"Shall we check on him? Do we abort?"

"Negative," he clips, knowing they have a job to do.

He moves through the growing crowd of people, noting that several of them are wearing variations of masks. He did not know this was intended to be a Masquerade. Of course, judging from the lack of them, not everyone knew or has elected to participate. He gives passing thought to this, wondering why some are covered and some are not. The masks also vary, some hiding nearly the whole face, some leaving but the mouth free, whilst others are more decorative, not much shielding the wearer's features at all.

The boss also notes this, some minor concern entering his mind. He also does not know why some of them are so bedecked. He leans in close to Yelena, whispering in her ear as she interacts with some of the party-goers, "Why do some wear masks?"

She merely gives him that smirk of hers. He stands as though stone, thinking this must be some surprise of hers in the making. He is not amused. He makes his way through the throng, bodyguards in tow, leaving her to her more apt socializing. He does not note the intense gaze of the woman standing midway up on one side of the grand staircase. She knows this mark will take much more work than did Soosaar.

Volkov is not completely ignorant of the function, having given approval to Yelena at some point, else it would not have happened. He also got involved to some degree, and not only with funding. Still, this is not his type of soiree. Too many people.

He notes several very physically appealing young men and women working through the crowd, especially up here on the second floor where less people congregate. They are dressed quite nicely, but they stand out from the regular guests. There is something different, something more sensual and revealing in their mode and measure of appearance. He realizes they are not those on the select list of invitees but intended as favors. This suspicion is nailed home when he sees a couple, obvious guests, abscond to privacy with one of the young women, not much more of an introduction than a light grab of her arm.

Appetites, he realizes. This party is but an expensive, elegant buffet. He is more curious now, resolving to explore further. He knows he is being followed, for he may hardly move anywhere in such a public venue without his 'guardians' nearby. He does not know, though, of the man and woman who have joined in the wake. They arrived together, but now they follow somewhat separate from one another.

SWORD OF THE BUTTERFLY

Tomas knows where Livie is. They trail in such a way as to give themselves potential for exploiting opportunities as well as watching over one another. They have done this before. Still, he is anxious about Nenad's sudden silence. The sniper may well have been found, but then he wonders why Volkov would not be vacated from the premises. He lets it nag at him that they may need to do the same. Risks and more risks.

Volkov continues his wandering, gaining notice from some but largely remaining a passerby. He sees people in the throes of varied imbibing, whether alcohol, drugs, flesh, or some combination thereof. He continues on his way, noting the growing energies as he delves deeper into the estate. There *is* something here, he realizes, though he is still not sure what. He follows, like a dowser, sensing a surge nearby, one he realizes is not such a swell but has only appeared so to him, and he opens the door, entering the dark, comfortable-seeming room.

The masked man in the center plays a theremin, arms held poised, hands moving, even his fingers undergoing deft, subtle movements, as though deliberately plucking delicate strings that hang invisible in the air. Volkov watches for a time, noting that the small gathering of people in here portrays a spectrum of responses. Some are rapt, paying close attention, others look bored or confused, while a tiny subset have taken to a distant, shadowed corner, engaging in more attention of each other, perhaps somewhat fueled by the music.

"It sounds like crying in the fog," Volkov says, noticing that Yelena has appeared, standing next to him, peering as though desirous of his reaction.

"I thought you might like it."

"The theremin is not an easy instrument, and he plays it well. How did you find him?"

Her lips curl, noting his interest - a fish nibbling at the hooked morsel.

"I know him," is all she gives.

He holds more interest in the music than her mysterious answers and seductive ways. The tune ends, the small crowd giving forth a smattering of applause. She sees that he also joins in, his hands slow, deliberate, sincere.

"What else would you like to see?"

He looks at her, thinking passingly on why she does not offer to introduce him to the musician. Perhaps the masked man does not want his privacy intruded upon. Some artists may be eccentric. Or perhaps she knows he'd walk over there himself if he were so inclined.

"I will see more," he replies, moving out of the room.

She follows, as do the others.

Tomas has seen many things in his time, especially considering the path for which he opted and his current choice of employment, but he's never been to a party quite like this. He is not here as a real guest, of course, but he lets his imagination work toward that scenario. He is a man of control, but he still wonders what it might be like to partake of the many offerings. This event is a temptation, but it is not just one of the flesh. He finds himself taken by things he does not fully comprehend. Still, mind on the job.

"Any word from Nenad?"

"No," Alex speaks.

"Have you informed Eldon?"

"Would you like him to?" Livie speaks after a short pause for her and Alex to converse in their mother tongue.

"Not yet," Tomas decides after a short time of thought, "Stick with the target."

The music changes significantly as they careen through some hallways and happen upon a large room, viewing it from a walkway that curves around the edge of the entire circular chamber. Tomas peers over, noting several people on the lower floor, but he sees nothing producing the somewhat eerie, electronic sounds, not even a piano or keyboard, though there are such recognizable tones within the strange miasma. He thinks, then, that perhaps it is not so different from the theremin, all of it meant to invoke something in particular, though he knows not what. This music, though, is being piped in from elsewhere, perhaps pre-recorded.

There is a naked woman below, sitting in a rather regal chair atop a pedestal. Well, she is not technically naked, as she wears jewelry upon her fingers, wrists, and toes, and she wears an ostentatious mask, stopping just above her richly red-painted lips. A man in an equally rich red cassock intones words that seem fit for a religious ceremony, then inviting people to step forward and take something from a silver tray

SWORD OF THE BUTTERFLY

situated between the woman's spread legs, a communion of sorts, or a perversion of one. It takes a moment, but eventually someone approaches, taking one of the morsels. The woman smiles. The ice thus warmed, others move forward, a queue eventually forming, as though aspirants waiting their chance to worship.

"What are these trappings?"

Yelena looks to her boyfriend, his face somewhat wrinkled in judgment.

"Oh, they are just having fun," she replies, "These people like to pretend they are into some secret as they engage in their debauchery, like the Hellfire Clubs of Britain."

"You invited them, did you not?" he throws back, "You set this up."

"Da."

He studies her, then huffs, "The one playing the theremin was much better."

Volkov turns, heading away. He does not see the delicious grin that takes her lips.

Tomas keeps on the tail, playing it casual, giving gentle smiles and nods to some as he makes his way through the manor. He continues to keep a mental blueprint of the place, realizing it proves more expansive and complicated than he had earlier assessed. He hopes to make it quiet and be able to slip out unnoticed and reasonably unhurried, but this method inherently brings a great deal of risk. He already feels pressed with Nenad's sudden disappearance. He again contemplates aborting the mission, but he does not issue the order.

"Hello."

He looks up to see two gorgeous women in front of him. He had all but completely missed them, moving to go around without thinking, as though they were a lifeless obstruction. They are both dressed in a display of finery, both looking as though they stepped off the runways of a fashion show. They remind him of Volkov's lady friend, looking quite predatory.

He gives a smile and a quick nod of his head, making to continue on his way.

"Are you in a hurry to get somewhere?" one asks, and he detects an Eastern accent to her words, though he cannot exactly peg her origin.

301

"Mmmm," the other purrs, a hand moving languidly up her friend's naked arm, "If you know something exciting going on, please take us with you."

"I…" He grins more openly, a stunted exhale trying to open his lips. "I am just exploring. It is a very nice house, don't you think?" he tries, then again going to step by them.

He glances over, realizing he has lost sight of his prey. He curses mentally, wanting to be away from these two ladies, so he can check if Livie is still on him and pick back up the trail.

"It is," one of them agrees, her words elongated in obvious seduction, "May we accompany you and see what you find?"

"Excuse me," he says, being more final but still coating his expression with some measure of manners, then slipping away.

He steps more rapidly than he likes, not wanting to catch anyone's attention and give cause for alarm. The two ladies see this, of course, watching as he departs, their subtly lecherous grins not faltering from the seeming rejection.

He moves into the hallway, noting it is darker here, devoid of people. He continues, somewhat surprised when it curves rightwards and also feels as though it is descending. He wonders what desire and will would lead to someone putting such a passageway into a home.

"Livie," he whispers into the com.

Nothing.

"Alex," he tries, voice more demanding.

Nothing.

He guesses there must be something obstructing his efforts here.

He finally reaches the end of the hallway, and the door there is locked. He emits a sharp, frustrated snort of air through his nose, then looks about, realizing how dark it is. His eyes must have adjusted as he descended. And even with this realization, he does not see from what emits the very limited illumination. He tries the comlink again, and again, nothing. He decides it is time to get back up out of this strange hallway, but he gives it one more try. The knob turns.

He blinks, brow wrinkling. He heard nothing to indicate it had become unlocked. He wonders if someone may be waiting just inside,

SWORD OF THE BUTTERFLY

but he can always play the lost guest. He pushes the door open, walking in slowly, looking about.

He can make out shapes in the dark room, but none of them are people. He glances up, noting the ceiling is so tall he has trouble making it out, wondering if he is playing tricks with himself. He decides to take a further risk, and he pulls out his mobile, using it as a makeshift torch, the modification to it producing a quite decent amount of illumination. If there is anyone here, they remain silent, for surely he has now announced his presence.

He realizes the ceiling is not so impossibly high up as the darkness initially gave his mind to think, but what he sees gives him pause. Painted around the uppermost portions of the walls are eyes, or the suggestion of such. They all look hastily drawn, more perhaps like symbols or sigils than true depictions, but they all stare at him, made of their bold, daring red lines, as though defined by blood. He notes the sheen reflected by his light, suggesting the insignia are fresh. He wonders what this is, all of his, the entirety of it suddenly scratching at his awareness, for his duty here has kept him from truly pondering the oddity of the gathering.

He navigates slowly, noticing the blocky, non-descript furniture, almost suggesting this is some storage room, though there is enough deliberate arrangement to it to make him wonder if that is indeed the case. Several steps in, and he spies the less blocky and more bulbous thing toward a far wall. It is covered, and he doesn't like what his gut tells him. He moves over, still going slow and quiet, though he wonders if such stealth is any longer necessary.

His instincts prove correct, and once removed, the shroud reveals the body of a person, a person he recognizes.

"Eldon," he says, speaking the seemingly dead man's name, wondering how and when their leader got here, or was more likely brought here.

He shines the light over him, noting he is nude, but what makes Tomas recoil is the condition of the man's abdomen, being rent open and leaking of its innards. He ponders the feeling he held a mere moment ago, from whence it came, and he feels fortunate his own intestines are still intact. He'd like to keep it that way. Time to abort. He turns to leave.

"You almost discovered our secret, didn't you?" speaks a cultured voice in a Transatlantic accent.

He starts, going rigid, one hand moving toward the blade he has hidden on himself, the other moving to shine the light of his phone. He sees a well-dressed man standing there, wearing no mask. He might even think him a mere guest if not for the words he has uttered.

"I'm … lost," Tomas tries, putting on one of his charming smiles, those that mingle a self-assuredness with enough vulnerability to evoke trust.

"Oh, no doubt of that," the man says, studying the other, "You know, you'd almost be good enough for us."

Tomas blinks, perplexed. "Us?"

The other man grins. "Yes. Us."

A moment stretches, the two merely studying one another. Tomas does not like the man's calm or confidence.

"I'm afraid you can't be allowed to succeed," the man says, and he sounds almost apologetic, "There is more going on here than your employers realize. It is really quite insignificant that they are unhappy with some rogue capo coming here to set up his own shop … I suppose 'capo' is the wrong term for the Russian mob, but it doesn't really matter."

He fixes his eyes back on Tomas.

"We still have more work to do."

Tomas studies the man, his own hand now having reached his hidden weapon. The distance between them is not so far as to rule out sudden surprise attack. Despite the man's manner, he does not appear armed and both his hands are in view. Tomas decides to act.

He moves his hand, quickly shining the light from his phone into the man's eyes, hoping to at least startle if not blind him momentarily. He also moves forward sharply, pulling forth the small knife. It all takes an instant, but he is suddenly on his knees, his hands empty, pain beginning to seep out from his wrists and the backs of his legs.

He makes no noise, not bothering to cry out or whimper. He hears the footsteps of the other, and he sees as his mobile is retrieved from where it stopped on the ground, the light used now to shine on him.

SWORD OF THE BUTTERFLY

"You have no chance here," the man says, and Tomas sees the subtle, though diabolical curl to the lips. He glimpses a shine of deep red light toward the hand not holding the phone, something held there, something dripping with a portion of his own blood.

"Who are you?"

"It doesn't matter who I am," the man replies, smoothly, the hungry grin gone from his handsome face, "What matters is that at least one of you has to get away."

Tomas blinks, feeling somewhat woozy from the leaking blood.

"What?" he manages, the word almost a breath.

"Yes. One of you must get away," he continues, as with the air of a collegiate professor, "Tales and folklore, even legend, are all very important now, aren't they?"

Tomas tries to speak again, but his befuddlement is evident, the continued loss of his vitae an also obvious deterrent to his focus. His heart continues pumping, that strong organ now working against him after so many years of tireless service.

"Ahh, well I sense your confusion. Don't worry, you've no hope. There are others."

Tomas glances up, the pain of just such worry etching his face.

"Livie ..."

The man smiles, the expression almost warm, but something underneath robs it of sympathy.

"You care about her. How ridiculous. As I said earlier, you're *almost* good enough. I was more referring to the other. Alex is his name, yes? He'd make a much better teller of tales, so no, I am afraid your dear Livie will share a similar fate as you."

Tomas hangs his head, his desire to know what all is going on leaving him with the unabated flow of his blood. He feels cold. It takes him a moment to realize the man has come right up to him, crouching. He raises his eyes, feeling a tremendous weight to do so.

"Your end will prove more painless, though," the man remarks, bringing up his hand, and within it he holds a rather wicked-looking dagger made of black glass.

He moves his forearm with a smooth grace, perhaps more as though conducting a symphony than ending a life. The razor sharp edge of the obsidian slices easily through Tomas' neck, blood thrusting out, though its power and profluence is lessened from the already significant loss.

The executioner steps back as the man slumps.

"I do hope you at least enjoyed my playing of the theremin."

*****

She sees her standing there, looking obviously distraught, even through the general façade she usually projects, the one where she seems of stone, as though nothing, not even tears, would erode her stoic expression. Of course, they have come to know each other better over time, in so far as a teacher and student may do so. It might surprise some how much people in these roles do learn of each other, especially with the type of training they are doing. Still layers, privacy, secrecy yet remain.

"Therese," she greets, walking up to the dark-haired girl, putting a bit of sympathy and a question mark on the word, though more a tentative approach than anything overt.

"Lilja," she says in return, then, "Hi."

Lilja wonders if she has ever heard her student use that word.

"You weren't in class," she notes, hoping this may jar the lid.

The hacker just looks at her, then shakes her head.

"Is something wrong?"

Therese swallows, her jawline belying the clamping of teeth, more a steeling than anger. Her lips then part, the exhale that comes forth showing a slight stutter.

"I want to talk to you about something … If that's okay?"

Lilja blinks, then nods, her mind abuzz with what this may be. "Okay."

She wonders if Therese will resume her accusations and demands regarding her being the vigilante. Of course, she was correct, but Lilja never admitted it. As far as she knows, her student has never confirmed it, despite her obvious talents. Lilja readies herself, knowing she doesn't want this sort of thing thrown at her and the guilt it brings, especially now.

SWORD OF THE BUTTERFLY

"I ...," the other girl tries, then she tucks in one side of her mouth, playing with the snakebite piercing there. "I found out some bad news, and ... I look up to you, you know?" She suddenly shifts gears, and Lilja continues to just stand there, eyes on the woman. "I don't really have too many people in my life that I do. No one else, really, so ... I was hoping I could talk to you ... if you've got a minute?"

Lilja nods, slowly, paying close attention to Therese without necessarily appearing to do so. She watches for signs, minutiae in movement, anything that may tell her if Therese is perhaps ill, in danger, or even a danger herself.

"Tell me what happened," she bids.

"I went to visit someone in jail recently," Therese reveals.

Lilja blinks, pondering, wondering if she is about to hear of a close friend or relative having been apprehended. Perhaps Therese is upset about something like that and just wants to talk. Maybe she even needs some direction in what to do. Maybe that is all this.

"I ...," she again tries and again pauses, eyes studying the red haired woman before her. "I don't know if you are who I think you are, or if you can be what I want you to be, but I want to tell you this, and not just because of that, but because of how I feel about you."

Lilja gives more of the calm, hopefully comforting nod, "Okay, Therese," but she still keeps that underlying study and awareness, for she is becoming tense in expectation of the things implied and what may be about to be told.

"I've been keeping a watch on the problems in the city. You know that, and uhm, I've been trying to help others."

"Oh?"

The hacker nods, her dark, spikey hair a channel of the confusion she evinces. Then the movement stops, and Lilja watches, seeing the growing tension rise again. She feels a gathering pinch in the flesh of her face, a drawing in of her own concentration and worry. Therese is all but trembling, fighting the emotions she feels within herself.

"Did you ... did you see the ... news on the dead cop they found – Quain Contee?"

Therese had sent information, per her usual, through the network that feeds intel to the vigilante. She still believes in what she does, but the devastation she feels has forced her into an uncharacteristic diplomacy.

"Yes."

"It was my fault."

"What?" Lilja's head moves fractionally, belying her perplexion. She wonders if she is hearing a confession.

"I fucked up," Therese adds, "I really ..." She looks away and up, fingers clenching, eyes blinking rapidly, still fighting back the strange feeling of emotion. "I really ought to stop trying to do investigation outside of cyberspace."

"Therese?" Lilja finally speaks into the growing silence, "What do you mean?"

"I'd been working with ... that cop, Contee." She seems to have to force out the name. "I found ... something, a place, for him to check out. Well, I ... I'd been working with a P.I., and I sent him there first." She fixes a stare on Lilja, and the pain that resolves on the young girl's features sends a wave of empathy through the teacher. "I've just been sending people to the fucking executioner."

Lilja had seen the information from "Sparrow", Therese's online alias, but it had not said anything like this, merely being further and more detailed information about the murdered police officer, nothing about a private investigator. Therese fully intends to share more with her contact, but after what else she had learned, she felt compelled to come here and speak to Lilja directly.

"I found out that the cop's ex-partner was in jail," she continues, once regaining what she is able of her composure, "Corrupt cop, finally left the department and went full-on criminal, but then he got arrested and was going to give evidence against his boss."

Therese does not add that she saw the mug shot of the man, realizing he was the same who had helped kidnap her last year, leading to her second rescue by the vigilante. It had chilled her, and she felt as though some pieces of a larger puzzle were showing themselves.

"So, I went to visit the ex-partner in jail. To talk to him. I don't know why. I just felt like I needed to, but..." She turns her strained eyes again on Lilja. "They told me he killed himself," she states, almost cold, though not from anger or vengeance, but to still herself and the growing

SWORD OF THE BUTTERFLY

maelstrom she feels inside. "He was in protective custody, trying to help them. He left a note, blames himself for Quain's death. There's too much death, Lilja. Too much. It has to be stopped."

The two stand there, both looking almost frozen. Lilja feels the roiling current beneath the icy surface, an undeniable force that will eventually break through. All that is unknown is how it will be handled, what damage it will do.

Therese moves her head side to side, aggressively, as though shaking herself out of a reverie, her left hand going up to her face, formed almost into a fist, and she presses the knuckles of her clawed fingers against her cheek. She feels the burn there, the threat of tears, and she is left feeling alien for it, fighting it, subconsciously, doing what she thinks is a defense against the pain. Lilja wars with her own emotions, but she does not give any sort of physical display, only moving her hand forward to gently touch Therese's shoulder, gently sliding her hand down to the bend of the elbow.

"Sorry to have bothered you," Therese manages, her voice strained, "I just needed to tell someone." She glances at the redhead, her lips forming into a sort of grimace that seems an attempt at a smile, as if such an expression were an impossible foreign language to her. "It sucks not really having anyone to talk to."

"You can talk to me."

Therese locks eyes with her instructor, staring, unblinking. After a time, she nods, the gesture rapid, almost jerky.

"Thanks."

"Are you going to be okay? Do you need a ride home?"

Therese presses her lips together, drawing them inward, eyes moving away from Lilja. She truly ponders the first question. Has she ever been 'okay'? She supposes she has and ought to stop being so melodramatic, but the situation now is very real. There is a tremendous threat in the city, and she has done no more than send meat to the grinder. She wants help from the vigilante. She wants something from this woman standing before her.

"I'll be fine," she opts, eyes going back to those deep blue ones, "And thanks, but I have my bike."

Lilja nods, letting her hand drop as it seems her student is indeed calming. "Okay. Be careful."

Therese blinks, head rising on her stiffening neck. She finally nods again.

"Yeah. I'll stay out of it. I'll just stick with what I know," she decides, then turns and leaves.

*****

"Why did you leave Finland, Lilja? Did something bad happen?"

A dark miasma envelopes her, though she feels it like a haze, like something on the edges of perception. There is a solidity here, a convincing measure, even through the dim.

"Did you let someone die like you let those kids die?"

Tension roils, like sutures bleeding into her, too tight, the rough thread pulling through tender flesh, the slow creep of binding pain.

Doubt scratches at her, has done so for many years. Yet now, it is worse. It leaves more than marks. It gets deeper, peeling at scars, pushing at new places, and cracks form. They feel this like a lure, and they will use it. They know she is out there. They know of this new force that defies them, and they want to consume it. She has eluded them until now, but they have her.

"Why haven't you even visited the gravesite, Lilja?"

Smatterings of darker hues begin, dropping in mid-air on the outside of the place in which she has found herself, as though she is inside a bubble, seeing ink drops form outside. They spread, reaching out, then disappear, suggestions of a coughing sound.

The haze within her mind is not entirely of nightmare. She dwells now in the Dreamlands, a place told to her by her grandmother, a place that is more real than most may credit, a place where one's subconscious has reign. It is a place of confrontation unlike any other.

They may thrive here, riding upon the wispy waves of that in-between place. Such locales may be gateways for them, and they ever lurk, gnashing and scratching, looking for ways to get inside.

They have found one. "What are you afraid of? Why are you running away again?"

SWORD OF THE BUTTERFLY

Forms coalescing, taking shape, heads rising from shoulders, features hinting through the fog, like chaotic lines obeying and giving more definition, yet still abuzz with rebellion. She sees sorrow on one, a male, someone close to her, someone dear, yet he turns away in disappointment. She sees challenge on another, a female, someone who rivals her, pushing her with a precision that threatens to tear her apart.

Don't leave, don't leave, she tries to say, but her voice does not wish to properly work. She reaches out, trying to grab at the departing figure, to move toward it, but she feels stuck, her muscles paralyzed, her feet lodged in firming cement.

The unnatural fog seeps inside her apartment, coiling its way throughout, seeking, hiding. The creature it conceals sniffs deeply. Yes, there. It detects the sweet, enticing scent. That weakness, that fear, it was born of itself, but they fuel it, letting it grow. It yields more unto them. And now, finally, they have found her.

It wasn't my fault. There was nothing I could do! She cries out, trying to shout at the extent of her lungs, hoping to convince someone, anyone, perhaps even herself. Yet, there is barely any sound.

"You know that's a lie," the voice of fear resumes, grating into her, "You killed him."

No!

The demon gains more form, becoming a darker, weightier shape within the transdimensional mist. There is a suggestion of a bulbous, weighty body, a central core, appendages moving out, somewhat thin, though comprised of fibrous muscle, joints like hard knobs. Even as the monster gains solidity, it seems off, wrong, disproportionate. But it is not here to fully obey laws of this world.

The door opens without being touched, and there, within that room, that resting place, it sees her. She is trapped within herself, ready prey. A line forms across the front of the demon, a wide maw showing itself with the parting of absent lips, an obscene opening toward the upper part of the main mass, a crowd of teeth within, a tight array of thick needles.

It moves closer, hardly making any sound on its large, almost sloppy feet. It scents the fear now like a ripe bouquet. It inhales again, reveling in the allure. She is sweet, lying there on her side, red hair arrayed out like a pattern of sprayed blood. It wants her, and even though the desire is rich, the purpose plain, it lingers, giving more time to the enticing foreplay.

Close, so close now. Claim her. Eat her. End her. Deadly claws on slowly writhing, slender fingers, offset eyes wide with pleasure.

Dali suddenly springs out toward the demon's face, yowling and hissing, clawing at the eyes with a great ferocity. The monster howls in its unearthly way. Lilja wakes, body tensing with a sharp intake of breath, eyes going wide, confusion claiming her. She turns, hearing the sounds, seeing the dark shapes in her bedroom.

The beast grunts and growls in a manner unfit for this plane, grabbing the large cat with its taloned hands and throwing him against the wall. Dali cries out, falling to the floor, unmoving.

Lilja rolls away, going over the bed and landing upon bare feet. The demon reacts, turning to her, lunging. She ducks her head, using her bent legs to propel forward, staying low. Adrenaline rushes though her, but now that she is awake, her training takes hold. She knows she is under attack, knows Dali has been badly hurt, and she knows her life is being threatened.

The thing hisses, feet plodding with a lethal staccato on the floorboards as it rushes after its prey. She rises up, having gained some distance and takes to a determined sprint, knowing where she needs to go.

Why are you running away?

The demanding hisses both within and without, and she is not sure from where it comes. She falters, feeling it like a drilling buzz. The demon gains on her. She turns, barely missing being struck, and there it is, waiting for her, patient, ready, in its proper placed, cleaned and well-maintained, needful of its own purpose.

She grabs the katana from its stand, jerking it free of its saya, both hands on the hilt, turning on planted feet just as the demon attacks. She moves to the side and down to avoid the swipe of both claws, striking out with her own collected force, and the sharp blade of the sword digs in to the thing's side, going deep, lodging. It screams, moving away, taking the weapon with it.

Lilja reacts quickly, but a slim moment spared to realize the sword is no longer in her hands. She dodges away, rolling, using that momentum

SWORD OF THE BUTTERFLY

to regain her feet and face her opponent. Dark ichor leaks down the side of the monster, though it shows more concern for her than the katana stuck in it.

It attacks again, rushing her, flailing with flaying claws. The chaos and speed of it is challenging, but she moves away, using her own diminutive frame and speed to make herself a less easy target. She pivots, striking out with a powerful kick, her heel smashing against the Demon's body. It feels like a dense mass of vegetation, and it seems she does little more than annoy it. She is well versed in sensitive places on the human body, but she knows not how to pinpoint such weakness in this thing.

It unleashes a challenging, lustful growl from deep within itself, that wide, irregularly shaped mouth open and eager. It lunges again, arms out, as though hopeful of merely crashing its bulk onto her and crushing her. Lilja ducks down, low, keeping her feet, moving away. The demon collides with the wall.

The beast turns, yelling at her again, and she lunges in, grabbing the tsuka of the katana, pulling it free. A greater spray of the beast's vitae erupts, and it now cries out in what she hopes is pain. It rushes her, sensing her closeness. Lilja pulls her arms back, bending them, then presses forward with all her strength, sensing a surge of energy from deep within herself. She unleashes her own battle cry, feeling a wave coursing through her body, and there, flashing about the blade in that single, short instant - a blaze of colored light, and she jams it inside and up into the demon's mouth.

She dances back on fleet feet, holding the sword, the length of it dripping with the black gore. The demon stares at her, eyes threatening to pop out of its head, gaping mouth unleashing more of its fluid. It then drops forward. She moves away from this, sword held ready, point angled at her opponent, but it looks to be dead.

She then drops her sword, turning to rush to Dali, worry and panic now claiming her. She'll get him to a vet, she'll get her phone, call Skot.

This is not over.

CHAPTER THIRTEEN

They sit together on the sofa, close, embracing, just feeling each other's company in a way they have not in a while. The time apart has felt long. It has done her good, even as it filled him with longing and a nagging impatience. But Lilja has returned. She's moved back in, brought her things, especially the sword, placing it reverently in its holder.

She had collected Dali and rushed to the emergency vet clinic, hoping he'd be okay. He had proved to hold a resilience similar to her own, and though there would be more monitoring, the treatment had proven successful. He'd be fine.

Skot remembers that phone call with an alarming clarity, waking to the chiming of his mobile, seeing the number. In the instant it took him to answer, he figured it could not be so bad since she was the one calling, but then a panic gripped him – what if someone else was calling him on her phone? The relief which washed over him when he heard her voice did not match her tone of alarm. She quickly explained what had happened, telling him where she was, and he had gotten there as soon as he could.

He felt a nigh sickening miasma of worry and comfort that she was alive and well, but she *had* been attacked by a demon. They'd found her. If there had been any doubt as to whether or not they know her, such is gone now. He knows this is not just to remove the Book's guardian. This is to destroy someone they perceive as a threatening enemy.

"You know I've had a lot of training." Lilja breaks the silence, looking up at him as they loosen their embrace.

He nods.

"Part of that is learning to identify risks. I assess everywhere I go. I analyze. I evaluate tactics and strategies with every mission I undertake. You know how important that is to me. I suppose I came into a feeling of comfort." She pauses, pondering. "'Confidence' is probably a better word for it. I knew of the risks out there. I had identified them. I kept watch on them and on myself. I had it figured out.

"Then you showed me a whole new world, and it's kind of scary," she says, adding a short grin and exhaled chuckle, "and that risk ... well, it's much more difficult to discern."

She goes quiet, eyes moving away, thoughts turning inward. He keeps contact with her, watching, holding his tongue. He moves a thumb over her held hand.

"In the moment when the demon attacked me, I didn't think much. I just acted. And that's how it's supposed to be. I teach that to my students." She looks over at him. "Just as you and my sensei taught me."

He blinks once, wondering to be in such prestigious company, and he knows that he is not alone responsible for her new learning once she became a Hunter.

"After I had calmed down a bit, when I was waiting for you to come to the clinic, I felt a rush of feeling. I realized what had just happened. The training, the practice, over and over, and then, when it is needed, it just ... *happens*. I felt the power."

"What power, Lily?"

"The magick," she breathes.

"That's something within you," he replies, his brow furrowing, "You've always had it."

"Not exactly like that," she elaborates, "Like what you do with your sword, like Nicole has tried to teach me. I felt the power all around me, it flowed through me, flaring inside me, and coated my sword when I struck. Like I was channeling it into my attack."

Skot just looks at her, staring, and he eventually blinks.

"That's amazing, Lily." And he sees the huge, bashful grin appear on her face, and he pulls her into a firm hug. "I knew you had that potential. It just needed to, well, *happen*. Just as you say."

After a time, they part again, and he sees that a ponderance has again claimed her.

"Demons are a *threat*," she resumes, "not just a risk, anymore. I suppose they were always a threat, but I didn't fully accept that. My way of teaching is to handle the risks before they become a threat, since a threat is something that has to be handled immediately. Because this threat is so great, so new, so ... *hidden*, it just took me a while to get a hold of it. Longer then I realized. I thought I had it figured out ..."

Her voice trails off, and he realizes she is feeling apologetic, perhaps even disappointed of herself. He leans in, hugging her tight.

"Lily, it's okay. Don't be so hard on yourself. This is not an easy situation to digest, but trust me, you're doing well. Very well. You are amazing." He smiles at her.

"I don't feel amazing," she retorts, blunting the words with the suspicion of a smirk.

"Well, it'd be nice if you did, but it doesn't change it. I have seen this knowledge handled in so many different ways and with varying degrees of success. You are remarkable, and I'm glad you're safe and sound."

They exchange another embrace, adding kisses to the end. He is warmed to see the calm curl to her lips, that easy smile.

"I'm glad I'm back," she says.

"Me, too," he agrees, and this brings a blush to her skin, a soft bubble of laughter. "But," he adds, looking suddenly more serious.

"But?" she pitches when he does not continue.

"I hope it is not just out of fear. We can always ward your apartment better. I want..." He pulls in a breath. "I want you to be here ... with me ... because-."

She cuts him off, squeezing his hand. "I know, and I am. I *want* to be here ... with you."

They smile at one another, just gazing into each other's eyes.

"I was more scared for Dali than myself."

"I'm not surprised at all to hear that," he offers, and though it may seem something lobbed with humor, his expression and intonation sound serious.

"He saved me," she all but whispers, and he nods, having heard her say that several times when they were filled with anxiety, waiting on the feline in the emergency room.

"That he did, and he'll get a hero's welcome when he's better. And he'll be given all the comfort he wants here."

She nods, thoughtful, then a light smile traces her lips.

SWORD OF THE BUTTERFLY

"What?" he asks, his mouth finding the expression contagious.

"I just realized something," then she moves her eyes to his, "Dali and I are both guardians."

His smile increases, and he gives her a squeeze with his hands.

"We're all guardians, Lily. It's not about the Book or hunting. I'd be happy if the Book could just be a book, you know? Something interesting, mysterious, but ultimately mundane, or at least, useless. And if there were no more hunting. We're here to guard this world, to protect humanity. We're *all* Guardians."

She ruminates for a short moment, her eyes drifting in their focus. Then they snap back to his, her grin somewhat lessened, though she does not look as weighted as one might expect from such a realization, such a responsibility. She nods, slowly.

"Yes," and her voice sounds resolute. "We are."

And though things are now happier between them, the threats still remain. Not just the Infernal, either, but the very real, beastly things that humans may wrought upon one another.

She receives intelligence about another large building, similar to the apartments in which she was almost killed. Still, this is a place important to the crime ring, and she feels she must launch an assault. The information is checked and cross-referenced. It appears valid, and if so, it could be a potential crippling. She considers turning the information over to the police, but a feeling of guilt surges through her. She needs to let such wash away, like water over stone, but in the end, she decides to pursue this herself.

She leaves information for Skot, knowing he will be worried, displeased that she doesn't let him provide assistance, but this is how it is. They both understand that.

She's looked at blueprints, done some initial reconnoitering, and she feels ready. She let herself not rush this one, forcing a restraint to that uncharacteristic lack of patience. Having such a virtue had been important in her success in sniper training, and she realizes now how much of her underlying anxiety had been affecting that. Yes, she wants to save these children, but her rushing into things is not helpful. It pains her to think of what is happening to them. She doesn't want it to continue an instant longer, but plans must be followed, strategy must be careful.

She now sits atop her motorcycle, shrouded in darkness, looking at the target locale through her small, powerful binoculars. The structure is somewhat old, comprised of dark concrete and regularly spaced windows, nearly all of them paned, composed of half a dozen segments. These are all, also, shrouded. The top level, however, shows large, broad windows, single sheets of glass, and nothing is obscuring these.

The building is comprised of six floors, but where the apartment complex had been broad and squat, this one proves much narrower, reducing its breadth as it rises, the top four stories of quite less area than the lower section. She knows there is also something of a basement, and she had procured what public records she could, learning as much of the subterranean architecture as she could find. There had not been a great deal. She'd fancied using that as a way in, but what she found did not display such a ready avenue.

The place had likely been a modern marvel when first built, and she knows from records that it used to be a very legitimate office complex, though now pinpointing the ownership and function results in difficult data trails.

She has also received some intel on the security of the place, nothing very sophisticated. She used various modes on her binoculars to find a few cameras and plot a course. The doors in front are more tightly secured with lights and such security sentinels, and she has spied the movement of men just inside. She knows others are also within, but the front entrance is heavily guarded.

It appears she can make it to a maintenance ladder, and she heads out after engaging her bike's theft deterrents. She has her H&K G36C, suppressor affixed, subsonic ammunition at the ready. It is strapped to her torso, held tightly in front, and across her back is her katana. She doesn't expect to need it, but after the ordeal with the demon attack, she experienced some compulsion to bring it along. She feels somewhat weighted, having brought along many items she thinks she may need, not the least of which is the disposable cell phone she'll use to call the police once the building is secured. She doesn't know how many children are

SWORD OF THE BUTTERFLY

inside. This place is not just used for such activities, but she expects to find some.

As she nears the target, she ponders Skot's invitations to aid her. She has always felt protective of her independence, especially in these ventures, but she now has a moment of doubt. Her ego is not more important than safety, and even with only one other proper person here, the risk would be significantly reduced. Still, the time for such considerations will have to come later. Time to focus.

The maintenance ladder is some feet off the ground to discourage children or others from using it to gain access to the roof. Lilja draws upon her free-running experience, trotting up to the proper amount of speed as she nears the wall, the jika-tabi offering flexibility. She climbs, placing her hands and feet in the correct way, using her momentum to gain enough height to spring up and take hold of the bottom rung of the ladder. She pulls herself up, quickly climbing to the roof.

There is no access from here into the building, which is usual for the general architecture of the region. She moves about, keeping low, scanning the rooftop, noticing nothing out of the ordinary. She goes to the southeast side, the one most enshrouded in shadow, and she affixes the rope to the railing. She then lowers her goggles, turning on the night vision, and rappels over the barrier. She turns, going upside down, the black rope barely visible, and she peers inside the window. It provides her with an unexpected view of the area, a good portion of it in sight. There is a distant wall, showing that some portion of the level has been partitioned, but other than boxes and scattered furniture, she sees nothing. No signs of life. No signs of alarms or other intrusion preventions.

She releases her weapon, the strap keeping it tight and firmly in place, and she lowers herself more, slowly. She waits, and it still seems as though the inside of this topmost floor is lifeless. She retrieves the center punch tool, pressing it into the glass toward the bottom. The do not appear to have a mechanism for opening. She finally feels the give, hearing the light pop. Now that the glass is weakened, she quickly turns, going back to upright and pushes off the wall to get momentum. On the way back, she crashes through the window.

This is the biggest risk yet, as she releases herself from the rope, taking the rifle in hand, peering about, listening. Once she is confident she has remained undetected, she moves. Rushing is not the way, and the methodical check reveals that indeed there is no one here. It appears this floor is being used somewhat as storage, though even that shows sparse and haphazard. She finds the stairwell, the door unlocked, and she heads down.

She takes her time, the passing of it not much entering into her awareness, except that she knows she does not have all night. She keeps up the deliberate pace. The next floor proves more like what she might expect from an old office building, and she carefully navigates the hallways, entering each room she encounters, checking. They also hold no more than what one might expect from a dust-covered place of memory. Still no signs of guards, contraband, or children. She moves on to the next.

The third proves also not as expected, showing her a spacious chamber, like a ballroom, and she wonders as to the former function. She also begins to worry a bit that she has yet to encounter any signs of life or evidence of illicit goings-on. She knows the building is being used by the criminal organization, the intelligence she received even making it out as though the place is rather important. She saw signs of guards inside before she made her approach and entry.

She walks near a window, and though she'd not normally bother, the oddity of the situation compels her to look. She freezes, then steps closer, getting a better view. The police are out there, in force, and not just regular patrol. She spies special tactical units, some holding ballistics shields, many of them in armor, and they are making to surround and enter the structure.

"Fuck," she hisses, pulling back from the window.

She wonders what the chances are that the police are here for the criminals, and she just happens to be here, too. She just as quickly tosses that aside. She's been set-up, and even if not, they'd arrest her as a nice bonus to the raid.

She quickly mulls over what to do. She won't use force on the police. Besides the fact that they'd respond in kind, she will not willfully harm them. She is approximately in the middle of the building, about as close to the ground as the roof. But they may have sniper teams already in place.

She creeps further along, then dares to peek out the window again. She sees many vehicles, some with their lights on, though obviously they turned off their sirens when they neared. There are vans, of course, and many, many officers. Several small teams are making slow approach, holding submachineguns, shotguns, moving in tight formation behind a lead person bearing a shield. The others are keeping their distance, in cover. This means they've been alerted to an imminent armed threat. She's not sure how long they have been out there, but judging from the time she has been here and from what she sees, she expects them to be in the building soon, if they are not already.

It will take them some time to clear the structure.

She moves quicker, checking other windows, trying to see if they do already have the place surrounded. Of course, they do. She waits, peering, and there, yes, she sees a sniper team getting into position on a nearby rooftop. There may even be air support out there.

She will not fight the police.

She thinks on the basement level, but she knows she'd have to rush down the stairwell, hoping it leads to the underground portions. Maybe the elevator? She gets to it quickly, forcing the doors open, looking down to see the carriage waiting there on the ground floor, almost as if inviting her. She won't use it, though, but it means she'd have to make a risky entry into the lift and then out onto the ground floor, and one of the first things they'll secure is that very passage.

"I won't make it," she murmurs to herself.

The best thing at this point will likely be to disarm and surrender, letting them have her. There is enough risk already with how well-armed she is, and she doesn't want to give them any reason to use deadly force on her. She can lay her weapons down, step back, and wait. She knows how to be non-threatening and cooperative. She knows what they'll do, as she has been trained in the control and capture of potentially dangerous targets.

She wonders at the set-up. They must have leaked this information, hoping the vigilante's network would find it, check it, and deliver it. This token retinue of guards has been waiting in this building for how long now? And she obviously tripped something when she entered, and they called the police, probably reporting an armed intruder, maybe even mentioning the vigilante. She takes in a slow breath, shaking her head, feeling disappointed. How could she fall for this?

The police are coming. She's heard a few noises funneling up through the concrete and steel, distant signals of the impending presence. Soon those noises will get louder, more definite. Soon, they'll be here. She glances about the large room, wondering where the best place would be to surrender, and there, she spies something she missed before. Something out of the ordinary – a fireplace.

She goes over to it. It's large, and she wonders again as to the purpose of this room. Still, a fireplace means a chimney, and though she had largely dismissed the roof as a reasonable attempt for egress, there may be an option here. It's so large that she can get inside it, doing so by crouching, stepping fully in, and she bends, turning, and she looks up. There is no opening for exhaust.

Why would someone build a fireplace with no chimney? She looks around, moving her hands to the stone, as though feeling for answers. It makes no sense. She goes back out, still examining, despite knowing the police are on their way up to this floor. She runs her gloved hands lightly over the mantle, and there, she finds it. A small switch, a difference in the surface, a depression, and she hears the answering click in the depths of the dark fireplace. She goes back in, and there, she sees it. The back of it is a secret passage.

She opens the small portal with a push of her hand, leaning in a smidge and looking down to see a narrow passageway, a ladder beginning here and going all the way down. It's deep, and her best guess is that it descends lower than the ground floor, an obvious secret escape route. She is not sure what is down there, or how long this hidden pathway has been unused, but it seems a better option than waiting for the police. She slips in quite easily due to her petite frame, and she pushes the door back shut, hearing the small sound as it locks in place. She doesn't bother seeing if she could open it from here, instead beginning the slow, quiet downward climb.

SWORD OF THE BUTTERFLY

She sits up suddenly, the room temperature coffee in the cracked and chipped mug almost spills out, belying her drift into unfocused thoughts. She has a series of alerts set up, all sorts with myriad, complicated protocols, and she now hears and sees one of those to which she has given the highest priority, one she has never heard before.

Therese manages to set her mug aside without spilling any of its contents as she sits up straighter in the cheap chair. Her skinny body has gone rigid, tense, and her fingers fly over the keyboard, one hand going to the mouse, as she checks the tickler. One of her cyber-world contacts, one whom she has never met in person but trusts, has sent her a message of something happening that might involve the vigilante. This is not the only thing that has happened, as in the few moments since the alert hit, her computer has done some checking of its own, running scripts, validating, searching, cross-referencing, and this has added to the legitimacy of the situation.

Therese's eyes move rapidly, consuming the information on the screen. There has been a call on the police comms, a great deal of force sent out to a particular building, one known to be associated with criminal elements in the city, one which she quickly recognizes as a place of interest scouted by herself via many electronic channels. Reports of an intruder, quite heavily armed, and some casualties. The digging has also brought up mention of the "vigilante".

She runs some other scripts, and she is soon seeing the view from some nearby cameras. It doesn't show her as much as she'd like, what with the City not quite yet giving over to the ubiquitous cameras as with some other major metropolitan areas, but there are many about. The owners of these electronic sentinels, whether private or municipal, would not be pleased with her ease at piggy-backing their views, but that does not concern her. She studies what she can, seeing that several of the marked police vehicles are there, tape already put up to cordon the area. Most of the officers she spies are wearing armor, all of them in careful, defensive positions.

She sits stock still, save for her hands and eyes, just absorbing information, seeking out more. She knew the possibility always lurked of something bad happening to the vigilante. Of course, the very act itself is illegal and subject to risks and threats. Still, she had resolved into something of a comfort zone, perhaps naively. She's even made confrontations in the face of what she believed was failure of the responsible party. Now she wonders if perhaps that has led to greater risk-taking and this. Her thoughts go again to Macar, Quain, Alec. She experiences blame at all of those losses. Is she good for nothing more than putting people at risk, leading to their deaths?

An increase of tension may be noticed along her jawline. She does not toy with her snakebite piercing as she is often wont to do. Instead, her teeth clamp together as she imbibes as much information as possible, hacking into reports and comm-links with a subconscious-seeming simplicity.

The police have sent out their heavily armed response units, sniper teams, anticipating potentially lethal action. They've surrounded the building. Casualties have been spotted inside - men shot, dead.

Why would she do that?

Thoughts careen in her mind, like a tumultuous white noise, the occasional formed piece flitting into her awareness like a larger chunk of detritus, threatening damage.

Is she okay? Is she okay?

Worry further grips her. She no longer interfaces with her computer, having collected all worth doing so at the moment. She waits, perched on a precipice, wondering what the next news will say, wondering if she ought to do something.

Back before all of this began, such thoughts would cross her mind but in a different context. She's always felt like she is able to do something, and that is part of why she has gotten so deeply into hacking and cyberspace. But now her considerations include actions that involve going offline, leaving her tiny, comfortable apartment.

She feels like throwing on her clothes, hopping on her bike, and driving over there. But then what?

She can't very well demand that the police let her in. They'd as likely detain, then maybe arrest her if they realized how she came by her information or her connection to the vigilante. Does she really think she can do anything helpful?

Then another thought shoots through her mind, and she is stunned for a short spell.

SWORD OF THE BUTTERFLY

She knows Lilja's address.

It had not been too difficult to find, and upon doing so with such ease, she had been left to doubt her once solid surety that her self-defense instructor is indeed the vigilante. She'd never gone, not wanting Lilja to think her some stalker, but she had retained the information, just in case. She could go over there now, and if no one is home..?

And what if someone is? That would surely mean that Lilja is not the vigilante, but then what? What would she say to the woman? And even if she is not there, it doesn't mean she *is* the vigilante. Still, as she sits, thinking, fretting, she knows she is going to do something.

She gets up to hurriedly dress and be on her way.

Consciousness returns like a warm sunrise bringing sensation, the lull honing to a sharpness that also brings awareness and anxiety. She remembers going down the tube she found hidden in the fireplace. She made it to the bottom, yes, after a lengthy descent. During that climb, she had even passed by some areas where she swore she heard the police through the walls. She had remained still, quiet, not wanting to alert them to her presence. When she had made it to the bottom, it was dark. She'd gone to use her goggles when something had happened. Something had crept up on her, something nigh-invisible and then … nothing.

"You are awake."

Lilja looks over, blinking, and she sees him. They have never met face to face before, but she knows his appearance. He has, of course, never met her, and though he now looks upon her unmasked visage, he does not know who she is.

"Imagine surprise to find vigilante is woman," Volkov says, and though one might expect this to be uttered with some insulting bite of humor, his tone and expression sound quite deadly serious, "And this glorious hair of yours."

She glances side to side, noticing the telltale glimpses of the vibrant coloring of her locks. They've undone her hair.

"I could make a lot of money off you."

The moment lingers. Lilja knows what he is threatening, but she also knows that unless he used constant drugging, she'd make her escape. She feels the lingering effects of something, perhaps a gas used to knock her out, and she spends these moments testing the bonds. They feel quite secure.

She supposes he expends the moment to try to frighten her. It doesn't work. She merely continues in the assessment of her situation. She is tied, tightly. She is on the ground, on her knees, not only having her limbs restrained, but she also feels as though she is anchored to something in the wall. The rope is quite thick, tactical, like the rope she uses for rappelling. She won't easily get free.

As if to accommodate her intelligence-gathering, the lights come up. They are still quite dim, but she now sees that they are not alone. She makes out eight other men in here with her and the crime boss. The room is similar to the ones in the other building. The area is quite large, pipes visible at the ceiling, and there is no other furniture in here that she sees save the old, wooden table beside which he stands. The guards are armed, of course, and she has been relieved of her own weapons. The situation is quite bad.

"But I won't do that with you, no," he says, walking nearer her, but still, she notes, keeping sufficient distance. He does not seem to be a stupid man. "You would sooner die, I think, than be subject to that. As soon as you got chance, you'd kill yourself, or kill others and get away."

She drills her eyes into his, and he returns the gaze, unfettered. Neither show agitated on the outside, but the unspoken storm waits, churning just beyond the horizon.

"Still, a woman. I am impressed."

She remains silent, just keeping her eyes on him. Though she is bound, she will not be again taken unawares. And she is not gagged. She may yet cause damage with her head and teeth if given the chance.

"You have great power in you, hmm?" he says, perking his eyebrows, "I have seen much of this, so I know what I talk about. You will not be wasted by being cheap sex slave. I am glad you found secret passage and escaped our first trap. I would have been disappointed had you not.

"We called police. Even left them some bait to get them very interested," he says, speaking of the men he chose to sacrifice, having them assassinated by a more trusted guard when the time came to spring the gambit. "I was a little worried you would not find secret passage, but you did." He almost manages a tiny smile. "Second trap was much better, and it got you. Now, *I* have you. Good, good. We put end to this soon."

He looks to one of the other men, speaking in Russian. She knows something of the language but not enough to really make out what is said. The man nods, then heads out, two of the other guards in tow. Volkov then looks back at her, studying her in silence, just as she does to him.

"Your power will soon be mine."

Her brow knits the tiniest bit. She wonders what he means by this. Is he going to use the knowledge of her appearance against her somehow? Maybe he plans to release her image to the press, co-opt all she has been trying to do as the vigilante, but she is still confused by his intent. He captured her, on purpose, then let her regain consciousness when he could have easily killed her. What is his plan?

Another voice then enters the silence, that of a woman, and it is not her own. She shifts her eyes and sees the figure resolving from the darkness on the far edge of the chamber. She is speaking to Volkov in Russian, but her eyes are firmly fixed to Lilja's. She steps further into the light, and Lilja blinks, moving her head back.

Yelena looks at the bound captive. Her manner of dress is the same as always, as though she has just stepped off a runway. The sound of her stiletto heels is somewhat echoed in the room, and her darkly painted lips hold her ubiquitous smirk as she gazes upon the vigilante.

"You should not be surprised the vigilante is a woman," she says, switching to English, "I am not surprised at all."

She strides past her man, her steps slow, deliberate, getting closer to their captive. She then halts, bending at the waist, peering. Lilja scans over that face. The jaw is rather pronounced, strong, and it seems to press into further definition, as if the woman is grinding her teeth together as opposed to really smiling. Her eyes are a striking grayish-blue, her hair that white-blonde. Lilja also glimpses something else there, high up on the brow, as though the intent of the hairstyle is to hide something.

"Not surprised at all," she repeats, then stands back upright, looking back at Volkov, "Let us get to it."

Therese stands in front of the door, unsure. She's come this far, but now, she doubts. She can knock, of course, and part of her wants Lilja to be home while another part of her hopes she is not. She doesn't want anything bad to happen to her teacher, but she badly wants to be correct about her being the vigilante. She's not sure why she feels this way, almost as if she has somehow let this idea of the vigilante coalesce in her mind and now she juxtaposes it on Lilja along with desires she does fully admit to herself.

But if Lilja is home, she is safe, but what, then, does Therese say to explain her presence? She supposes she could just be honest, but she begins to question that almost as soon as the thought forms. She steels herself, deciding some action is better than nothing, and she knocks.

She waits, tense, almost feeling a nervous tremble of trepidation. She hears no signs within as though someone coming to the call. She knocks again.

And again, nothing.

A third time gains the same result.

Therese has acquired some non-computer skills during her time as a hacker, meeting other dwellers in that shadowy, gray world between the law and crime. She's sometimes traded knowledge for her expertise when someone wanted something but did not have the funds. Besides, some information and abilities are worth more than money. Though she has had little opportunities to practice, she did learn how to pick a lock.

She glances about, making sure her knocking has not garnered any notice. She then retrieves her tools, and though it takes some effort, and she begins to worry of being caught before even getting in, she manages to pass the bolt. She looks about again, and still it seems no one has taken interest in her presence. She gets inside.

She notices signs of a cat, and she wonders if the animal is hiding somewhere inside or might even come out to investigate her. She hears nothing as she takes a few quiet steps within. It's dark, and she wonders then if perhaps Lilja is home and maybe is a deep sleeper. What if she now wakes her highly-trained teacher and gets dealt with as an intruder?

SWORD OF THE BUTTERFLY

Well, she'd deserve it, so she tries to summon more courage. She moves further in.

The place is not too large, and though it is dark, she uses her phone, with one of its many apps, to offer similar illumination as a flashlight. She quite quickly notices signs of disarray and what she assumes to be a struggle. Alarm spikes inside her, pulse increasing. She freezes in place, as though willing her ears to hear anything that may be in wait.

Nothing.

She peers about, shining her phone hither and thither. There is upset furniture, what appears to be stains of some sort on the flooring, and even jagged tears on one wall. *What the hell happened here?* She gets down closer to the ground, peering at the stains, then gives a sniff. She wrinkles her nose from the rancid stench, and this only gives her more confusion.

She now decides that she doesn't care if she's caught. She has to know. She searches the entire place, which does not take long. She finds no cats, but the bedroom looks to also be in a state of disarray. This is not someone being negligent of cleanliness or orderliness. She can see from other parts of the apartment that Lilja is obviously not uncaring of such things. This is clearly signs of a struggle.

Her mind begins to race. What if someone found out she is the vigilante and attacked her here? What if she fought off the attack, then went for a counter-attack or revenge? It doesn't seem like Lilja, and the stains on the floor and wall are not that fresh. No, something else happened and not this evening. But why, then, would she leave her home in this state?

And what if it is still not related at all? Maybe there was an intruder, much as she just broke in. If someone was stupid enough to break in to Lilja's place, there would surely be a fight. Maybe she repelled the attack, but she got hurt and is in the hospital? She'll run a check on records.

She realizes she is also stupid to have broken in, and now she begins to think she should not be here. She is worried even more, not having gained any real resolution from this visit, and she decides it is time to go. She'll head back to her place and run those checks and keep a vigil on the situation at the building and hope against hope that Lilja is okay.

"How are you doing, dear? Are you okay?" Yelena asks of their tied-up prey, giving a lilting tinge of seduction to the end of her words.

Lilja does not respond, having remained silent throughout. She watched as the two had a somewhat heated discussion. It did not even broach an argument, but she could tell from their expressions and body language that tensions were rising. The woman wanted something, and perhaps she got it. Lilja is not sure, but at some point the boss dismissed the other guards, leaving just the three of them now in the room.

"She does not waste her breath on useless speech," Volkov notes, giving a small motion of his head as though complimentary of the silence.

He lets that very silence linger, standing there, looking down at her.

"Do you know much of folklore and myth? Religion?" he speaks, raising his eyebrows on the last. He waits a moment for her response, but none is forthcoming. "Lies, truth. I know something of the Truth that exists in this world, and it escapes many."

She feels that tension at her forehead, that confusion. She wonders what he means about power and now this, and then she snaps her eyes back to the woman. She merely stares in return, calm-seeming. Lilja moves her focus to Volkov, wondering what he knows and into what she's really gotten herself.

"Some say Eve had red hair, that it was sign of her Original Sin, a stain. I see your hair is not natural red. Your color is also stain. Some also say this stain was seen on her firstborn son, Cain." Volkov narrows his eyes, parting the polite-looking hold of his tattooed hands. "Do you know these legends?"

She moves her eyes again from him to the woman and back.

"You have mesmerizing eyes," he comments, "but you are not Russian. This much, I know. I wish I knew more about you, but what I do know will have to be enough."

Confusion now races through her mind. She tries to corral those thoughts, make some sense of them, find a light in the storm. This man is no mere local crime boss. The presence of *that woman* here confirms it. What's going on?

SWORD OF THE BUTTERFLY

"I did much research on you," he continues, "You have done good in this city. Thank you for dispatching predecessor. It opened door for me, opportunity, where I long wished to have one."

He pauses, noticing a slight reaction from her.

"Do not worry. You are not my pawn. I am not that powerful, but you have helped me. Thank you."

His tone is not at all sarcastic or taunting but sounds laden with dry sincerity. She tries to fight the confusion, the worry. She wishes she had some way to call Skot. She doesn't think this because of being caught, but because of what she now knows and senses even further of this man and what is going on. She has safety protocols in place. If she does not 'check in' by a certain time, Skot will receive a message and a password. He could use this to access the details of her mission along with a way to track her phone, but even with her lapse into unconsciousness, she does not think that time has yet come.

She realizes the two are speaking somewhat quietly in Russian. She finds this odd. As if she could decipher their words were they louder.

"No, there is something about her," Volkov pronounces, shifting back to English, looking her way, obviously wanting to include her in the discussion. "She is not entirely ignorant. I can tell. She is strong. Da, da, very strong."

"You know, don't you?" he continues, setting those hard eyes of his firmly back unto her own. "There are many bad men in this world, but they are sometimes driven by demons, no?"

She blinks, eyebrows perking, though she is trying not to give away too much by any sort of reaction. Still, with the presence of that woman, she supposes pretense is all gone. He may be speaking metaphorically, of course, and besides, even if he is not, what may she do now?

Even as she thinks this, she remembers what happened when she faced the Demon that attacked her in her home. She does possess abilities beyond the normal human kin. She tries to drive the confusion from her mind, trying to focus in hopes of bringing forth that magick. Perhaps she may use it to free herself or do something, anything that may help.

"What do you gain from this taunting?" Yelena steps forward as she pitches this question.

"I am not taunting," he looks over to her, a shade of confusion, almost defensiveness there as though how could she come to this conclusion. "I respect her power, even if she is not fully aware of it. Look at what she has done."

Lilja tries to ignore their words, even as they gnash and pull at her curiosity. There is so much more going on here than she ever anticipated, but now, she needs to free herself, fight back somehow. She continues to peer inward, trying to coalesce the very power of which this man speaks, of which she knows she holds.

"I know what she has done," Yelena replies, and she moves in closer, her hands touching Volkov, moving along his shoulders and back as she nears, pressing her body against his. "I know what she can yet do, just as do you ," she whispers into his ear, and as she does, she sends a sidelong glance to the bound woman.

Lilja does not respond to this, does not spend any more time on studying that woman. She continues focusing, trying to channel the energy within, hoping she can again manifest it. She needs to be free of these bonds. She needs to fight. She realizes that even as she does this, she is not just struggling against physical restraints. She has to find this strength within herself. She knows it is there. She knows she can do it. She just has to find it and use it as she will.

"We've wasted enough time," Yelena declares, still close to her man, and she moves somewhat behind him, as if being attached to his side like some leech prevents him from going to their captive and doing what he plans.

Volkov stares at Lilja. She looks up at him, having turned her own focus down to the floor as she works to gather her energy. She has felt nothing flare up as it did when she fought the Demon. She can sense something there, deep within, but it almost feels like her own voice catching in her throat, breath robbed from her even in the effort. She tenses, trying to continue normal respiration, readying herself for what is to come. She can read on his body language that he prepares to act.

"Blood, darling," says a voice, and Lilja's eyes narrow, for this has come from the woman. She has uttered it so quietly, yet it has reached her ears. "There will be blood."

SWORD OF THE BUTTERFLY

Volkov nods, once, closing his eyes briefly at the end of the gesture's motion. The woman's pronouncement did not sound like a question, and perhaps his response is not an answer but more an offering of respect to the prey at the time of slaughter. He again parts his hands, having moved them back to an interlacing aspect. He is full of careful, heavy attentiveness, but in the end, it proves to not be enough.

His eyes widen, staying held in this strained aspect. Lilja tenses, moving back as she is able, even though he is not yet near enough to touch her. She then notices the movement at his neck, just near his Adam's apple, and there it is, catching a certain light, casting a shadow, a shadow that is interrupted by a sudden and steady flow of blood – the metal item rises forth, having been driven into the back of his neck by the woman. She may hide her true hair beneath a very convincing white blonde wig, she may speak Russian with the expertise and sound of a native, she may call herself Yelena, but in truth, she is Anika Malkuth.

Lilja wonders why the man does not turn on his assassin, for even though this puncture of metal through his neck may be painful and lethal, it should not be so thoroughly debilitating. But then, this is a Malkuth doing the killing. She snicks her eyes to the woman, seeing that Anika stares back. Volkov's hands begin to move up, then they stop just above waist height, and the trembling begins. The fingers of his right have form the shape of a claw, defiance even in his death throes. More blood trickles and leaks from his throat, then he collapses to his knees.

He remains this way for a moment, a testament of his strength. Lilja again moves her eyes to Anika. She sees the once palpable shadow gone, and Lilja wonders what other magicks may have gone into the woman's disguise. She looks back at Volkov as he falls to the ground on his face, the momentum causing his head to turn, and she glimpses two glints of metal. That is how she ended him, then, and it means the one in his neck was unnecessary, for the suggested angle of the other thin spike shows it has been buried up into his brain.

She sets her eyes on the woman, wondering what shall now happen. Anika somewhat surprises her by moving forward and releasing the bonds. She gets some distance from the Malkuth once she is free, standing there, moving her limbs to regain proper circulation. She wonders if there is about to be another fight.

333

"No 'thank you', then?" Anika taunts, and Lilja notices how smoothly the woman shifts to her 'normal' speaking voice, or what Lilja presumes is that.

Lilja glances over at the fallen man, thinking of all the pain he has caused, the lives he has ended, and she thinks this is an inadequate end to him. Something does not feel right about it, but she will not mourn his passing.

"We've been with him for some time."

She shifts her deep blue eyes back to Anika as the words are uttered.

"Why?"

"Ah, so you do still possess the power of speech."

Lilja's eyes narrow, and she moves away, scanning about the room.

"I know where your things are, if you are looking for them."

"Where?" comes out the single word, not a plea but a demand, delivered in a firm tone that broaches no deny.

"We'll get them for you. You'll need them."

"Why?"

A moment of silence rises as the two stare, challengingly, at each other.

"As much as I'd enjoy another round with you, we don't have the time," Anika finally speaks, "The Guardian has been detained, and they are after the Book now."

"What?" Lilja's eyes widen, tension rising in her muscles.

"He was a warlock, for lack of a better term, but not a very good one. He knew of the Infernal, and like some empty-headed fool, he worshiped them. They tricked him, made him addicted to this 'power'."

"And you were with him the whole time, and you could have stopped him," Lilja almost growls, stepping in close to the other woman, achieving the necessary balance and position for combat, a natural flow and motion of her body even as her agitation clearly rises.

Anika glances her over. "I said we don't have time."

Lilja does not seem so eager to back off, merely standing there.

"We're not the Felcrafts," Anika reminds, "You need to get that through your head. Once I knew he intended to kill you, I killed him. Aren't you the least bit grateful?"

SWORD OF THE BUTTERFLY

A deep breath passes through the redhead, then she backs away a step. She glances back down to the cooling body.

"So, this was all meant to catch me."

"Don't flatter yourself," Anika clips, regaining the other woman's eyes, "The Infernal would have been just fine launching an assault with you there, but *he* was obsessed with you. How *convenient* that the vigilante happened to also be the Guardian." She delivers this with slit eyes, as though driving home an undeniable point. "Letting him trap you was something of a reward from them. Pathetic …"

Lilja blinks, a rapid series, as though waking, and she regains her focus. She looks from the corpse to Anika.

"We need to get to the library."

*****

Skot is not alone here, which is what he hoped. He wonders what else transpires this evening that has been planned by others and shall prove unanticipated by him. His thoughts also drift to Lilja, but he tries to remain focused. Yes, he is very concerned for her, very, but there is nothing he can do on that front.

He does not think it chance that she has gone off on one of her missions this very evening that the special alarms have been raised in the library. He hopes it is coincidence, hopes that her mission is going as planned, and she will soon be done and realize there is yet another matter begging attention. It won't prove easy on her, but it is better than several other alternatives. He called, left her a quick, concise message as he was rushing out the door. Now he stands here, just inside the front doors of the large library building, lurking in the shadows, watching.

The cleaning crew is here, and though he wonders why they'd still be at it at this hour, such detail seems incidental. They are here, going about their business as if nothing is amiss. For them, that is well how the evening may and should pass. Not only are members of the janitorial staff at work, but he has spied Marcel, Lilja's assistant. He is given to wonder why the young man is present, but perhaps he is just one of those who lives for his work, feels more comfortable here than even at home.

He lets doubt tickle at his mind, but there is no real reason to suspect him.

And to top it all off, there is the security. They are always about patrolling the college ground, and he has seen two of them inside, one talking to Marcel. He worries that the intrusion may have tripped one of the conventional alarms, giving security a reason to investigate. All of these "mundane" people being here only complicates matters. He has to get below and be sure the Book is safe, protect it if need be.

He's already summoned up some of his magickal abilities to scan the people here, feeling the hinting drift into another focus, the coiling warmth, and from what he can tell, none of them are compromised. He hopes to keep it that way, and he wishes there were something he could do to get them to leave. He knows, though, that revealing himself would only cause more issue, so he uses another preternatural skill of his to obscure his presence. He does not quite go invisible so much as unnoticed. He would, of course, be spied if someone gave him direct, steady attention, but it is surprisingly easy to avoid such, even without the aid of magick.

He grips his cane in one hand, ready to draw the hidden sword at a moment's notice, his shoulder holster also affixed, bearing of the two-toned Walther P99, loaded with that special ammunition, spare magazines on the other side of the harness. He has not brought a suppressor, so if it comes to firing, he will be easily heard. He hopes it won't, but knowing the special alarms have been tripped leaves him with scant faith of that.

He waits outside the door to the Rare Collections room, noticing it has not been opened. He knows how to access it. Part of the deal for the Malkuths to accept this resting place had been that more than just the university's personnel would be able to gain entry. He knows they still blanch at having lost this treasure, so they hoped to gain this bit. He had forced their acceptance by saying the Felcrafts would also know how to access the room. The Book is under Lilja and his Family's care, but he knows their rivals would love any excuse to take it.

He has gone into a slight trance, sending out more scans, and he does not detect anything in that room. His abilities in this vein are not the best, but he feels sufficient to this task. If there is no demonic presence in

SWORD OF THE BUTTERFLY

the locked chamber, then why did the alarms trip? He pauses, realizing another possibility. They may be preparing to launch a very serious attack, one which would take a measure of power he does not think they have here at the ready, but again, he is taken by the feeling of the unanticipated. Surprise attacks are meant to overwhelm the opponent, and they did lose their half-breed. Perhaps this is also motivated by revenge.

He heads back to the main room, trying still to maintain some semblance of obscurity. Marcel is there, sitting near the entrance as he once did so often as a student-volunteer. He is bent to some studious task. Skothiam thinks he has indeed realized something more about the young man and his feeling of home here. He could imagine worse places to experience such a comfort, but right now, the library is unsafe, and the unwitting assistant sits right at the entrance.

He hears some noises, looking to his left, and he spies two people chatting in the distance – a security guard and one of the janitors. They seem happy to pass some time with small talk or the like. It is dark, few lights on, quiet, and any ruckus would travel through the locale like a clarion. Skot takes in a breath through his nose, feeling a rise of tension. He wishes none of them were here, but wishing it will not make it so. He wishes Lilja were here, too, but again, such a desire does not cause her to suddenly appear.

She tears through the streets on her motorcycle, the stealth mode engaged, and she hopes against hope that she will not garner any notice of the police. As if this were not risky and unusual enough, she has a passenger clinging tightly to her back, one Anika Malkuth, who just recently saved her life. She abhors feeling indebted to the woman, but that will have to wait. She speeds recklessly through the streets, keeping off the main thoroughfares, trying to maintain sharp senses to notice vehicles, pedestrians, any other potential obstacles.

They manage to reach the library, and she stops the bike quite close to the entrance. She notices lights and motion inside, so she does not get as near as she had planned. She has already re-donned her mask, also wearing her goggles for the ride. Anika slips off the motorcycle quickly, and Lilja follows, gathering her items from her bag.

"I don't suppose you've a spare for me?"

Lilja looks over.

"I *did* just save you, and we are in a hurry," Anika interjects in the ensuing silence.

Reluctantly, Lilja hands her sidearm to the other woman, offering the Glock, which Anika takes with a little twist to her lips. She gives the weapon a cursory examination.

"Conventional rounds," Lilja notes.

Anika gives a little look, as though this is just further disappointment, but she takes hold of the pistol with a show of experience, moving her eyes to the entrance of the library.

"We can't go that way."

"Why not?"

"There are people there," the redhead answers, her voice muffled by the balaclava.

"Why are there people here at this hour?"

"I don't know."

"This is the most expedient place of ingress, and we've more important concerns than some young man who shouldn't be here. For all we know, he's-."

"He is not," Lilja cuts her off, sending a firm authority into her voice, well acquainted with the Malkuth attitude toward innocents who happen to be at a scene.

"Fine." Anika gives in, obviously unhappy with this. "This is your place of work, your charge. How do we get in?"

"This way," Lilja says, but the tail end of her statement drifts into something she did not intend. Just as she completes the utterance, Marcel's head rises, quite suddenly, and he peers into the distance, face moving forward with it.

She and Anika watch, quietly, neither at an angle to discern what has gathered the man's attention, but he gets up from his place and walks further inside.

"Fortuitous," Anika clips, heading for the entrance as though she is no longer interested in any discussion with the other woman.

Lilja quickly follows.

SWORD OF THE BUTTERFLY

"What the bloody hell?" comes frustration from Anika as she finds the door locked.

Lilja gives a quick eye roll, pushing the woman out of the way with the intrusion of her own presence, disengaging the lock. She leads the way inside.

None too many steps within, and Lilja pauses, glancing back to note that Anika has stopped.

"What is it?" she sends out an insistent whisper.

Anika looks over. "You don't feel it?"

"No. Feel what?"

"They're here."

Skot is not yet aware that his love has arrived, bringing with her an unlikely guest, but he is aware that the Infernal are now, indeed, here. He has felt it, drifting into awareness with a disarming subtlety, like a slowly encroaching mist that thickens and billows, turning to obscuring fog. It does not take long before he senses more, shapes hiding within the haze, lesser demons, but still a threat all the same. He is able to continue to conceal his presence from them, for these are little more than ravenous beasts, and he doubts they have been sent to secure the Book. It is more likely they are merely advance troops or scouts of some sort, sent to harass anyone that may be present or even to serve as sacrifices to the special deterrents in place.

They will sense the others, though, for Marcel and the mundane humans are not in position to hide their presence or offer any sort of real resistance save their own force of will. These lesser, bestial demons are not entirely corporeal, using the fog and the power it conveys to drift in where they might normally be unable. But just as with hauntings, they may use this to indirectly affect the humans here, potentially causing great turmoil.

He has to do something.

He sends out a subtle touch of magick, resulting in a collision of energies and forces on some nearby books, causing several of them to shift, one to fall. This gains Marcel's attention. Skot continues the "show", a slight flicker of amber light, more rustling of the books. He realizes this very thing might be perceived as ghostly activity, but he'd rather the young assistant's experience with the paranormal be of this more benign nature than what gathers now in the invisible fog.

Still, such beacons may attract more than intended, and Skot curses himself as he realizes that some of the as yet intangible creatures have also taken notice.

They scuttle over, two bypassing Marcel as though unaware of him, more interested in this sweeter promise, but a third does pause, appearing as though to sniff in what may pass as such an orifice to sensory reception. It then *nudges*, managing to make contact with the young man on some level. Marcel stops, looking down in the general direction of the squat, stocky thing, confusion on his face, something drifting toward fear.

Skot curses again, realizing his attempt to distract and remove Marcel has only put him at greater risk. He moves then, easily avoiding the other two that shamble to the upset books, sniffing and slavering as though on the trail of wounded prey.

There is a shift, something that may be there but seems to not quite be. Marcel blinks, head rising up on stiffening spine. He looks around, though not back toward the area of the entrance. He senses something, and a shiver runs up his back, causing tension in his jawline. He feels unsettled, uncomfortable, unsure.

Skot has swept by, using more powerful magicks to further obfuscate himself, though he knows that the fog, the demons, and Marcel's state have added to this stealth. He drew his sword in the quick passing, the momentum of the unsheathing causing an arc of force, and he had cleaved the beast in two as it rose on elongated, disjointed feet to get closer to Marcel. There had been an accompanying flash of light, quick and sharp, and the thing now lies on the ground, squirming in pain, giving forth cries of anguish in an unheard tongue.

Marcel blinks again, wrinkling his nose, but he just stands there.

Move, Skot thinks, willing it to happen. The other demons are still somewhat rapt in their exploration of the very diversion he had intended for Marcel, but they shall soon look back at their dying brethren.

"What's going on?" the young man sends out a whisper laden with suspicion.

"Marcel?"

Skot looks over to see that security guard who had been earlier speaking with the janitor has come over, concern laced on his features.

"Is everything okay?"

"Oh, yeah, Billy. Thanks." Marcel puts on a weak smile for the other, who is not too many years his senior.

Billy peers, narrowing his eyes as though he does not buy this at all. He looks ready to walk closer, but to Skot's relief, Marcel goes to him.

"I just thought I ..," he begins, then looks back, obviously unsure of himself.

"You what?" Billy pushes, though he bears more an aspect of friendly helpfulness than any stern pressure.

"I don't know. I thought I saw something."

"Where?"

Just then, the other two creatures turn, seeing their dead fellow, and they go into an aspect of alarm, scuffling over, leaning in close, opening their own versions of sensory organs to try to discern what has happened.

"There." Marcel points where the demons have just left, and Billy peers, seeing nothing out of the ordinary. He meanders over.

"Looks like a book fell is all," the security guard says, bending down to pick up the one that had been sent to the ground by Skot's magicks.

"Yeah." Marcel huffs out a short, embarrassed chuckle, also drawing near. "I guess I'll take that."

Billy offers a smile, handing the book over, and Marcel proceeds to reshelf it.

"Skot?"

He moves his head, having been watching with rapt focus as the two demons inspect their fellow's corpse, snorting and sniffling about, knowing they will eventually take notice of Marcel and Billy. He sees something he had hoped for and something else quite entirely unexpected, adding to the mysterious nature of the evening.

"Lilja!" he all but cries out, recognizing her even with the mask, and he goes to her, giving a quick hug.

She returns it as best she is able, what with all her gear and the current situation.

"You killed one?"

He looks at Anika, then back. "You're alright?" he asks, and Lilja nods. His eyes go to the Malkuth, his aspect changing, "I'll need to know why *you* are here."

Anika smirks, not giving a centimeter under the scrutiny of the Head of the Felcraft Family.

"But first, we have a situation."

"You don't s-," Anika begins, voice coated in sarcasm, but she is cut off.

"If you are here to help, good, but if not, then leave now," Skot commands.

She offers no further words, showing her response in how she holds the pistol, looking around to assess the situation, then giving a perk of eyebrows and indication of her head toward the two demons. Lilja notices Marcel and Billy, and she feels the sharp sense of concern rising to a greater peak. She doesn't want anything bad to happen to these people. She quietly draws her katana.

"I can take out those two," she whispers.

"There are more."

She glances at the woman, then to Skot, and he nods.

"She's right. These are just a vanguard. The fog is thickening. More are here, more are coming."

"They're after the Book."

He nods to Lilja, noting the increased etching of concern on her features.

"I've checked," he informs, "They have not gotten down there yet. Our measures ought to force them through this way." He indicates the entrance.

"Ought to?" Anika pitches, but it seems they are not inclined to pay much attention to the jab.

Lilja nods to Skot, once, resolute, then she moves.

He and Anika observe as the masked redhead goes to the other two creatures. They fidget, about to make a move of their own, but Lilja acts first.

She swings with a vicious arc, rising up from the shadows, and one of the beasts recoils, a strange-looking spray of its vitae spews out as it is deeply rent, collapsing. The other screeches in its otherworldly voice,

SWORD OF THE BUTTERFLY

and Skot barely hears it. Its mouth gapes nearly as wide as its neckless bulb of a head, teeth crowding around the edges, looking to angle outward with the force of the yell. It goes to attack, but another swipe, as strong and efficient as the first, results in a diagonal cut across its shape, and it falls to the thickening, odiferous pile.

"She is quite good," Anika admits, the volume of her voice low.

"You knew that already."

"She's also the infamous vigilante," Anika presses, toying, "I suppose that adds to her resume."

Skot just gives her a look, his eyes slit, then he glances back over. Lilja has left the area, but her strikes resulted in a glint of light and movement, some even showing the hint of that amber sheen, and the two men have walked over. They investigate, though they cannot quite make out what is going on, but the dark energies are mounting. They scratch and annoy at the awareness, coiling in deep, causing potential fractures like vines growing through concrete.

"What's going on?"

Billy looks up at Marcel on the tail end of those whispered words. He sees confusion and fright there, and he feels some of his own.

"I don't know, but I'm going to check the entrance. Stay here."

Skot looks over, and indeed the front of the library has become like a billows, steadily pumping in its effluvia as if a throbbing, pulsating vein were coming straight from the heart of the Infernal. He spies more creatures clamoring forth, some like the thick, low-set beings already slain, others smaller, skittering about like large, grotesque insects, none quite fit for this world, still mostly insubstantial, but they are merely more of the advance. If that wave takes hold, it will allow more of them and more expression of power in this plane.

Anika makes to move that way, but she is halted by a hand on her arm. She gives that touch a pointed look then slips her eyes to Skot.

"Do not harm the innocents," he iterates.

She fights to not roll her eyes and scoff. Though they are both invested in the protection of the Book, this is officially Felcraft ground, and they are in charge, especially with their Head here. If it were just she and Lilja, which she had hoped on the way over, she'd be able to abuse more leeway. Of course, the man himself is not an 'innocent'. Mayhap something unfortunate would happen to him during such a concentrated and potentially chaotic attack as this.

She gives him a single nod, her aspect not at all betraying her quick thoughts, and she creeps toward the entryway.

Skot melts back further into the shadows, keeping up the obfuscating magick. He has eyes on Marcel, the young man waiting there near the rapidly disintegrating yet still quite fetid pile of demon corpses. He again wishes the assistant would move, for that very spot reeks with negativity. Once this is done, the library will need to be cleansed. He has already given some thought as to how the Infernal learned of this in the first place, having sent their precious half-breed to his death. They knew such an attack was imminent. Still, such analysis and resultant actions will have to wait.

"Everything looks in order," Billy comments, having gained the main doors, finding them secured, but his voice trails off at the end.

He feels something, though he is not sure what it is, his forehead wrinkling. He gets closer to the transparent double doors, peering out, expecting to see something. He wonders if perhaps some students are out there, trying to play a prank. He turns around, moving back in.

"Maybe I should go out and see if-," he begins, but he pauses, blinking, for he has felt something.

Skot sees it, wishing that the security guard would just get out of here. He sees the shape of a demon as it stands right beside Billy, baring its hideous teeth, moving its fingers like the tendrils of an anemone. It is trying to influence the man, trying to generate feelings of unease, negative emotions. He can all but see as the shape takes more form, as though it were an empty vessel filling with substance from the roiling fog. He spies Anika somewhat nearby as she watches. He can tell she wishes to attack the beast, but she is holding back due to his command. Her eyes find his, widening as she pushes her face forward, insistently, though quietly, asking for permission to engage.

Skot exhales through clenched teeth, shaking his head at Anika as the other security guard comes over to check on his colleague.

"What's wrong?"

"I don't know. I … thought I heard something."

SWORD OF THE BUTTERFLY

Skot knows the man has amended his words, having rather *felt* the presence, but he understands why the untried guard would explain it as such. The demons likely are happy to see these mundanes here, hoping to devour them as some sort of snack as they go to acquire their real prize.

"And I thought I saw something."

Both officers look over to the approach of the assistant, Marcel. Lilja wonders why he is here, but just as with Skot's analysis of the situation, such concerns will be postponed. She is not as attuned to the hidden world, but she knows enough. She has kept to the shadows, acting very much as she might in her capacity as the vigilante, and though she has not yet seen more of the beastly intruders, she knows they are out there. She has heard the sounds of the cleaning staff, but they are thankfully occupied on a higher floor, the noises of their work travelling down the open stairwell as she moves nearby.

"What did you see?" the other guard asks of Marcel.

"I'm not sure. I actually heard something first," he elaborates, and this gets a look from the officer to his coworker, "Some books fell off the shelf."

"Is that unusual?"

"Well, yes," Marcel admits, "It's never happened before that I'm aware of. It's not like they're loosely or poorly stacked or left near the edge of the shelves."

The man looks at him, quite interested in the tale despite its potential. Marcel has some trouble reading him, feeling a touch silly all of a sudden, unsure, thinking he is now making a big deal of nothing.

"And then, when ... Billy and I were over there. I thought I saw something else."

"Something else?" the man asks. He again glances to his colleague who is looking around, anxiously. "What was it?"

"I'm not sure, like some motion in the shadows, some weird flashes of light."

"It sounds like some kids could be playing pranks," the guard admits, moving his eyes again to his partner, "Hey, Billy, what's got you spooked?"

"Huh?" Billy snaps out of his scanning. "Nothing," he says, somewhat defiantly, getting a little grin from his buddy.

345

"The kids that go to this school are smart, some of them are too smart for their own good, and we've had trouble before. Maybe we ought to check-," he begins to suggest, then he blinks, looking in a slightly different direction, "What the hell?"

"What?" Billy and Marcel ask in unison.

"Now *I* see something … I think," he amends, eyes narrowing, face moving forward, then he shakes his head. "Okay, something's up. Billy, let's look around, inside and out," the more experienced guard decides, "Would you check the cleaning crew?"

"Yeah, sure," Marcel agrees, seeming to be suddenly deputized.

The demonic forces have continued to coalesce throughout, seeping in and gathering strength. The three men are indeed being watched, and not just by those unearthly creatures, but also by the three Hunters. Those eyes see as the monsters linger about the men, already trying to further influence them in their as yet less tangible ways.

"What are we going to do?"

Skot looks over at Anika who has made a quiet return to his position, but he doesn't say anything.

"You said to not harm the innocents, but if we sit here doing nothing, they are going to be harmed."

He still does not answer, glancing down at her pistol.

"It's Lilja's," she whispers, noting his gaze.

"She gave you her sidearm?"

"I'm afraid it's loaded with conventional ammunition, though," she adds, then lets her eyes travel to his holstered weapon. "I don't suppose you'd let me borrow-."

He shakes his head slowly, giving a clear, resolute answer. Anika shrugs, looking back over at the mounting scene. Marcel has left to check upstairs on the janitorial staff, and Billy heads over to unlock the front doors in order to investigate outside. Skot stares, trying to will the security guard in leaving. He'd prefer they all exit, but at least getting some of them out of this vicinity would be a great improvement.

But it doesn't happen.

Billy pauses, doors unlocked, one of them partially opened, his eyes wide, frozen in place by whatever it is he sees. Skot notices this, but he doesn't have the proper angle to tell what suddenly has the security guard's attention. He creeps forward, and just then, he feels it. Where the arrival of the Infernal vanguard is like a subtly seeping fog, this is a storm.

Billy also sees it, like an approaching current, but the confusion it brings is evident. He also thinks he sees something there, something dark and low to the ground, moving fast. He blinks, shaking his head as though unwilling to accept the reports of his eyes.

"Ow!"

He looks back inside the library to see his colleague standing there, holding his right arm.

"What happened?" Billy rushes over, though he spares a quick glance back to the open door.

"I must have ran into something," the other security guard says, moving his hand away to reveal a rather nasty cut on his forearm, the sleeve of his uniform torn, blood seeping from the fresh wound.

"Shit. That doesn't look good. What'd you run into?"

He looks down, searching for the corner or piece of metal or whatever it may have been. "I ... don't know."

The Hunters know, and the demon that has managed to infiltrate the corporeal world enough to have caused this wound is now veritably tittering and slavering, wanting more. Skot rises up from his crouched position.

"What are you doing to do?" Anika bids, her voice sounding more laden with challenge than curiosity or concern.

"Protect them," he says to her, making ready to approach.

"Alright," Billy continues, unaware of the others, "Let's just get you back to the station and get this cleaned up." He pauses, looking up, noticing the fixed stare of his partner. "What?"

"Someone ... someone's there."

Billy looks over, and he also notes the outline of a human shape in the shadows, but before he may say anything, the double doors of the library crash fully open.

A flood of powerful wind gushes forth and into the foyer, barely preceded by the shapes of the loping beasts, three large wolves rushing in, claws clicking noisily on the floor. They seem to almost be riding the storm. The security guards blanch, gripped by sudden fright. They both fumble for their deterrents, mace and stunners being pulled and readied.

Anika has moved further back, fully aware of what is now happening and wanting to not be in the middle of it. Lilja's position still holds unknown to the others, but Skot approaches the fray as the lupine animals move with a sure agility, growling, biting, bodies shifting with the close of the hunt. To the eyes of the untrained, they appear to carry on a ferocious battle with empty air.

"Stop!" calls out a commanding voice, and the two guards look over. "They are not here to harm you."

Neither recognize the man, and both feel ready questions on their lips. But the feeling of danger is great. Skot steps closer, hands held out, palms displayed within splayed fingers, trying to show that he is no threat even as he attempts to ease the feeling of such from the animals.

The wolves continue to growl and gyrate, moving in their predatory purpose of attacking the demons. They are able to see the beasts, and their actions bring results, the insubstantial creatures now going on the defensive as some are caught and ripped asunder.

These animals are specially bred and trained, the main pack living on the grounds of Felcraft manor, though these had been brought here temporarily once certain activities on the part of the Infernal had been discerned. To those with some sight, a luminescence may be seen along their healthy coats, gleaming in their eyes and flashing from their fangs. They exist simultaneously on both planes, drawing from a similar ability possessed by cats and other animals, though these benefit from their breeding, training, and the presence of their nearby master.

The winds howl in, coiling about and becoming like a funnel within the library. Most of that magick is also unseen by the guards, but the fierce currents cause upset in the physical world. The main brunt of the force crushes many of the monsters, corralling them within, keeping them from fleeing even as the barrage begins to rip the odious flesh from their unnatural bones.

Billy fires his conducted electrical weapon, striking one of the wolves in its hindquarters. The animal unleashes a sharp yelp, trying to flee the hit. Its prey takes the moment to scamper free.

"No!" Skot calls out.

SWORD OF THE BUTTERFLY

"Don't come any closer!" the other guard demands, now angling his spray.

Skot pauses, hands still held out. "They are not here to harm you!" he tries again, the noise of the forces rising up, now even affecting the ears of all those present.

"He's armed," the one says, finally spying the holstered weapon.

"Drop your weapon!" Billy commands, turning, having dispelled the cartridge from his first shot, readying the CEW for another fire as he steadies his aim.

The winds seem to crack the barrier of worlds, but in truth, they are revealing what is hidden, and larger, more grotesque and dangerous looking demons peel forth, as though having always been there, lurking invisibly. They yet remain unseen by the guards, but the wolves go to quick work, though their task is much more difficult with these. More yowling and cries rise forth.

"Wh-what," Billy says, eyes darting about, "What's going on!"

"Back away from the area," Skot says, trying to maintain some control, "Just calm down."

Billy realizes he has just heard something that he is supposed to say, and he steels himself, even as he hears those horripilating sounds, feels the rising pressure of that outré wind. None of this should be happening, but he at least has training in how to deal with threats. He holds steady, his finger readying to pull the trigger.

"Get on the floor! Lie face down, hands-," Billy says, and his voice is cut off as he crumbles.

The other guard looks over in time to see his colleague fall, and he barely makes out the darkly-garbed figure clinging to Billy's back, arms about his neck. His eyes widen, but despite this, he blindly fires the spray. Lilja moves quicker and with much more focus, quickly subduing him. Soon enough, both men are unconscious, wrists and ankles zip-tied.

"Sorry, Billy," she whispers, then looks at Skot as he comes up beside her, "What's happening?"

Before he may answer, a figure comes through the doors, appearing to float, carried upon those preternatural winds. She is ethereal-seeming, her clothing flowing like drapery on the forceful air. Her long hair also flips about, though it appears unnatural, not as chaotic as one might expect, more waving about her as might the serpentine hair of a gorgon. She is aglow with power, and as though she were the nexus, the heart, the intensity of the magick rises. The remaining demons are drawn in and ripped apart.

The storm then calms, the wolves sniffing and looking about for remnants of the enemy, finding none. The woman now stands on the ground, as calm and controlled as might be someone at a garden party, not a hair out of place. She sets her eyes on them.

"Nicole," Skot says, voice flat as he rapidly steps to her "Why are you here?"

"You needed my help."

Skot tenses, moving his face to the side, as though beginning to shake his head and stopping it just as it begins.

"Thank you," he manages, "but I had hoped to keep this inconspicuous."

"I shared that hope," Nicole intones, "but the situation has worsened." She sets her eyes on a particular point in the shadows, drilling the spot with her vision.

Anika walks forth from that place, looking slightly sheepish. Lilja notes this, realizing the Malkuth woman is more afraid of Nicole than anyone else. Nicole studies her for a short time, but she says nothing.

"How has it worsened?" Skot finally presses.

His sister turns her eyes to him, still maintaining her poise.

"The skin wearer is here."

"What?" Skot blinks, and though they had somewhat anticipated it, there had been hope that it would not happen.

"Where?" Lilja interjects, stepping nearer to the powerful woman.

A tense moment passes as Nicole appears to inwardly focus, then she finally speaks, "At the Book."

Lilja turns immediately, rushing away and toward the stairwell. Skot prepares to follow.

"Skothiam?"

He turns back to the beckon of his sister, eyes on her.

"There are more on the upper floors. A threat to the humans."

He gives a single nod, anxious to help his love and to deal with this situation.

SWORD OF THE BUTTERFLY

"I have also discerned the source from which they are launching this attack."

He gives another nod, "A gateway? Is it near?"

"It is close, yes," she replies, her voice smooth, a slow pace that is almost infuriating for those wanting to be off, but it manages to leech some of that tension. "I shall tend to it."

He gives another nod, and then his sister is away, again appearing to glide on ethereal winds, if not more composed of them than physical form. He readies once more to follow Lilja, but he spares a glance to the Malkuth.

"She's not going to help us?" Anika asks, and he might think this some subtle way to find out if Nicole is no longer an obstacle, but it feels different.

"She is. By closing the gateway."

"She didn't say it was a gateway."

"I know that."

He wishes to know why she is here, why she is suddenly acting this way, but he also knows Lilja is off, alone, to hurl herself headlong into the face of a very serious threat. He moves out, hearing the sound of Anika's footsteps as she follows. They pause at the stairs.

"I ..," she begins, sounding uncharacteristically unsure of herself, "I'll go upstairs, deal with those there."

"Alone?"

She nods.

"With no more than a conventional weapon?"

"This is not my only weapon," she says, and it does not sound like the typical Malkuth boast.

He desperately wants to get to the Rare Book Collections room, but he is not comfortable with this, either.

"That ... Demon," Anika continues, eyes shifting to the downward sloping stairs then back to Skot, "The skin wearer. It's very strong, very dangerous. You weren't there. It almost killed me, and I never even saw it coming."

He realizes now. She is afraid, and she had probably hoped Nicole would be dealing with the powerful monster. He also realizes that Lilja is down there with it, alone.

351

"Get upstairs," he says, all but giving her an order, then he heads down as quickly as he is able.

Lilja had sprung into action immediately upon hearing the words uttered by Nicole, no thoughts given as to whether anyone might be following. Perhaps such is reckless, perhaps she ought to value her own life more than the security of the Book. She is not even fully aware of what knowledge or power is held in that old tome, but she feels the enormity, the deep responsibility of keeping it out of Infernal hands. She is also the Guardian, and she will not permit this theft.

She had somewhat cleaned and re-sheathed her katana after slaying the lesser demons. She knows she is not armed with the special ammunition she needs, but she grips the assault rifle readily, moving on silent, quick feet to the door to the Rare Collections room.

It is open.

She crouches, listening. She hears noises within, and were it not for the late hour and situation, she might find the unobtrusive sounds to be nothing alarming. She moves her masked head just enough to peer with one eye. She sees nothing, for not only is the room shrouded in darkness, but the area where the most valuable books are kept is further within and obscured by shelves.

She creeps in, going silent on her jika-tabi. She is not sure exactly what to expect, knowing only what she has been told of this very powerful Demon. She holds her G36C close and at the ready, pointing the barrel as if a herald that leads the way. She finally comes to the point where she will arrive unto the place of the Book. It seems almost holy now, a shrine, a sacristy. She remembers when she stood in almost this exact place, a very similar situation, readying to face the strange half-breed and former student, Pothos Wilbraham. She feels much more forewarned and forearmed this time.

Peering about shows another large, human-looking shape, obviously working at the defenses and trying to get at the Book. The misshapen half-breed had been inelegant, awkward, but this one is all muscle and surety. She notes the telltale signs of some of the supernatural measures having been triggered, leaving a scant detritus in the area that would be

SWORD OF THE BUTTERFLY

missed by most. Where these deterrents hindered the ex-student, this intruder appears none the worse for having breached them.

She also notices a rising glow. The person is big, and she corrects herself, for this is no "person". Its expansive, well-muscled back is to her, so she figures it is busy with its hands at the shield over the prize. Some magick is being used to break through and get to the tome. She knows there is more than just this, and other quite lethal traps are in place. Still, she doubts, not wanting to just leave this one to such. This one seems to either be immune or has bypassed them altogether.

She steps about, carefully aiming the weapon. "Stop what you are doing," she issues in her commanding tone of voice, "Put your hands on your head."

The intruder complies with the first, giving an immediate cessation of signs of movement. The glow, which had been steadily increasing in brightness, also tapers off, though it does not disappear entirely. Instead of placing hands on the head, the creature turns, fully facing Lilja.

It looks human, though something in the eyes hints otherwise. The short hair is dark, angled chaotically, the brow heavy. The chin is lowered as it shifts its gaze down to the petite one issuing orders, such is the height it possesses. Those cracked lips spread into a large grin.

"Ahhhh, the Guardian," it utters, voice rising from the very bowels, grating and deep, "So, our trap failed."

"Put your hands on your head." Lilja persists, her index finger moving closer to the rifle's trigger.

"This is fortunate. Some of the traps you have here have also failed, but this last safety is proving bothersome, but I am sure you know how to get to the Book." So said, it raises its hands, though instead of placing them on the head, the thick fingers curl and tense, and that emanation of light sparks back into greater luminosity.

The Dark Claw of Botis, she ponders, remembering the name given to the spell the half-breed used on her. She had been told such magicks were generally quite deadly, and she was fortunate to have resisted. She was also told this skin wearer is possessed of great strength and power, and she wonders if the magick preparing to be unleashed might supersede that she once faced.

353

Realizing she is quite out of her depth, she pulls the trigger, squeezing it many times, unleashing multiple three-round bursts. Some of her shots hit, but she is not sure which is more unbelievable, that her adversary moves so quickly, so suddenly, that he appears to be able to dodge some of the shots, or that the ones that do hit hardly affect him. Before she realizes it, the distance has been closed, and with a powerful swipe of an arm, her rifle is ripped free from her hands, the strap snapping as the weapon flies away from her torso, clattering onto the ground some distance away.

She lunges back, instincts kicking in, honed by countless hours of practice. The Demon sets its eyes on her, the 'disguise', if the form is still meant to be such, giving up more as those orbs take on a sheen of scarlet luminescence. The face remains as stone, save for this change, eyes of a predator on its prey. Lilja shifts her feet, improving her stance in these scant moments the beast has seen fit to give. She watches it as closely as it watches her. Her body has shifted to present less of a face, less of a target, her left hand held forward, ready for blocking, as her right inches back to the hilt of her sword.

It moves again with that sudden speed, but this time, she is better prepared for it. She springs backwards from the attack of its clawed fingers, unsheathing the katana in the same motion, striking out. She feels the blade hit flesh, and when she comes to rest again, eyes still on her opponent, a dark fluid oozes down the blade.

The Demon stands back, glancing down at its forearm, noting the deep cut across the dense muscles. Lilja might have expected this strike to completely shear the limb of a normal opponent, but this has only resulted in a rather nasty looking slice.

"It stings … a bit," the thing utters, more commentary than any true bother.

She wonders why it is spending any time at all on words, hoping that the moments it wastes will result in an opening she may exploit. Help may also arrive, but she does not want to count on that. Just as she ponders these things, it attacks again.

Its speed is phenomenal, and not only that, but it evinces little concern for itself in the method of its attack, plunging headlong. She shifts to the side, the movement elegant, like that of a dancer, and she

SWORD OF THE BUTTERFLY

swings, the arc of the attack moving upwards. She is surprised, though, when it manages its own effortless dodge, and the blade swipes through air. It turns about, angling a clawed hand at her exposed torso, and she presses on her back foot, pivoting, pushing back and away from the counter.

It carries the offensive, swiping and grabbing at her. She recalls it asking for her to give access to the Book, and she wonders if it is trying to capture her. Its massive attacks seem full of lethal promise. She had held some small hope that it wanted her alive and thus might have to hold back in its force, but if this is holding back, she wonders what, indeed, a full hit might entail.

She is not sure if she now knows, but when its punch hits her in the chest, it hurts. She flies back, colliding with the nearby bookshelf, almost falling to the ground as she feels her breath knocked away and the pain of the strike taking her. She wonders if she has suffered a fracture, though the main force has been in the region of the breastbone. She clutches her chest with one hand, gasping for breath, still maintaining some hold on her sword, angling it out toward her foe.

It moves its fingers a bit, as if they were tentacles feeling the air for some sign of weakness, then they again set into the fierce shape of those claws. It bends its knees, preparing for another attack.

"Demon!"

Two sets of eyes look over for the source of that commanding shout. Skot stands just inside the doorway, his cane held in one hand, his drawn pistol in the other. Once he sees he has the beast's attention, he squeezes the trigger, firing multiple shots, each alighting the air with that particular amber hue tracing the trajectory. Some of the shots hit, but the creature uses that same incredible speed to retreat, going into hiding in the darker places of the chamber. Skot keeps his pistol aimed as he rushes over to Lilja.

"Don't worry about me," she says, and though he, of course, does, the tone and manner of her voice lets him know she is reasonably okay. "We have to stop that thing."

He nods once then rises fully to his feet, Lilja doing the same. The two know the creature is there. They can hear it breathing.

"Aaaahhh." The voice curdles up from the darkness. "The Head of House Felcraft. Did you like the present we left you?"

The tone of its voice holds obvious taunting. Skot and Lilja give each other a glance then spread out, making careful approach toward the hiding place. They both know that this particular Demon is very powerful, possessed of physical as well as magickal strength, and with it hidden in shadow, they must be wary. It may seem the two Hunters have it cornered, but this may not necessarily be a position of weakness for the monster.

Skot knows the thing is referring to his cousin Charles, whom it slaughtered, as well as the condition in which they left the body. He tries to block such thoughts from his mind as he and Lilja continue their careful approach.

"I see you both," it reveals, "and I invite you both into the darkness with me."

They continue moving, and Lilja fans out, trying to make an angled approach even within the limited space of the room. She hopes to flank the thing, or at least widen the coupled angle of their potential attacks.

"You are both strong. I can smell it. The other was a morsel," it says, referring to Charles, "but your *father* ..."

Skot's step hesitates. Lilja shoots her eyes over, looking at the man she loves, hoping he doesn't lose his focus to this.

"Yessss," the Demon hisses, "Your father was giving us too much trouble. He was *too* strong, such fortitude, but we got him in the end."

Don't listen, she wills, continuing to move, hoping to get to the thing first now, hoping her presence will distract it, keep it away from Skot. She dares to shift her eyes to him, and she sees that he is still approaching, being careful, slow, gun held at the ready. He looks unfazed now, but she can sense a tension. She knows he is a stalwart man, much like his father, but no one is full proof. A crack may lead to a crumble.

She wishes she had her rifle, but she remembers how ineffective that proved. Skot's weapon at least holds the specially-crafted rounds. She readjusts her grip on the katana, and she feels a rising anxiousness pushing her to get to the Demon first. She knows that is not good. This

SWORD OF THE BUTTERFLY

should not be rushed. She also knows she has that power inside her. She just needs to again tap it.

"We exploited his weakness. The same you all share."

She uses its voice as a target, but she can tell the thing is also moving. She knows it is toying with them both, for there are moments of silence, then when it speaks, she can tell it has moved. It is capable of remaining completely quiet, so it does this to upset them. She also worries of that enshrouding darkness, for it looks too dark, perhaps even that it may be growing.

"You so highly praise your pathetic 'hunter genes', but your very humanity, those genes, that is your taint, your stain, your weakness."

She glances over again, and she can no longer see Skot. She freezes, panic threatening to take her. She resists it, easily, but she knows it is there, simmering deep within. She wonders that she can no longer spy him, and she thinks the darkness is doing it, blocking her view. She also notices a tiny movement in that same area of shadow, and she prepares to lunge.

"We got to him," it grates, "It took many years, but the pain and suffering … ah, it was so exquisite, so worth it. We let death waste him before he even died, and we'll do it again-."

Shots ring out, coming rapidly. She looks over, the illumination allowing her to see Skot, and he is not that far. They have both managed to indeed come up on varying sides of the unnatural blackness cultivated by the Demon, her angle more than perpendicular to his. The special bullets fly into that area, the firing flame from each shot causing quick flashes of brightness. She sees the thing, and it looks more bestial, its dark skin more ashen, the etching lines of its muscles more defined, and a hideous grin has its lips, showing teeth bared in enjoyment.

She springs toward it, blade ready. In that same instant, another illumination flares, a dark fire of purples and blues, and the Demon unleashes a wild magick. It erupts, and she feels its force, though it proves mainly aimed at Skot. It hits him quite squarely, and he goes flying, his pistol and cane dislodged from their hold.

The power sends her back, though not as terribly as Skot. The Demon propels itself, going toward her man. She cannot tell how he fares, but she knows that he is now without physical weapons. She knows also that he possesses other abilities, but she is not sure if he even now possesses consciousness … or life.

"Skot!" she cries, hoping to get the beast's attention as well as some arousal of response from him.

A sudden thought hits her, and she runs, clambering, moving with speed of which she did not know she possessed. The Demon is going to kill the man she loves. It seems to no longer care of the Book or her, but it wishes to destroy one of its chief adversaries. She feels that rush of concern filling her, and it gives her preternatural speed and focus.

She gets to her desk, forcing open the drawer with a strength that bypasses its locked state. She rips through the contents, opening the false bottom to retrieve the H&K USP45CT, the handgun loaded with eight rounds of the specially treated bullets. She racks the slide, taking careful aim at the shape of the Demon, and she feels that power welling within herself. She fires, and not only is there the twinge of outré light that follows the bullet, belying its state, but another surge of magick erupts from her core, enveloping her arms and adding to the round.

The first hits the Demon in the temple, and though one might not expect the force of such a gun to so strongly impact a thing of this size, its momentum is completely redirected as it falls to the side. She moves over in a rapid, steady walk, maintaining aim with both hands, firing bullet after bullet. Each hits its target, each flies out with that extra power that comes from within herself. She feels it now, pushing with it, as though she held a small cannon. When she is done, the Demon lies in a heap, collapsed in on itself, fluids leaking profusely, holes torn in its massive body, cavities revealing the ruined shine of organ and blood.

She stands close to it, gun still pointed, though she is out of bullets. She feels that power still coursing within her. It struggles to raise its head. The motion is jerky and quivering, the thing obviously on its last threads. It tries to focus its eyes, ooze gurgling from its mouth. Perhaps it is trying to speak, to taunt further.

With a fluid motion, Lilja draws her sword, swinging out as she goes down with bent knee, and she shears the Demon's head from its body. The sharp rise of colored light is quite visible when the metal connects with its target, a focused explosion of power. She flicks the blade, sending the clinging vitae flying away in a rain of black droplets.

SWORD OF THE BUTTERFLY

Quickly sliding the weapon back in its scabbard and dropping the pistol, she goes to Skot.

"Skot? Skot?" she calls, "Are you okay?" Her hands move to check for wounds.

"I'm fine."

She goes in, wrapping her arms about him tightly, and he returns the hug just as intensely.

He then looks over at the dead beast, then eyes back to her. "That ... was amazing."

She cannot stifle the curl that takes her lips, and the two share the moment, giving forth to a short series of light laughter as the tension leaks away.

*****

They are back in their home, sitting comfortably on the couch, enjoying some hot tea. She snuggles in close to him, nestled in his embrace. He has one arm about her, the other free to touch of her gently or take hold of his mug. They sit there for a time, just enjoying the feel of peacefulness, being close. She looks up after she has more of her drink.

"So, Volkov was with them the whole time?"

Skot nods, thoughtfully. "So it seems. He was a dark magician, a warlock, if you will, though we don't generally like that term. He possessed the Hunter genes .., and they found him first."

"Who did?"

He emits a weighty sigh, and Lilja looks more up at him. She then scoots back to better see as they talk.

"The Infernal. They ... coerced him, seduced him, made some sort of deal, and he dedicated himself to them."

"People really do that?" she asks, her brow wrinkling, "Sell their souls to the Devil?"

"Sometimes, and I hate to sound trite, but they know not what they do."

She sips more of her tea, knees tucked in close to herself, both hands holding the mug. Her eyes peer at him as she does, piercing the rising the steam from the hot brew.

"The Infernal, as best we can tell, are not interested in human souls or servants. They use humans as they are able, of course, but mainly, they just seem to see us as enemies, ripe for slaughter. They don't appear to want any resources from us, as one might see in conventional wars. This is more about a total conquering, a complete eradication of a species.

"Of course, as I have mentioned, most people are unable to perceive the Infernal, or when thrust into a situation where they can, that generally results in death. But they sensed the ability in him, and they used him. His actions here allowed them to launch that attack on the Book."

She still says nothing, just drinking and listening.

"The Malkuths also found him." Skot emits another sigh, obviously displeased with this. "And they decided to watch him to see what he, what *they*, were up to."

"He was bait. Like Ernst," she ponders, "Risky."

He shows his own agreement.

"I don't like how they do that," she adds, eyes having drifted away into her thoughts.

"Me, neither."

He then sets his eyes on her, and she looks back. She smiles lightly, but his expression is different. She blinks, moving her face forward and to the side, eyes narrowing in a silent inquiry.

"I almost lost you, Lily," he says, "I owe the Malkuths for saving your life. Even if we disagree with their methods and end goal, if Anika had not been there …"

"If the Malkuths had done something about Volkov when they found him, none of it would have happened. None of the children being prostituted and murdered. You don't owe them anything."

He senses the underlying fierceness in her tone, and he nods, slowly. He understands and agrees with her point, but the truth is that she was saved by Anika. He feels the debt.

"She also helped at the library," he mentions, and he wonders why he would be taking such a tact, namely looking for the positive in the woman who saved Lilja's life.

"The Malkuths want to stop the Infernal," Lilja replies, her calmly uttered words like a shrug.

"Yes, of course. I spoke further with Anika and even Asenath, and they were surprisingly forthcoming, which makes me suspicious," he adds as an aside, "They had infiltrated Volkov's inner circle, putting Anika in the forefront, of course, but they had some others inside prior to that, probably evaluating the man and seeing the best way to get their claws in. Asenath admitted to at least two other women who acted like Anika's friends. It seems that once Anika was 'in', she brought more as a part of some *entourage*."

"Is Denman back in the City?"

"She would not say."

"It upsets me a lot that they let it happen. Volkov was torturing and killing those children to harvest their 'power', and it was all for the Infernal and to launch this attack for the Book. They let it happen."

"It's horrible," he agrees, "and it also upsets me that again we failed to notice it. It turns out that in your role as the vigilante, you were closer to the actions of the Infernal than we were."

She looks up at him, and he returns the gaze. He lets a curl touch the edges of his lips, and she eventually returns it, even slighter than his own. She wants to be a part of that 'we', but she yet hesitates. She knows he is fully committed to their relationship, but she still has her reservations.

Silence descends for a moment, the two of them lost in their own mental meanderings.

"What are we going to do about the library thing, anyway?" she pitches, eyes on him as she samples more of her tea.

"Well, it's a bit tricky, but it could seem that the library was hacked, passcodes compromised, leading to attempted entry, triggering of alarms, and it may have all been an unfortunate student prank, what with the gas they leaked inside the front door. Who would have known that an employee and some security guards were just inside?"

"A student prank?" she counters after her own moment of pontification, but he lets it simmer, watching her. She slowly nods. "I guess that works. I mean, you have more experience in this sort of thing than I do, but how does a student prank explain what the guards saw? I even had to choke two out."

"That is a concern, but it was dark, confusing, and there is the gas. It won't be perfectly clean, but it can be explained. Memory is fallible and may be manipulated. I don't like doing it, but the alternative is worse."

She nods slowly to this, hardly moving her head, as if accepting holds a weight.

"I don't really like any of this."

"What do you mean?" he asks.

"I don't know," she finally admits after some time of thinking, "I feel tired. We spend so much energy, your family fighting the demons, me fighting the criminals, and we fail."

"We haven't failed, Lily," he tries, moving a hand to touch of her forearm. He hopes she will reciprocate, but she just sits there.

"Skot, you have mentioned how Infernals can sometimes use your fears and emotions, even memories, against you, right?"

"Yes." He nods carefully, wondering where she is going with this. "That's correct."

"That Demon attacking me in my apartment just got me thinking of something ..."

He looks at her, waiting for more, but she remains quiet, so he gently presses, "What is it?"

She moves her eyes up to his. "I need to book a ticket to Finland."

"Why?"

"I have some demons inside myself I have to face."

EPILOGUE

She exists in a miasma, a whirling dreamscape, though it is filled with darkness, confusion, a nightmare of the mind. There is pain, a torture of it, but it is not like normal pain. She does not even remember who she is or why she is here or what this even is, but she feels the maelstrom. It has gone on for so long now, this dark, misty embrace, that she has accepted it, being borne upon its course like a mote adrift in a black, endless sea.

She is kept in this quasi-living state, this always-dreaming womb, by her captors, so they might use her as they wish. She is a rare gift, indeed, and once found, they'd not let her free. She is used as they desire, for she did agree to such, though she knew not what she did. She has already produced at least one viable result for them, though the ultimate end to that was not as they intended. Still, there is time, and she shall be kept enslaved through drugs, alchemy, and other torturous magicks, prolonging her life unnaturally, using her and using her until she is withered, then they shall dispose of what remains.

Or so they had planned.

The two men found her, taking advantage of the Infernal's focus on things happening in the City in effort to take the Book. They had followed clues and trails and breadcrumbs so small they almost turned to dust in the fog, but they have found her. It was not easy, and in truth, one of them did much more than the other.

As the two gaze upon the poor woman, the form of her so wane and nigh colorless, as though she has been bleached of vibrancy, one of them hands a wrought stiletto to the other. The blade winds as the body of a snake, artful, the handle ornate, though without any bejeweling, merely bearing of designs carved into the dark metal. It is called "The Weeping Dagger", and it proved a rare and treasured find of theirs some generations back, one they have kept in secrecy until its particular service is needed.

Duilio takes the weapon from David, looking at the man. "You want me to kill her?"

David nods solemnly. "It's a kindness," he says, though he notes the other man's hesitation. "Surely you've killed someone before?"

"Well, yes," he responds, somewhat sheepishly, "Haven't you?"

"No." David slowly shakes his head, as though they are having a casual conversation. "I've never killed a human. So, you see," he adds, a strange curl to his lips, "you're the more experienced here for this."

Duilio perks his thick eyebrows. "Perhaps it is time you learned …?"

"It's better for it to be you," the Hunter responds.

And Duilio wonders if this is because he works for the Malkuths, so the dirty work is left to him, or if it is because he has really done so little to contribute to their task up to this point. He is not sure, but as he gazes at the young woman, seeing how she is contained, her exposed body riddled with scars and wounds, her vacant eyes milky with lost sight, he knows the man who has become something of a partner of his is right – this will be a kindness.

The Interpol agent has seen many things, many things he'd rather not have ever known, but now it is too late. He will resign his position at the internal law enforcement organization, for he now has a new purpose. He gives a short, almost jerky nod, closing his eyes into it. When he reopens them, they gaze at the bound woman, and he is now filled with a calm, steely sense of what he must do.

The blade entering her *is* a kindness, one she does not even feel. Her consciousness slips away, followed by her life, and she is finally free.

ABOUT THE AUTHOR

Born in Houston, Texas into the temporary care of a bevy of nuns before being delivered to his adopted parents, Scott discovered creative writing at a very young age when asked to write a newspaper from another planet. This exercise awakened a seeming endless drive, and now, many short stories, poems, plays, and novels (both finished and unfinished) later, his first book, *Dance of the Butterfly*, is being published.

The seeds for this tale began with dreams, as many often do, before being fine-tuned with a whimsical notion and the very serious input of a dear friend. Before long, the story took on life of its own and has now become the first book in a planned series.

Having lived his whole life in the same state, Scott attended the University of Texas at Austin, achieving a degree in philosophy before returning to the Houston area to be closer to family and friends. During this time, he wrote more and even branched out into directing and performance art, though creative writing remains his love.

Please follow me for updates and information regarding new books at:

Scott's website/blog – www.scottcarruba.wordpress.com/
Scott's Facebook - www.facebook.com/AuthorScottCarruba/
Scott's Twitter – www.twitter.com/scott_carruba
Scott's Tumblr – www.scottcarruba.tumblr.com/

CHECK OUT THE OMP WEBSITE FOR
A COMPLETE LIST OF OUR TITLES

WWW.OPTIMUSMAXIMUSPUBLISHING.COM

BOOKS ARE AVAILABLE IN BOTH PRINT
AND ELECTRONIC FORMATS

The Optimus Maximus Publishing Shield Logo, the character of OPTIMA, and the name Optimus Maximus Publishing are registered trademarks of Optimus Maximus Publishing LLC. The OPTIMA character is also the intellectual property of Jeffrey Kosh Graphics.

RICKY FLEET
HELLSPAWN
SERIES

10.35 AM, September 14th 2015. Portsmouth, England.

A global particle physics experiment releases a pulse of unknown energy with catastrophic results. The sanctity of the grave has been sundered and a million graveyards expel their tenants from eternal slumber.

The world is unaware of the impending apocalypse, Governments crumble and armies are scattered to the wind under the onslaught of the dead.

Kurt Taylor, a self-employed plumber, witnesses the start of the horrifying outbreak. Desperate to reach his family before they fall victim to the ever growing horde of shambling corruption, he flees the scene.

In a society with few guns, how can people hope to survive the endless waves of zombies that seek to consume every living thing? With ingenuity, planning and everyday materials, the group forge their way and strike back at the Hellspawn legions.

Rescues are mounted, but not all survivors are benevolent, the evil that is in all men has been given free rein in this new, dead world. With both the living and dead to contend with, the Taylor family's battle for survival is just beginning.

Book 1 in the Hellspawn series.

Kurt Taylor and his family have battled the living and the dead and now find themselves on the run, their home reduced to ashes. With unimaginable horror lying in wait around every corner, the onset of winter and the plunging temperatures only add more danger to their precarious existence. They decide to forge ahead and try to reach the protection of others who have hopefully survived the zombie apocalypse. If this fails, their only choice would be to try and reach an impregnable fortress, a sanctuary that has stood for a thousand years.

Standing between them and salvation are the villages and cities of the damned, a path that will test their spirit and resilience unlike anything they have faced before. More companions are rescued from the jaws of death and join them in their perilous journey. Mysterious attacks befall the group and it becomes clear the dead aren't the only things that lurk in the darkness.

Tempers fray and personalities clash. The group starts to fracture and Kurt is forced to commit acts that cause him to question his own morality. Can they survive the horror of their new existence? Will they want to?

The Hellspawn saga continues.

BALLYMOOR, IRELAND, 1891

Patrick Conroy, a young American student of medicine in Dublin, decides to take a break from the hustle and bustle of the big city and spend a month in the quietude of the wild and beautiful Glencree valley, County Wicklow. However, surrounded by local legends and myths, he is soon dragged into an ancient mystery that has haunted the village of Ballymoor for centuries. Set on the background of the tumultuous years preceding the War of Independence, and colored by Irish folklore, the Haunter of the Moor is a ghost story written in the style of Victorian Gothic novels.

To Fight Evil with Evil

England, 1392.
As the Black Death quickly spreads through the kingdom, the little hamlet of Blythe's Hollow suffers under the yoke of a sadistic Lord. Desperate, the villagers decide to seek out the magical help of a local witch, causing the wrath of the Church. Torture and murder befall on those accused of being in league with the Devil, adding more sorrow to the beset folk of Blythe's Hollow. Yet, one man will rise against the tyranny; a man willing to learn Black Magick to fight back.

A modern dark urban fantasy, telling of two powerful families who uphold a secret duty to protect humanity from a threat it doesn't know exists.

Though sharing a common enemy, the two families form a long-standing rivalry due to their methods and ultimate goals.

Forces are coalescing in a prominent Central European city criminal sex-trafficking, a serial murderer with a savage bent, and other, less tangible influences.

Within a prestigious, private university, Lilja, a young librarian charged with protecting a very special book, finds herself suddenly ensconced in this dark, strange world. Originally from Finland, she has her own reason for why she left her home, but she finds the city to be anything but a haven from dangers and secrets.

Book One in a planned series.

Meet Mason Ezekiel Barnes, former NFL tackle turned successful author of the naughty ninja adventure series Mia Killjoy. Mason is obsessed with winning a Pulitzer and is thwarted by his fellow author and nemesis, the twerpy little gnome Conrad Bancroft.

Perk Noir is full of comedic relief, pop culture, NFL, jazz, a little touch of romance, and flashbacks of Lightning and his family during both the first half of the 20th century and later during the Civil Rights movement. Mason and Shelly and their adventures is a fun filled thrill ride that will appeal to all readers, there is something for everyone at the Perk.

Two hunters pursue the same prey.
Fate has forged the slayer, Trey Thomas and the Sandrian vampire, Adalius, two natural enemies, into an uneasy alliance against an evil more powerful than either have ever faced. Only together do they stand a chance of defeating Anna; if they don't destroy each other first.
As they pursue Anna, the apprehensive Lycan watch as a confrontation looms on the horizon between vampires, the New Bloods and the Old Guard, which threatens to plunge the vampire world into civil war and trigger an all-out supernatural conflict which in the end could destroy them all.

Killing is the sole province of the religious fanatics, an axiom as true today as it was some five hundred years ago; and no nation, region or person is immune.

Europe had clawed its way out of the Middle Ages with the dawning of the renaissance, only to be plunged once more into darkness, as the dogs of war circled to destroy its resurgence during the 16th century. The Islamic successor to the Roman Byzantines, the Ottoman Caliphate, flexed its muscles to conquer much of Western Asia, North Africa and South-Eastern Europe. Christian Europe shuddered when the once invincible bastion of the Knight's at Rhodes were defeated; and now trembled as the Ottoman army rattled the very gates of Vienna. No Christian army, it seemed, could withstand the ferocity of the Azabs, the Akıncı, the Sipahis, the Janissaries, and ruthless Iayalar's of the all-conquering Islamic hordes.

This then is the cauldron into which Gideon de Boyne is unwittingly thrust with his small army of dedicated Christian warriors. On the hostile island of Crete, at the doorstep of the Ottoman Empire, Gideon must face not only the overwhelming force of Muslim warriors but his own inner conflicts of the futility of war and his very Christian beliefs.

Will he succeed and come out of it unscathed?

Collected tales of Madness and Terror

Maximus SHOCK

An OMP Magazine

Complete Collection

MAXIMUS SHOCK 0

16 Mind-Shocking Tales!

RICKY FLEET   JEFFREY KOSH   EMIR SKALONJA
KEITH MONTGOMERY   SCOTT CARRUBA   CHRIS GARSON
LORRAINE VERSINI   MAURA ATKINSON BUTLER   MATT HAY
LEON BROWN   WK POMEROY

EDITED BY
CHRISTINA HARGIS SMITH

Made in the USA
Columbia, SC
21 June 2017